# Fear No Evil

John Gordon Davis was born in what was then Rhodesia of English parents and educated in South Africa. He became a member of the Seamen's Union and his university vacations were spent at sea, with the Dutch whaling fleet in the Antarctic, and on British merchantmen. He took degrees in political science and law and joined the Rhodesian Civil Service. After the success of his first book, *Hold My Hand I'm Dying*, he left his work, by then as a barrister in Hong Kong, to write for his living. His books include *Hold My Hand I'm Dying*, *Years of the Hungry Tiger*, and *Leviathan*.

He now lives with his wife Rosie on a farm in southern Spain for half of every year, while the other half they spend researching future books.

John Gordon Davis

# Fear No Evil

HARPER

HarperCollins*Publishers*
77–85 Fulham Palace Road,
Hammersmith, London W6 8JB

www.harpercollins.co.uk

This paperback edition 2014
1

First published in Great Britain by HarperCollins*Publishers* 1982

A catalogue record for this book
is available from the British Library

ISBN: 978-0-00-757444-5

MIX
Paper from
responsible sources
FSC® C007454

To my lovely wife Rosemary

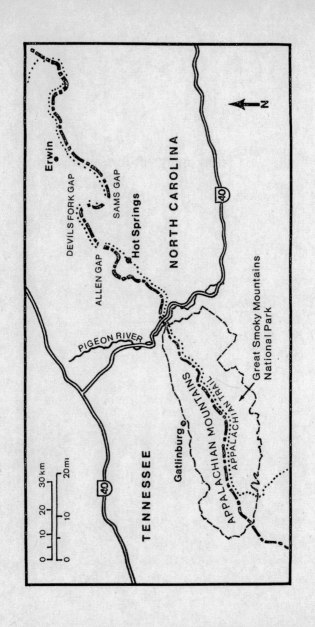

# part one

## one

Just over there, through the trees, was Fifth Avenue: cars and buses roaring, people hurrying, apartments, shops; the trees were budding, everything turning green, and there was a feeling of life in the sharp air around Central Park Zoo. It is a pretty little zoo, red brick covered with ivy, and at the entrance is a charming rotating clock tower: our childhood animals, cast in bronze, each are playing a different musical instrument, and as the clock turns it chimes a tune: the hippo is playing the violin, the kangaroo the trumpet, the goat the pipes, the penguin the drum, the jolly elephant the concertina.

This Saturday afternoon a young man was standing in Central Park, just outside the zoo gates, listening to the musical clock. He was twenty-eight years old, average height, lean, his thatch of hair jet-black, his skin clear and unlined; he was wearing a tracksuit and sneakers and his face was flushed from running. It was a strong, nice-looking face, but what struck you most were his eyes: they were beautiful—bright, deep blue, almost mauve, in certain light nearly black, and penetrating, and very warm, with thick lashes and dark eyebrows. Now his eyes were on the musical clock as it chimed five, and they were sad.

For down below in the zoo is very different from the musical clock. Over in the corner the great, solitary polar bear paced up and down in his cage, pad pad pad to the corner, blink, turn, pad pad pad back, blink, turn, pad back to the corner again; over and over,

7

and over and over. His feet covered exactly the same spots, and his body went through exactly the same turning movement every time. All day, every day, for the rest of his life. In the Elephant House the great mammals shuffled back and forth, back and forth, their great trunks curling and slopping, curling and slopping, nothing to do, enormous feet shuffling over the same few yards of concrete, big eyes blinking. Sometimes they trumpet, an old primitive scream out of the great forests that crashes back off the Victorian walls. In the Big Cat House, the lions and the tiger and the jaguar and the snow leopard and the panther are prowling back and forth, back and forth, powerful hunting animals pacing four paces to the corner, blink, turn, four paces back, blink, turn; over and over. The lions are fortunate, for there are two in one cage, but in their pacing they get in each other's way and have to make an identical movement to avoid each other, a terrible ritual, over and over. The other big cats are alone in their cages, and they cannot see each other. The puma is always trying to paw down the steel partition to get in with the jaguar. For the rest of their lives, four paces up, four paces down. It would make a difference to the big cats if they could just see each other, for solitary confinement is one of the worst punishments. But opposite their row are the cages of the gorillas, big hairy animals each twice the weight and size of two very big men, with faces and eyes that are almost human, and the male gorilla can see the female gorilla in the next cage just fine, but they just sit there and stare and eat their own excrement.

As the clock chimed an old black man came down the path.

'Hello man.'

The young man turned with relief. 'Hello, Ambrose.'

Old Ambrose looked up at him worriedly, then nodded his silvery head at the gates. 'You not goin' to knock this place over too, are you?'

'No.'

Ambrose took a deep, apprehensive breath, and glanced sideways. He reached up to the young man's top pocket and dropped a bunch of keys in it.

'Thanks, Ambrose.'

Ambrose looked up at the young man anxiously.

'You only got an hour. Midnight to one. While we're all havin' dinner.'

The young man nodded.

'And,' Ambrose said, 'the east gate will be open.'

The young man nodded again. 'Thanks, Ambrose.' Then he pulled two letters out of his tracksuit pocket. They were both stamped, and had express delivery stickers. 'Will you mail these? Tonight, as soon as it's over?'

Ambrose took the letters without looking at them and stuffed them in his pocket. He looked up at the young man, and now he had tears in his old eyes.

'For God's sake, Davey, do you know what you doing?'

'Yes.'

Ambrose stared at him, then blurted: 'They'll shoot you, Davey—like an animal yourself . . .'

Davey just shook his head slightly. Ambrose blinked, then grabbed his hand emotionally.

'Lord bless you!'

He turned and hurried back down the path.

# two

Down in the vast basements of Madison Square Garden, seven long-distance haulage trucks were lined up. One each was painted in big, old-fashioned Western lettering, *The World's Greatest Show*. The crews were hurriedly loading circus gear. Four of the huge vehicles were for the animals, each divided into adjustable compartments, with sides that folded down to form ramps. But at this moment all the animals were upstairs in the circus ring, parading in the grand finale.

Applause roared above the oompah-oompah of the orchestra. At the front, two elephants pranced on their massive hindlegs. The big male held a top hat in his trunk tip which he waved to the crowd, while the female flounced in a massive polka-dot skirt and held a parasol in her trunk tip. Hanging onto her tail was a baby elephant called Dumbo, dressed in dungarees. Behind them came two huge grizzly bears, also on their shaggy hind legs, dressed as people, and behind them pranced a little bear dressed in a pinafore, waving to the crowds with his paw. Next came four chimpanzees—three big females and one small male—dressed as cowboys, brandishing sixguns, Stetsons jammed down over their ears, and chomping on cigars. Behind came the magnificent performing horses, prancing in time to the music. On their backs rode three African lions and a Siberian tiger, leaping from back to back in time to the orchestra's beat; then came the sea lions, flapping along, balancing balls on their snouts, and the clowns clowing and the trapeze artists somersaulting and the leggy girls wearing sparkling tights, and the jugglers juggling.

And in front of the whole parade strode a tanned, handsome, middle-aged man in a scarlet coat and a white pith helmet, smiling and waving to the crowd. The name he went by was Frank I. Hunt, and he was the ringmaster.

A few minutes later it was all over. The animals hurried down the concrete ramp into the neon-lit basements, their keepers running alongside. They herded up the ramps into the trucks, and into their cages. All three elephants climbed into one truck, and their keeper chained them to their iron ringbolts. The lions and the tiger leaped up into another truck; the three bears scrambled after them into their compartment, then the chimpanzees. All their equipment was hefted in, blocks, barrels, seesaws, and hoops. It was quick and efficient.

The first truck rumbled up the exit ramp, out onto the streets of Manhattan. Then the next, and the next, at one-minute intervals. The convoy of the The World's Greatest Show went rumbling uptown through the night, spread out on Amsterdam Avenue, heading for the George Washington Bridge.

The last two trucks to leave Madison Square Garden carried the elephants, the big cats, the bears and the chimpanzees. They drove slower than the others, trundling along with their extraordinary cargo. Finally they approached the cloverleaf system for traffic turning off onto the bridge. But they did not take the turnoff: as soon as they reached it they accelerated and kept going, hard.

Miles across town from the Washington Bridge is the Bronx Zoo: two hundred and fifty acres of rolling, rocky woodland in the heart of the city, with winding roads and paths for people to stroll along while they look at the animals.

It was just after midnight. The zoo grounds were dark, the trees silhouetted against the lights of New York. There was a faraway noise of traffic, and sometimes you heard an elephant trumpet, a wolf howl, a big cat roar.

Suddenly, through the trees, appeared a shadowy figure of a man. He stopped, listened. Then he disappeared in the darkness.

Five hundred yards away through the dark trees, past the reptiles and the elephants and the apes, was the Victorian big cat house.

Outside, the young man reappeared. He crouched, unlocked the door. He stepped into the dark smell of the cats. There was a shattering roar.

Ten pairs of feline eyes opened wide, ears pricked, bodies tensed. The young man went quickly to the snow leopard's cage. The great cat was heaving herself against the bars, purring voluminously; the young man swung over the guard rail and leaned through the bars. He clasped the big head with both arms and hugged her and scratched her back as she writhed against the bars, trying to push herself against him.

'Hello, Jezobel—yes, you're beautiful . . .'

The big snow leopard could not get enough of him, pushing and rubbing, and all down the row of cages the other big cats were pacing excitedly in anticipation.

He pulled out a small flashlight and hurried down the row of cages, into the keeper's office next to the Siberian tiger's cage. He pulled out a bunch of keys, feverishly selected one, inserted it. He swung open the steel door and stepped inside. There was a sound of swiftness in the dark, and a mighty weight hit him on his chest with a snarl.

He crashed onto his back, half-stunned, with the huge tiger on top of him in a mass of jaws and claws going at his head, and he was laughing under the rough slurpings of her tongue, whispering 'Velvet paws, Mama!—Velvet!—'

He hugged her great striped chest as she stood over him, licking his face, then he shoved her firmly over and scrambled up. He pulled off his leather belt and looped it around the excited cat's neck, buckling it firmly as she writhed against him. Then he put his arm around her shoulders and began to stroke her neck hard, to soothe her.

'Sh—sh, Mama, sh—sh, Mama . . .'

Then he stood up and led her out of her cage, through the keeper's office and out into the hall. The Siberian tiger padded excitedly beside him. He swung open the big door, and the cold night air flooded in.

He paused on the threshold, peering into the darkness. Then, holding the tiger by the belt, he started to run.

The old cow elephant sensed who it was as soon as she heard him at the lock. She flapped out her great ears, and gave a squeak, lumbering up to the bars of her cage. She snaked her trunk through, urgently sniffing: the young man unlocked the door and stepped into the smell and gloom of the Elephant House.

The cages were divided with walls so the elephants could not see each other. The cow elephant was pressed against her bars, trying to see him, and the two adolescent elephants were reaching out with their trunks, snorting and snuffling. Across the hall the solitary hippopotamus was staring wide-eyed into the darkness, her nostrils dilated.

'Hello, Jamba . . .'

The young man scrambled through the bars of the cow elephant's cage. Her trunk curled around him; delighted, snorting, she lifted him off his feet. 'Yes, Jamba, yes, my beauty . . .' He lay against her face, hugging her and grinning, and the great animal shuffled and squeezed him. Then he whispered, she released him immediately, and he slid back down her trunk.

'I'll be back in a minute, my lovely . . .'

He hurried down the row of cages, touching the trunks that were groping for him, greeting the elephants by name. In the far corner the hippopotamus had her square snout jammed through the wide bars, shoving with her haunches. The young man climbed through the bars, and she reversed massively and lumbered against him. He put his arms around her big fat neck and hugged her. His eyes were moist, and the hippopotamus's eyes were rolling with delight.

'I'm sorry, Sally ... I'm sorry, old lady ... You'd be fine in the summer but not in the winter ...'

Big fat Sally, the only hippopotamus in the zoo, was huffing and grunting, her huge mouth slopping as she shoved herself into his embrace.

He gave her one last hug, then turned and scrambled tearfully through the bars. Sally lumbered after him, and floundered into the bars, her flanks quivering; he strode across the hall and wiped his wrist roughly across his eyes. The old hippopotamus stood there, squeezed against the bars, and she gave a big heartbreaking snort. The young man did not look back.

He hurried back to Jamba's cage, pulling out his flashlight and a wrench. He flicked the light on the locking mechanism, and set to work to open the elephant's door. All the time the hippopotamus stood rammed against her bars, grunting at him, her intestines half-clogged with the coins, lipsticks, and marbles the public had tossed down her cavernous mouth over the years.

The young man was running out of time. He unlocked the door of the Ape House and ducked inside. In the keeper's office he snapped on the switch for simulated jungle daylight.

The big silver-back male gorilla, the females and a baby blinked, scattered under their concrete tree. The male scrambled up onto all fours, staring intently; he bobbed excitedly and shook his head to show nonaggression, then came lumbering. He shoved his black hands against the glass panel, bobbing and shaking his head, and the young man grinned and bobbed and shook his head too.

He dashed back into the keeper's office, inserted a key, swung open the cage door—and the gorillas crowded around.

'Hello, King!'

He dropped to his haunches, his eyes moist. He could only take two. There was no more room in the trucks.

# three

It was two o'clock in the morning.

The circus gear lay abandoned on the grounds of the Bronx Zoo, a mess of barrels and seesaws and hoops and ladders.

Fifty miles away, on Highway 22, the two big circus trucks were hammering through New Jersey. The Western-style letters, *The World's Greatest Show*, had been hastily spray-painted out.

In the back of the first truck the three elephants from the zoo were squeezed in with the three elephants from The World's Greatest Show. The compartments of the other truck held all the lions and the tiger from the circus, the tiger from the zoo, the circus bears, the chimpanzees and the gorillas. Most of them were lying down to steady themselves, wide-eyed in the darkness, their adrenalin pumping.

In the cabs, the engines were loud, the radios playing. The driver of the second truck was a big strong man with a big gut, a wide face and straight black hair. Until an hour ago he had worked for The World's Greatest Show as an animal keeper and driver. He was tense, but sometimes a little smile played on his wide mouth, sometimes he whistled distractedly along with the radio. His name was Charles Buffalohorn and he was a full-blooded Cherokee Indian. On the sleeping bunk behind his seat was a knapsack, stuffed full, a sleeping bag strapped to it. These, plus maybe a few hundred dollars in the bank, were all he owned in the whole wide world.

Four hundred yards ahead were the taillights of the other truck. David Jordan's face was gaunt, his eyes frequently darting to the wing mirror, watching the truck behind. Every time the music stopped on the radio he tensed for a newsflash. Now and again he changed stations, listening hard.

Up on his bunk there was also a knapsack and a plastic bag containing a pig's carcass, bought that day from a wholesale butcher. On the seat beside him was Champ, the male circus chimpanzee, fast asleep. Champ was supposed to live with the other chimpanzees, but he liked to sleep in the cab with the young man, whenever he could get away with it.

On the floor of the cab slept a big furry dog. He looked like a husky, or maybe a German shepherd, but his face was almost pure wolf.

The elephants were crammed tight, great gray flanks pressing. Sometimes a trunk found its way out of the congestion and groped around, sniffing and feeling, and then it was a difficult business to recurl it, squeezing and shoving. The three circus elephants were dismayed by the strangers suddenly in their midst, for instead of the enormous territory an elephant needs, they had this piece of truck, their only permanent place on this earth.

But Jamba, the old cow elephant from the zoo, stood quietly, forehead jammed between two massive rumps, eyes blinking in the dark, but her heart thumping in excitement. Because the man she loved had come back, had taken her out of her cage amid the electric excitement of the Elephant House and out through the big double doors into the starry night. Suddenly she had been in the open, fresh night air and the smell of the earth all about her, and she was running beside him, his hand holding her trunk tip, running away from the Elephant House into the wide open world, and with each lumbering footfall her incredulous excitement had thumped harder and higher.

And squeezed into the back of the truck, squashed between elephants' legs and bellies, wide-eyed and wheezing, was the big, fat, old hippopotamus called Sally.

For, back in the gloom of the Elephant House, with the sounds of the young man heaving open the cages and then leading the elephants out one by one—excited silhouettes lumbering into the wonderful starry night, all that animal eagerness in the air—in those long, tense minutes the old hippopotamus had sensed what was going to happen, that the man was taking them away with him forever. Each time old Sally had thought that her turn would be next, and she had stood there massively quivering, nostrils dilated, lumbering around her cage in agitation and anticipation. Then he had come up to her cage, and looked at her standing there huffing and trembling with excitement, and he had said hoarsely:

'I'm sorry, Sally . . . I'm terribly sorry, my old hippo . . .'

Then he had turned and walked quickly back through the big double door, and he was gone.

And suddenly she had understood: that she was being left behind, he was not taking her with him after all; and up her old chest there swelled an incredulous rumble-cry of anguish, and her square mouth gaped and her eyes rolled and then out broke her hippopotamus bark of heartbreak and appeal, a croak that erupted in long staccato grunts from the bottom of her old belly, and David Jordan had stopped.

He had reopened the door, and the starlight had shone in again, and Sally had lunged against her bars in incredulous joy, snorting and blundering, her eyes rolling wide.

'All right, Sally . . . we'll do the best we can . . .'

# four

Every time he saw headlights in the wing mirrors his heart thumped; he would give Big Charlie a warning flash of his taillights, and they would slow down to the speed limit, waiting for the police siren.

The two trucks drove on through the night. They were in Pennsylvania now, on Highway 81 south, two hundred miles from New York. The road signs flashed by, towns, gas stations, connecting routes. Homesteads, barns, silos, belts of trees, the distant glow of town lights. Five miles away, on their left, was the dark silhouette of the Appalachian Mountains, undulating almost the whole length of the United States, from Maine in the north down to the Great Smoky Mountains in the south, and beyond into Georgia.

He looked at his watch. Three A.M. Another four hours at the most before the zoo would discover the animals were missing and the alarm would sound.

He glanced at his fuel gauge. It was half full. Above the music he feverishly calculated they would have to refuel about sunrise—near Roanoke, Virginia. He wanted to stop only once to refuel, so he had to wait as long as possible.

The two great trucks of The World's Greatest Show roared along, head lights beaming up the wide swath of highway, radios playing; and in the backs the animals were wide-eyed in the vibrating darkness, grunting, huffing, snorting.

Big Charlie Buffalohorn's broad brow furrowed, and he muttered aloud: 'Usin' an awful lot of gas . . .'

Huge signboards flashed past, advertising motels, garages, tires, skating rinks, batteries, Exxon, Texaco, Shell, banks, Southern Fried Chicken, hamburgers with a college education. The Shenandoah Valley stretched ahead into the night, and just a few miles to the east was the black silhouette of the Shenandoah National Park.

David Jordan knew the number of year-rings on the giant stumps of ancient trees up there that had taken hundreds of years to grow and a few hours to hack down; he knew what the rocks were made of and that they had been there since the oceans covered the land. Through this wilderness swept the Skyline Drive, with its overlooks and picnic sites and campgrounds and comfort stations and grocery stores and gift shops and laundries and camping stores and ice sales and firewood sales and stables and gas stations, and signboards everywhere telling you to stay on the trails and make sure you have proper footwear and how dangerous the wilderness is. And down here the eight-laned Highway 81 swept through the Shenandoah Valley, and all the way the signboards signboards signboards for the people people people. And across the mighty land, the pollution hanging in the air in a haze, factory smoke and the exhaust fumes of automobiles and airplanes.

But roaring through the night in the stolen truck, his face tense, his heart jumping every time he saw headlights, his mind darting over and over the same things, he was feverishly grateful for all the roads turning off up to that long black ridge of mountains. Those mountains were what he had to get into if the police cars tried to force him off the road: he'd just keep going

17

flat out to the next turnoff, with the police car bouncing off his side.

At four-thirty he saw Big Charlie's headlights flashing him, and his heart tripped.

He slammed his foot on the power brakes and swung off onto the emergency lane. The other truck pulled in behind and Charlie jumped out of the high cab and worked himself under the engine. He reached up into the machinery. He brought down his hand, then showed it to Davey. It shone with diesel fuel.

'How much you got left?'

'Nearly empty.'

He ran back to his truck and leaped up into the cab. He revved the big engine and slammed off the brake. His heart was pounding and he felt sick.

He drove hard, willing the truck to go faster, racing the moment Charlie's lights would flash at him again. That meant disaster: trying to fix it themselves, patching up the leak, and siphoning fuel from his truck to Charlie's, parked wide out in the open highway.

At twenty minutes to five Big Charlie's fuel gauge registered empty.

At quarter to five he saw a sign, GAS FOOD LODGING 10 MILES, and he felt a surge of relief.

There was a long hill ahead, stretching away in his headlights. The accelerator was pressed to the floor, he was praying feverishly, *Please God not this hill* ... Black yellow tarmac swept up and up endlessly, and all the time the diesel was squirting out of Big Charlie's fuel pump. Then at last the headlights picked up the hilltop, and far away on the horizon he saw the signs, a hundred feet high: *Shell*, *Texaco* and, higher than them all, *Exxon*. Then his teeth clenched: there was another hill to climb.

His eyes darted to the mirror, willing Big Charlie to make it. He was halfway down the first hill now, and he still could not see the lights of Big Charlie's truck. He wanted to bellow out, *God, help us now!*—and Big Charlie's headlights came over the crest. He sighed and trod on the accelerator.

Davey roared up the new hill, his headlights searching for the top. Then, five miles ahead, he saw the signs gleaming like lighthouses, and he had never been so grateful to see American commercialism blighting the landscape. Then he gritted a curse as he saw one more long hill before those truckstop lights. Big Charlie's headlights came into his wing mirror. Davey started up the last long hill, and the crest came into view. He roared to the top, and Big Charlie's headlights were in his wing mirror all the way. Just three miles to go: he started downhill towards the lights, thanking God, and Big Charlie was still hammering up the other side of the hill, and his truck gave out.

Suddenly the engine coughed, and Big Charlie trod on the accelerator. The truck jerked, the animals lurched, and the huge machine started to shudder. It came to a grinding standstill in the emergency lane of Highway 81. David was pounding down on the other side of the hill, watching desperately for Big Charlie's headlights. He came to the bottom, with the hillcrest half a mile behind him; then he swung the truck into the emergency lane and slammed on his brakes.

He stared into the mirror for half a minute, praying, *Please God* ... The eight-lane highway was divided by a wide ditch of no-man's-land—it was impossible to drive across. Then he clenched his teeth and rammed his truck into low gear. He roared the engine and heaved the wheel into a U-turn. He swung his huge truck right across the highway, then jammed his foot flat. He pulled back into the emergency lane, then roared the massive truck northward up the southbound lanes, his eyes bright with fury, praying *Please God no traffic for just two minutes!*

He drove flat out, hunched over the wheel, heart drumming. The long black hill stretched up ahead of him, on and on. He was almost crying. At last his headlights showed the top. He leaned on the horn, and came over the top of the hill.

There, halfway down, was Charlie's truck. Davey tore down the hill, praying to God to keep the traffic away, then he drove out across the highway into another U-turn.

He swung his huge truck right across the four lanes, desperately checking the long hill for headlights. His wheel was hard over, the great truck was coming around, and he thought he was going to make it in one swing. His right fender was coming around, around, around—and then it was not going to make it. He slammed on his brakes and jerked his engine into reverse. Teeth clenched, he twisted the wheel and let out the clutch.

Big Charlie bellowed, *'There's a truck coming!'*

Suddenly a big beam lit up the sky beyond the crest of the hill. The truck full of elephants was stretched across all four lanes. David kicked the accelerator flat and his truck screamed backward as the terrible headlights burst over the crest, blinding bright. Then Big Charlie was running at them, shouting and waving his arms. David rammed his gears, roared the engine, and let out the clutch; the truck leaped—and it stalled.

It jolted to a stop across all four lanes. The other truck was three hundred yards off, hurtling down on them at sixty miles an hour. David bellowed, wrenched out the decompressor and slammed his foot on the starter. The truck was two hundred and fifty yards away now, and the driver still had not seen him. David shoved back the decompressor, and the engine roared to life. He revved it for all its might, took his foot off the clutch, and the massive vehicle surged forward.

The truck was a hundred and fifty yards off when the driver saw the long side. At sixty miles an hour a vehicle travels a hundred and fifty yards in five seconds. The driver leaned on his horn and jammed his foot on the brakes. There was a screaming blast and a shattering hiss of brakes, the roaring of engines and the screaming of tires. The other truck came tearing down the highway toward his side, twenty yards, fifteen, ten, five—blasting and screeching—and the driver swung wildly to the left; David roared his truck full of animals across the road, and the truck hurtled past, missing Davey's by a yard, blasting a wall of wind in front of it, the driver bellowing obscenities. Davey brought his vehicle to a stop in front of Big Charlie's and slumped over his wheel, ashen-faced, eyes closed.

Fifteen minutes later the two trucks of The World's Greatest Show crawled into the all-night truck stop, one towing the other.

It was a big complex, scores of massive vehicles parked shoulder to shoulder. Some of the trucks still had their engines running, exhausts spewing, while their drivers were in the cafeteria, and the cold night air was dense with diesel fumes. David towed Big

Charlie's truck into the farthest corner of the big parking lot. Then they set feverishly to work. Davey wriggled under the engine with the wrench while Big Charlie held the flashlight. He began to unbolt the fuel pump.

'Where's another Fargo?'

They found one, and Davey scrambled under the hood and stole its fuel pump.

# five

The two trucks of The World's Greatest Show hurtled down the eight-lane highway.

The first gray was slowly turning pink above the Appalachians; then came the golden red spreading across the starry sky; and now the trees on the Appalachian ridge were flaming silhouettes. Then the tip of the sun came up, setting the east on fire, beaming down into the Shenandoah Valley, casting long shadows through the trees and the farmlands and across the highway, shining golden into the cabs of the two trucks and into the tired faces of David Jordan and Big Charlie Buffalohorn as they hammered down Highway 81. And for those moments the world beyond this ugly highway was young and beautiful; those purple and gold early morning mountains stretched southward in the sunrise, and Davey knew every river, stream, glade and gulley, and he was glad with all his heart for what he was doing.

For once upon a time, and not so long ago, the great mauve forests stretched right across the mighty land, trees with trunks wider than a coach and four, and firs and spruce, elm and pine and chestnut, towering forest peaks and valleys and great plains rich in waving grass, like an ocean, as far as the eye could see. There were herds of bison, and deer and bears and game; and rushing rivers and tumbling brooks and waterfalls and rapids and canyons, all of the purest water. The air was clean: from the vast blue lakes of Canada in the north, to the Gulf of Mexico in the south, from the mighty Rocky Mountains in the west to the Appalachians here in the east. That was how God made it, and it had taken millions of years to do it; it was beautiful, and it would have gone on forever, for He made it to stand all the ravages of time; but He did not make it to withstand the gluttony of Man.

Davey Jordan drove the truck of animals down the highway in the sunrise, the towns and cloverleafs and signboards flashing by, and those mountains up there were all that was left of the wilderness. The only pioneering that was left for a man was to get to the next gas station, his only survival problem the price of a hamburger.

At seven o'clock they heard it on the radio. Suddenly the jolly wakee-wakee music was cut off. His heart crunched and the disc jockey said excitedly:

We interrupt your favorite program to bring you this amazing newsflash. Now you've heard it all, folks. You've heard of huge bank robberies, all kinds of hijacks and sky-jacks and kidnaps and stick-em-ups, but this has got to be the zaniest of them all! Now get this: the Bronx Zoo has been robbed!

Yes, you heard me right! The Bronx Zoo has been robbed, but not of its cash box!

Yes, sir, the elephants, lions, gorillas and that *bi-i-i-g* tiger have been stolen in the night, and right this red-hot moment all those dangerous animals are at large somewhere in the *U*-nited States! The mind-boggling theft was discovered at six-thirty this morning. Police all over the eastern part of the United States have been alerted—

It was a quarter to eight, and a beautiful Sunday morning.

Every fifteen minutes they heard the excited newsflash again, but there were no new details on any station.

Twenty miles ahead, at Troutville, the Appalachian Mountains curved to the west, and Highway 81 continued south through a wide treeless plain: if a police car chased them in that plain, there was nothing he could do. But a hundred miles farther the mountains curved back again, at Wytheville, and that was where he was going to swing onto Route 21, heading for the Iron Mountains, then drive like mad down toward the Smokies on the backcountry roads. Once they were on those roads they would be only about a hundred miles

22

from the Smokies; and right now they were only one hundred miles from Wytheville. In one and a half hours they would be off this highway and into the back country—*please God just another hour and a half* . . .

Then at eight o'clock came a different newsflash:

It has now been confirmed that two trucks belonging to The World's Greatest Show, which left New York last night, have failed to arrive in Boston, and that circus equipment which came from these vehicles has been found abandoned in the Bronx Zoo! Police believe that the drivers of these two trucks will be able to assist them in their inquiries and have called for the public's help in finding them. Here is a description of these two men. . . .

Davey's heart was pounding; his foot was flat on the accelerator, and he tried to jam it flatter.

# part two

## six

The zoo was in an uproar, policemen everywhere. Outside the locked gates were reporters and television crews. The professional staff had gathered in the conference room adjoining the director's office.

'I've met him once,' Dr. Elizabeth Johnson muttered, massaging her brow. Just to sit still, while the director kept interrupting the meeting to accept telephone calls, took a supreme effort. She had not even combed her hair, and her damn panties were on back to front—she had slammed down the telephone, scrambled into the nearest clothes, flung herself into her car and driven furiously down to the zoo. 'And I found nothing remarkable in him,' she added. Which wasn't true—but she was not about to admit anything in the bastard's favor. A raving lunatic.

'Remarkable, I assure you,' the curator of mammals muttered distractedly while the director barked into the telephone next door. 'Quite fearless. Used to get into the big cats' cages with them.'

That wasn't news; it was one of the first things she'd heard when she came to work here. 'That shows he *is* crazy.'

'But, he didn't *seem* crazy. Just ... I don't know, I liked him—everybody did. And obviously very intelligent.'

'And rude.' Her accent was English.

'Was he? I'm surprised. Very gentle man, I always thought. No-nonsense and quick, but ... never rude. *Gentle*. And,

somehow, absolutely trustworthy. Now? . . . look what he's done
. . .'

The director waved at them to shut up. He was a tall, horsey man
of about fifty, eyes large behind his glasses. He was saying, 'Really,
Mr. Worthy . . . Please, Worthy, it is highly likely that your stolen
trucks will be stopped on some highway with the animals safely
inside them—but if this man Jordan manages to release them
somewhere, I assure you that the recapture operation will be
methodically mounted under my personal supervision, with the
assistance of the US Wildlife Department and other experts. *All*
other civilians will be excluded . . . Mr. Worthy, there are numerous tried and proven methods of capturing wild specimens, and as a
zoologist I assure you I am familiar . . .' He took an impatient breath
and shoved his glasses onto the bridge of his nose. 'Mr. Worthy—
you will be consulted when necessary, but I am *un*aware that circus
personnel are experts in the capture of wild animals—now . . . yes, I
will keep you informed, now good day, my other phone is ringing!'

He banged down the telephone and snatched at the next. 'Professor Ford,' he snapped.

Dr. Elizabeth Johnson could sit still no longer. She muttered
impulsively to the curator: 'Buzz me at the surgery when this
meeting gets going.' She got up and walked out of the room,
heading grimly for the Animal Hospital.

Professor Jonas Ford had banned the press, but outside the gates
a group of reporters was speaking to one of the keepers.

'Of course we all love the animals, but Davey was somethin' else
again. Man, he could almos' *talk* to animals.'

'What do you mean, "talk"?'

'I mean *talk*, sir,' Ambrose Jones said earnestly. 'I don't mean
just makin' their kinds of noises, though Davey could make any
kind of animal noise you name—canary, hippopotamus, monkey,
elephant, you name it.' He shook his old head. 'But what I mean is,
Davey knew what was goin' on in an animal's *head*. . . . He *knew*,
an' he could go up to that animal an' if you was listenin' real close all
you could hear was a kind o' mixture of noises, know what I mean,
like breathin' through his nose, snortin' soft, and whistlin' and
some of the noises the animal makes, like purrin' if it was a cat or
squeakin' if it was the hippo, and then some English, real soft and

26

friendly. And so *confident*, man ... and I ask him once, Davey, I said, How you do it, 'cos I wanna be able to do it too; and he says, animals got more *senses* than we got, that's obvious because they can do things we can't, and one of those extra senses is *feelin'*, he says ... *feelin'*. I mean telepathy, kind of.'

Ambrose shook his graying head. 'I ask him to explain plenty of times, but he just came over all complicated. And then he used scientific words too, 'cos, man, that Davey reads books; he's studied more books about animals than Professor Ford, even.'

'But what unusual things have you seen him *do* with animals?'

Ambrose said: 'I mean, he used to spend hours just sittin' with his animals in their cages, playin' with 'em and just watchin' 'em and talkin' to 'em and ... just *bein'* with 'em. That's the only way to know an animal, he said, by studyin' it, everythin' it does. And be its *friend*. ... He did that in the wilderness too, plenty of times.'

'Did Jordan ever get into the big cats' cages?'

'*Particularly* the big cats,' Ambrose said. 'And the elephants and the apes and the rhinos—and those rhinos, sir, they don't take to nobody, but they like lambs with Davey. But the big *cats?*—they went mad for him.'

'And other keepers can't do that?'

'No, *sir*,' Ambrose said. 'Certainly not. When the keeper has to go into the cage to clean it, first he chases the cat into the other section and seals her up in there. He don't go stickin' his hands into her cage. One time'—old Ambrose said, warming to his theme—'one time the big tiger's got to go to the doctor, see, but in the surgery she escapes. And she's runnin' all over the compound, snarlin' and roarin' and we're all runnin' round hollerin' and gettin' the tranquilizer gun—an' Davey comes in; and he jus' walks up to that tiger and says one word and puts his arms around her and leads her back into the cage like a little lamb.' He added: 'He loved that tiger. Mama. And Professor Ford was always tearin' a strip off him for gettin' in the cages, sayin' they were dangerous.'

'But was he a troublemaker?' the reporter asked.

'No sir! *No*. Davey was a real quiet man, and he did his job better'n all of us.'

'And the other man, Charles Buffalohorn, did you know him?'

'Big Charlie?' Ambrose said, 'Sure. He and Davey been pardners

27

a long time. But he didn't work here. But he came to the zoo plenty, to see the animals.'

'What's he like?'

'*Nice* guy,' Ambrose said. 'Real nice. And real gentle. And big. He makes Davey look so small. But Davey's . . .*smart*, I guess. And he's so . . . *sweet*. Maybe that's the word . . . but *tough* too.'

'You mean sweet-*looking?*'

'No. Well, yes, that too, but I mean . . . sweet-*natured* . . . sweet-thinking, like . . . he's got beautiful thoughts . . .'

'And Big Charlie?'

Old Ambrose smiled. 'He don't talk much. But he ain't stupid. You know what those two do? Go up to trappers' country, up to Canada and right here in the States. And,' Ambrose said proudly, 'they'd steal the traps! And throw them in the rivers.'

'How do you know that?'

'It's no secret. Davey's very hot against trappers, those animals takin' days to die, and chewin' their own legs off to get free, and the thirst and all that, it's terrible, ain' it? Why can't an animal at least get a decent death in a civilized country?' he says. And the whaling—and the seals, that's another thing. Every year,' Ambrose said, 'Davey goes up to Canada, to the Saint Lawrence when they're butcherin' the seal pups, right? And he joins them Greenpeace guys and the Friends of the Earth on the ice. He been in plenty of fights up there with those Norwegian sealers—the Greenpeace guys don't fight, you know, they just obstruct by standin' in front of the little pup lyin' there helpless, and Davey don't like fightin' either, but he says there's a time when a man's just got to stand up and fight when he sees somethin' terrible happenin'—he's got the *duty*, he says. Like when you see a mugger beatin' up a little old lady. Well, it's the same with the seals. And one time,' Ambrose smiled, 'he gets so mad he goes running out onto the ice with a big whip! And he cracks it over the heads of those butchers, like this, and he chases 'em back to their ship.'

'Didn't they retaliate?' the reporter smiled.

'Sure, and some come at him with their clubs, but Davey has 'em dancin' all over the place with his whip, and he drives 'em off. Then,' he said, 'they reported him to the Mounties.'

'What happened?'

'It was in the papers,' Ambrose said proudly. 'The Mounties took him in front of the judge. And Davey says, "It's amazin' what a fuss big brave men make about a little bit of whip cracking when they busy butcherin' defenseless little seals with clubs, an' skinnin' 'em alive . . ." It was all in the papers. And there's such a fuss that the judge just warns Davey, and binds him over to keep the peace, 'cos he didn't actually hit nobody with his whip, he just frightened 'em off. And you know what Davey says to the judge?'

'What?'

' "But I *am* keepin' the peace, your Honor—God's peace!" '

Suddenly, as he came over a long hilltop, there was the big flashing sign: POLICE CHECK—ALL TRUCKS PULL INTO EMERGENCY LANE.

Half a mile ahead of them was a wooden barrier across the highway, several police cars parked on the verges. A row of trucks was being inspected by policemen before being allowed to proceed under an elevating boom. Davey Jordan's heart pounded, and he jerked his foot off the accelerator.

He looked desperately into his wing mirror for Big Charlie's truck, and flashed his taillights in warning. His mind was racing. He was slowing to forty miles an hour, and the row of trucks was only five hundred yards away—now four hundred yards away, now three hundred . . . Now the last truck was only two hundred yards ahead, and the barrier one hundred yards ahead of that. And Davey trod on the accelerator and slammed his hand on the horn.

The blast of it split the morning like an express train, and his truck leaped forward, roaring down the highway again, blasting straight at the barrier.

Shocked policemen were scattering and waving and shouting, and Davey kept his foot down flat and his hand on the horn—roaring and blasting straight at the barrier, his headlights blazing, and Big Charlie roaring along behind him. Davey gripped his wheel, white-knuckled, his face ashen, his eyes wide and his teeth clenched. All he could see was that red and white barrier hurtling nearer and nearer, forty yards, then thirty, then twenty, filling his vision—and then he hit it.

With a crack like a cannon above the blasting of the horn, the barrier burst and flew like grapeshot, big shattered timbers flying high and wide into the Tennessee morning; Big Charlie's truck hurtled through after him, leaving shocked policemen scrambling for their cars.

A quarter mile ahead was a turnoff to the town of Erwin and the Appalachian Mountains. Desperately Davey Jordan swung his truckload of elephants onto it.

# seven

He kept his hand on the horn, tearing through the town like a locomotive—houses flashing by, people and dogs and cars scattering. Ahead was an intersection, the traffic light green. He heaved the wheel and swung into Main Street, the whole massive truck keeling over.

He roared up Main Street, leaning on his horn, storefronts flying past, cars screeching and dodging, people scrambling and staring and yelling, and Big Charlie right behind him. Two hundred yards behind came the first of the police cars, lights flashing and sirens screaming.

The two trucks went hurtling through Erwin, heading flat out for the Appalachian Mountains, with the police cars wailing behind them. Ahead was another intersection, lights yellow. Davey roared across it. At the next one the light was red and he kept his foot flat, his hand on the horn. A car squealed to a wild halt halfway across; Davey swung his wheel desperately and the truck hurtled through, Big Charlie still behind him. The first police car was almost level with Charlie now, siren screaming and a cop yelling out the window brandishing his gun, and Charlie just kept going. The car overtook Charlie's truck and went wailing on after Davey on the wrong side of the road, and now the second police car was screaming up on Charlie's flank.

The first car was drawing wildly alongside Davey, the cop yelling, 'Pull over or I shoot!' Davey jerked down behind the wheel and kept on going. Two hundred yards ahead was the turnoff to the mountains, and he headed for it, hunched over his wheel. The police car swung howling in front of his fender; there was a deafening crash of metal, and sparks flew. The truck jolted, and the police car bounced off, tires screeching and cops yelling. Davey kept his foot flat and swung into the intersection. His huge truck swayed and the police car swerved out of his thundering way, going into a wild skid. Big Charlie thundered across the intersection also, and the second police car crashed into his side, banging and bouncing off, then the driver swerved to avoid the first police car skidding toward him, and they crashed into each other. Sideways on, with a wrench of metal and screaming sirens, the two massive trucks roared into the suburbs of Erwin.

They hurtled along, horns blasting, hedges and fences and gardens and churches flashing by, dogs and cats scattering and astonished housewives clutching laundry, groceries and children. Back at the intersection the two police cars disentangled themselves and went racing furiously after them again, battered and howling. The two massive trucks full of animals hurtled past drive-in banks, and supermarkets and restaurants, laundromats and gas stations, heading for the Appalachian Mountains. Then one of the police cars was drawing alongside Davey's cab again, and he ducked, his foot flat, his horn still sounding. There was a jolt and a screech, and the police car bounced wildly off his fender. The driver bellowed and swung the screaming car back at the truck. There was another crash above the siren; in the second car the cop was shouting into his radio 'Pete's jus' bouncin' off—there he goes again—these bastards're too big to head off—Now he's goin' to shoot—' And there was the cracking of gunfire above the wailing, and the bullets went ricocheting off Davey's heavy-duty tires; fifty yards back the second car's windscreen suddenly shattered like a spider web, and the car skidded to a stop against the curb.

The front car swung back toward Davey's truck. There was a wrenching crash, its front wheel wobbled, and the car went into another skid. It skewed wildly across the road; then it nose-dived into the picket fence of the No-tell Motel Drive-in 'n' Nite-Club.

Elizabeth Johnson slammed down the telephone in her office, grabbed her medical bag, and dashed out. She scrambled into her

31

Volkswagon. She drove fast out of the zoo grounds, heading for the airport in New Jersey.

# eight

Up in the Appalachians, a few miles from Erwin, there is a disused bridge across the Nolichucky River. It is one lane only, over the sheer cliffs of the gorge, which drops to the river below.

David Jordan roared his truck up the crest, then brought it to a hissing halt. He shoved her into reverse, and the huge truck swung backward off the highway, down onto the bridge. He leaped out of his cab, ran to the back, wrenched out the bolts and dropped the big tailboards. There stood the elephants and Sally, jam-packed, blinking at him.

He gave an imperative whistle. Rajah squeezed himself around and started uncertainly toward him, shoving past the hippopotamus.

It only took two minutes to get them all down the tailboards and onto the narrow, old bridge. Davey climbed back into his cab feverishly, and drove his vehicle out of the way, to allow Big Charlie to reverse his truck into the same position.

Five minutes later all the animals were on the bridge. The big bewildered elephants, the wide-eyed lions and tigers, the bears, the gorillas and Sally, blinking and frightened. Davey ran to the other end of the bridge and whistled, and Big Charlie began to shoo them from behind. The circus elephants began to lumber after Davey, then the bears and circus lions, then the others followed. Across the bridge they went, then they were scrambling up the steep dirt track into the Appalachian Mountains, Davey in front with Champ the Chimpanzee beside him, and Big Charlie and the wolf-dog, Sam, bringing up the rear.

For the first two miles they ran uphill, into forests of pine and laurel, the long line of animals huffing and panting, their nostrils dilated at all the smells, adrenalin pumping, flanks heaving. Davey ran, his knapsack bouncing, his heart pounding with exhaustion, his eyes bright with fury that this had happened, just one hundred miles from the Smokies—just two more hours in those trucks. He ran and ran, following the narrow dirt path that was the Appalachian Trail, looking over his shoulder, gasping at the animals to follow, but they were right behind him: the chimpanzee galloping hard on his heels; and Mama the zoo tiger; then Rajah and the circus elephants, trunks swinging; then the zoo elephants and the performing bears and, at the rear, Sally the hippopotamus, wheezing. Davey knew they would follow him, and anyway Big Charlie was herding them and Sam would bring back any that scattered off the trail. He kept glancing back only to urge them to hurry, desperately putting as much distance as possible between them and the abandoned trucks. He ran and he ran, then at last he slowed to a rasping jog.

He shuffled along the crest, his arms hanging loose, his heart thumping against his chest. He knew that a few miles ahead, near No Business Knob, there was a spring. About a mile beyond that, a creek. The animals needed water. But the spring was too small; it would take too long; they needed the creek ... and he had not brought the pig's carcass for the lions. Nor did he have a rifle.

'But ole Professor Ford's right,' Frank I. Hunt drawled, eyes closed. 'I'm not an expert.' His makeup girl was putting the finishing touches to his tan.

'But to *them* you are,' Charles Worthy said. He jabbed his finger downstairs at the Hilton Hotel lobby. 'You're the big lion tamer to them, and don't you forget it, Morris.'

'And don't call me Morris,' Frank sighed.

'And those grizzly bears, everybody's scared of grizzly bears. Even those elephants are dangerous—that's what you got to tell them. And *you're* going to get them back.'

'Sure,' Frank said.

'You know much more about those animals than that Professor Ford—' He jerked his thumb at the television screen. He tossed his showman's head: '"I am unaware that circus personnel are experts ..." Well, I tell you something you're going to make him aware of.

He just keeps animals like museum pieces for people to ogle at. But we—we bring the animals *to* the people! We bring *knowledge* of animals. Entertainment. Happiness. Most kids in this world would never *see* an elephant or a lion unless we brought them to their town. And we're proud of that! Zoo?—they just keep animals in cages. Us?—we go into the cages!'

'Sure,' Frank Hunt said wearily.

'Are you *listening*, Frank? We're not going to take that insult from Ford lying down!'

'Certainly not.'

'And something else Ford's unaware of,' the old man said vehemently. 'He's not going to steal the show, Morris! Hell, they're mostly *our* animals that's been stolen, *our* trucks, *our* gear thrown all over the zoo, *our* circus that can't go on! What's he lost? One tiger and a coupla gorillas and three or four elephants, and bet they're all as miserable-looking as he is.'

'Actually,' the makeup girl said, 'I thought he was kind of cute. All serious and cuddly.'

'Whereas *you?*—you're photogenic, Morris. You go into that ring, and you knock all the ladies dead. And the kids love you, you make everybody happy. And *you're* the expert. I'm not saying you *must* go down there to those television cameras and cash in on what's happened … That wouldn't be … in keeping with our proud tradition. All I'm saying is … there's going to be an awful lot of publicity—and if it rightfully belongs to anybody it belongs to us—not to Professor Ford, Morris … This is very important to put across Morris!'

'Morris isn't a very photogenic name. Try Frank I. Hunt.'

'What's the *I* supposed to stand for?' the girl asked.

'Ignatius,' Frank said.

'*Ivan*,' Worthy said testily. 'Can't you take anything seriously? Listen, Frank—you don't seem to realise what this means. The whole world's watching, Frank! We're going to hold their attention for weeks while those animals are recaptured. And you, sir, are going to be a national figure—the guy who goes into the cages, remember that!'

'It's getting the animals *back* into the cages that I'm not wild about.' Frank looked at himself in the mirror. 'Am I or am I not,' he said, 'a dead ringer for Tony Curtis?' He blew himself a kiss. 'Or Dean Martin?' he added reasonably.

'Be serious for once!'

'Serious? . . .' He reached for the bourbon and sloshed some into his glass. 'I am deadly serious, Chuck. I an *not* a big white hunter. Never have been, you know. Ringmaster, that's me.'

'You're not a comedian either!'

'Comedian?' Frank mused. 'Maybe that's what I should have been. Or an escape artist.'

'You don't even care that we've lost our animals! Even if they're shot!'

Suddenly Frank Hunt looked serious. 'Is that so?' He took another big slug of his whiskey. 'Well, I'm here to tell *you*'—he jabbed a finger—'that I *do* care.' He jabbed his finger again. 'I want all those big cats safely back in their cages! And that tiger. Because I, Chuck,' he tapped his chest, 'trained the bastards. *I*, as you so correctly pointed out, go into the cages! Not you—*me*. And I don't want to start all over again with new sonsabitches who want to eat me for breakfast every goddam morning!'

He shucked on the jacket of his white safari suit, then clapped on his leopard-skin-banded hat at a rakish angle.

'You know why I'm so happy? Because I'm not going into the ring with those cats tomorrow.' He turned to the girl and said pensively, 'Maybe I should have been the Human Cannonball?'

Then he opened the door with a flourish and strode down the carpeted corridor to the elevator, Worthy hurrying behind him. He stabbed the elevator button and waited jauntily. The doors opened on an elevator full of people standing solemnly. Frank gave them a businesslike smile and intoned, 'I suppose you're wondering why I called you all together? . . .'

# nine

'Why not?' Dr. Elizabeth Johnson demanded indignantly.

'Because, ma'am,' the air-hostess smiled, 'we're not allowed to serve alcohol over the Bible Belt.'

'But we're twenty thousand feet up!'

'In the Bible Belt it's dry all the way up to heaven, ma'am.'

'Good God ...'

Then that gave her something new to worry about: the Bible Belt. She had heard about this funny country down here in the South, its hillbilly brethren who thought the world was flat. Didn't they have people up in these hills who still spoke Elizabethan English? Backwoods people like those in that movie *Deliverance* ... God ... What would people like that do to jungle animals let loose in their mountains? Not counting American hysteria, and the great American hunters she'd read about, who were going to descend with a whoop and a holler on the sudden bonanza of exotic targets to blood their mail-order guns on. Oh, God, the hue and cry that was coming, and the bloodbath ... And a lot of policemen in this country were supposed to be trigger-happy. And who was going to be masterminding the recapture operation? Dear old Jonas Ford. ...

She closed her eyes. *That* in itself was enough to make her need a drink.

That was unjust of her. Jonas was a fine zoologist, one of the world's best. A good administrator, too. Maybe he could handle this crisis, maybe he was just the man. Maybe he'd get in there and mastermind the whole thing as magnificently as he performed post mortems.

She lit a cigarette and blew the smoke out hard.

She wished she could believe it. Dear Jonas ... *fine* Jonas ... honorable Jonas ... distinguished and successful Jonas. And even—for the right girl, one day—*lovable* Jonas. But, oh, dear me. ...

She sighed out smoke. Heavens, he treated life—people—as he treated his animals. 'Exhibits.' That's what he called the animals in his zoo. 'This is a fine exhibit.' 'Is this exhibit sick?' 'What about the female adult exhibit?' And that's how he treated people in his earnest, uptight way. That's how he had treated that press interview and put everybody's back up—didn't he realize that this was also an *emotional* crisis, that not everybody approved of zoos, that the cages *were* too small, that the zoo was going to come in for a lot of criticism? Didn't he realize the crying need right this moment to appeal for calm and *goodwill?* To make the public feel *love* for the animals, so they'll cry out for *restraint* ... She felt the dread and impotence well up again, and closed her eyes. *Keep thinking about Jonas* ...

She had caught Jonas's television interview in the transit lounge in Cook's County airport (where she could have got a drink if only she'd known about the Bible Belt lurking ahead, zapping its deadly laws up into the stratosphere). And oh, dear, Jonas meeting the press on television about this terrible thing, this insanity committed against her poor animals ... He had spoken as if the reporters' questions were a personal affront.

She sighed. And, yes, she felt sorry for herself. Because until she saw him on television she had begun to think—*hope?*—that something could come of it between them. For an instant she had even felt proud when she saw him striding so authoritatively into the press conference—but as soon as he began to speak with his serious-scientist authority ...

She exhaled smoke. No ... Jonas and she just weren't meant for each other by dear old Mother Nature. In that instant she had glimpsed all the things about him that gave her the willies. Jonas and his half bottle of California wine. His nervous expression when she consulted the menu, in case she chose anything too expensive. Jonas opening windows when she lit a cigarette. Jonas inspecting the cutlery for stains. Jonas and his sudden bumbling ardor every time he tried to make love to her. Jonas jumping up afterward to wash his hands. Jonas and his determined dignity. Jonas and his bloody *tactlessness*—'You drink too much, my dear, that's why you're putting on weight.' 'You smoke too much, my dear, you're losing your complexion.' Just the thing a girl likes to hear.

She smiled wearily. Dear Jonas ... Good man. Good scientist. Well-off, bachelor, social standing. But she had been a fool even to try to make a go of it. She should have kept the relationship on its original level—intellectual; just somebody nice to talk music and poetry and books and films with—somebody nice and safe. But no. She had been trying pathetically to put her life back together ever since the Big Heel suddenly had kicked her out. It had been very nice, after her dismal failures in the singles bars (Oh God how dismal), after her pathetic efforts at being with-it—a shrinking violet on the meat market—to be wooed by her new prestigious boss, very nice to write home to England, so that the Big Heel would hear about it, that she was having a ball in the Big Apple of New York and having a wild affair with one of the world's leading professors of zoology—how would his blonde Singapore dumbbell look then?

Then she sighed at herself scornfully. But bitterly all the same. Because Bernard wouldn't care. And the sad fact was that she shouldn't care either! A whole bloody year—she should be over it by now!

Enough! She felt the tears burn, and she got up impulsively to stop herself thinking. She hurried down the aisle to the toilet, trying to compose herself. She locked the door and slumped against it.

She sighed deeply. There were a few other hard facts to face.

And one was that she dreaded ever having to show herself to him now—to have herself compared to the blonde from Singapore. Because she *was* too fat now, just as Jonas said. She was a godawful mess! Look at you! And even your panties back to front still!

She unzippered her jeans, kicked off her shoes. She pulled the jeans down over her hips, wrestled them down over her thighs. So tight! Two sizes bigger than last year! She sat down on the toilet and struggled out of them. She pulled off the offending panties, then made herself look in the mirror.

God, she looked dreadful. And she wasn't talking about her distress, her red eyes and her hair all over the place. She stood there naked from the waist down, twenty thousand feet above the Bible Belt. Plump thighs—and she used to have good legs. Look at your hips. Dimpled bottom. Even her shoulders were chubby. She had put on so much weight that her bust looked smaller, though it wasn't. She used to have almost classic high cheekbones. Now? A year ago she was positively *thin* after eating her heart out for two awful months in their heartbreakingly empty house in London hoping Bernard would return to his senses and come back to her. 'I'm afraid I've fallen in love,' he had announced on the telephone from the airport, 'I'm not coming home.' A few stop-overs in Singapore, and he'd fallen in love—prepared to kick over five years for some peroxide blonde he'd met in the Shangri-La Hotel. And now what she had done to herself—overweight and a smoker's cough!

She closed her eyes. This was ridiculous . . .

She *looked* ridiculous, standing there. She pulled on her panties, then her jeans. *Ridiculous, bare-assed over the Bible Belt feeling sorry for herself.* She jammed on her shoes. She peered into the mirror to patch herself up, then sighed. She'd left her bag on her seat; she didn't have her makeup.

Oh, what the hell! Why should she care what she looked like, nobody else did. Except dear old Jonas Ford. She didn't care if she was too fat, if she ate too much, and if a few whiskys and a bottle of wine every evening were making her fat, to hell with it—what else was there to look forward to in her crummy apartment at the end of a day? *She did not care any more.*

Then she looked at herself grimly.

Well—that was wrong. She was going to start caring again, from now on. She was going to stop feeling sorry for herself. So, her husband had jilted her. Big deal—it had happened to millions of other people. Think *positively* . . .

She ran her fingers through her hair, bit her lips to get some color into them, then opened the door. She returned to her seat, collected her handbag and walked back to the toilet.

She brushed her hair vigorously. She powdered her nose and put on her lipstick.

There . . . she looked much better. Her hair was still good—wavy and shiny and a lovely chestnut. And her green eyes were still beautiful. And her mouth. In fact, she had a lovely face—you could still see that. *She was going to get herself back into shape.* Think positively. So she could stand comparison with the Singapore blonde.

She returned to her seat and stared out of the window.

And her heart sank again as she looked down at those mauve

Appalachian Mountains. Oh, how vast. They just went on and on forever. How on *earth* were they going to get those animals out of there? It was going to take a massive military-style operation just to *contain* the animals in any given chunk of it, let alone get in there and *find* them, track them one by one. Then get them *out* ... No roads and that massive, steep, rugged, timber country.

Then she thought of her dear animals loose, frightened, bewildered, lost, their beautiful eyes darting fearfully in all directions and their hearts hammering, crouched in hiding and slinking about, terrified of every rustle of leaves and snap of a twig, desperately looking for food and not finding any, getting hungrier and hungrier, not understanding what had happened to them, getting thinner and thinner and wild with fear—*and not understanding*. *Defenseless*. And her heart surged in impotent anger at David Jordan.

She did not know what good she was going to do, impulsively jumping on a plane like this and getting down here. Bernard had always accused her of impetuosity. Too easily steamed up. 'Drama, Liz—you're a sucker for drama.' But she knew she just had to—she just had to *try*, somehow try, to get in there and *do* something. Be available, to help, to try to prevent. To ... *succor*. ...

# part three

## ten

A creek ran down a ravine, through thick hemlock and laurel, disappearing into tangled green and dappled shadows. The animals were invisible from the Appalachian Trail, fifty yards up on the crest. A man loses sight of another within twenty paces in those forests.

It was early afternoon. The animals clustered around the little creek, waiting for Jamba, the old zoo elephant, who was still drinking. David squatted on the bank, sweat shining on his forehead, eating a bar of chocolate, his eyes restlessly darting over the animals, constantly looking in the direction of the Appalachian Trail.

Champ sat on one side of him, Sam in front, ears cocked, tongue slopping, his wolf eyes riveted on every movement of the chocolate from hand to mouth. Davey's face softened and he fondled the dog's head. Sam thumped his tail once, then he was all eyes for the chocolate again. Davey broke off a piece and tossed it to him. Sam snapped it up in midair, gulped it down, then was all rapt attention again.

'You didn't even taste that.'

But Sam would have nothing to eat tonight, and nor would the big cats because he'd left the meat in the trucks. That whole business with the trucks was a crying-out shame. Just two more hours, and they would have made it. . . .

He breathed deep, to stop himself thinking like that. They'd made it this far, and they'd make it the rest of the way.

He looked at the big cats—they were expecting him to feed them about now. They were tired. But they were in good physical condition. They were all watching him intently, except Mama, the Bronx Zoo tiger. She sat beside him, flanks heaving, tail twitching as she watched the circus cats. He put his hand on her big head and stroked her; for a moment she put her ears back and shoved her head up into his hand, then she was glaring at the circus cats again.

'Mama? It's all right, Mama.'

She looked at him a moment distractedly, her eyes just twelve inches from his, and he felt the old thrill, the pure marveling at such beauty and animal perfection, her magnificent tigerness, her eyes piercing deep and dangerous, her face three times the size of his, every hair and line of it perfect, her black nose exquisitely shaped, her big jaws so magnificently and efficiently designed to kill. Then she turned back to the circus lions again.

They were crouched together, panting, eyes alert, ready to whirl around and run. Tommy, the big lion, was in the middle, the lionesses scattered about him, long tails flicking. Sultan, the tiger, sat slightly apart, only tolerated by the others because of the circumstances. They were not frightened of the other animals, they knew most of them: it was the forest, the unknown. Their eyes darted around, ears cocked, but mostly they were staring at Davey, big yellow eyes piercing into him, waiting to be fed.

'I'm sorry, my friends. Just rest. Lie. Lie, Tommy.'

Tommy lay down reluctantly. The lionesses followed suit. Sam lay down too. Davey looked at him and then pointed across the creek.

'Guard, Sam. Guard.'

Sam got up and jumped across the creek, and went a few yards into the forest, then sat down and looked about him at the animals. He knew what was expected of him and he tried to look business-like, but he was thinking about the chocolate. Davey smiled at him.

But he was worried about the big cats and he cursed himself again for not bringing a gun. There was a brand-new rifle waiting for him in the Smokies, buried months ago in preparation for this day, so he could feed the big cats until they could look after themselves—but, why, oh why, had he been so stupidly confident as to think he did

42

not need another gun in the truck for this kind of emergency. How was he going to get them meat over the next few days?

He sighed tensely. Soon there were going to be plenty of guns in this forest, looking for *them*.

'Come on, Jamba.'

He got up impatiently and plodded into the shallow stream. Jamba stood in the middle, laboriously sucking water up her trunk, blinking at him. 'Come on, old girl!' He crouched down and scooped out a little dam for her, and stuck her trunk tip in the muddy hole. Jamba sighed and sucked the little dam dry in one exhausted slurp. Davey looked up into her sad, affectionate eye, and he felt a rush of emotion for the dear, old, kind-hearted animal. 'Oh Jamba,' he whispered, 'I love you.' He put his arm around her trunk and squeezed. 'You're going to love it down there.' Then he winked and cocked his head furtively at Rajah.

'Hey—what do you think of *him*, then?'

Old Jamba just sighed and slurped.

'All right, Jamba, hurry up.'

Sally stood in the stream behind Jamba, her head hanging, her fat flanks heaving. The young zoo elephants were clustered together uncertainly, waiting for Jamba. She was their natural leader still, and she wouldn't reject them until she went into estrus and mated with Rajah.

Davey looked at the big circus elephant. Rajah stood massively, eyes closed, trunk hanging. He looked completely relaxed. The cow Queenie was swinging her trunk restlessly, waiting for orders in this strange terrain. Dumbo was edgy too, standing close to her. He had been hanging onto her tail as they lumbered along, as he had been taught to do. But good old Rajah looked unperturbed by all this, and Davey smiled with relief.

Good old Rajah. Maybe he thought this was something to do with his job. But no, he was so intelligent, he knew what was going on. He knew they were running away. And the feeling in the air—the electricity, the sense of urgency, the run run run and the necessity to obey.

He knew. But he was such a cooperative old war-horse, and so experienced, that he didn't fluster easily. Davey had told him to rest, so now he was resting. He had been trained as a logging elephant in India before The World's Greatest Show had acquired him; he was accustomed to working without supervision. He knew how to stack logs neatly on top of each other, when to swim out into a river without bidding and unblock logs, how to heave railway cars into position, haul trucks out of mud, heave on ropes. At the circus he would perform heavy-duty jobs if he was shown what was wanted. He even performed tricks willingly enough. All he wanted in exchange was a fair deal; what he hated was the crack of the ringmaster's whip, the shock of the electric prodder; and his massive body yearned for space.

Well, Davey thought, he could ride on Rajah when he got exhausted.

'How're you, Charlie?'

The big Indian was lying on his back higher up the slope, eyes closed, chest heaving.

'Okay ... I saw the elephants along the trail snatching some branches and eating.'

'Yes, no problem with their feeding.'

'Nor the gorillas.'

King Kong, the silver-back male from the zoo, was on all fours, his big knuckles folded, intently watching, his brown, worried eyes alert. The chimpanzees were gathered together nervously. Davey glanced at King Kong; then smiled and averted his eyes and shook his head to show nonaggression. King Kong shook his head and glanced away, then looked back at him anxiously and waited again.

'What about the bears?'

'They'll start eating soon—bears are always hungry.'

'They don't look like they want to start nothin'.'

The great performing bears were on all fours, heads up, dish faces immobile, suspiciously sniffing. They sensed his attention, and they looked at him expectantly. He knew what they were feeling, hanging on his word, waiting for him to tell them what to do: he was their keeper, their friend; they were devoted to him in their big, single-minded bear way. They were not frightened by the wilderness, Davey knew; they were just suspicious and bewildered. They were the natural monarchs of the wilderness, and he was not worried about them adapting back. Gradually, they would leave him, and even each other. And revert to the solitary monarchy that was their nature, wanting no one, steamrollering through the wilderness, huge thousand-pound beasts standing ten feet high on their hind legs, able to leap twenty feet and gallop faster than the best man can run, able to kill a charging bull with one swipe of their claws ...

Just then he heard it. He stiffened. There it was, faraway but certain: the chopping drone of a helicopter.

Davey stood still, trying to locate it. It was coming from the south, from the Great Smoky Mountains. Both he and Big Charlie threw their heads back, searching the chinks of sky through the overhead boughs. The droning became louder. Then it was upon them: a terrible roaring monster suddenly blacking out the sky fifty feet above them, blasting the forest so that trees bent and dirt flew, and the animals scattered in all directions, bounding and blundering, terrified—then as quickly it was gone, roaring away over the treetops.

'Come on!' Davey gave a piercing whistle and shouted: 'Sam—herd!'

He started running up the mountain, looking back over his shoulder, whistling to the animals. Big Charlie was rounding them up, Sam herding from behind. They started blundering through the undergrowth after Davey.


# eleven


In the early afternoon Elizabeth drove up to the Nolichucky River bridge in her Hertz rented car. There had been efficient police barriers across the highway on both sides of the Appalachian Mountains, but they had let her pass when she had explained who she was. The deputy sheriff and two patrolmen were guarding the bridge with rifles. The two trucks of The World's Greatest Show were still there.

'You the vet they radioed us about?' the patrolman said, chewing gum.

'Yes. And please point that gun elsewhere.'

He lowered the gun and scratched his cheek. 'Nobody don' go through. Wal ...' he said, 'there's the trucks. Since eight o'clock this mornin'.'

'But have you seen *them?*'

'Nope. Only person seen 'em is Sergeant Hooks an' his pardner an' they both in bed, sore'n a gumboil.'

The deputy sheriff came over from his car. He raised his hat. 'What can I do for you, ma'am?'

'Has anybody tried to *track* these animals, officer?' she demanded.

'Sure have, ma'am. I was first on the scene after Bert Hooks got himself overturned. Tracked 'em for two miles, then the sheriff radioed me back, orders from the zoo.'

'Where was the spoor heading?'

'Straight down the Appalachian Trail, ma'am, far's I seen.'

'But you're throwing a cordon round the area?'

'Sure are, ma'am. Over forty men in there already, and the state troopers are arriving any time now, and the militia.'

She closed her eyes. 'What are their orders?'

'Stop the animals gettin' out into civilized area, ma'am, till the experts arrive.'

'How?' she demanded. 'By shooting them?'

'Only as a last resort, ma'am. We can't have lions and tigers coming into town.'

'*Noise!*' she cried. 'You've got to shout and beat a can to chase them back—never shoot! Where's the Sheriff?'

The lawman sighed. 'He's up there, ma'am. With some very good men, don't doubt it.'

'Up there? In a helicopter?'

'No ma'am, not in a helicopter. Those woods are too dense for that.'

'Well, I have to go in there, officer.'

The Deputy stared at her.

'Ma'am,' he said quietly, 'you're not going anywhere. Only authorized personnel.'

46

'I *am* authorized! I'm the vet!'

'Ma'am,' he said firmly, 'I'm not letting you go in there. You won't get nowhere with those shoes anyhow. That's tough wilderness in there. I'm not letting you go in without an armed escort—and I'm not supplying that, ma'am. We ain't got enough men for this job as it is.'

'I can look after myself!'

The officer sighed and put a weary hand on his hip.

'Ma'am—you cannot look after yourself, vet or no vet. They're wild animals at large in there! And two very wild men! In very wild country. With those shoes'—he pointed at her feet—'and unless we're very smart there're goin' to be a good few other wild folk in there with their guns—and they're no better than animals, ma'am.' He looked at her sternly. 'I don't know where you come from, but this here's the United States of America—haven't you heard what gun-mad SOBs we are!' He glared at her. 'And I'm not letting you loose amongst that lot!'

She felt her stomach go cold. She was not going to argue with him. Wherever they were, the animals weren't near here. They'd be as far away as possible from the trucks. She turned and grabbed her roadmap out of the rented car.

'What's the next road to the south that crosses the Appalachians?'

The lawman sighed. 'Highway Nineteen W, ma'am. At Spivey Gap.'

'How far south?'

''Bout ten, twelve miles, ma'am. As the crow flies.'

'Is that barricaded by police too?'

'Sheriff's workin' on it, ma'am. You won't get through that way either.'

'How do I get there?'

'Back through Erwin,' the patrolman said resignedly.

On her way back to Erwin the cars had been lined up at the police roadblock, newspapermen and sightseers and at least a dozen cars full of men, armed with rifles, volunteering to help.

Elizabeth sped through the town onto the interstate highway, then took the turnoff to Spivey Gap. Her dread turned to anger. There were *still* no police barricades on this road! She wound up

47

into the mountains. At the crest there were only two police cars, the patrolmen keeping the traffic moving. They waved her through.

*A cordon around the area, my foot!*

She drove past the police angrily, her eyes darting at the forest to left and right, looking for ... for what? Signs, spoor, elephant droppings, broken bushes—my God! Like looking for a needle on the edge of a vast haystack.

She felt absolutely helpless. Hopeless ... Looking for any indication of the animals' having crossed the road. She drove slowly, peering at the road, at the edges of the forest. Nothing ... If there were something, she'd miss it, like this. Hopeless ... She'd have to get out and do it properly. Then, around a bend in the highway, she saw the small metal signpost of the Appalachian Trail.

She stopped her car on the verge. She hurried across the highway, to the point where the Appalachian Trail came out of the forest and crossed the road. She looked at it. It was just a tangled dirt path worn through the undergrowth, a foot wide. No spoor that she could see. Silence, everything motionless. She took a deep breath and started to climb the bank of the highway, onto the trail.

Dr. Elizabeth Johnson was no expert tracker, but she had been on two zoological expeditions to Africa, and one to the Rockies, and she knew what to look for. She kept her head down as she climbed the narrow, winding trail, searching the ground, eyes flicking sideways to the undergrowth. Within two minutes her legs were aching. She toiled up the slope through the forest, frequently stopping, her heart hammering from the unaccustomed exertion.

After half a mile she stopped, sweating, her breath coming in gasps.

She had not seen a single sign of animals. She crouched, panting, and examined the hard earth for her own footprints. My God—even *they* were hard to find. Just a tiny scrape here and there. The light was so difficult for tracking, the trail dappled with shadow, sunlight shifting through the boughs. She stared helplessly at the unyielding trail; but she did not believe that twenty-odd big animals, including elephants, could have passed without leaving *some* mark.

She straightened up, and listened. Just the rustle of leaves, the twitter of a bird. She could not even hear the vehicles on the highway, only half a mile back down the trail. She probably would not hear a man approaching until he was ten paces away. The silence was vast, the world muffled by the wilderness.

She could only see twenty paces into the forest. An elephant could be walking thirty yards away, and she could not see it.

She felt absolutely helpless. Vast ... The forest stretched for at least five miles down the slopes of the Appalachians on either side of the trail. It was over ten miles from where she stood to the abandoned trucks. It could take an expert tracker days to make visual contact in this dense forest.

She stood there, sweating, getting her breath back.

Well, there was only one remote chance, apart from going back to the Nolichucky and starting from scratch: go into the forest in a straight line and look for the spoor. If the animals had headed this way, if David Jordan was trying to get them out of this area but was avoiding the trail, she might cross their spoor.

She plunged off the trail, into the undergrowth.

It was late afternoon when she found it, half a mile down the steep forested slope on the North Carolina side of the mountain.

She clung to a tree, elated, exhausted, her arms covered with scratches, muscles aching, hair sticking to her neck and forehead. She stared at the spoor.

She could hardly believe it. ... That a caravan of big animals could have left so little sign of themselves! There was just *one* sign of elephant, and that was a conspicuous lump of dung. The undergrowth was so thick and flexible, the dark earth so hidden and spongy, the light and shadows so difficult.

She crouched and touched the dung with the back of her fingers. It was cool.

She looked feverishly about her in the shadows for more signs. *None.* She knew that a whole troupe of gorillas could pass without leaving obvious sign of themselves—even an elephant over certain terrain—and if she got to her knees now she would find more spoor—but this terrain was so difficult ...

She leaned against the tree, getting her breath back; then she started plodding after the spoor. She crept along for five minutes, then she clenched her fist and started stumbling across the mountain slope in the direction she thought they had taken. Surely they were headed out of this area of the woods where the sheriff was after them.

Exhausted, the underbrush grabbing at her, her ankles buckling, Elizabeth was desperate. With her poor physical condition, with the incompetence of her fellows—where was Dr. Bigwheel Ford while she beat her brains out and broke her neck?

After a hundred and fifty yards she slumped to a stop, gasping, heart pounding.

She could see no more spoor.

She looked back; she could not see even her own tracks in this undergrowth and she could see no more than twenty paces in front of her.

An hour later she heard the muffled sound of a vehicle, and she realized that she was near the highway again. Suddenly, twenty yards in front, was the open sunshine.

She knew now. She had long since lost the spoor, but *that* was where they would have gone: across the highway, into the forest beyond. While that sheriff and his men bumbled around on this side.

She slid down the bank. She wasn't going to waste any more time looking for tracks here.

She toiled up to her car.

The Appalachian Trail continued on the south side, directly opposite, leading steeply up into the forest again. She reached into her car for the road map.

The next road to the south that crossed the Appalachians was Highway 23, at Sams Gap about eleven miles away. She took a big breath.

She started plodding up the narrow dirt trail again, head lowered, looking for spoor. Within thirty paces she was hidden from the highway, ascending steeply into pine forest and hemlock.

Suddenly she stopped in a patch of sunlight, and her pulse tripped with excitement.

She was not looking at an animal's footprint. But the hard ground had been scraped by something: by a bunch of leaves, used like a broom.

She crouched, heart pounding, examining the mark. Then she

50

stood and jogged back down the steep trail. She scrambled into the car and did a hard U-turn, back toward Erwin.

She pulled up in front of a sporting goods store. There were several pickup trucks parked outside, gunracks on the back. She hurried inside.

'You accept these things?' She held up her American Express card.

'Sure do, ma'am.'

'Where're your knapsacks?'

There were a dozen men clustered at the gun counter. Some had their shirts off, showing tattoos; there was loud discussion and laughing. She selected the cheapest knapsack, and a sleeping bag, cursing herself under her breath—she had all these things at home. She found a cheap canteen kit, a pair of Pro-Ked basketball shoes and thick socks, a large-scale hiker's map of the area. She hurried back to the counter and slapped down her credit card.

'Hi, Sugar!' a voice said. She ignored him. 'Excuse me, ma'am?...' She turned to the man disdainfully, then jerked wide-eyed as she looked straight into the muzzle of a rifle.

'Bang!' The young man grinned. 'Right between the eyes!'

'Put that thing down!'

'Bang!' the man repeated, sweeping the gun across the shop. 'Bang!—bang!' There was laughter.

'Or like this,' a youth snickered, holding an imaginary machine gun at his hip. '*Er-er-er-er.*'

Elizabeth stared, shocked. 'What are you boys buying guns for!'

'You the noo sheriff, ma'am?'

'She's from the Bleedin' Hearts!'

'Now listen here!' She held out a trembling finger. 'I know what you boys think you're going to do—go and hunt those animals that were let loose today . . .'

'Only in self-defense, Sugar.' Hairy hand piously on hairy breast.

'Now listen to me—'

'She's from the Bleedin' Hearts,' the youth said. 'The No-Killum Club.'

'You listen to me! I'm an officer of the Bronx Zoo and you're not allowed into those mountains and by God if anybody shoots one of those animals they're going to jail!'

'Ooo-oh!' the gunman said, then they all chorused, 'Ooo-oh.'

She was shaking. 'I've warned you,' she whispered, 'and I'll give evidence against you. Not only do those magnificent animals belong to the Bronx Zoo, it would be a barbaric crime against nature!'

'Aaaa-ah . . .'

She was aghast. Then she tried to look at them witheringly. 'Why?' she whispered. 'Why this despicable human appetite to go out and kill your fellow creatures at every excuse?'

'She's from the No-Trapums, No-Killums, Poor Little Thingums.'

'Good God . . .' She turned and signed her name shakily on the credit card slip, and gathered up her things. Then she turned on them. They pretended to cringe back.

'I've warned you . . .' she said. She turned and started for the door, feeling sick.

'Bang!' the young man said, and they all pointed imaginary guns. 'Bang! Bang!'

'Got her right up her fat ass!'

Elizabeth hurried fearfully into the supermarket. She bought half a dozen cans of corned beef, some rice, two dozen bars of chocolate, some vitamin pills. On her way back to the car she passed a package store. She hesitated, then dashed inside.

*To hell with you Jonas! Why aren't you down here instead of shooting your mouth off on television?*

She ordered a fifth of whiskey; then changed it to a pint.

'Where's the nearest butcher, please?'

'Just down the road aways, ma'am.'

She got back in her car and drove to the butcher shop.

'Can you sell me half a pig, please? Or a whole sheep, whichever is cheaper.'

'You in the barbecue business, ma'am?'

Mystified, he hacked the pig's carcass into chunks as she directed, then stuffed the pieces into a sack, and carried it out to the car for her.

She scrambled back into the driver's seat, and began to study her new hiker's map. It shook in her hand.

It was a huge area—about a hundred square miles of wilderness. But there were several dirt roads up into it, crossing the Appalachian Trail at several points. There was even a picnic area slap in the middle, and a road that led to a mountain called Big Bald.

She concentrated on the best way to get up there.

About fifteen miles away, on the other side of the Appalachians, the helicopter was parked behind an old barn on an abandoned farm.

Three men crouched on the grass, and they were also studying a large-scale surveyor's map of the area.

They were wearing camouflage fatigues and hunting boots. Each man held a top-quality, big-caliber rifle. Inside their helicopter were more rifles of different calibers, all with telescopic sights and silencers.

# twelve

An hour before sunset Davey reached Tumbling Creek.

He watched the animals drink. Big Charlie was spreading out a collection of edible roots and berries and fungi.

'If I could light a fire,' he rumbled, 'I could make a good stew.'

'No fire.'

He hated all the dirt roads through this part of the mountains. A posse could penetrate very deep, very quickly, by vehicle. He wanted to get out, across Sams Gap and into the mountains beyond. It was only seven miles away—three hours, if they stuck to the Appalachian Trail. There was no point in sidetracking—nobody could track them in the dark. By tomorrow morning somebody would have found some spoor, and realize where they were heading. By tomorrow morning the authorities would be organized. *So the important thing tonight was speed. Get as far away as possible down the easiest trail.*

Davey pressed his fingers to his eyes.

Oh ... if only they could have got to the Pigeon River in the trucks. Right on the edge of the Great Smokies ...

He slowly dragged his hands down his face.

Well, they were only eighty, ninety miles from the Smokies. Less than five days, at twenty miles a day.

He could keep the animals together for five days. Fifty, if he had to. He was not worried about that; what he was worried about were all the highways he had to lead them across.

Sams Gap, seven miles ahead.

Then Devils Fork, fifteen miles.

Then Allen Gap.

Then Hot Springs, on the French Broad River.

Then the Interstate 40 and the Pigeon River. With the Great Smoky Mountains across it...

The important things were to keep going as hard and as long as possible.

And rest ... just for an hour.

He was hungry, but his hunger did not matter. What mattered was that the animals rest and eat. He ferreted in his knapsack and pulled out a bar of chocolate. He began to eat it distractedly.

None of the animals was in condition for such hard work. Sam and Champ were both intent on the chocolate. He sighed and pulled out another bar and unwrapped it. Sam's wolf eyes were agog with anticipation. Davey held the chocolate out to him.

'Try,' he said, 'to at least taste it.'

Sam grabbed the chocolate and in two gulps it had vanished. He thumped his tail once and looked hopefully at his master.

Champ croaked and looked at him with big eyes, then held out both hands, cupped.

'Chocolate,' Davey advised him, 'is not what chimpanzees like. Chimpanzees like grass, leaves, roots and similar.'

He should not have done it, but he felt sorry for Champ. The little animal did not know whether he was a human being or a chimpanzee. In the circus ring he thought he was a chimp; with Davey he thought he was a person. In both situations, Champ had an

54

inferiority complex because he was so small. Davey scratched the animal's small head as it chewed the chocolate with relish.

Sally was standing all by herself, in the mud, huffing. It only covered her big blunt toes. She had tried to lie down in it, and her flanks were black with mud.

*Oh why, for God's sake, had he weakened?*

If he had known this was going to happen . . . He could not bear to think what was going to happen if she could not keep up. How could he leave her? It made him desperate just to think about it. . . .

He heaved himself up, plodded into the mud and crouched beside her. Sally opened her eyes, startled.

'How're you, old lady?'

Sally sighed.

'I'm sorry, old Sally.'

Sally wheezed long-sufferingly. 'Let's look at your feet.' He tapped the back of her knee, lifted her hoof and peered in the bad light. It felt rough. But he knew hippos grazed over many miles in Africa, and they could run fast and far, lungs as tough as saddlebags for all their underwater work. But Sally was an old hippopotamus.

'But when we get there, you'll love it, Sally,' he whispered. 'There're beautiful clean rivers for you and even a big lake, and all kinds of things to eat.'

Old Sally groaned, listening to the soothing voice of the only friend she had ever had. Her eyes began to droop.

'And it's warm down there now. Sally. You're going to have a lovely time this summer. It's all going to be worth it.'

He hugged her big fat neck.

And when the winter came, and the rivers got freezing? He felt his throat thicken. Because when winter came, it would not matter. When winter came, old Sally would not be around anymore.

'All right, Sally . . . Sleep, old lady.'

He stood up, stiffly, and looked through the dappled light at the big cats. Mama was waiting for him, next to his knapsack. The circus cats were together on the opposite bank, staring at him, still waiting to be fed.

'I'm sorry.' There was nothing he could do about their food tonight; he had to put it out of his mind.

But the elephants were all right, and the gorillas and the

chimpanzees. The elephants were feeding now, huge gray shapes shuffling wearily, their trunks reaching up, curling round a bunch of leaves, then down to their cavernous mouths, then chomp, chomp, chomp. Old Jamba had assumed natural dominance over the young zoo bulls. When she moved on, they moved.

He sat down again, next to Mama. He just wanted to collapse onto his back, but he had not yet finished rounding up his worries. Dear old Mama. He scratched the back of her head, and she arched her neck and back. Sometimes she gave an angry moan at the circus cats. 'Come on, Mama, they're all right.' He nodded at Sultan, the circus tiger. 'How do you like the look of him?' he whispered. But Mama wasn't having anything to do with Sultan.

Davey's heart went out to Sultan. The lions did not want to have anything to do with him either, although they worked with him. They barely tolerated him. He had to be caged apart because the lions would bully him and wouldn't let him get anything to eat. Even in the ring they snarled at him. Old Sultan wanted to be part of the lions; they were the only family he had ever known. He even thought he was a lion. In the ring he had a hard time from Frank Hunt, too, because he was not the brightest tiger. Sultan performed with bloody-minded reluctance and only because he was terrified of the whip and the electric prodder and because he knew that was the only way he was going to be fed.

He sat all by himself, with a nervous, long-suffering aloofness, watching Davey, waiting for his supper. He blinked and averted his head as Davey crouched in front of him, and took his big furry cheeks in both hands.

'Never mind, Sultan. Tigers are smarter than lions really. And you've got another tiger to live with now.'

Sultan just sat there pessimistically, eyes averted, having his cheeks scratched, feeling sorry for himself. Davey stood up, wearily.

The lions were all watching him. Nervous of the darkening forest, waiting to be fed, waiting to be told what to do. Big Tommy sat in the middle, staring, as if ready to come padding straight at him to kill. But Davey knew that killing was the last thing on Tommy's mind. Tommy wouldn't know how to kill a chicken if it were thown at him squawking, except by playing with it. It was

56

going to be difficult teaching them to hunt. Except maybe Kitty.

As if reading his mind, Big Charlie said, 'Don't worry. Kitty will catch on quick. And show the others.'

Davey nodded. Kitty's eyes never left Davey, her thick tail poised.

'But she's the one I'm worried about,' Big Charlie rumbled, watching her. 'Got the devil in her heart.' He added, 'She's the only one I won't turn my back on.'

Davey shook his head and smiled. He did not believe for a moment Kitty would turn man-hunter. But he never turned his back on her either, in her cage. She would come creeping up on him. Not to attack, but to pounce and play, four hundred pounds of jaws and claws. One pat with those paws could tear off a man's face. He was careful with her; Charlie didn't mess with her; Frank Hunt was downright frightened of her. And Princess, the other lioness, hated her.

Tommy liked Kitty, but Princess picked on her. It happened now. Kitty started toward Davey, and, as she passed, Princess hissed, ears flat, fangs bared and a big paw ready to swipe. Kitty stopped, eyes half closed, ears back, head averted. Her paw was ready too, but she did not rise to the challenge, nor even hiss back. She just waited for Princess to subside. Charlie and Davey smiled. Kitty was not afraid of Princess; she was indifferent. Princess was the matron of the pride; Kitty accepted the fact and did not care.

'Okay, you two,' Davey said.

Princess turned and stalked away angrily, and Kitty padded menacingly over to Davey. He held out his hand, and she arched her back and wiped her big flank along his leg, tail up. He put his hand under her whiskery chin and scratched. 'You're not afraid, are you, Kitty? I'm relying on you.'

He straightened up and sighed.

'You okay, Charlie?'

'Sure.' He lay on his back. 'Stop worrying now, Davey. It's happened.'

Davey shook his head. 'A few more hours, and we would have made it in the trucks.'

'It's happened. Ain't nothing we can do about that. But we'll still make it. Now, get some rest.'

Davey smiled at the big Indian.

'Come on.'

He gave a low whistle and started to lead the animals back up the steep mountain to the Appalachian Trail at the crest. Then he started to jog, his face tense, his arms hanging slack, but it was twice as fast as walking, and he could keep it up for hours.

The sun was setting. A minute later, as he came around a bend of laurel, he saw the man.

His heart lurched and he started to spin around to shout a warning, but he cut it off.

The hiker had his back to him, one hand on his hip, looking impatient. The next instant Davey saw a girl emerging from the bushes, head down, pulling her jeans over her thighs and muttering. Davey turned desperately, to lead the animals off the trail, and the same moment the man turned.

He could not believe his eyes. His jaw dropped, and he went ashen, speechless. He was a keen backpacker; he carried Ed Garvey's famous book on the Appalachian Trail like a Bible; he had hiked other wilderness trails; but *nothing* had prepared him for what he saw: a wild-looking man with a huge elephant behind him. He started to scream, but it just gargled in his dry throat. At that moment his wife looked up, and she screamed for him.

Her eyes widened and her mouth opened to its fullest and the cords stood out on her neck and she clenched her fists to her bosom and her jeans dropped and she screamed. A wild female wail of paralyzed horror that galvanized her husband into action. He grabbed at her arm to plunge off the trail, and at the same moment she turned and fled in the opposite direction.

The man flung himself off the narrow trail into the steep undergrowth, stumbling, out of control, gasping for his wife—and she fled down the trail wild-eyed, her jeans below her buttocks, bellowing her terror to the sky, and Davey yelled, '*It's okay—get off the trail!*' But she could not hear him, and she could not run with her jeans bunched at her knees, and she stumbled and lurched, desperately trying to yank them up, looking wildly over her shoulder and the more she could not run the more terrified she got—then Davey plunged off the trail on the opposite side. With a piercing whistle to his animals, he ran down the steep mountain, leaping and bounding, the animals lumbering and blundering after him.

For a hundred yards he crashed down the mountainside, then he swung south again, parallel to the Appalachian Trail.

Until well after dark he kept them trekking doggedly across the wild mountainside. It was killingly slow going. His legs trembled, and his stomach was a knot of exhaustion. He bitterly regretted not having just blundered on down the Appalachian Trail after the screaming woman until she had thrown herself off it, out of the way. But he could not bear to see her so frightened, and she could have fallen and been trampled; as it was he was worried that she might have run so far that she could not find her husband afterward.

When it was properly dark they stopped and threw themselves down, to sleep for four hours.

King Kong was fully grown, and the hair on his back had turned to silver. He weighed six hundred pounds, and his shoulders were thick and powerful. He stood nearly six feet tall, and his shaggy arms reached below his knees; his knuckles were twice as broad as a man's, and his jaws were big and strong. In the zoo, nobody had dared go into his cage without elaborate precautions, except David Jordan. When they asked him how he did it he had replied 'because he knows I understand.'

A gorilla understands very well. King Kong did not remember much about his life in the Congo, but he remembered the green things and the space, the joy of climbing through the trees. For ten long years he had sat in his cage with the other gorillas, under a neon light, with a concrete tree and a concrete floor, and he looked at the people who came to stare, and grin, and make faces at him; he knew they were the same kind that had massacred his clan to capture him, but he also knew they could not get at him in here, and time had numbed his fear. But every day of his life his great body yearned for space, to stretch his limbs, to walk and run; for green things growing, and real earth, and trees to climb, and sun and wind and sky.

And that is what Davey Jordan understood, and most zoo men do not. Zoo people will sincerely say that their animals are happy, because they are fed and safe from predators; that they neither remember much nor instinctively yearn. But David Jordan had the gift, the heart and the compassion to be able to put himself into the big black breast of the gorilla, and feel what he was feeling, so that he felt like a gorilla himself. When he sat in their cage, and talked to them, and even made their sounds, King Kong knew that David knew what his gorillaness wanted and needed and yearned for. But even more: King Kong knew that Davey was not a gorilla but a creature superior to him. And to everyone in the animal kingdom, superiority is important.

Now King Kong understood what had happened, although it was very confused in its urgency. He knew he had been set free, and he sensed the fear and the excitement of the other animals, and he was frightened. There was not yet any joy of freedom, but he sensed that he was running for his life, and he would keep on running forever, following his leader in this desperate race.

Now his leader was asleep, and King Kong wanted to sleep also. But he was frightened of the dark forest about him. He wanted to be up above the ground. He did not yet remember how to build nests in trees, although he knew he wanted to.

He looked up at the trees uncertainly. He knew how to climb a tree. But he also knew, just by looking, that in these trees he could not lie down to sleep. The big gorilla looked around at the darkness apprehensively, then, uncertainly, he began to do the best he could: he began to scrape the leaves and twigs into a circle about him.

The other gorilla watched him. Then slowly, uncertainly, she began to do the same. King Kong lay down on his side in his nest, and tucked his shaggy legs up to his shaggy black stomach, and he crooked his arm under his big worried head as a pillow.

# thirteen

A forest road crossed the crest of the Appalachians, through a treeless sag at the base of Big Bald Mountain.

It was after midnight. Dr. Elizabeth Johnson sat, locked in her rented car, on the dirt road, hidden in the trees on the edge of the sag. Trying vainly to sleep; waiting for first light. She had bumped her way over all the crisscrossing tracks, peering into the darkness for the shining of eyes, the flash of movement; she had even gotten out and tried to examine the road for spoor in the headlights: it had been hopeless. Scores of miles of winding tracks through a hundred square miles of wilderness. She had been frightened every time she got out of the car.

She was frightened now, locked inside it, sick with the fear the deputy Sheriff had instilled into her, the horror of the men in the Erwin gun shop. She had wrapped her new sleeping bag around her shoulders. She had eaten, and had had a good few nips of whisky. But she could not sleep. She had a lot of tramping around to do tomorrow if she hoped to find them before the gunmen of Erwin. But she was too desperate to sleep.

She sat in the dark, nerves screaming with exhaustion. Big Bald rose treeless to the south, ghostly silver in the moonlight. It was completely still. Spooky. O God, the wilderness was spooky. She had tried to dismiss her fear contemptuously, then to examine it logically. But it was man's primitive fear of the wilderness itself, its wildness, that she was afraid of, just as much as a madman with an ax. Driving up here, she had been fearful that demons would leap out of the shadows. *Demons*—the same that had frightened cavemen and the Pilgrim Fathers and made them set out grimly to 'conquer the wilderness,' turn it into a garden, to take its primeval menace out of it. *Childish* . . . But no—it was the primitive man in her.

She took a deep, tense breath, and reached for the whisky bottle.

If Bernard could see her now . . . Then she felt foolish for even thinking about him. She lit a cigarette with shaky fingers, and inhaled grimly.

She took another sip of whisky, and almost gagged. Then she could hear Jonas Ford saying, 'Whisky isn't a very feminine drink, my dear.' Well to hell with you, Jonas, it tastes damn good, and it's making me feel a whole lot better. Where the hell are *you*? While I sit here scared witless . . .

She sighed.

She was not being very reasonable. It had been *her* wild decision

61

to hurl herself onto a plane and get down here. Jonas was doing the right thing, staying to organize things. And what good did she think she was going to do here, anyway? What was she going to do even *if* she found David Jordan and the animals?

She massaged her forehead with her fingertips.

She did not know.

Except somehow stand between the animals and a bloodbath, somehow shout the hillbilly gunmen out of shooting, somehow warn David Jordan about them, somehow shout some sense into him ...

David Bloody Jordan ... A fat chance she had of talking any sense into *him*. She remembered him clearly, and he was obviously very bright—even Jonas Ford had once described him as 'very intelligent,' and coming from Jonas that was quite something. The keepers had talked about him with such awe, and all the stories—like the time one of the grizzly bears had got his paw jammed in a tin can that some idiot had thrown into the pen. He was going berserk, and the staff was trying to lasso him to tie him down and there was a terrible hullaballoo, and apparently David Jordan had just walked into the den, cool as a cucumber, grabbed the enraged animal's paw and wrestled the can off. 'Quite fearless,' the curator of mammals had described him. 'Damn stupid,' Jonas Ford had said. But even Jonas had described him as 'quite a remarkable fellow,' and the previous vet had said that he had 'almost a Saint Franciscan ability with animals.' She had heard a good deal about him before he had unexpectedly turned up at the zoo.

She'd heard the commotion in the Big Cat House, and gone over to investigate, and there was the great Davey Jordan going from cage to cage, and the cats were beside themselves with excitement, purring and rubbing themselves against the bars. She had watched, fascinated. She had read a good deal about people who can do wonderful things with animals. Quietly she had walked up to him. He paid no attention to her, just stood there, in his own private world of the animals, and he was smiling and talking to them softly; she could not catch the words but they were loving, and the look on his face was? ... It was a beautiful private world she had glimpsed, of love and understanding between a man and animals, which she felt she had no right to enter, an inter-feeling she would never achieve with animals no matter how hard she tried. It had been an intrusion on her part when she finally tried to talk to him. He had been vaguely aloof, almost abrupt, as if he couldn't waste his precious moments.

She could not remember now what she had said as openers—doubtless something corny—but she remembered he had said: 'It's not that animals are like *us*—it's us who're like *them*. If you put it the other way around you're denying the theory of evolution. We're all part of the same animal kingdom ... every Behaviorist from Flaubert to Desmond Morris agrees there's hardly an aspect of animal behavior that isn't relevant to ours.'

And with that he had excused himself, leaving her feeling foolish. And she had been astonished at the articulate wisdom falling from the lips of a circus hand.

Which, afterward, she had resented. After all, she was the veterinary surgeon around here, it was her domain. But she had never forgotten the look on his face, the sweet vision she had glimpsed behind those eyes.

But, by God, she resented it now, with anger and fear in her heart, sitting like a fool again in her rented car in the middle of the wilderness in the middle of the night. Why was she always such a ... *sucker*? For the ... grand emotional gesture?

She lit another cigarette, and longed for daylight.

At three o'clock she was suddenly awake with a start, realizing she had been asleep. Her eyes darted about in the silent moonlight. Then they widened, and her stomach contracted.

A mass of moving blackness was coming out of the black forest onto the open grassy sag.

A man was jogging in the lead, and behind him were the big cats, ears back, tails low, then the elephants, then the gorillas, then the enormous bears, and behind them all was a huge man loping along with a dog. She gasped and wanted to run. All she knew was the raw human fright of wild animals coming at her. She cringed and stared. Then came the astonishment; such a disparate mixture of animals all following one man! She sat rigid at the spectacle of the magnetism some rare people have ... then David Jordan glimpsed her car on the edge of the forest, and he stopped.

She collected her wits, and rolled down her window frantically. 'Mr Jordan!'

He turned and started running for the forest, and the animals whirled around and followed him. She scrambled out of her car.

'I'm the zoo vet—Dr. Johnson—I'm alone!'

He disappeared like a shadow into the forest, the animals crashing through the undergrowth after him. She yelled, 'Wait—' and stumbled into the open. 'Mr Jordan! Look, I'm alone—I'm unarmed!'

She waited for his response, heart pounding, frightened. Then his hoarse voice came out of the black forest.

'What do you want?'

She was so relieved she was almost crying. 'Please—I've got to talk to you!'

'What about?'

'About the animals! This is a terrible thing you're doing. You've got to give them back, for their own good!'

'They're not going back.'

She cried desperately across the moonlight: 'You've got to listen to me! They're going to be *shot*. I've seen the gun-crazy hillbillies in Erwin! I've *seen* them, I tell you—buying guns! And at the roadblocks. And the police are after you, and they're not much better. You're going to be surrounded!'

Davey crouched in the dark forest, his sweat glistening. 'Where are they?'

'I don't know exactly. Last night they were at the last highway back there!'

'They're crazy if they shoot, that won't get the animals back.'

'Even the police will shoot! They're frightened, don't you understand? They aren't used to wild animals here!'

'Tell them they're not wild animals—they won't hurt anybody.'

Suddenly, a man called out behind her. 'Okay, nobody else here.'

She spun around with a gasp, and stared up at the biggest man she had ever seen. '*Who're you?*'

'I won't hurt you, ma'am.'

Davey stepped out of the forest, the big cats slinking behind him. She stepped back toward her car.

'Please tell them everything will be all right if they don't interfere,' Davey called.

She cried, 'What are you trying to prove?'

'Just tell them to leave us alone.'

She cried, 'This isn't where these animals belong. They can't fend for themselves!'

'They'll learn.'

*'The police are after you, I tell you. And the hunters—you know what they're like. You'll be shot to ribbons!'*

He broke into a jog, and the animals started after him. She stared in amazement all over again, then shouted desperately, 'Listen, I'm a vet; I know what I'm talking about. Don't you remember me—Dr. Johnson?'

He did not answer.

She cried: *'Where are you taking them?'*

But he did not answer. He jogged across the sag, the animals lumbering behind him.

She yelled: *'I've got meat for the cats.'*

Davey ignored her. She turned desperately to the big Indian. 'Where are you going with them?

Big Charlie's eyes were on the column of animals. He turned to follow them, but she grabbed his arm. 'Where? . . .'

He looked down at her. 'To the Garden of Eden.'

Her fingernails dug into his arm. 'There is no such place! They're going to die!'

He looked at her, then gently pulled his arm away.

'Wait!' She turned, flung open the back door of the car and grabbed her doctor's bag. 'Carry that!'

'You can't come with us, ma'am.'

'The hell I can't! Those are my animals, and I've got to look after them.'

She seized her new knapsack and sleeping bag. Charlie was staring at her, clutching her doctor's bag. She hauled the big bag of meat off the back seat.

'You can't come with us.'

'It's a free country. Can you carry this meat?'

The animals were fifty yards away now, lumbering up the grassy slope of Big Bald in the moonlight. All senses were alert, the cold

65

night air was moving over their bodies and into their nostrils. Elizabeth could still hardly believe what she was witnessing even though, as a scientist, she knew there were such people as David Jordan. Before she could hesitate she started jogging desperately up the grassy slope after them. Charlie Buffalohorn stood, holding her doctor's bag and the meat, staring after her.

Then he started up the slope.


# fourteen


It was some time before dawn.

Davey lay in the undergrowth on the edge of the forest, peering down onto Highway 23 at Sams Gap. The road was a black blur, ten feet below the embankment. Beyond it, the forest rose again.

He could see no vehicles, no people. He lay, panting, sweating, trying to press his exhaustion into the earth, waiting. For a match to flare, for a voice, for a shadow, for a vehicle to come along the highway out of the forested night and light up the road. For five minutes he waited, then he stood up, quietly as an Indian, and retraced his steps.

The big cats were scattered about in the darkness devouring the meat.

Elizabeth sat well away, slumped against a tree to cover her rear, her legs shaking. Her exhaustion was nothing compared to her fear of the huge dark shapes of the animals in the moon-dappled forest. For one moment she had looked straight into the eyes of the Siberian tiger; those big, carnivorous eyes in that huge killer face with that menacing body behind it, staring straight at her without any bars between them, and she had felt a terror so pure that all she had known to do was throw her arm across her face and cringe. Then Davey had tossed the tiger a hunk of meat, and she had grabbed it and turned away. Then he had turned away himself and melted into the darkness, and she had wanted to run after him for protection, to beg him not to leave her alone. She waited desperately for him to return, her knapsack clutched in front of her as a shield, listening to the sounds of feeding. When she saw David Jordan come back she felt a wave of relief so enormous that it was almost sexual in quality—*he was her protector*.

She tiptoed nervously over to him. He was squatting, his face in shadow.

'Mr. Jordan? Please listen to me . . . for the animals' own good.'

'I'm listening.'

She swallowed, feeling inarticulate.

'How do you think you're going to get away with this?'

He did not look at her. 'I'm not trying to get away with anything, Dr. Johnson. I'm just doing what is right.'

She cried softly. '*Right*? How can it be right to throw defenseless animals back into the wild?'

'You asked me a question,' he said quietly, 'so listen to the answer.'

She took a quivering breath to contain herself. His voice and manner were so quietly determined they were almost military. His whole presence inspired confidence. 'You're a vet, you should know. It's not right to keep an animal in a cage. You've seen them at that zoo of yours—you must've seen them in plenty of zoos.' He shook his head at her across the dappled darkness. 'Pacing about, in those tiny cages. Why are they doing that, Dr. Johnson? Mama, here, the tiger. Up and down, up and down. Why? Is it natural for a tiger to do that? Or is she doing it because she wants out? Because she wants space? Because her nerves and body and soul are crying out for freedom?'

'But Mama doesn't *know* about freedom! Any more than a child who grows up in Manhattan knows about Africa! She was *born* in captivity.'

He said quietly. 'Then why does she do it? For fun? Because she's enjoying herself? No, Dr. Johnson. She's doing it because she just naturally *knows* she wants out. She's *yearning*. And the other big cats in your zoo—they weren't all born in captivity. They remember, just as you and I remember, natural things like freedom. They long for it. And the elephants and the hippo. And the gorillas . . .' He shook his head. 'Jamba—she wasn't born in captivity, was she?

67

And look at her tiny cage. Nor the two youngsters . . .'

Big Charlie said out of the darkness. 'Cats finished eating.'

'Mr Jordan, please listen . . .'

'We're going now, Dr. Johnson,' he said quietly. 'Thank you very much for the meat. You better go back to your car. I don't think you'll keep up with us; you'll be left behind. It would be much better if you went back and told them to leave us alone.'

She cried. 'Where are you going?'

But he turned away from her and made a low whistling sound. All about her in the dark the big animals turned and shuffled; then he was moving among them like a shadow, making soft muttering noises, touching them and calling them by name. She grabbed her knapsack, too desperate to marvel at what she was seeing.

They slithered down the embankment at Sams Gap, and scrambled onto the highway. Davey ran across the road and leaped up into the forest on the other side, and the animals loped and lumbered urgently after him, followed by Big Charlie and Sam. Last of all stumbled Dr. Elizabeth Johnson.

Davey slogged up through the black forest, across the mountain-side, the animals strung out behind him. Elizabeth gasped. 'Mr Buffalohorn!'

Big Charlie hesitated, then stopped. She toiled up to him, and dropped her medical bag.

'You better quit, ma'am.'

'I'm coming, dammit!'

She was bent double, hands on knees, head hanging. He hesitated, then picked up her doctor's bag. He turned and started after the animals.

She straightened, exhausted, then started stumbling doggedly after him.

Just before sunrise Davey stopped. They were in dense forest about a mile down-mountain from the Appalachian Trail. Somewhere, above the thudding of her heart, Elizabeth could hear a waterfall. He said, ahead in the dark, 'We're sleeping here.'

She looked exhaustedly about for a good spot. She badly wanted to sleep near him, or Big Charlie, or both.

But she was not going to ask. She wasn't going to sleep surrounded by animals either. She went plodding back up the

68

mountainside, struggling through the undergrowth, for about twenty paces. Then down she slumped.

She woke with sun on her eyelids. And the dread.

She blinked; all she could see was dense foliage. She struggled out of her sleeping bag, then her heart suddenly tripped as she heard a branch snap. She jerked around and stared, heart pounding; then closed her eyes. *They were still here*—that was the sound of an elephant feeding.

'Mr. Jordan?' she whispered.

The elephant jerked and blundered farther into the forest.

It was completely silent but for the hammering of her heart. She stood there, feeling helpless, afraid. She started rolling up her sleeping bag. Then out of the corner of her eyes she noticed a pair of black hairy legs. She jerked up, and looked straight into the blinking face of a chimpanzee, holding Big Charlie's hand.

'Oh, thank God . . .' She closed her eyes. 'Where's Mr. Jordan?'

Charlie nodded downhill. 'Asleep down there aways. Don't do anything to wake him.'

'And the animals?'

'Down there too.' He looked at her uncomfortably, eyes hooded in his brown face: 'You'd better quit and go back today, Dr. Johnson. For your own sake.'

He had said it kindly. There was nothing she'd like better than to quit.

'Well, I'm not going to . . . my own sake doesn't matter. I'm staying for the animals' sake.'

He built a tiny fire of dry twigs between two stones, balanced a little tin can of water and made coffee.

'How long are you staying here?'

'Until sunset. The animals need a good rest.'

'And then?'

He did not answer. She wanted to cry out, *For God's sake tell me where you think you're going.*

'The Garden of Eden, you said last night.'

Big Charlie fed twigs into the tiny fire. 'Yes.'

She blurted, 'There's no such place.'

He did not answer. She closed her eyes in frustration. 'Oh, for

69

God's sake give it up. They're going to be shot to pieces. You know what a beast the American so-called hunter is! And I saw them, getting ready . . .'

He was staring into the little fire. Her hands were clenched; she stared at his big profile. He turned and looked at her, kindly.

'It's no good talking about it, Dr. Johnson.'

'*Where?*' she whispered fiercely. 'And how the hell are you going to get there?'

'It's no use, Dr. Johnson. And it's no good trying to talk to Davey about it, either. He's got enough on his mind.'

She snorted. 'Of course I'm going to talk to him; I don't care how angry he gets.'

Big Charlie shook his head.

'He won't get mad. Takes an awful lot to make Davey mad. He just won't argue with you, that's all. He'll just walk away.'

Big Charlie stood up and turned away himself.

'Where are you going?' she appealed.

He stopped and looked back at her. Then she understood.

'All right—I won't talk about it anymore. Please don't leave me here . . .'

'Okay. Come with me.'

He started walking back up the mountain. She started hurrying painfully after him.

About half a mile up the mountain, on a rocky outcrop, sat Sam, on guard, thumping his tail in welcome.

She would remember it disjointedly: her body aching, her head light from not enough sleep; the unreality of the forest, the animals, the twittering of the birds through her harried thoughts; the whole extraordinary thing. The big Indian sat, waiting. The gentleness behind his bulk, the quiet strength that did not need to be leashed because it was so . . . confident? So gentle that she did not want to upset him by breaking her bargain. She would, she had to—but at the right moment.

And the strange, beautiful wolf-dog, Sam. He was so serious, ears cocked, staring fixedly up the mountainside. Suspicious of her, tolerating her only because of the Indian's presence. She wanted him to accept her, she wanted to stretch out and fondle him, tell him he was a good dog. But she didn't—it would almost have been a presumption, an intrusion into such professionalism. But all the while was the frustration of waiting.

'Does Sam understand?'

The wolf laid his ears back, but did not turn.

'Sure.'

'That he's on guard for pursuers?'

Big Charlie looked at her. 'Of course. He's trained.'

Of course. It seemed a silly question now. 'What'll he do if he sees anybody coming? Bark?'

'Run and wake Davey. He knows he's got to keep his mouth shut unless it's a real emergency.'

Oh, lovely Sam . . .

'Is he very fierce?'

A wisp of a smile crossed Charlie's face.

'He's pretty friendly.'

'But would he attack?'

'Only if he had to. Then he'd be fierce. But usually his bark's worse than his bite.'

She smiled. 'How does he like the other animals?'

'He likes them fine. He's used to them.'

'But he's never had to herd them before.'

'No. I guess he's not too crazy about that. They're all pretty big.' He added. 'The big cats, he's not too keen on them.'

For the first time in a long time she smiled, and tears burned in her eyes. Oh, *Sam* . . .

'I don't blame him,' she whispered. 'Does he chase ordinary cats?'

'If he gets the chance. But with these big ones? He's not stupid, Sam.'

They both smiled. It was a little shared amusement at Sam's expense. Then the moment passed. Charlie looked solemn again.

'And the other animals? Do you think they understand what's happening?'

Big Charlie looked surprised. 'Sure.'

She felt almost foolish.

'But how?'

He looked at her. 'Because they know. That they're out of their cages and running away: Davey's telling them to run.' He added,

71

'They can *feel* what each other's feeling. They know. There's a—sort of bond between them. To follow and run. Can't you feel it?'

Yes, she could. But no, she did not believe it. Not a bond, a common purpose, to run away from their cages. Surely they wanted to be back *in* their cages, where it was safe; they were frightened, that's why they were running. They were only keeping together because they were frightened, and because they were trained animals, and because Davey Jordan was the only security blanket they had.

The silence returned. Just the occasional cheeping of a bird. The vast, eerie wilderness. Her nerves were tight with the waiting—waiting for David Jordan to wake up so she could try to talk him out of this madness.

Then, completely silently, he was there. Sam's tail thumped in greeting; she looked around, and he was standing behind her: a lean young man, with the most penetratingly gentle eyes she had ever seen.

Afterward, when she tried to remember what she said, how she said it, whether she had spoken too forcefully or not, she was unable to reconstruct it fully. She was articulate; she had been on her university debating team; she knew what she was talking about; she could be forceful when she wanted to be—overly emotional perhaps, but she defended herself and what was right. What she would remember was feeling blustery and impotent against this quiet, gentle man, who refused to argue with her, who listened to her politely enough but who did not want to talk to her at all, who did so only as an act of hospitality. He was a private man who seemed to know what she was going to say, who had heard it all before; a man who had made all his decisions, and no matter what she said and pleaded and preached, would remain unmoved.

But she remembered him saying, almost reluctantly, 'I was there the day those baby elephants arrived from India. At Kennedy airport, in the middle of the night. They were reaching out for each other with their trunks, for comfort. Pushing their trunks into each other's mouths, and everybody was saying. 'Ah, aren't they cute!' But nobody felt bad for taking those poor animals away from their natural home.' He'd looked at her, and she would remember his quiet intensity. 'Because people are strange, Dr. Johnson. Somehow they think it's all right to make animals unhappy, and treat them as curiosities. I remember the vet saying, "I got a real live baby elephant." ' He'd looked at her, puzzled. 'In *prison*, Dr. Johnson. For life. And yet that vet was a kind man.' He shook his head. 'Every day you see those animals in their cages—pacing up and down, up and down. For the rest of their lives . . . You've seen it in your zoo, seen it in the Central Park Zoo.'

She would remember protesting, 'Kindly don't compare us with Central Park. That zoo's a disgrace.'

He said quietly: 'All zoos are, Doctor. Your Bronx Zoo is worse. Because you're the famous New York Zoological Society, with all the money and all the university degrees. But you've got all those tiny cages. Outside in the grounds there are hundreds of acres for people to walk around enjoying themselves looking at the unhappy animals . . . innocent animals, who've committed no crime.'

She had started to interrupt, but he went on quietly.

'And we look at that miserable animal in its cage and say, 'Isn't that interesting—look at the elephant.' What kind of creature are we, that takes pleasure in another creature's misery? Even though we *like* that animal . . .'

'That's not all there is to it. Mr. Jordan. Zoos do a great deal toward *conserving* animal life—and educating the public.'

For a moment he had looked as if he were going to argue with her, then he just said, kindly, 'I can't understand you, Dr. Johnson. You're a vet. All the *good* things you can do. Heal animals . . .' He looked at her in real puzzlement. 'You're a kind person. But you're really a *prison* doctor. You're a doctor who wants to keep his prisoners forever, Dr. Johnson. Not send them home when they're better—just keep them in prison forever so you can admire them.'

She had been absolutely indignant. '*Rubbish!*'

'It's as if you went to Africa and captured all kinds of black people, brought them back here, and stuck them in cages as Montezuma did, so people could go and look at them on Sundays with their children.'

'Rubbish! There's no comparison. Animals aren't people.'

But he'd withdrawn, as if he regretted having let himself be

73

drawn out at all, sorry for having hurt her feelings unnecessarily, because she would never understand.

Later, cooled down, she tried again.

'But what are you trying to *do*, Mr. Jordan? I mean—please believe me, I love these animals as much as you do, and I deeply resent your calling me a prison doctor. But what are you trying to *achieve*? Are you hoping to make such an *impression* with this extraordinary feat that the whole world is going to be up in arms against zoos and somehow just turn their animals loose in the forests around London and Los Angeles and Tokyo? If so you're wrong.'

But he was not going to argue about it, because she would never understand. When he spoke it was not in reply, but rather an articulation of a private thought.

'There is a way of life, a way of thinking, of . . . behaving toward other men and your fellow creatures . . . toward *all* living things . . . toward the whole earth, and the sky, and the sun . . . that is based on love. On compassion. On *respect*. On cherishing everything there is around you, because it's wonderful. Unique. It's natural and . . . *good*, and it evolved that way all by itself. It's got to be cherished. And if we think like that, and live that kind of life, we can all have our freedom, we can all have our happiness. . . . We can all feel the sun, and smell the grass and smell the flowers and look upon each other with . . . appreciation . . .'

"That's the Garden of Eden. It doesn't exist anymore. Maybe in parts of Africa. But you can't try to re-create it in the United States of America.'

For the first time he almost argued with her. 'Not in the richest, the cleverest, the most . . . inventive . . . the biggest, the most successful country in the world? Or can man only be successful when he hogs the whole world for himself?'

'Are you suggesting we revert to a state of nature?'

He said quietly, 'It's a state of mind, Dr. Johnson. A state of heart. A state of soul. A state of God, maybe.'

He stood up. The discussion was over.

She would remember that day as a kind of dream.

There was a little grassy glen below the waterfall she had heard last night. Sam was left on guard up on the mountain, while Big Charlie slept beneath a tree, the chimpanzee called Daisy sitting nearby. Most of the other animals were in the forest. Elizabeth glimpsed them through the trees from where she sat, near the waterfall, her body stiff and aching, her nerves tight with frustration and anxiety about the gunmen that must be closing in on them now. Only the big cats were in the open glen, except Mama, the zoo tiger, who crouched near Davey and balefully watched the other big cats. Mama wasn't going to have anything to do with them. On Davey's side sat the little chimpanzee. Elizabeth thought it was a pathetic, colorless little animal.

The waterfall cascaded into pools; the sun dappled gold through the treetops, sparkling on the cold clear water, warming the rich earth; and the spring air was crisp and soft and clean.

And Sally wallowed in the gurgling pools.

Wallowed and huffed and sighed, big fat old Sally who had exhausted herself stumbling along at the rear of the troupe of animals, her old heart pounding and her hooves sore and scored. Now she had slept off her exhaustion, lying flat out like a felled ox, and when she woke up she had heaved herself up and waddled down to the stream, and stood there in the misty sunlight, staring at the first running water she had seen in her whole life: real sparkling water, tumbling and swirling through real pools, with real weeds and reeds and mosses. Sally had never seen, nor smelled, all these wonderful, almost frightening things, and she stood on the bank and sniffed and hesitated, showing the whites of her eyes. She knew this place was good, but still she was nervous. Then, finally, she tentatively put one sore hoof into the water. She flinched at the cold, but she wanted the water, cold or not; wanted to plunge her great weary body into the buoyant balm of it, wanted it to soothe and support her. For a long quivering moment old Sally hesitated, then she sort of bunched up her big haunches, and she plunged.

With a resounding splash, and a snort, she thrust her head down, and then she was gone in a flurry of hooves, her fat old body suddenly streamlined, surging like a submarine. Sally swam, the water churning about her, and she no longer felt the cold—just joy, of her body working naturally as a hippopotamus's body is meant to do; she no longer felt her aches, and her hooves did not hurt anymore. Sally swam underwater, her eyes wide at the rocks about her, her ears filled with the crashing of the waterfall; then she came up to breathe, surging and huffing. The water cascaded down on her black shiny head, and rainbows sparkled about her in the morning sun.

She sank back under the stony bottom of the swirling pool, and pushed by the current, she walked, bumping against the smooth boulders, peering all around, nosing and nudging around the rocks, into dark places, all for the sheer pleasure of it. Then she broke surface with a gush; her ears pricked, her eyes widened and her nostrils dilated; then she turned, and plunged back under and swam into the current again, churning back to the waterfall.

Sitting on the bank, Elizabeth could almost feel, through her frustration and fear, the old hippo's happiness, almost feel the pleasure of the water surging about her body, the joy of doing what she was meant to do—and in all the beautiful space, with the sunshine and the rainbows and all the green things growing.

And Elizabeth's face softened, and she smiled.

Davey would not talk about it any more.

He had not said so, but she sensed and saw it: in his apartness, although he sat only a few paces from her; in his privacy; in his absorption in the animals. It was like an unspoken agreement between them that she could stay a while and rest, and even, he hoped, enjoy, provided she did not try to argue with him. He was in his own world.

She wanted to cry out, *What about these men following you?*—but she just sat, stiffly, trying to bide her time.

She worried for them all, but, after Sally, she worried most about the big cats: the bears could feed themselves, so could the elephants, the gorillas too—but the lions and the tigers could not.

They were grouped together uneasily in the middle of the glen, Sultan sitting disconsolately apart. They were all scared to venture closer to the trees—if there were a cave they would be huddled into it; the only reason they weren't huddled around Davey was because Mama was glaring them off. Mama was tense, aggressive, clinging catlike to her only security, the man she knew.

While he sat, immobile, watching with patient silence, Elizabeth worried herself sick. How did he do it, just sitting there?—didn't he

76

know all hell was about to break loose? He was almost . . . *military*, in his self-control. While Big Charlie slept, and the birds twittered, and the waterfall cascaded and Sally huffed and surged.

But then, as Elizabeth stiffly watched, Kitty, the lioness, began to play.

Suddenly she rolled onto her back and presented her belly to the sunshine, paws in the air; then her eyes rolled wickedly, and, with a sudden twist, she was on her feet: crouched, poised, tail flicking, looking for something to pounce on; and suddenly she pounced.

Onto nothing. She was springing up and crashing down on her forepaws, rump up in the air. She swatted her imaginary quarry with her big paws. Then she whirled around and went racing up the glen in furious mock flight, skillfully dodging invisible assailants. Then she whirled and raced back to Tommy and Princess. She skidded to a halt in front of Tommy, her tail held high. Princess sprang up and hissed and raised her paw, ears back dangerously, but big Tommy just looked at her. Kitty ignored Princess and jerked provocatively to galvanize Tommy into action, and she growled deep in her throat; Tommy just turned his head and looked disdainfully away.

So Kitty whirled around, and fled up the glen again, and swung around and stopped. Crouching low, head just poking up above the grass, waiting for Tommy to pursue her. But Tommy lay down elaborately and sighed. Then Kitty's gaze fixed on Sultan, and every muscle tensed; she began to stalk him. Treacherously, head low, killer paws padding, eyes boring. Sultan sat alone, and miserably watched her out of the corner of his eye. He knew what was going to happen. Closer and slowly closer Kitty stalked, her killer gaze fixed murderously on the unhappy tiger. All eyes were watching her. Sultan sat there on his haunches, rigid, head up, tail wrapped protectively around his front paws, his nose pointed fixedly across the glen, but gloomily watching Kitty.

For Sultan knew that she was going to bully him, challenge him, humiliate him, and finally pounce on him and make him run away, stripping him of such dignity as he had. This is how it had been in the circus all his life. He watched Kitty stalk him, and he pretended to ignore her with the last of his dignity, his heart sinking. Closer and closer Kitty crept, her heart pounding joyfully; then, when she

77

was three paces from him, she froze and stared at him.

Her eyes didn't waver; every muscle was tuning itself up for her sport, and Sultan sat, agonized, tensed for humiliating flight, but postponing it until he absolutely had to. Kitty jerked, and Sultan suddenly jerked too. Then Sultan, to his own and Kitty's astonishment, did something he had never done before: he made a preemptive strike.

Suddenly Sultan was unable to bear the suspense any longer, and in one terrified spasm he threw himself at Kitty with a roar, all jaws and paws. Kitty scrambled up in disarray, and Sultan hit her full on the chest. He bowled her over in a snarling crash before she knew what had hit her, and in a flash he was at her throat. Kitty kicked, roared and twisted, and scrambled up to flee; then Sultan, who had been doing so well, who should now have persevered and put Kitty in her place, spoiled it all and fled himself.

He turned and ran, in horror at his own audacity, and Kitty collected her scattered wits and whirled around in hot pursuit. Sultan fled up the glen, making for Davey as fast as his legs would carry him, with Kitty bounding furiously after him. Elizabeth cringed in terror, and Sally, who had temporarily vacated the pool for a breather, blundered back into it with a mighty splash and disappeared gratefully to the bottom. Sultan came racing flat out to Davey. Then Mama entered this fast-moving scene.

Suddenly Mama reacted to the invasion of her territory, and she sprang from Davey's side and bounded at the offending Sultan, who found himself running from one terrible tiger slap-bang into the awful wrath of yet another one; and he swerved at full tilt and went racing at a tree.

Now, Sultan knew nothing about trees, but he instinctively threw himself at the nearest one and clawed his way up it. Which, unfortunately, of all the trees in the forest he might have chosen, was built as unhelpfully as a telephone pole. But Sultan hurled himself up this tree with the professionalism born of terror, and Mama bounded at Kitty instead.

All Kitty knew was that she was joyfully putting one impertinent tiger to flight, when suddenly, out of nowhere, she was attacked by an entirely different one. She skidded to an astonished stop, whirled around and fled back across the glen toward the rest of her pride,

78

Mama galloping furiously after her. After ten yards Mama stopped and glowered at Kitty, tail swishing, and Kitty stopped at a safe distance and glared back. Then Mama turned, satisfied that she had made an impression.

Meanwhile, back up his telephone-pole tree, there was Sultan, stuck—clinging with all his might, ears back, tail trembling with the effort. He gave a deep-throated moan, looking down at the unyielding earth and Mama, who was looking malevolently up at him. For a long moment Mama stared; then, ominously, she lay down, in a dangerous-looking crouch, never taking her eyes off him. Sultan gave another moan of despair.

Davey had not moved, but a smile played on his mouth. Big Charlie had awakened, and he was watching the little drama. Elizabeth, still flinching inwardly at Mama's proximity, could not believe their quiet amusement.

'Do something, Mr. Jordan!' she whispered.

Davey just shook his head.

'Call her off,' Elizabeth whispered.

Davey did not look at her. 'He's got to learn.'

'All he's going to learn is about crashing out of a tree! And being set upon at the bottom!'

Davey suppressed a wider smile. 'He'll learn about choosing better trees, Dr. Johnson. It's all the law of nature.'

She hissed at him, 'To hell with Nature! He's going to get slashed to pieces.'

But Davey only said, 'Let them sort it out, Dr. Johnson.'

Elizabeth's heart reached out to the desperate tiger, and she was angry with the man who could have put a stop to it but who refused to interfere. She wanted to command Mama off, as she would her dog, but she dared not. Not only because Mama terrified her, but because she simply dared not countermand the great Davey Jordan's orders.

That was his effect. Despite her degrees, despite all her expertise, she felt under his authority; she was a woman in the wilderness surrounded by dangerous animals and not only was he a man—a physically stronger human being—she was also out of her league *scientifically*. In short, he was the authority; the only person who could control what was going on. She did not know what she despised most in herself: her fear of Mama or her fear of annoying David Jordan. She was transfixed by the plight of poor Sultan, marooned up his tree.

Then suddenly he came sliding down—not voluntarily, but induced by gravity. Sultan's aching claws could cling no longer; the bark of his unhappily chosen tree began to give way; there was a loud rending of wood above the new moan of anguish from his throat, and Sultan slowly descended, tearing great strips out of the tree trunk. Mama eased herself up to a menacing crouch, and a moan of bright outrage came from her.

Elizabeth started to yell at Mama, then Sultan's screeching claws could stand the strain no longer, and he let go with a yowl of terror, twisting in midair in a desperate bid to face his awful adversary. Mama scattered backward under the spreadeagled jaws and claws, shocked, and Sultan flattened her. Again involuntarily, but effectively nonetheless. There was an outburst of roars and flying paws as Sultan disengaged himself; then he turned and fled.

Davey had been right: Sultan had not squandered his time while up his tree; he had looked around for a better one, and he staked it out. Now he bounded up it. He scrambled onto a stout, solitary branch half way up and turned around and snarled.

Nobody could get him now. From his branch he dominated the tree.

# fifteen

The afternoon was warm and golden green. Butterflies were fluttering, birds chirping. Sally emerged from the pool and moved cautiously down the glen to graze, her big square mouth chomping like a lawnmower. The lions were all luxuriating in the sun, on their backs, paws in the air, and every now and again Kitty tried to box the butterflies.

The gorillas and chimpanzees had retreated into the trees when Elizabeth came to sit beside the waterfall. Now, first the chimpanzee called Daisy came back, cautiously bobbing behind bushes and peeping at her. Then one by one the others began to appear, brown eyes anxiously peering and ducking in inexpert counterintelligence. But then they began to relax.

Daisy was plucking at the greenery, holding it up in her thumb and forefinger and examining it quizzically, then popping it into her mouth and munching experimentally while she kept an eye on Elizabeth. One by one, the others followed. Only the zoo gorillas remained tense, standing on the fringes of the trees, staring at her suspiciously: they remembered her. She wanted to give them her most winning smile and call out, 'Come on, King, don't be frightened.' But she just wagged her head to show nonaggression and ostentatiously averted her eyes.

Then Daisy began to play the fool. Suddenly she threw her handful of leaves into the air with gay abandon and gave a short bark, slapping her hand on the ground with all fangs barea; then she threw herself into a cartwheel. Whirling in the sunlight, head over heels, crashing through the undergrowth; around and around Daisy went, hands and feet flying. Suddenly the other chimpanzees were copying her, throwing themselves into their circus cartwheels out of the infectious joy of the forest. For the moment Elizabeth forgot her fears of the hunters, and she wanted to clap her hands. The gorillas stared, astonished. Then Daisy spun into a somersault, landed smartly on her feet and galloped straight at King Kong; she leapfrogged over him, slapping her hands on his shoulders, flying over him before he could dodge indignantly. Then Florrie was racing at him.

King Kong jumped aside, and Florrie swerved after him, waving her arms; Daisy cavorted twenty yards up the glen, pretending to run in terror of big King, looking back over her shoulder. King Kong stood uncertainly, flustered and staring. Daisy's challenge had been cheeky, and he did the only thing he knew to impress her; he rose up onto his hind legs with some misgivings and beat his hairy chest. But Daisy just cavorted more provocatively and came scampering straight back. King Kong blinked in mid-thump, gave a disconcerted grunt, and charged.

Daisy fled gleefully across the glen, and King Kong pounded after her, disconcerted because he was not gaining on her. Now Florrie was joyfully beside her, and then Candy. Nervous little Champ scrambled up from Davey's side and went galloping off to join them. Daisy, Florrie, Candy, and Champ raced down the glen, then into the trees beyond, with King Kong pounding breathlessly after them, scattering the lions in all directions.

Kitty had flung herself flat as the hairy humanoids thundered past her, but now she sprang over the undergrowth after them. King Kong went thundering through the trees in hot pursuit of the chimpanzees, with Kitty bounding after him.

Then something began to happen in King Kong's big, serious, sooty breast. Suddenly it felt like fun to be crashing through the trees; it felt wonderful for his great body to be running and chasing. The forest felt like his territory.

Just then Kitty bounded at him with a shattering roar right in his earhole. King Kong flung his shaggy arms over his head and spun around, shocked at the sight of the huge lioness flying at him. He reeled backward wildly and collected his wits, and he reared up onto his hindlegs.

Kitty skidded to a stop and froze, backside up, head down, ears back uncertainly, and suddenly this had become serious. Even the chimpanzees stopped their cavorting, eyes wide.

King Kong and Kitty faced each other in the sudden silence, both hearts thumping. King Kong wanted to have nothing to do with lions, and Kitty didn't want to have anything to do with bad-tempered gorillas twice her size. For a long, shocked moment King Kong and Kitty stared each other down, one poised at full height, the other crouched low, mutually alarmed at what they'd got themselves into.

Then Kitty's nerve broke.

Slowly, her back arched, and she hissed; then she began to creep backward, never taking her eyes off King Kong's. King Kong glared at her all the way with intense relief. Then she turned and took to her heels. She burst into the open glen, and stopped. She looked back at him, tail swishing, then she sat down and proceeded to wash her face.

King Kong glared at her balefully, turned and headed

purposefully back into the forest, satisfaction in his heart.

Then they heard the helicopter.

Davey and Big Charlie tensed; it was a faint, faraway throbbing. Elizabeth's heart was thumping.

Davey and Charlie were looking at each other, twelve paces apart, listening intently, assessing. The sound was getting louder, but it was muffled by the forest.

'There.' Big Charlie jerked his head down the mountain.

Davey nodded. 'Going that way.' He pointed north, toward Erwin.

They listened, hardly breathing. For a long minute the sound seemed to stay at the same level, and her heart hammered as it occurred to her that it was hovering to lower men; then the noise began to diminish. She closed her eyes and exhaled. Davey and Big Charlie relaxed visibly.

Davey checked the position of the sun, nodded, and Charlie disappeared into the forest, heading up-mountain.

'Where's he going?'

'Just to have a look.'

She clenched her fist and massaged her brow.

'O God . . . How much longer are you staying here?'

'Until the sun starts going down. They won't find us with helicopters.'

'Mr Jordan,' she quavered, 'that helicopter was not police. The Sheriff told me; it belongs to *hunters* . . . and it can lower men all over the place.'

'They'd have to be very lucky to find us that way, Dr. Johnson.'

She wanted to cling to that assurance. 'But aren't you worried?'

It was a silly question. He lay back and closed his eyes. 'Of course. Please relax, Dr. Johnson. The animals will pick up your vibrations, and they'll get nervous too.'

She could hardly believe this. Here they all were, at large in America, romping in the forests—even she had been carried away with the magic of it—while the net was closing in on them, hunters drawing closer and closer: yet there lay David Jordan, eyes closed, relaxed. Like Sir Francis Drake finishing his game of bowls while the Spanish Armada hove to on the horizon.

But no, he was not crazy. That was the extraordinary thing. He just has this ... she was going to say 'crazy idea,' but that wasn't right either, because even she, for a while, watching the animals, had been caught up in it, the beauty of it—she had glimpsed the world he wanted, and it was not only possible, it was *happening*.

But no—it was not possible. *She had to talk him out of it.*

Then she realized the bad logic: she had concluded his venture was crazy because *Man* would come down like the wrath of God— *Man* deemed it crazy and would not permit it. But who was Man? The circus owners. The Sheriff of Erwin. Even Jonas Ford—who called his animals 'exhibits.' Who were *they*, to make the rules?

She stopped herself and took a deep breath. Her nerves were stretched so tight she felt like screaming. What was she talking about? Of course it was crazy. *She had to make him see it.*

But there was his exasperating refusal to talk about it! He almost turned the other cheek. She longed for the protection of darkness. For five minutes she sat in silent turmoil.

She carefully tried another approach. 'Mr. Jordan? Do you believe in God?'

He lay still, eyes closed. Just when she began to think he was going to ignore her, he opened his eyes and looked at the sky.

'There's a poem I read once. About the man who was sent up to God to complain, because the people on earth were suffering.' He hesitated, then, almost shyly, he began to recite.

> *I travelled far and, lo, I stood*
> *In the presence of the Lord Most High*
> *Sent thither by the sons of Earth*
> *To earn some answer to their cry*

And the Lord listens, puzzled, then He says:

> *The Earth, sayest thou? ... A race of men? ...*
> *By Me created? ... Sad its lot? ...*
> *No—I have no recollection of such place*
> *Such thing I fashioned not!*

But the man cries:

> *But Lord, forgive me if I say*
> *You spake the word and made it all! ...*

So God thinks a bit; then He says:

> *Let me think . . .*
> *Ah . . . dimly do I recall*
> *A tiny shape I built longst back*
> *—It perished surely? . . .*

Davey turned and looked at her, then he ended:

> And the man cries out:
> *Lord, it existeth still!*

She was staring at him. She remembered the poem, from Professor Joad's book, *God and Evil*.

'So God's forgotten about us, has He? And you're going to recreate the Garden of Eden? You're His instrument?'

He looked away, embarrassed.

'I'm not God's instrument, Dr. Johnson. I'm just doing what is right. Setting free the animals. Where they'll be happy at last.'

Then he got up quietly and started walking down the glen, with Mama padding behind him in the dappled sunshine.

Sultan took the opportunity to come scrambling down out of his tree.

Little Smoky was only little in comparison to the great grizzly bears he performed with in the circus, and when he wore his dungarees and scout hat and danced behind them with his fire extinguisher, and held paws, he did look little and awfully cute. When he squirted his fire extinguisher on cue, messed up Winnie's pinafore and knocked off Pooh's hat, and they whacked him, he did look just like their baby grizzly bear. But he was really a fully grown black bear, and he weighed nearly five hundred pounds; he stood five feet tall on his hindlegs; he could swipe eight feet high with his clawed paws, and he could run faster than the best man can sprint.

Smoky did not remember the forests of his cubhood, nor his mother, with her big, furry, grunting, dangerous protection; all he remembered about those days was the sudden deafening bang, the terror of being suddenly alone and running for his life, then the terror of being caught. They had put him in a cage and fed him milk from a bottle. The cage had become smaller and smaller until he could hardly turn around in it; then one day they'd sold him to the circus. He had not seen another black bear since the day of the terrifying bang.

Now, indeed, Smoky thought he was a grizzly bear, just as the public did. But he thought he was a puny grizzly, and he had an inferiority complex. But he did his job well enough in the circus because bears like to show off once they understand how. The trouble for Smoky had been in understanding how. It had taken a long time to understand what the man wanted him to do, and he'd suffered lots of electric prods and was terrified of the cracking whip. When he'd finally understood what he had to do to earn the reward, the fearsome man started teaching him something new and incomprehensible. It was very confusing and frightening, and he did not know, each time he was taken out of his cage, what was going to be expected of him. Only when he saw the crowds around the ring did he know that it was an old trick he had to do, one he understood. He dreaded the man with the whip, and he was nervous of Winnie and Pooh because of the authority their great size bestowed. The only friend he had was his keeper, and he was devoted to him. His keeper fed and groomed him; he sat in his cage with him and played with him. Smoky would have done anything for him, as long as he understood how.

Elizabeth, watching Smoky, was frightened of him—and terrified of Winnie and Pooh with their huge, expressionless, powerful presences. But her harried heart went out to them all.

From her readings she knew of the Americans' mentality about the wilderness and their natural heritage, and that no other animal so filled the American mind with dread as did the legendary grizzly bear, even though, once tamed, grizzlies become absolutely devoted to their keepers. Almost certainly the bears would come down out of the forests wherever Davey abandoned them, in search of familiar human protection and food; they would set the fear of God into Americans and have the whole town out to blast them off the face of the earth.

Watching them, her fears were confirmed. They were rooting around, but they were staying within sight of Davey. Every few minutes one of them would look back at him to make sure he was still there.

But, as the afternoon went on, little by little they ventured farther; and finally they were out of sight, grubbing and grunting through the undergrowth, snuffling under fallen logs, nudging over stones. There were lots of things that bears like to eat—roots, berries, fungi, sprouts and grasses—and there were many exciting smells.

For the first time in his life, Smoky found that he was not trundling after Winnie and Pooh. They were not shoving him aside and nudging him away from the food; there was enough to share, with so much space to lumber and huff and bustle through. Slowly, Smoky began to feel like a real bear.

It was a wonderful feeling, of being strong, of bulldozing importantly, shoving aside bushes, flattening shrubs, rolling over logs and burrowing into the rich earth, with no Winnie or Pooh to boss him around. Then Smoky discovered something else: that black bears can climb trees, and grizzlies cannot. And something else: that bears like honey, that he was just naturally good at getting it, and that grizzlies are not.

Suddenly, as he was rooting around, his snout full of earth, he smelled something delicious. He eagerly followed his nose, and saw Winnie and Pooh standing on their hindlegs, swiping up into a tree with their forepaws. Bees buzzed angrily about their heads; in a fork in the tree was a hive.

But the hive was well out of the big bears' reach. Pooh was trying to climb the tree. He lunged at it, chest first, and flung his forelegs around it. He jumped, and for an agonizing instant he clung there, hairy and bulbous, his hind claws frantically trying to find purchase. Then he slid down with a thump. Winnie tried, taking a lumbering run at the tree trunk, hind paws massively scrabbling. Then, *crash*, down she came too. Smoky looked at all this hirsute activity, and he just knew what to do.

He knew nothing about trees and nothing about honey; but he knew that he could climb a tree to get it. Smoky lumbered around Winnie and Pooh, giving them a wide berth, looking up into the tree, sizing it up; then he bounded.

His claws sank into the bark, and up he went, effortlessly. He was halfway up before Winnie and Pooh realized it, and was into the beehive snout-first, long tongue licking, claws clinging tight. The bees went berserk, swarming about his furry head in a cloud. The

87

smell of honey flooded down to Pooh and Winnie, and they were beside themselves. Smoky was getting stuck into what they couldn't reach, and Pooh hurled himself at the tree trunk with anguish and came crashing down again, grunting and thumping. Pooh tried to paw Smoky down out of the tree by jumping and swiping. Winnie joined in, and they bumped into each other in their agitation, but their paws whistled harmlessly beneath Smoky's rump. The bees were zapping furiously into his nose, his ears and his deep shaggy fur, but it would have taken strong machinery to pry Smoky out of that tree.

He clung tight, his heart thumping joyfully, his eyes screwed up and his snout stretched out, his pink tongue slurping in and out of the beehive. There was honey all over his chops and face and drooling down his neck, and it was absolutely delicious. His nose was a big black sticky swollen mass of stings, he had swallowed scores of bees, but Smoky did not care. Now honey was running down the tree in thick long drools, and Winnie and Pooh were pawing at the trunk, their long pink tongues gratefully licking the bark.

None of them had ever been happier.

# sixteen

Elizabeth jerked, eyes wide, hand to her throat.

'Oh! Hello . . .'

'Hi.' Big Charlie squatted self-consciously five paces away. 'Sorry.'

'How do you move so quietly?'

'Sorry. Where's Davey?'

She pointed down the glen, her heart still palpitating. 'He went down there about an hour ago. I think I offended him.'

Big Charlie shook his head slightly. She did not know whether it was in denial, in regret, or even perhaps in sympathy. But right now, the less said the better. She had shot her mouth off with that impetuous remark about God's instrument—she'd had him talking, and she had blown it. She found herself nursing the hope that if she shut up and stuck with them long enough they would simply not have the heart to reject her. *Then* she could do some good, when she had won their confidence. O God, she wished it would get dark quickly.

'Did you find anything up there?

Big Charlie shook his head. 'No, Dr. Johnson.'

'Please call me Elizabeth.' Big Charlie looked embarrassed. She added, 'We're all in this together.'

Charlie looked uneasy. He picked up a twig and fiddled with it; then said, 'We're going soon, Dr. Johnson. You won't be able to keep up with us.'

She took a big breath and closed her eyes.

'Let me worry about that. I'm a big strong girl, haven't you noticed?' She tried to make a brittle joke: 'Maybe too big, you think, hmm?'

Big Charlie smiled, and blushed. 'I didn't mean you're too big.'

*She had him talking.*

'Yes, you did—too fat.'

'You're not too fat, Dr. Johnson.'

'Just fat, huh?'

Big Charlie squirmed in smiling embarrassment. 'You're just right for me.' Then he looked horrified, as if he wanted to slap his hand over his mouth. 'I mean—for my liking.' He floundered. 'I mean ... I think you're great like you are,' he ended, covered in confusion.

She smiled and felt tears burn for a moment.

'Thank you, Charlie.'

Big Charlie looked desperately down the glen for Davey. But there was no rescue in sight; he pulled himself together and crumbled the twig.

'But we will worry about you, Dr. Johnson. And ... we've got enough to worry about right now.'

'Charlie—don't let's talk about it. Let's wait for David. Let's just talk ...'

A glint came into his hooded eyes.

'It's not just for Davey to decide, Dr. Johnson.'

She could have bitten off her tongue for the tactless way she had put that.

'I know . . . I'm sorry . . . but please—can we just talk?' She shook her head. 'Tell me about yourself. Or I'll talk about myself. Are you married, Charlie? Have you got a girl friend? Where is she? Or let's . . . tell me about the animals.'

Big Charlie looked at her with disappointment. That she thought she was fooling him. But he was too polite to say so.

'I'm not married,' he mumbled reluctantly.

'Is Davey?' she said brightly.

'No.'

'Have you got a girl?'

Big Charlie looked at the ground, and then a rueful smile twinkled across his face. 'Sometimes . . .' Then a smothered laugh rose from his chest: 'When I get lucky.'

She was smiling again. Oh, poor Charlie! 'And Davey?'

Charlie shifted and looked at her apologetically. 'Can we talk about the animals?'

She clutched at this change of subject. She cast about for something not provocative.

'The elephants . . .'

Big Charlie waited. 'What about them?'

She marshalled her thoughts urgently. 'I watched that lion play today. And then the chimps. And . . . it was truly wonderful.' She shook her head sincerely. 'It's been a wonderful day, really. I've learned a great deal. But about the elephants . . . I mean the zoo ones. Your circus elephants. They're accustomed to traveling, to new places and all that. And to teamwork. So maybe all this isn't such a shock for them. But you saw how nervous the zoo tiger is, for example—she doesn't want to mix. So what I'm saying is, I'm sure that the zoo elephants are feeling the same way. I know those elephants—as individuals. I know they must be very frightened. Of —she waved at the forest—'the vastness . . . the lack of security.'

Big Charlie stared at the ground, self-conscious at being asked advice by a fully fledged veterinary surgeon. He found it difficult to say, you're mostly all wrong.

So he said, 'You're partly right, Doctor.'

*

In his cage in the zoo, Little had learned almost nothing about being an elephant. He had learned what time of day he was going to be fed, when he was going to be chained up again by his foot, that in daylight people came to stare at him. He was not allowed to play with Clever: sometimes their chains were just long enough to be able to reach each other with their trunks, but mostly they were chained too far apart, facing opposite directions. For the rest of the time they just rocked on their great feet. When the people came to look at them, they reached out their trunks through the bars, groping for some friendly contact. There was nothing else to do.

He could not see Jamba behind the next gray wall. But he could smell her, and hear her. Sometimes, he could stretch his trunk out through the bars, reach around the dividing walls, and maybe touch trunks with her. Then they sniffed and groped at each other. He yearned to be with her, for her company, her comfort, and her natural authority. Jamba yearned with all her elephantine instinct to mother him and yearned for his fellow elephantness. But they could not see each other. The only way to express themselves was to trumpet, a frustrated, old sound of the jungles that fell back on the Victorian hall.

Now Little had been released from his cage, and he was with old Jamba, in her important elephant company. Although he felt the urgency in the air, he was not really very afraid. He was only very anxious to do the right thing, to keep up with the running, close to Jamba and Clever, so as not to be left behind. After the first long, confused burst of running on the first day, what he mostly felt was a nervous exhilaration—for the sun, the sky and all the green, for all the space and the glorious sense of using his body.

But Jamba was afraid. Not so much of the wilderness itself, but because she knew they were running away from a wrong that had been committed, and that they would be pursued and punished if caught. For an old elephant understands very well what it is and is not allowed to do; she had learned very well from twenty-five years in a cage that she was not allowed outside; she knew that they were being chased. Only for this reason was she afraid of the wilderness, for the perils it had of her terrible pursuers.

Jamba was just naturally responsible for the young elephants now, for Little and Clever. All her life she had yearned for a calf to mother; for years she had bothered and fretted, and had called out to them in the next cage. Now she had them with her, and along the Appalachian Trail she kept them in front of her where she could discipline them, making sure that they kept running from the dangers behind: for that is an old elephant's natural duty with inexperienced and foolish young elephants. And when they had arrived at this place and all the animals had thrown themselves down, Jamba had not gone to sleep. Not until the first birds began to twitter and she could see again had she fallen asleep, exhausted, but still on her feet, her big ears listening.

Nor had she relaxed her vigilance when they all woke. She had started feeding, urgently, stuffing her belly while she had the chance, before she had to run for her life again. She made sure Clever and Little were in front of her all the time. If one of them went too far ahead she called him back with an imperative squeak: if one dropped back, she curled her trunk around his rump and shoved him forward. She wouldn't let them get too close to the circus elephants. She did not want to have too much to do with them yet, especially Queenie. Queenie was big, she had tusks, which gave her authority, for might is right in the kingdom of elephants. Queenie watched Jamba balefully.

But not Rajah.

Oh, no, Rajah wanted Jamba to come closer. Old Rajah had never been allowed to have a mate. In the circus, when Queenie was in heat, they were kept well apart, which drove Rajah mad. He had trumpeted and wrenched on his chain and endlessly curled his trunk, his great penis dangling as he tossed his fodder about disconsolately. If ever Queenie had gone into heat unexpectedly, and Rajah had tried to mount her, he got the whip cracked across his face, or the electric prodder. That's how it had been for over fifteen years. Now Rajah was very aware of a new female, and although he knew she was not in heat, he was interested. Huffing and sighing, and blinking mournfully, he had tried to edge closer to her. But Jamba was having none of that nonsense, and she made sure that Clever and Little stayed near.

But now a new throaty noise came from Jamba's belly: it was contentment. For slowly, as her huge belly began to fill and nothing happened but the warming of her back by the dappled sunshine, the urgency gave way to the pleasure of feeding. Of the marvelous abundance of food growing all about her, food she could wrap her trunk around and pluck in a real elephant way. She loved the satisfaction of the crisp feel and the living smell of it, and of all the different tastes. With each step it became more pleasurable to choose, to smell and taste. Slowly, she discovered the joys of movement and of space—space to swing her head and her trunk, the feeling of being huge in a limitless place, of boughs bending before her body, of earth beneath her feet, and the many, many smells.

Jamba's stomach began to rumble; then, one by one, the other elephants' stomachs joined in. It was an infectious community of feeling, an agreement passing between them that all this was good, that all this was lovely to an elephant's way of thinking.

Jamba did not feel so shy any more of the circus elephants. She edged closer toward them as she fed, and what she was feeling now was an elephant's desire to be acknowledged. She raised her trunk in greeting, to show her respect for Queenie's tusks; she curled her trunk up over her head in a salaam and lowered it with a sigh. First Rajah and then Queenie greeted her in return, with smaller salaams. Finally, they stood in a group, slowly blinking and sniffing at each other with their trunk tips.

In the late afternoon Davey came back and sat down with Charlie and Elizabeth. She heaved a sigh of relief. She wanted to know if he had seen anything suspicious, what he was going to do about the hunters—didn't he believe that she had seen them gleefully getting ready in Erwin? . . . And what about the helicopter? . . . But she controlled herself.

The elephants came out of the forest, stood in a solemn line at the water's edge and drank. It was the first time in years that any of them had had so much water, and each knew just naturally what they were going to do with it. When they had drunk enough, they sucked their trunks full, then curled them up over their heads, and jetted the water over their backs—and again, between their legs, over their bellies, and again and again till their whole bodies glinted in the afternoon sunshine. The abundance of water on their bodies was like the very space of the forest, and the sunshine was filled with their sighings and the rainbows of their spraying.

As the sun lowered, the other animals began to gather around the pool near Davey. Like cows gathering around a gate at milking time, Elizabeth thought. Despite her fears, she sat enthralled.

She was in awe . . . for, rationalize about security blankets as she would, the impressive fact was that these were not domestic cattle but a group of widely different animals, and it was overwhelmingly evident that they were gathering around this man because they loved him.

*They loved him.* She could *feel* it, as one can feel it between people. She could see it, in the way they looked at him, in their whole demeanor, shuffling close, hopefully waiting, pulled toward him. First came the bears, their power bulging in their furry shoulders and shaggy legs, their clawed paws padding ominously, silently, their big dish faces expressionless; and Elizabeth felt a cringe of fear again. But Davey was smiling at them with such a gentle look in his eyes she was ashamed.

'Hello, Pooh . . . Hello, Winnie . . .'

They came snuffling up to him, nudging him with their noses, their furry bulks blocking out the sunset, grunting as he fondled their heads, and his smile was radiant. As if on command, they both sat on their haunches like dogs, towering shaggily over him, looking expectantly at him, huge, lovable thousand-pound beasts that had filled man with dread since time began. Her nerves still cringing, Elizabeth smiled and wanted to stretch out and touch them, and fondle them too.

Next the lions came pussyfooting across the glen; then the chimps and the gorillas. Finally came the elephants, gathering around in a ragged phalanx, great gray animals with slowly flapping ears, their trunks curling, their brown eyes gentle and wise, slowly blinking at Davey, waiting for him to tell them what to do. Davey gave a whistle, and a minute later Sam came bounding into the glen, tail wagging and tongue slopping.

Big Charlie said softly, 'Call the birds, Davey . . .' Then another wonderful thing happened.

Davey extended his arms, uttered a long, trilling whistle, and the birds stopped singing. It seemed as if the whole forest held its breath; the animals became still.

Then came the birds. First one, swooping down from the trees and fluttering in front of Davey; then two more; then from all directions. Wings swooping and beating, they flew around his head, fluttering and twittering excitedly, bumping into each other, their wings whirring; and they began to land on his outstretched arms. In a minute his arms were laden with birds, twitting and jostling; they were on his shoulders and perched on his head. Still more birds fluttered about him. They were sitting on the ground about his feet and perching in the boughs above his head.

Elizabeth could hardly contain her feeling of awe; her heart turned over; she wanted to clap and laugh and cry. She had read about such rare, lucky people as David Jordan, but she had never believed she'd see one. The animals stood so still, listening to his charm; the elephants, bears, gorillas, lions and tigers, all pent, with the birds twittering, the sun turning the sky golden red, the forest mauve.


At sunset they set off upward in a long caravan, plodding through the undergrowth, heading for the Appalachian Trail on the crest.

Elizabeth still did not know whether she was going to be allowed to stay; Davey had said nothing, and she had kept quiet. She was intensely relieved that the dark was almost upon them, with a mist wisping through the trees.

Within half a mile, her legs could climb no more. Her gut had knotted even though Big Charlie was carrying her kit. Davey called a halt, ordered Dumbo to kneel, and told her to climb astride his neck. She did not argue.

Now, gratefully riding, she felt Dumbo's warm body beneath her, his bristles prickling through her jeans. She felt a thrill like a child's, almost glee, an overwhelming affection for the animal who was so willingly saving her from the agony of climbing and the terror of being left behind. She wanted to put her arms around his neck, thank him and praise him. And she was still under the spell of the birds.

And, oh, despite her fears, she wanted to go with these animals wherever David Jordan was leading them. Just to be with them—to help them! The sunset grew more beautiful the higher Dumbo climbed; she had had a most wonderful, extraordinary day. She felt a rush of affection for big Queenie laboring up the mountain in front of her, for old Rajah, whose tail Queenie was holding with her trunk tip; she looked over her shoulder and smiled at Little and Clever toiling earnestly on either side of Jamba, and she loved them all.

She knew that Dumbo was enjoying carrying her. He let go of Queenie's tail, curled his trunk over his head and groped for contact. His snuffling trunk tip found her plump ribs so that she giggled and jerked; then he found her hand and curled his trunk around her wrist. Elizabeth was delighted, and tried to squeeze him back. Dumbo could feel her happiness and affection in her voice, and he was eager to please. He was also very pleased with himself, because in the circus only Rajah and Queenie carried people. All he ever had on his back were the chimpanzees and the big cats.

Then Little groped for her also. For Little had had a wonderful day too. Seeing Elizabeth ride on Dumbo made him want to carry her too, so he lifted his trunk and tried to wrap it around her waist, to catch her attention. Then Clever also wanted to play; he tickled her. Elizabeth laughed and wriggled, and Clever pulled his trunk back. She grabbed it to tell him it was all right, and Clever plodded along beside her, holding her hand.

Smoky was lumbering shaggily up the mountainside, his bee-swollen snout down, still sniffing all the earthy smells, honey still in his ears. Ahead, Daisy, Florrie and Candy loped ahead of the anxious gorillas. They had all had a lovely day. Kitty had thoroughly enjoyed herself too, despite everything. Winnie and Pooh had had an excellent day, although they were very wistful about the honey.

And Sam was loving all of it. He just loved herding: chasing, challenging and earning his master's praise. In fact, as Sam trotted along beside Big Charlie, bushy tail high, tongue lolling, what Sam really wanted to happen was for somebody to put a foot out of line so he could go bounding off indignantly, and head it off valiantly—as long as it wasn't one of the big cats.

Sam definitely did not want to have anything to do with those big cats. Little ones, certainly: he loved chasing little, reasonably-sized suburban cats to the point where they fled up a tree and were mercifully out of reach. Since time immemorial, that has always been the perfectly satisfactory cat-dog relationship, and in the circus, where the cats were well caged, Sam had done nothing to disturb history. Nothing, therefore, had prepared Sam for this potential holocaust of uncaged big cats. He was very pleased that they were way up front with his master, and that he was way back here with Sally.

Now Sally lumbered up the mountainside, her bruised hooves hurting and her big gut aching with Sam panting right behind her black backside. She ached and wheezed; all she wanted to do was turn around and go blundering back down that mountainside, Sam or no Sam, and plunge her massive body straight back into that pool, letting herself sink to the bottom. But she also did not want to be left behind, so she just had to keep on going. Nevertheless, Sally had had a lovely day too.


The sun had set when they reached the crest.

They were strung out in a long line along the narrow trail. Elizabeth could not see Davey ahead, nor Big Charlie behind; they all were jogging, and she had to cling to Dumbo. Her aches and weariness came back. The darkness did not seem to provide protection against the dreaded hunters of Erwin anymore. It was after midnight when they reached Devils Fork.

Davey left the animals five hundred yards into the forest and went to reconnoitre the highway. For ten minutes he lay on the edge of the treeline overlooking the sweep of road, waiting—for a match to flare, for a voice. But he saw and heard nothing. He crept back to the animals.

Elizabeth was propped against a tree. He crouched beside her and said apologetically, 'We're leaving you here, Dr. Johnson. When daylight comes, make for the highway. A car will soon stop for you.'

She looked at him. O God, to give up now, just to lie back and sleep sleep sleep and not have to get up and run again.

'No,' she said.

# seventeen

Davey came down the steep embankment onto the road, the animals scrambling behind him. He started running up the highway to find where the trail resumed. He had covered fifty yards when the lights suddenly came on.

Suddenly the black highway was ablaze in the headlights of three cars parked on the crest. The animals were bathed in dazzling light: elephants, apes, lions, bears, Sally, all blinded. David Jordan waved and bellowed, 'Don't shoot! Don't shoot!'

He gave a piercing whistle and lunged across the road, calling the animals, and then Big Charlie was running flat out up the road, waving and shouting. 'Stop! Turn off the lights!' David leaped up the steep bank, the animals blundering after him.

And then the firing started.

First one wild shot, then a ragged volley, shattering the night. Little squealed in the headlights, trunk upflung, and lurched around to run; another bullet smacked into his head, and he stumbled and fell. Daisy was screaming, blood on her neck. She tried to run and sprawled. And Smoky was staggering in the dazzling headlights, and Queenie was squealing, and Mama had sprawled, blood pumping from her back as she blindly tried to claw herself forward, and all the time the gleeful cacophony of rifles shattered the night. Then Big Charlie reached the first car, running furiously. He kicked in a headlight with all his might and spun around to kick out the other. Then Elizabeth came stumbling down the embankment.

She leaped wildly onto the road screaming, '*Stop!*' She ran frantically toward Mama, screaming '*Stop it, you bastards!*' She fell onto her knees beside the tiger, and Mama twisted and snarled, trying to raise herself. Big Charlie kicked out the other headlight, and the firing suddenly stopped. He lunged at the nearest gunman, grabbed his rifle in one hand and his collar in the other, and furiously slung him across the highway. Then he lunged at the car behind, swinging the rifle with all his might, and the headlight smashed with a crash of glass. A figure leaped at him, and Charlie chopped him down; then he swung the rifle at the other headlight. The third car was roaring and reversing out of his way, and Big Charlie slung the rifle at it, smashing in one of the retreating headlights. Then he plunged off the highway, into the forest.

And in the retreating headlight was the carnage, the huge form of a spread-eagled elephant, and Mama trying to claw her way across the road. Elizabeth clambered up, gasping, her face creased in fury; she screamed, '*You hillbilly barbarians!*' She cast about desperately for her doctor's bag, saw where Big Charlie had dropped it, and ran for it, sobbing. Then she dashed back to the writhing tiger. She snatched out a syringe and a phial. Silhouettes were coming down the highway toward her. She looked up and shrieked, '*Barbarians!*'

'Hey, she must be a vet.'

'Hey—what you doing with my tiger, lady? Stand back!'

'Get away!' she screamed. She plunged the syringe into the phial.

'You get away, lady. I shot that tiger, an' you ain't killin' it.'

'That's my tiger,' another voice shouted.

Mama rolled her striped head and tried to roar, wildly clawing herself forward, and Elizabeth scrambled after her, yelling, 'Get away you savages!' The man hollered, 'Stand back, lady,' the other voice shouted, 'That's my tiger,' and the shots rang out again.

Elizabeth screamed, and there was nothing in the world but the frenzied crashing of the guns. But the hunters could not see in the half darkness, and the first bullet whacked into Mama's neck. She lurched, roaring, pumping blood, and the second broke her jaw. Elizabeth threw herself hysterically at the nearest gunman, screaming, her fists like clubs, and his shot went wide, and she kicked out at his shins; then she flung herself wildly at the next man, kicking and flailing and screaming, and Mama was still trying to claw herself away through the cacophony with the bullets thudding into her. Then a voice hollered: '*Got it between the eyes!*'

The tiger lay sprawled in the car's headlight. The men were clamoring around her, laughing and arguing about who had shot her, and Elizabeth sat slumped in the blood, sobbing hysterically.

Then Little began to get up.

For none of the bullets that had hammered his huge honeycomb skull had hit his brain; they had only stunned him. Suddenly he was scrambling to his great feet again with a groggy noise, lurching high and terrible. The hunters scattered, terrified, and Little lurched forward, his bloody trunk swinging and his ears flapping; then a hunter recovered and fired.

The bullets smashed into the base of Little's trunk, and he lurched, eyes closed; then he tried to turn to run away from the terror, and he crashed onto his knees. His trunk outflung, his eyes wild, blood pumping out of him, the hunters whooping after him and Elizabeth screaming, 'Leave him,' Little scrambled up again.

He started to stagger frantically forward, and a bullet thudded into the side of his face. He lurched and tried to turn the other way, and another hunter fired. The bullet smashed into his jaw, Little staggered around to try to defend himself, and they all opened up on him.

From all sides, bullets thudding into the grunting elephant's face and shoulders amid the stink of cordite and Elizabeth's screams. Little's trunk was flung up over his head to ward off the blows, and he flapped out his bloody ears to increase his size to frighten his tormentors. He tried to trumpet, and the blood spewed out of his trunk in a spray. He stumbled forward into the bullets, his eyes full of blood and his face a pulp of holes, and the hunters scattered, whooping and hollering. Little tried to charge the nearest figure, to ram his down. He lurched three staggering paces; and a bullet smashed through his eye, and he fell again.

Little collapsed onto his knees, one eye shot out and his other rolling; then he started to scramble up. Again and again the young elephant tried to get up from his knees, lurching and crazed, his trunk up and the crack-crack-cracking of the rifles and Elizabeth's screams filled the night again. Then one wild bullet smashed into his skull in front of his brain, and Little crashed on his side for the last time.

But still he was not dead, for the bullet had only fractured his brainbox. He lay on his side in the headlight's glow, his bloody flanks heaving and his trunk bubbling blood with each breath. The hunters scrambled around his head, firing at him. It took another six shots to kill him, because the hunters of Erwin did not know how to kill elephants.

Then they scrambled on top of him, laughing and joking, and took turns being photographed. Elizabeth was stumbling down the highway, and she filled her lungs and cried out *'David Jordan—now will you believe me?'*

The happy hunters were still photographing each other when three strangers appeared out of the darkness. They strode up to the carnage, and one shoved an Erwin hunter off Little's head.

'Get out.'

The Erwin hunter sprawled in the elephant's blood, shocked. 'What the hell?'

'Get out of here,' the second man rasped.

'Now listen here . . .'

There was a slow, slick click from the third man's rifle.

'You heard,' he said quietly. 'This is *man's* work.'

The men from Erwin all stared, then scattered. The sprawled hunter began to clamber up. Then his teeth suddenly clenched, and he hurled himself, one hand outstretched, the other drawn back in a fist. The newcomer jerked, his arm whirled, there was a flash of a blade, and the hunter sprawled again, gasping. He lay on the road, clutching his hand, his face contorted, staring at the stump of his knuckle.

'You cut my finger off!'

The newcomer slowly bent and picked up the bloody finger. He held it up, dripping.

'Next it's your guts. Now get out of here, boy.'

The blood was pumping out of the stump. The young man stared at his hand, aghast. 'I'm goin' to the police . . .'

'Yeah, and you tell them you shot the critters and go to jail . . . Go ahead, boy . . .' His foot swung, and he kicked the hunter in the ribs. There was a thud and a gasp, but the hunter scrambled up. He started crouching away backward, holding his bloody wrist tight. The newcomer held up the finger.

'I've got your fingerprints, boy . . .' He shoved the severed digit into his pocket. 'Only reason I'm not shootin' your tires out is I want you out of here—but don't push your luck . . .'

He turned and flicked a torch over the carcasses. 'Find the tracks,' he snapped. His two companions started searching the embankment with their flashlights.

The man went over to Mama, crouched down, and heaved her over. He put his razor-sharp knife to her chest and began to skin her.

# part four

# eighteen

Eric Bradman was a member of the Fund for Animals, Friends of the Earth, Greenpeace, the Sierra Club, and he was once one of the most popular men in America. He was a television journalist, and in his day his encyclopedic knowledge of world affairs, his wit, sincerity, powers of debate, and the charm and merciless skill with which he had interviewed people were so admired that many people said he should be president. Politicians feared him, youth idolized him, housewives loved him. His energy had been boundless. Then he had been smitten with throat cancer.

Now he could speak no more than a few minutes without getting hoarse. He could not be the ubiquitous commentator anymore. Now, he made his own films about the environment, the energy crisis, endangered species and man's gluttonous rape of the earth. Over sixty, he was still very popular. He occasionally appeared on panels when the subject was close to his heart, but he had to save his voice. Politicians now dreaded the moment when his voice turned hoarse, and the veins began to stand out on his neck, and the viewers' hearts went out to him. Eric Bradman was the Grand Old Man of the public forum, and one of the letters which David Jordan had given to Ambrose had been addressed to him.

On Monday morning the story of the stolen animals was on the front page of almost every newspaper in the world, and a new word had been coined: *Zoo-jack*. The headlines were all sensational, some hysterical, inspiring dread of the scourge of beasts let loose upon the land. There was almost applause for the zoo-jackers, if one read between the lines of some, and a rash of editorials severely criticized zoos. To add insult to Ford's injury, the *New York Times* had published in full their letter from David Jordan, condemning zoos in general and explaining why he had set the animals free. Jonas Ford had been appalled at the 'vulgar' sensationalism, indignant at the slur upon his administration, and outraged at David Jordan's letter. To add further insult, the radio today was full of Elizabeth Johnson's story, implying that if she could get herself down there and try to stop the massacre, why hadn't he?

Professor Ford had no intention of letting his press conference last more than ten minutes. He had imagined a dozen or two people at the most, but the hall was packed with journalists from around the world. He strode to the lectern, cleared his throat and without more ado read his prepared text in his no-nonsense style. After condemning the reaction of the media and deploring the massacre at Devils Fork earlier that morning, he continued:

'The government, while placing at our disposal all the help by way of personnel and equipment we need, is leaving the recapture operation entirely in my hands, in collaboration with the chief wildlife officer of the United States. We have been in consultation the whole of yesterday, working out the details of the operation, which is to be called Operation Noah. Briefly, they include the following:

'One: The entire perimeter of the wilderness area where the animals are will be cordoned off by troopers by the end of today. This involves several thousand men. This cordon will contain the animals while Operation Noah commences. People living nearby, therefore, have no cause for alarm.

'Two: Recapture will be effected by firing tranquilizer darts into the animals, containing a drug known as M99. Within a short time this drug will cause the animal to drop into unconsciousness for several hours, when it will be recovered, bound, taken to a holding stockade, and as soon as possible returned to its proper place.

'This whole process is likely to take several weeks. The animals have to be individually tracked and recovered. There are over twenty involved, all different in the amount of drug and handling required.

'Three: The public will be prohibited from entering the cordoned area. This is not only to protect people from their own folly, but ensure there is no recurrence of the tragedy, nay the atrocity, which has occurred. Not only are these specimens private property, they are priceless national, indeed international, assets. To hunt them is not only a barbarity but highly dangerous. It must be realized that these are highly dangerous animals, of which the American hunter has no experience.'

Professor Ford looked up from his text, then said abruptly: 'Any questions?'

A reporter said, 'Professor, what are you qualifications for being in charge of this Operation Noah?'

'I was on Operation Rhino in Zimbabwe some years ago, trans-locating black rhinos to game reserves, and on a similar operation in Zululand in South Africa . . .'

'Were you in charge, or? . . .'

'I was an observer, but I participated in every stage and wrote a scientific paper about it. I have also been in the Congo studying the lowland gorilla. I have also been on numerous zoological expeditions, assisting in the capture of specimens, in South America, Asia and in Alaska and Canada.'

Another voice said, 'Frank Hunt of The World's Greatest Show gave us the impression that he would be—or *should* be—in charge. Have you any comment?'

Jonas Ford shoved his glasses up the bridge of his nose.

'Mr. Hunt is under no such impression now. We have been in consultation with him and the owner of the circus, Mr. Worthy. They are making a number of vehicles available for transporting back specimens, which is a convenience, but Mr. Hunt trains animals which is a far cry from capturing specimens. However, his personal knowledge of his individual animals may prove useful. He will be *accompanying* us.'

Another reporter said, 'Professor, you say your troops will have cordoned off the area by tonight. Why not earlier? Why not *last* night?'

'Because,' Ford said impatiently, 'it is a huge undertaking to mobilize the local troops. They have to be called in from all over the countryside. It takes a lot of organizations. Maps have to be studied, supplies arranged. Transport. Tents. Fuel. But I authorized the local sheriff to raise as many local men as he could to contain the situation—we did the best that could be done at such short notice.' He glared at his audience. 'Large numbers of troops are en route to the scene right now. And members of the Wildlife Department.'

'But the sheriff did not contain the situation at all. Why is it that David Jordan managed to cross twenty miles of wilderness—*and* two highways—without your men even spotting him, let alone containing him?'

'You should ask the sheriff. But in his defense may I say he did the right thing. He set out to locate the animals by tracking them, which is the only reliable way. But it is dense wilderness, and he was hours behind them. He did his best. And *nobody* can track in the dark.'

'So how are you going to improve on the sheriff? Are you going to search for them by helicopter, for instance?'

'My dear sir, helicopter search is useless. The forest is thick; one can't see the ground. The *only* way to find an animal, unless you're lucky and just stumble upon it, is by tracking it. That is what I shall do, and Wildlife officers are at the scene now, tracking from Devils Fork where they crossed this morning.'

'And then?'

'Then, sir,' Ford said with an impatient sigh, 'we will keep track of them every day, darting one at a time, recovering it, flying it out by helicopter to our camp, where it will be placed in a stockade.'

'Where's your base camp?'

'It hasn't been set up yet. But it will be by tonight. In a suitable place near the area of operations, obviously.'

Another reporter said, 'When exactly are *you* going to get down there, sir, to take charge?'

'This afternoon. Or tonight at the latest.'

'Why so long, Professor? Dr. Elizabeth Johnson managed to get down there the day before yesterday, and by the small hours of yesterday morning she had found them.'

Professor Ford looked at him with glowering dignity.

'It is difficult,' he said, 'not to say highly uncomfortable to be in two places at once. Dr. Johnson just abandoned her duties here and rushed off. She found them not by tracking, but by luck.'

'And with *pluck!*' a reporter shouted from the back.

'Indeed. I am not belittling Dr. Johnson's courage, nor her good intentions. But I could not simply abandon my post on an emotional impulse; I had to organize the recapture operation. Do not underestimate the size of that task. It has been done in thirty-six sleepless hours. And though a handful of the sheriff's men and I might have stopped the massacre had we, with the benefit of clairvoyance, been at Devils Fork, we could not have contained the animals. We would only have hoped that them *seeing* us would have frightened them into staying on the other side. *If* they had seen us. A handful of men in that huge area. In the dark. That is why we need a lot of troops, to act as a conspicuous human fence.'

'What are the troops going to do if the animals aren't deterred by them?'

Ford took a deep breath. 'It is not our intention, sir, to indulge in a debate on operational tactics. That will only provoke endless and possibly emotional discussion on something which, with all due respect, you know nothing about. Suffice it to say that these very points have been the subject of lengthy consideration.'

Then Eric Bradman spoke for the first time:

'Well, it seems to me that making a human fence out of thousands of troops who know nothing about animals is inviting confusion, panic, and a possible bloodbath.'

Everybody waited for the professor's reply. 'Is that a question, Mr. Bradman?'

'Unfortunately not,' Bradman grumbled. 'You made it clear that you won't entertain questions on tactics. But I do have a question, please . . .' Everybody waited. 'According to Dr. Johnson, to whom I've spoken by telephone and whom I'm going to be joining later today, the animals are following David Jordan through the wilderness as if he were the Pied Piper. Can you, as a zoologist, explain this?'

'There is nothing Pied Piperish about it, Mr. Bradman. Nothing very remarkable at all. These are *tame* animals, and they *know* him because he used to work with them. Indeed, most of them are highly trained circus animals. In the animal kingdom, one animal, usually the largest male, becomes accepted by the others as the leader, or *alpha*, as it's called. In a zoo, the keeper becomes accepted as the alpha. The same in a circus. The animal also *likes* its alpha and is to a great extent emotionally dependent upon him. Furthermore, the keeper, the alpha, provides food. When such animals are thrust back into the wilderness, as has happened now, they are frightened and completely at a loss. So, naturally, they will follow their alpha—who, in this case, is Jordan. That's all there is to it.'

His eyes darted over the other faces challengingly.

'But,' said Eric Bradman, 'are there not certain people who *do* have remarkable powers with animals? Who empathize with them to such an extent that the animals adore them, people who can *communicate* with animals in their own language, as it were?'

'Supposedly. In the same way as there are spiritualists, hypnotists, mystics, people with extrasensory perception; I have not had anything to do with them.'

Eric Bradman let the zooman's dismissal hang, then he said quietly, 'Why did you ban David Jordan from the zoo?'

Ford had not imagined he would have to defend himself.

'There are certain perverse people who make a pest of themselves in zoos. They torment the animals, or feed them, or try to touch them. I ban such people—as do zoos everywhere. I can understand the public's morbid curiosity in this man Jordan, but I am not about to have any administrative judgment debated.'

'Of course . . . But is it true, Professor, that the animals used to show great excitement when he arrived, make a noise and try to reach him through the bars?'

'I believe so. Then he'd break all the rules and touch them. Highly dangerous, because the public is then tempted to try the same thing. You can't treat them like dogs and cats.'

'I see . . . they should be left alone in their cages?'

Ford look at him angrily. 'The obvious answer is yes, Mr. Bradman. Only a fool would say no. But I do not like what you imply.'

Bradman said mildly, 'Professor, I am not condoning what this man Jordan has done. I do not like zoos—that is what I implied—because is it not immoral, Professor, let alone *cruel*, to imprison our fellow creatures for the amusement of the public?'

He was prepared for the question.

'Zoos, Mr. Bradman,' he said with a hint of triumph, 'are more necessary today than they have ever been in history. For never before has the animal kingdom been in such danger of being overrun, sent into extinction, by man. Zoos are a *sanctuary* for animals, Mr. Bradman. They *breed* under protection, and one zoo trades off surplus stock to another. And zoos, Mr. Bradman, are *not* there simply for the public's amusement. They are there for the public's *education*.' He glowered at him. 'For the fact is that ninety-nine percent of the world will never see these specimens *except* in a zoo. And *seeing* them makes them *aware* of ... their worth.'

Bradman said earnestly, 'Professor Ford, as a zoologist, do you feel *sorry* for animals in distress?'

Ford knew what was coming. 'Of course. But none of the Bronx Zoo animals is in distress, Mr Bradman.'

'Then why is it,' Bradman said reasonably, 'that—for example— all the big cats are constantly striding up and down their cages? A human being, constantly pacing up and down in a confined space, would be considered in distress.'

'There is no parallel. A man has a highly developed brain. An animal has no powers of reasoning. As it knows nothing but its cage, it is not reacting to his *captivity* by pacing.'

'It is not instinctively searching for freedom?'

Jonas Ford said triumphantly, 'No! The desire for freedom is *not* an instinct. There are only *five* basic instincts, meaning things which animals do entirely alone without learning from others or by experience. These are eating, sleeping, keeping warm, mating and self-preservation. Anything else an animal does or knows, it gets by experience or imitating others. So, Mr. Bradman, a tiger pacing in its cage is *not* doing so because it has *learned* about freedom, because it has not experienced it. And it is not doing so in an *instinctive* desire for freedom, because freedom is not one of the five instincts.'

Eric Bradman was staring at him, amazed at this clinical but obviously sincere scientific analysis.

'Then *why* is the tiger pacing, Professor Ford?'

'Perfectly natural. All creatures walk about.'

'Natural? Is it happy?'

'Perfectly. It is well fed and cared for. It has no enemies to prey on it. And it knows no different life.'

'But the tiger in the jungle doesn't pace up and down.'

The tiger in the jungle must hunt for its food. When not hunting, it sleeps or relaxes. As the zoo tiger does not have to hunt, it paces about to work off its excess energy, as it were.'

'It's not bored stiff?'

'No.'

'Nor unhappy?'

'I have answered that question.'

'Nor restlessly seeking freedom because freedom is not an animal instinct? Nor is it lonely?'

'The tiger is a solitary animal, Mr. Bradman.'

'So it is simply being a tiger—expressing its *tiger*ness?'

Everybody was hanging on the sharp exchange. Bradman's eyes were blazing, and Professor Ford was glaring.

'As a scientist, I am not sure what you mean by "tigerness." '

'I see.' Bradman let the admission hang theatrically. Then he went on, almost wearily. 'And the elephant, Professor—is that a solitary animal?'

'No . . .' Ford began.

'And the hippopotamus?'

'No.'

Bradman shook his head, like a wise old magistrate. 'Indeed,' he said quietly, 'both are very gregarious animals, are they not, which live in herds, highly loyal and affectionate to each other?'

Professor Ford opened his mouth but Bradman continued: 'And we know that elephants roam thousands of miles a year. Now, to quote David Jordan's open letter to the *New York Times*, why is it that the New York Zoological Society—the expert on animals—sees fit to keep their elephants, these gregarious animals, among the greatest mammals ever seen on earth—in separate cages the size of a human being's bedroom?'

Ford was trying to control his anger.

'Elephants, Mr. Bradman, only cover large areas in search of *food*. The wild elephant has to spend sixteen hours a day feeding. The rest of the time it spends resting. In the zoo, where it is well fed, it does not need much space.'

'How many hours a day does an elephant feed in the zoo?'

'About three.'

'I'm trying to find out what your elephant does with its free time. If it only feeds three hours it must spend twenty-one hours resting. Is it correct that an elephant only *sleeps* about six hours a day?'

Ford shoved his spectacles up on his nose. 'It is.'

'So your zoo elephant has fifteen hours a day when it's neither eating nor sleeping?'

'Your mathematics are correct.'

'What do—or did—your elephants do with their fifteen hours every day?'

Ford was uncomfortable.

'They rested.'

Bradman let this hang too, then said quietly, 'From what were they resting, Professor?' Ford glared at him in answer, so Bradman went on quietly. 'Oh, Professor, doesn't an elephant ever like to *play*?'

'All animals play to a certain extent.'

'Doesn't it want to feel the pleasure of space about its massive body? Feel the fresh air and the sun and the breezes? Doesn't it want real trees to feed from? Doesn't it want to roll in the sand and dust itself and squirt water over itself? And doesn't it want companions, its herd?'

'There are two other elephants right next door to it.'

Bradman's voice began to go hoarse. 'But in a separate cage. With a great concrete wall between them so they cannot even see each other! *Why?* ...'

'Because,' Ford said, 'the cages were built that way a hundred years ago—somewhat *before* my tenure of office.'

Bradman cried, 'But in the name of pity, why haven't you knocked that wall down, so at least the elephants can *see* each other—touch each other, just *be* together?'

Ford said uncomfortably, 'Because of the expense. And it's a question of space ...'

'Space?' Bradman echoed incredulously. 'But the Bronx Zoo has two hundred and fifty acres of parkland, as David Jordan points out. And you allot a piece of concrete the size of a bedroom to an elephant. Is a zoo for animals or for people?'

'These things take time and money ...'

The veins stood out on Bradman's neck.

'How can you justify inflicting misery on an animal, the screaming misery of solitary confinement as David Jordan says, to save the expense of knocking one wall down? Can't you imagine the frustration of it, the heartbreak of it—year after year, the misery of being in a cell every day of its life, without even the company of its own kind, yet knowing there are elephants just next door; being able to *hear* them and *smell* them but unable to *see* them, unable to *join* them! Imagine, the stultifying *boredom*, the *yearning*. . . .'

'They have the company of their keeper, and every day hundreds of people come to visit them.'

Eric Bradman stared at him incredulously.

'Good God . . .' he breathed.

Jonas Ford folded his notes theatrically.

'Enough of your sentimental ignorance, sir,' he said grimly. He strode angrily out of the building.


# nineteen


That same morning, when the sun was coming up over the mountains, gold and misty through the trees, Smoky sat and let Davey examine his wound. But, as he parted the heavy fur, Smoky barked and reared, his eyes wild, and he scrambled backward, looking at Davey fearfully, flanks heaving, blood on his fur, the pain thudding through his chest. Davey approached him again, whispering urgently, and the bear stood, quivering. But as soon as Davey tried to part the bloody fur he scrambled back again, confused and terrified, pain in his ribs, chips of bone grinding with each breath.

Now Smoky lumbered along the Appalachian Trail behind all the other animals, panting and gasping; with each thud of his paws the pain jolted through his flank. There was nothing he could do but follow, and there was nothing Davey could do to help him.

The bullet had hit the socket of Queenie's tusk, skidded along it and lodged into her jaw. Now she lumbered down the trail, blindly following the others, shaking her head against the elephantine toothache, her ears flapping. With each footfall the agony jolted through her jaw, and she shook her head harder trying to get it out. Each shake aggravated the pain, so she shook her head harder and squealed, trying to run away from it. All she knew was that she had to keep running after the man who was hurrying her away from that terrible place where it had happened. For three miles she had blundered along, shaking her head; then at last they had stopped.

Queenie knelt down when Davey ordered her, groaning and blinking. He examined the bloody bullet hole and could see the hump where the bullet was lodged in her jaw. It was probably only an inch beneath the swollen hide. If she would let him, he could probably cut it out himself. But when he had touched it with his finger she had squealed, flung up her trunk, and tried to scramble up. There was nothing he could do to help her, to take away the pain, and she could sense the fear and fury in him.

The bullet had smashed into Daisy's shoulder and flung her onto her back. Blinded by the headlights, deafened by the rifles, she had tried to run and she had crashed. Her left arm had buckled under her, and she had scrambled up, screaming, and terrified out of her wits, and fled into the forest on her hind legs and one arm.

When they stopped, the sun was up. Whimpering, her brown eyes wide in shock, ready to cower, she let Davey examine her.

There was only a small hole in her shoulder, but her arm dangled powerless. She looked up at Davey with big, desperate, pleading eyes, lips curled back over her teeth. King Kong stood on all fours, chest heaving, his eyes darting suspiciously. When Davey had tried to bind her arm against her body to support it, she had barked and tried to scramble aside. There had been nothing he could do for her.

'I'm sorry, Daisy, O God, I'm sorry ...'

He could not bear to think of what he had to do, nor how he was going to do it, nor when, to put her out of her misery. The only thing he had was a knife.

And he wanted to shout his anguish and his fury to the heavens.

Now Daisy stumbled along on three legs, her shattered arm dragging, head down, whimpering.

Thus they fled down the Appalachian Trail that Monday

morning, wild-eyed, nostrils wide, flanks heaving, the big Indian bringing up the rear with Sally, Smoky, and Sam.

# twenty

The sun was getting low.

One police car had been at Allen Gap some hours with four deputies under the leadership of a worried young patrolman. Two truckloads of troops had just arrived and were taking up positions. Frank Hunt and Charles Worthy were standing with the patrolman and the lieutenant in charge of the troopers, Frank wore a safari suit and a broad-brimmed veldt hat with a leopardskin band. Chuck Worthy was watching the road, hoping for a television crew to arrive. 'How dangerous are they, sir?' the patrolman asked. He suffered from acne, and his eyes were burdened with responsibility.

'Very.' Frank drew on his cigarette. 'Very,' he added sincerely.

The patrolman rubbed his chin. 'Even with you? Would they go for you?'

'You should see their eyes when I get into the ring with them every morning.'

'You go in alone?'

'With an assistant. Guards my back.'

The patrolman glanced at the forest. 'How's this guy Davey Jordan doing it, then?'

Chuck Worthy snorted. 'Him? He's not a human being, he's some kind of fairy.' He tapped his head. 'You can see it in his eyes.'

Suddenly Frank's eyes widened.

'*It's that goddam Indian,*' he whispered.

Everybody swung around.

A hundred yards away, Big Charlie stood on the high bank above the road. They stared at him, astonished.

'Hold everything!' he shouted.

He held his hands above his head. Then he started along the bank toward them.

The patrolman slowly pulled out his gun, and there was a ragged click of gunbolts. Frank yanked out his forty-five, his eyes darting across the forest for animals. Charlie was fifty yards from then now. He shouted hoarsely, 'Is the vet here . . .?'

The patrolman wet his lips and shouted, almost politely, 'No.'

'Please call a vet. We want to hand over three animals. In pain. We want to make a deal.'

There was an astonished silence. Then Frank called huskily, 'Where're the animals, Chief?'

'I'll show you . . . if it's a deal . . .'

The patrolman recovered himself. 'What's the deal?'

Big Charlie panted, 'Got your $CO_2$ gun, Mr. Hunt?'

Frank nodded warily.

Big Charlie said, 'You dart the three animals, for the vet to fix. The rest of the animals you leave alone. They stay free . . .'

'You got to be joking . . .'

'If you guarantee that . . . to leave the other animals free, me an' Davey, we'll give ourselves up.'

The patrolman was openmouthed.

'You're full of crap . . .' Frank breathed.

Big Charlie said, 'You got a radio. We want it guaranteed by the governor of Tennessee.'

'Holy smoke . . .' Frank Hunt whispered. 'And if we say no, Chief?'

'Then it's no deal. We just stay in the forest.'

Frank could not believe the impertinence. 'And what makes you think we won't shoot you when you try to run back to the forest?'

'Shut up!' the patrolman bellowed. He glared around at them. 'I'm the only law officer around here right this moment. And until a more senior one arrives, I'm in charge!' He held a trembly finger up at Big Charlie. 'And I'm telling *you*, Mr Buffalo, that it's a deal.'

He turned shakily to Frank Hunt.

'You going to dart these three animals, or am I?'

Frank stared at him.

'Then gimme your special gun.'

'For God's *sake*, man! You can't just go in there and face dozens of wild animals.'

The patrolman grabbed at Frank's holster and yanked out the $CO_2$ gun. 'Okay, Mr. Buffalo—where're they at?' He turned and shouted hoarsely at the lieutenant in charge of the troopers. 'Get all your men up here on the double.' Then to his deputy: 'Get onto the radio and tell the sheriff.'

He started running down the highway, following Big Charlie, followed by the troopers. Charles Worthy grabbed Frank by the sleeve of his safari suit, his face thick with anger.

'You get your ass up there, Morris. *Get your goddam gun back and get in there!* This is *our* show, Morris!'

They crept through the forest, forty soldiers tiptoeing in a line, eyes wide, guns ready. Big Charlie was in front with the patrolman, Frank Hunt picked his way behind them with his six-gun, Chuck Worthy was at the rear. They were on the Tennessee side of the mountain, about a quarter of a mile down from the Appalachian Trail, about five hundred yards into the wilderness.

Big Charlie waved the soldiers to a stop. He beckoned to the patrolman, and whispered, 'They're over this rise, about another three hundred yards. Tell your men to stay here, you and me go on.'

The patrolman's eyes were wide.

'Why not the troops too?'

'The noise. The animals'll run. Maybe Mr. Hunt better come too.'

The patrolman beckoned nervously. Frank looked at him in alarm, then crept warily forward.

They moved on through the dense undergrowth for another two hundred yards, toward the crest of the rise. Charlie stopped and whispered. 'Very carefully now . . .'

He turned and went on another ten yards. Then suddenly he froze, listening intently. All Frank could hear was the pounding of his heart.

Big Charlie signaled the patrolman to stay where he was. He crawled forward another ten paces, silently, peering ahead. He stopped again. He listened. Then he beckoned the patrolman to follow.

They were almost at the crest of the rise. Big Charlie stopped, listening. Then he motioned to the patrolman to wait.

He crept on again, into the undergrowth. Out of sight. The patrolman and Frank Hunt waited breathlessly.

And they waited.

And waited.

A mile away, on the other side of the Appalachian Trail, Davey Jordan came down the embankment onto the empty highway and ran across it and up into the forest on the other side, the animals scrambling behind him.

Back on the other side of the mountain, the patrolman and Frank Hunt waited. They waited almost an hour before they realized that Big Charlie was not coming back.

# twenty-one

That night the pain in Queenie's tusk was very bad. Where the bullet was lodged there was a lump the size of an orange.

She lay alone against a tree, trying to rest, blinking slowly in the dark, legs folded beneath her, trying to endure her toothache, taking deep groaning breaths.

She could hear the other elephants feeding, wrenching at the leaves. She was hungry and exhausted, but the pain in her mouth was stronger. She had hardly eaten since the attack, and she needed to eat over three hundred pounds of vegetation daily. Lumbering along the Appalachian Trail, she had grabbed at leaves, but the agony had streaked through her jaw and tusk as she tried to chew, and she had squealed in agony.

When they had stopped, she had tried to drink. She had sucked up a trunkful of water and squirted it in, but the agony of the ice-cold water against the root of her tusk was excruciating, and she had shaken her head and that made the agony crash harder, and she squealed, and scrambled backward, and then just had stood there, waiting for the pain to subside. She had fearfully slurped up another trunkful, but the agony had stabbed again and she squealed and scrambled again, her heart pounding from the shock. Her body had cried out for water. At last she had got it right, pushing her trunk tip deep into her mouth before squirting, exhausted by the confusion of it.

She knew what had become of her, who had struck her this terrible blow: the same creatures who had come to watch her in the circus, the same that had kept her captive. She knew she had to flee and be cunning for her life; and she knew that her only hope lay with her keeper, that only he could be trusted, that he was trying to take her through these perils. But this she also knew, in her blood and bones: she was a mighty elephant, bigger and stronger than all other creatures; if any other creatures tried to hunt her she would charge them and smash them to the earth, and seize them in her trunk, and swing them on high; then club them down to the earth; and she would crash her great knees down upon them, and crush out their life.


Davey leaned against a tree, exhausted, his eyes glistening.

Ten yards away Big Charlie was deep asleep. Near Davey lay the big cats, the lions on one side, Sultan on the other: all sleeping except Tommy, who sat, head up, ears pricked, eyes wide in the darkness, listening. He was hungry. Sam was asleep at Davey's side, legs twitching; he was probably dreaming of chasing something to eat. Champ lay on his side, his head in the crook of his arm, his back against Sam's. Somewhere out there in the dark the two grizzly bears were foraging, and even Smoky was feeding somewhere. On the edge of the stream lay Sally, flat out on her side, snoring long-sufferingly. But Davey was thinking of none of them; he was watching Daisy.

She sat on the other side of the pool, in the moonlight filtering through the trees. The other chimpanzees slept, their heads resting on the crooks of their hairy arms. The gorillas had made makeshift nests of leaves and twigs scraped into a circle.

But Daisy sat alone, her back hunched, her right hand holding her chest, blood oozing between her fingers, her broken shoulder hanging. Her mouth grimaced, and her eyes were shocked as she stared across the pool at Davey. She could not sit, nor lie, nor stand without her shattered shoulder taking the weight of her whole arm.

Davey watched her, tears glistening. He had tried, again, to bind her arm to her chest, but she had cried out and jerked away, her bloody hand clutching her cowering face. He had tried to comfort her, had held her good hand and talked to her, making sympathetic noises, trying to lull her to sleep. His own body was crying for sleep, but he would not, could not, until she fell into merciful unconsciousness. The tears were running down his face as he waited for that, and his heart was breaking for what he had to do.

*Oh, Dr. Johnson, where are you now? ...*

And, O God in heaven, to sink into oblivion and not to have to do what I have to do. And when I wake up, maybe You will have done it for me.

But God did not.


Slowly, slowly, Davey pulled out his knife, and slowly, tremblingly, opened the blade. He took a deep trembling breath and looked at Daisy sitting in the moonlight; he whispered, 'Oh, forgive me, Daisy ...'

Then the cry broke in his throat, and he slumped forward and sobbed. He wanted to fill his lungs and bellow, *Savages! You savages!*

He tilted back his head again, tears running into his mouth.

Why didn't they leave you in the jungle where you belonged, Daisy? Where you had every right to be, where God made you to be, why did they have to come to your piece of the world and catch you and put you in a cage so people could come and laugh at you? *What right did they have to do that?*

He wept at her across the pool in the moonlight, and Daisy sat hunched in the dappled darkness, silently crying at him, her eyes bright. He screwed his eyes up tight and forced his head against the tree, trying to feel pain himself. He thought of her racing through the glen, leapfrogging over King Kong, cartwheeling, somersaulting and cavorting for joy through the trees.

O, God, maybe I shouldn't have done it ... *O God, what have I done to her? Please God, help me now ...*

He slowly got up.

He walked shakily toward her across the darkness, the knife concealed in his palm.

'Hello, Daisy . . . Hello, girl . . .'

She watched him all the way. He crouched, shaking, his throat thick. He slowly put his left hand under her good armpit and gently, ever so gently, lifted. Daisy looked at him, begging not to move, but he lifted a little harder, and she got up, with a grunt, clutching her shoulder.

Silently, he led her, hobbling, through the dark undergrowth away from the others, down the slope.

'Sit, Daisy.'

Daisy sat, holding her bloody shoulder, looking up at him beseechingly. He knelt in front of her, tears shining on his gaunt cheeks. Gently he scratched her head. Daisy sat there, hunched, suffering.

*Please God help me to find the right place.*

Daisy opened her eyes and saw the glinting knife in his hand, but she did not understand. All she knew was the agony, and the human she loved trying to comfort her. She looked at the knife dazedly, then raised her eyes and looked into his, pleadingly. The grief erupted in his throat.

*Don't just stand there, God . . .*

He took a deep juddering breath, slipped his left hand over her eyes, and lifted the sharp point of the knife to her bloody breast. He felt her move her head, and look at him, and he hesitated—for grief, for the feel of life, his hand trembling in front of her breast. And then she understood. In that terrible moment she saw that death was about to strike, that this man she loved was about to kill her, and her eyes widened in incredulous horror and her mouth opened to scream, and he squeezed his eyes and plunged the knife.

In one horrified lunge he rammed it to the hilt in her heart. There was one huge killer jolt of agony, the incredulous shock in her eyes. She fell backward and he came down on top of her contorting body. He wrenched the knife out and rammed in into her again with all his horrified might, and pulled it out and plunged it in again. He pushed back her chin blindly and plunged the knife into her throat and slashed it open. Then he collapsed on top of her inert body, and buried his contorted face into her bloody chest, sobbing, gasping.

# part five

## twenty-two

Highway 25 sweeps through the Appalachian Mountains, down to the steep wooded banks of the French Broad River. It crosses the bridge into the village of Hot Springs, then sweeps back up into the forests of Tennessee and the Appalachians again.

Only a few hundred souls inhabit Hot Springs. The stores are well spaced, green vacant lots between, and lanes lead to a few houses. Half a mile or so downriver, there is a railway bridge. There is a railway shed, a post office, a general store, one cafeteria, and a liquor store. On the outskirts, up the mountain slopes, is a Jesuit mission, a brick building with two bunkhouses, where people who hike the Appalachian Trail are welcome to rest awhile. It is a pleasant little hamlet, nestling by the river, surrounded by steep forests, peaceful and sleepy.

It was four o'clock on Thursday morning, but at the Jesuit Mission all the lights were ablaze, and there were dozens of cars in the driveway. On the lawns stood three helicopters, and people slept in bedrolls on the grass. The liquor store had never done such business, and the cafeteria, which usually closed early, had been doing a roaring trade till well past midnight.

Professor Jonas Ford had made Hot Springs his base camp for Operation Noah, and the Jesuit Mission had opened its doors to him. On the riverbank beyond the sheriff's office were parked four long-distance haulage trucks of The World's Greatest Show and numerous wildlife department vehicles; in the campground, in the trees beyond, were great piles of iron scaffolding for the stockade to hold the animals.

Sheriff Ernest J. (Boots) Lonnogan was a big man with a big face, lined deeply from years of much heavy scowling and much wide smiling, and what he didn't know he thought he knew. But, for all that, he was a good lawman. Lonnogan had known since he was a boy that one day he was going to be sheriff of Hawker County, just like his pappy. 'LAW ENFORCEMENT HAS BEEN OUR FAMILY BUSINESS FOR TWO GENERATIONS,' his election posters read, 'AND THERE'VE NEVER BEEN ANY COMPLAINTS EXCEPT FROM THE CROOKS.' It was true, and it *was* a family business. Every New Year the Sheriff sent out publicity calendars displaying four photographs of grimly smiling people: Sheriff Ernest J. (Boots) Lonnogan, Deputy Sheriff Ernest J. (Kid) Lonnogan, Patrol Officer Fred C. Bushel, and Priscilla Lonnogan, Secretary. The joke around Hawker County was: 'How did this ringer Bushel get on the force?'

Lonnogan's other election poster showed him delivering a straight left punch, with an explosion around the fist: 'SHERIFF LONNOGAN KEEPS YOUR COUNTY PEACEFUL!' And in his no-nonsense way he sure did keep the peace, and there were no real complaints. Lonnogan may have had a big mouth and looked one hell of a dude in them cowboy boots without a horse, but he knew his business, his heart was in the right place, and he didn't hassle you none if you didn't bend the law too hard. The only complaints came from his fellow lawmen in neighboring counties who said that Boots Lonnogan kept Hawker so clean he was a pain-in-the-ass busybody in other folks' counties, trying to help. Lonnogan loved being a sheriff.

Hawker County is about a hundred miles away from Hot Springs, on the other side of the Great Smoky Mountains, beyond Cades Cove. Lonnogan had no official business in Hot Springs this night, but he was there, just visiting his colleague, the sheriff of Hot Springs, and in case he needed any extra help, he brought along Kid Lonnogan and two other men he often deputized—Jeb Wiggins of the *You-Wreck-'em-We-Fetch-'em Garage* of Hawkstown, and his brother Fred Wiggins, who had the *You-Bust-'em-We-Buy-'em Scrapyard* just opposite.

The local sheriff of Hot Springs had deputized a number of his own townsmen, and had posted three at the highway bridge, with rifles and sandbags, and three more at the railway bridge half a mile downriver. Lonnogan had inspected these defenses and found them insufficient. He had gone to advise the local sheriff, but the sheriff was in bed, so he had driven up to the Mission to advise Jonas Ford, but he too was in bed. Lonnogan was now urging the local deputies to beef up their defenses when a solitary figure appeared on Main Street from the direction of the Mission.

It was Eric Bradman. He was whispering his notes into his pocket tape recorder. Later his wife would edit and narrate them into the filmtrack.

'Confusion. And red faces.

'Professor Ford refuses to give press conferences anymore. Just terse releases.

'But . . . he *has* arrived, with his entourage of experts, consisting of wildlife department personnel and Frank I. Hunt and . . . wait for it: ranking members of the Boone and Crockett Club, and the Coin Club!

'Who're they? Well, ask my reader of those macho magazines about rifles and hunting. Named after those famous American hunters, Davy Crockett and Daniel Boone, the first club was founded by Theodore Roosevelt to, quote, "Promote Manly Sport with the Rifle," unquote. That very same Theodore Roosevelt who wrote in his memoirs about the sporting pleasures of shooting African ostriches sitting on their nests. And the Coin Club is that American big-game-hunters' club for whom the jungles are, quote, "the cathedrals where we worship," unquote. Indeed, Professor Ford has been inundated with offers from hunting organizations all over America, such as the Rod and Gun Club—which, in Ohio, volunteered to a man to form Gary Gilmore's firing squad. They offer to solve his problems . . .'

Bradman paused, thinking.

'Anyway, Ford first flew to Allen Gap, only to learn that Jordan had tricked them all there, including intrepid Frank I. Hunt, by using accomplice Charlie Buffalohorn as a decoy. The impertinent rascals.

'Seething with righteous frustration, Ford flies on to the next gap in the mountains, namely the French Broad River and Hot Springs. Here he will draw his line of defense . . .

'And a good choice, too. Because the wide river draws the line for him.'

He stopped in the middle of deserted Main Street, and confided, 'Barbie, take lots of local shots. The width of river. Steep mountains. Sleepy hollow suddenly all ajitter. Windows boarded. Sheriff coping with first-ever traffic jam. Liquor store almost cleaned out. Bible Belt country. Townsfolk agog. Et cetera . . . Cut to the Mission. Emphasize the good Catholic fathers. Prayers for the animals last night in the chapel. God's beautiful creations. Then add a few quotes from Jordan's letter along the same lines. Horror of solitary confinement. Etc., etc.' He paused, then added: 'Emphasize the tranquillity of these mountains, and of the Catholic fathers for that matter. Then cut to your footage of all the police armed to the teeth. Then to the map table in the bunkhouse, the helicopters, circus trucks, the stockade being built . . .'

He took a deep breath, and walked on down Main Street.

'But Ford has at least called off the troops. Only a few truckloads will be used for guarding remote homesteads, manning roadblocks, diverting traffic. What on earth did Ford or the President of the United States hope to achieve by mobilizing all those soldiers? To *contain* the animals? As for keeping the public out, quote unquote: it's a massive area, and it's so dense you'd need a soldier every five yards to stop a determined hunter slipping through.'

He was approaching the bridge now. He slipped his tape recorder into his pocket. Sheriff Lonnogan was staring at him in the lamplight.

'Say, ain't you Mr. Bradman—seen you on TV?'

'Right,' Bradman admitted reluctantly.

'Hey fellas—Eric Bradman himself!' Lonnogan straightened in case a cameraman should appear and stuck out his big hand politely: 'Howdy, sir. Sheriff Lonnogan, Hawker County, Tennessee. And this here's my son, the deputy sheriff. Say howdy to Mr. Bradman, son.'

'Hi,' said the boy. They shook hands. Kid was a big youngster, carrying too much fat and a pair of pearl-handled six-guns his father had had specially tooled for him. He too wore cowboy boots. He was maybe twenty, but he still had pimples, and Bradman guessed he got through a lot of Coca-Cola and candy.

'What you think, Mr. Bradman?' Lonnogan smiled.

Bradman shook his finger and pointed at his throat. 'What do you think?' he said softly, to save his voice.

From the look of the man, Bradman was expecting some broad southern-cop bombast. But when he spoke, although the words came up to expectation, the voice was impressively low-key. 'Like I was sayin', Hot Springs ain't none of my territory. But if this was my town I'd sure have more deputized men out. I said to my friend the sheriff—more deputies, I said. An' really *wal*lop this wild man Jordan and his Indian friend. There's duly-sworn-out warrants for his arrest, ain't there? Why ain't we in there executin' them warrants? If we did, the animals'd stop runnin' all over the country like hound dogs an' we can apprehend them, or easily shoot 'em, as the case may be. And stop 'em terrorizin' the country an' disturbin' the peace. I, for one, don't want to see decent law-'bidin' folk gettin' et. What is this, the Wild West? But no. Professor Ford says nobody to execute those warrants without his say-so, an' me, personally, I doubt the legality of such orders.'

'Professor Ford is acting under powers conferred by the president of the United States,' Bradman said quietly.

'Sure, Mr. Bradman.' Lonnogan was calm. 'I understand that. But I'm a lawman myself, and I learned the constitution of the U-nited States on my pappy's knee an' I'm tellin' you that I have my doubts. A man's right to defend his hearth an' home an' to make a citizen's arrest to prevent same is fundamentally en*shrined* in our Constitution. An' I'm tellin' you, not only as sheriff of Hawker County for many years, but as a woodsman who was *born* in these here hills, that the presence of these wild animals at large constitutes a violation of rights to peace an' security of person an' property. I'm here to tell y'all—includin' Mr. Ford an' the president of the United States—who I greatly respect an' uphold—that *grizzly* bears, an' lions an tigers, constitute a terrible threat inasmuch as they *killers*, Mr. Bradman . . . Not to *mention* elephants.'

Bradman nodded, encouragingly. Just then a pickup truck drove down Main Street. Three men sat abreast in the front seat. Lonnogan watched it wheel slowly toward the bridge.

'An' I'm here to tell y'all that if this Wild Man Jordan comes any closer to *my* terri-tory, if he brings his wild animals anywhere *near* the Great Smoky Mountains like folks're saying he's headin' for . . . well, sir, I'm gettin' me a posse of deputies an' I'm goin' in there after him, Mr. Ford or no Mr. Ford. Because what's Mr. Ford done in the last three days except make a lot of noise an' playin' soldiers? Has he upheld the peace an' security of person an' property? . . . Well, sir—I'm duly *sworn* to do that duty. I'm not goin' to see decent folk gettin' et . . . Excuse me, Mr. Bradman . . .'

Lonnogan tilted his hat and strolled toward the pickup truck. The three men sat and watched him come. They were all between forty and fifty years old, rugged but prosperous-looking men, in superior woodman's clothes.

'Howdy. Can I do anythin' for you guys?' Lonnogan smiled.

The biggest man shook his head. He had a scar on his cheek which gave him a dashing air. Lonnogan nodded. He had noted the number plates and the gun rack. No guns were visible, but he had noticed three knapsacks.

'You gentlemen figuring on hikin' some place?'

'Nope.'

'Huntin' somethin', maybe?'

'Nope.'

'Well, now,' Lonnogan said, 'what would three men from Sylva, North Carolina, be doin' round here at four o'clock in the mornin'? Just joyridin', maybe?'

'We breakin' some law, Sheriff?'

'Well,' said Lonnogan, 'that's what I wouldn't like to see from three respectable men who're hidin' their rifles under the front seat. How come, gentlemen?'

'That's a crime, to bear and carry arms, officer?' This man had thick eyebrows and a square, purposeful jaw.

'Nope. But right this red-hot moment huntin' around here happens to be a crime. Unless,' he said, 'you just happen to have a permit from Mr. Jonas Ford himself?'

'Why should we have?'

Lonnogan decided to cut through it all.

'Now listen here, gentlemen. Just settin' foot in these woods right now happens to be a crime around here. And as for ever *thinkin'* of huntin' any of those zoo animals—that's a very serious offense . . . Now, I can see you're all responsible, right-minded citizens who just want to do your natural duty protectin' your hearth and home. But you guys better leave all that to the experts and the law . . . I know how you feel, but imagine if the woods were full of civic-minded hunters like you? Now—I got a long memory for faces and number plates. So will you gentlemen kindly go back to Sylva? Or do I book you on suspicion? Or do I impound this here pickup for a roadworthy test an' let you walk home?'

The first man grimly started the engine. Lonnogan stepped back, touched his hat with exaggerated courtesy, and watched the truck U-turn and drive slowly back up Main Street.

# twenty-three

At that moment, a mile away, Davey lay on the edge of the forest at Lovers Leap Ridge, overlooking the French Broad River. The railway bridge was below him.

He did not think there were troops on the other side of the river. He had been watching for half an hour, and there had been no trucks. There were definitely no troops along the riverbank immediately below him. If there were soldiers he would hear them, see their flashlights, their cigarettes—they had no reason to conceal themselves. The railway bridge was unguarded, at least on this side.

Davey closed his eyes and sighed, sick in his guts with fear. And exhaustion.

He had to cross this railway bridge before it got light.

He did not know how steep the embankment was above the railway tracks at the other end of the bridge, whether all the animals could climb it. He could not go east, away from Hot Springs; there was a virtual cliff. The other way, along the tracks toward Hot Springs, he seemed to remember, the tracks were hacked into sheer rock. But there *must* be somewhere, some break, some gully the animals could get up in the half mile before Hot Springs.

He breathed deep. It was a dark night; it would be hard to see a gully until he was right on top of it. But this much he did know; the railroad storage depot just before the highway bridge was built on a wide piece of bank: he could get into the forest behind there. But it was only a hundred and fifty yards before the highway bridge.

They all badly needed rest and a safe place deep in the forest where they could throw themselves down and sleep.

But they could not; today the trackers would be onto them. They must be organized by now. In a few hours that railroad bridge would be cordoned off, if it wasn't already. And then they would never get across, they would be trapped on this side.

Davey wished he could see the other end of the bridge. But he could see no lights.

There was nothing else for it. The last thing he wanted to do was to fight, to hurt anybody. But he had to go across that bridge and make sure it was clear.

He heaved himself up, and whistled for Big Charlie.

It was cloudy; there was no moon.

Big Charlie and Davey crept silently over the railroad bridge, one behind the other, crouching against the steel girders. Frequently Charlie stopped, peered, listened; they could hear nothing except the murmur of the river, see nothing but the big black shape of the mountain. They were halfway across when they saw the sudden flare of a cigarette lighter, a man's face flickering.

They crouched, breathless; waiting for another flare, a voice, something to tell them how many there were. But nothing: just the pinprick glow of one cigarette.

Then Big Charlie squeezed his bulk between the girders, and disappeared. Davey followed.

Soundlessly, they began to claw along the outer side of the bridge, their fingers clutching the girders, their feet clinging to the lip of steel.

The deputy sat in the middle of the tracks, staring moodily, thinking of his nice warm bed back home in Hot Springs. Behind him, on a narrow verge of gravel, lay his two fellow deputies, in

128

sleeping bags, fidgeting in uncomfortable sleep.

Forty yards away, four sets of fingertips groped their way along the bridge.

When they were thirty yards from the end of the bridge, Big Charlie stopped and tried to peer between the girders. Davey clung behind him, knuckles white, his legs almost jerking with the muscular tension, feet wedged painfully on the narrow lip of steel. They heard the deputy cough. A voice said, 'What's the time, Dick?'

'Four-twenty.'

There were the muffled sounds of a man getting out of his bedroll.

Big Charlie turned, and nodded down at the river. He began to lower himself from the bridge.

Below him a steel pylon dropped straight to a big concrete base just above the water. Big Charlie clung from the girder, legs dangling, feet groping. They found the pylon and wrapped fiercely around it. One hand let go of the girder and searched under the bridge for the pylon. He clung to it, his other arm upstretched; then he let go of the girder and his body lurched. He skidded down the pylon for ten feet, hands and feet scraping; then he stopped. He clung to the steel, then slowly slid down to the concrete base.

Davey started to follow, and the voice said sharply in the darkness, 'Hear that?'

'What?'

Davey clung, his heart pounding. He heard somebody slowly, hesitantly, walking out onto the bridge. Then, 'Halt! Who goes there?'

A flashlight beamed on.

Davey hung on in the shadows of the girders, white fingertips clutching the bridge. ·

'Jus' J.J. snorin', Dick . . .' Then a snicker. 'You seen that in the movies, huh? 'Halt, who goes there"?'

'Heard somethin', I tell you.'

At last the flashlight went out.

Davey closed his eyes in relief. He began to clamber down from the bridge. He clung with both hands, face screwed up in effort. His legs dangled, and his feet groped desperately for the pylon. He wrapped his legs around it. Then the flashlight blazed again. He hung by one hand, his other groping for the pylon. Then he lost his grip, and he fell.

Suddenly there was nothing but the terrible clutching at air and the strangled gasp in his throat. Davey fell through the blackness, spread-eagled, and his last horrified thought was that Big Charlie couldn't handle the animals alone if he was killed on the rocks; he twisted in midair, hit the icy black water with a splash, and disappeared.

Up on the bridge lights flashed everywhere—over both sides of the bridge, down into the black rushing river. They flicked up, down, and all over.

Directly below, Davey clutched the concrete base of the pylon, only his plastered head above the water.

For almost ten minutes he clung in the rushing water while the flashlights flashed, and Big Charlie pressed himself against the pylon, while up on the bridge it was opined that there weren't no fish in the whole *world* as big as that.

Finally the lights went out, reluctantly.

Then Big Charlie lowered himself gingerly into the water. He faced up into the current and kicked himself away.

The deputies sat in a line across the tracks, just waiting for dawn when they would be relieved. J.J. had his legs inside his sleeping-bag because he had the most doggone arthritis. One moment they were just amuttering and complaining and aminding their lawful business when out of nowhere came these hands. Their mouths were clamped shut, and they were held in the most doggone headlock. Through their bulging-eyed, muffled struggles Big Charlie's message rasped in their ears: 'One holler an' I'll set my *lions* onto you.'

They were bound and gagged with their own shirts, belts, and suspenders, dragged off the track, and propped against the rock face of the embankment. Big Charlie rammed one of their pistols into his pocket and hurled their other weapons into the water.

The first gray light was coming into the east over the black mountains as they came scrambling down the steep banks out of the forest, hooves and paws slipping and sliding, down onto the railway tracks. Then they were running for the bridge, Davey in front, the animals lumbering after him, followed by Smoky, Sam, and Big Charlie.

Davey ran head down, trying desperately to see the tracks, gasping Please God . . . He ran and he ran, the animals strung out along the bridge. At the other end of the bridge the three trussed deputies struggled wildly. J.J. was bound half in his sleeping bag, like the bottom end of a resuscitated mummy, staring boggle-eyed in the direction of the terrible rumbling. Then out of the blackness they came.

First the massive shapes of the elephants pounding out of the darkness, the Wild Man running in front; then the terrible monsters were almost on top of them. Thundering off the bridge and around the corner of the tracks in a terrible mass of heads and bodies and legs and tusks and fur, and J.J. kicked in such terror that his hands wrenched out of the suspenders binding his wrist, arthritis or no arthritis and then Smoky saw him and stopped.

The bear's heart lurched and he blundered to a stop, and Sam almost went into him; Big Charlie just managed to swerve around them. Then Smoky whirled and fled. The other animals went thundering off the bridge down the tracks into the blackness, and Smoky made off in the opposite direction before Sam collected his wits and turned and chased after him.

Smoky galloped blindly back across the bridge, and he did not feel his pain in his panic. Sam raced to catch up with him, snarling, the hair erect on his back. Smoky was snapping at him wildly; Sam swerved and raced ahead of the panic-stricken bear to cut him off, but Smoky just charged straight at him, wild-eyed. He bowled him right over and fled on. Sam scrambled up and chased him again, but Smoky was almost at the beginning of the bridge now. Sam raced alongside, and Smoky lunged at him and burst off the bridge.

He scrambled frantically up the embankment with Sam frantically at his heels and plunged into the deep undergrowth. He whirled around and swiped at Sam furiously with his clawed paw.

Davey slowed to a jog, his heart hammering, looking desperately for a gap in the dark rock embankment. He could not see the lights of

131

Hot Springs from here; he jogged on, gasping, looking. Then the tracks curved with the river, and the town's lights came into view again, five hundred yards ahead. He could make out a car parked at the highway bridge, and the silhouette of the storage depot a hundred yards in front. He stopped, chest heaving, trying to count the people. But he was too low to see. He turned back to Rajah.

'Lift!'

Rajah sighed, curled his gnarled trunk under Davey's buttocks. He heaved him over his head and deposited him astride his great neck.

'Walk, Rajah.'

The elephant started shuffling down the tracks, the other animals following, panting.

Four hundred yards back, J.J. was hopping around in his sleeping bag, trying to untie his gag. At last he spat it out. He filled his lungs and hollered the first word which came into his head:

'ALERT!'

Then he grasped his pistol which Charlie had not found and hollered, *They's comin!*

He fired blindly into the darkness down the tracks, again and again. Queenie squealed as a bullet smacked into her rump, and the animals stampeded.

Davey clung to Rajah's neck and bellowed 'Whoa,' but his shout was drowned in the wild cracking of the pistol and the animals stampeding past him, Queenie in the lead. He struck Rajah's neck, and the elephant broke into a run, thundering toward Hot Springs.

At the highway bridge all hell was about to break loose. They had not heard J.J.'s shout, but they sure had heard his gunfire; then the pounding of feet. Coming out of the blackness, getting louder and louder. Lonnogan and the deputies stared, listening, incredulous. Then everybody scrambled for cover behind the sandbags and behind Lonnogan's car, hearts hammering, guns ready. The noise grew louder and louder. Then into the lamplight at the storage depot they burst, a great mass of thundering animals with the Wild Man on top of an elephant in their midst, shouting and waving. The lawmen could not believe their eyes, the most terrible sight they had ever seen.

They came thundering down the tracks, Queenie in front, her great ears outflung, her trunk swinging, her eyes wild, the other animals galloping behind her with David Jordan bellowing 'Whoa Queenie!' But Queenie did not hear him. She was only aware of the terror, the agony in her jaw, the stampeding panic, and that Davey was no longer leading her. She had to run for her life away from this terrible danger, and she only knew that she had to charge the lights, use her massive strength any way she could. Then she saw the human beings, and her heart lurched in renewed terror and outrage, at more men blocking her path and threatening her, the same who had thrown blinding lights on her and struck terrible pain to her jaw. All Queenie knew was that she had to charge and kill them before they killed her.

Queenie flung out her great ears to increase her size, and she curled her trunk under like a battering ram, and she charged, trumpeting and thundering straight at Lonnogan's car. Lonnogan scattered backward, aghast, his six-gun held up before him in both hands, and he fired wildly. There was stunning brightness in Queenie's head; and her legs gave way, and she crashed.

Queenie collapsed onto her chest in the middle of the railroad tracks, and the animals blundered over her, leaping in the lamplights. Now Rajah was in front again with Davey desperately bellowing *'Don't shoot!'* Ahead was Main Street; Davey bellowed 'left,' and slapped Rajah on the right ear to turn him. Rajah swerved and went thundering up Main Street, straight toward Professor Ford's car.

Jonas Ford was coming down the hill from the mission when the animals came into his headlights: a sudden mass of hides and hooves pounding up the tarmac in a terrible stampede. All he felt was sheer animal terror despite the protection of his automobile. He slammed on his brakes and swung his rented car desperately across the street, and there was a blinding jolt as the car crashed into a telephone pole. Jonas Ford gargled in horror and tried to open the door, and the animals were on him. They were leaping and swerving, and pounding, panic stricken, in a terrible mass, and Tommy roared and sprang onto the hood and off the other side; then all the big cats followed, tawny bodies outstretched and jaws agape, so the whole car shook. Next came the gorillas—galloping and screaming, fangs

133

bared in black contorted faces—and the bears, a huge mass of muscled fur leaping. Ford crouched behind his wheel, arms clasped over his head. Then he saw the big male gorilla.

King Kong was galloping up Main Street like a giant humanoid dog when he saw Jonas Ford's face at the window. He opened his big fanged mouth and roared, jumped up onto his hind legs, and beat his hands on his black chest; Jonas Ford flung himself flat.

And down at the railway tracks, Queenie lay spread-eagled in the lamplit dawn. Lonnogan and the deputies were cautiously peering above the sandbag; Ford uncurled his arms and began to raise himself. Then Queenie began to get up.

She clambered to her feet with a snort, blood running out of the hole in her forehead as she lurched and squealed and flapped her ears. Lonnogan and the lawmen scrambled for cover again, and Queenie realized that she had lost the other animals and she screamed in terror and ran.

She staggered up Main Street, throwing her great head to shake out the agony, running from the terrifying human beings. She only knew she had to catch up with the others, and she raised her trunk and trumpeted desperately for them to hear her; then she saw the car across the road and Jonas Ford's frightened face, and she shied.

She swung aside, ears out, and turned, her massive hindquarters tucked in. She started running back toward the river, and the lawmen scattered for cover again. Lonnogan crouched, held his six-gun in both hands, and fired again. Queenie lurched and ran back up Main Street. Jonas Ford frantically twisted the ignition, rammed the car into reverse and it roared to life. It leaped backward, and crashed into the pole on the other side.

Queenie saw the terrible machine across her path of flight, and she filled her lungs and screamed. She flapped her ears back, curled her trunk, lowered her bloody head, and charged at the car. Jonas Ford saw the enormous bloodied head thundering down on him, the most terrible sight he had ever seen. He jerked out the clutch and the car leaped forward. It stalled, and the elephant hit him.

Queenie hit the car at full charge, and there was a crack like cannon. The glass shattered, the car reared up onto its side, and then went over with a bone-jarring crash. Ford was thrown on his head. Queenie screamed in fury and lashed her trunk at the car like

134

a sledgehammer; more glass shattered and metal crunched, and then she charged it again, hitting the side with all her remaining might. The car skidded across the road. She screamed after it, head down like a bull, and hit it again. The car crashed over onto its other side, and she hooked her tusk under the chassis and heaved. The shattered car went rolling and smashing onto the shoulder of the road. Jonas Ford was thrown around, shocked senseless, and the car plunged into the drainage ditch. Queenie turned and started blundering up Main Street as Lonnogan grabbed a deputy's rifle, and another shot rang out.

The bullet smashed through Queenie's spinal column just above her tail, and her whole hindquarters gave way beneath her. She collapsed onto her chest, both her hindlegs paralyzed behind her; she screamed, her eyes wild, and tried to scramble up; and she collapsed again, onto her side. She squealed and twisted onto her chest, and her trunk lashed the road, groping for something to drag herself forward by. Her forefeet pawed the tarmac, and she moved herself forward twelve inches, frantically trying to flee from the terror behind and to follow the other animals. The terrified elephant heaved and thrashed, dragging her bloody hindquarters, and then Lonnogan and the deputies were running up the road, guns ready.

At the top of Main Street appeared the car of the sheriff of Hot Springs, awakened by the gunfire. Cars full of journalists were swinging down the bend from the Jesuit Mission, and citizens of Hot Springs were tiptoeing up the sidestreets in their nightwear and hair curlers, armed with guns and garden rakes, peering incredulously. In the drainage ditch the battered car's door creaked open, and Professor Ford began to crawl out.

Queenie saw them all and screamed, and she threw up her great bloodied head and her trunk, and lunged her forefeet as she tried to heave forward. Her chest was dragging raw on the tar, her paralyzed hind legs were sprawled behind her. The people converged on the street, ready to run for their lives, and the journalists' flash bulbs started popping. Sheriff Lonnogan dashed into the middle of the road, his rifle at his hip, and through her terror Queenie knew that he was going to kill her. She squealed and tried to scramble to her feet again. Lonnogan leaped backward and hollered at Ford, 'I give you one minute to do something about this here elephant!'

Six hundred yards away, Elizabeth was running down the road from the Jesuit Mission. Queenie flapped out her ears and threw her trunk at Lonnogan. She tried to scramble up and crashed back onto her chest while the photographers darted about; with each blinding flash the elephant thrashed. Sheriff Lonnogan was walking backward in front of her, his gun leveled on her, while Jonas Ford stumbled around her trying to assess her injuries. Then Lonnogan hollered, 'Your minute is up!'

The flash bulbs went, and his shot boomed down Main Street in the dawn.

# part six

# twenty-four

The Great Smoky Mountains are only about thirty miles from Hot Springs, down the Appalachian Trail.

Not until nine o'clock that Thursday morning was the Operation Noah team assembled, because the Wildlife Department trackers had spent the night in the forest around Allen Gap, fifteen miles away, and had to be air-lifted out. At sunrise Professor Ford had sent other trackers ahead up the mountain looking for spoor, but it was nine-thirty when the principal team set out, following the spoor out of Hot Springs.

Timmons, the Department's best tracker, was in the lead, carrying a Cap-chur dart rifle, followed by Dawes, another tracker, and Professor Ford, also carrying his own Cap-chur rifle and the zoo's tranqu-pistol. Behind him was another wildlife officer called Milton, who knew these woods pretty well, and behind him was Frank Hunt, nursing a hangover. He had his .45 six-gun in one holster and his $CO_2$ pistol in the other. All of them were carrying walkie-talkies. There were also three staff members of the Bronx Zoo, one of whom was old Ambrose Jones. They were carrying water bottles, knapsacks of high-energy food, and cooking utensils. Behind them came three troopers carrying rope, axes, saws, and a field radio. Straggling behind were a journalist and a television director with his cameraman. The remainder of the press and television people were back at the Mission, awaiting their turns.

Elizabeth was one of the zoo personnel, toiling behind Frank

Hunt, carrying her doctor's bag. Apart from her fury over the killing of the elephant, she felt like hell. She too was nursing a hangover. In fact, Hunt was to blame, and Eric Bradman.

She had intended to go to bed early last night, but had ended up drinking a bottle of wine in the refectory after dinner with Eric and Barbara Bradman and a priest. They had discussed environmental problems, then the morality of zoos, from there the morality of what David Jordan had done, and finally—with a third bottle—metaphysics in general. Eric Bradman had opined that 'animals share with us the privilege of having a soul,' quoting Pythagoras, and the priest had been inclined to agree, because 'Scripture foretells for animals "a glorious liberty, and the compassion of heaven will not be wanting to them." ' And the lion would lie down with the lamb; we would beat our swords into plowshares. It had been good, heady stuff, and it had been late when she had gone to bed.

But she had been unable to sleep, worrying about the animals. She still agonized about the horror of the Devils Fork slaughter. She also was still under the spell of that beautiful day in the glen. And now she was surrounded by guns, hardware, and roadblocks; sandbags, lawmen, troops; and excitement and fear in the air. She desperately wanted the animals safely recaptured, but she resented all these people; she dreaded their incompetence; she didn't want them manhandling and terrifying her animals. She could not dispel a sense of foreboding. Finally she had got up and gone to the bunkhouse kitchen to make some hot milk to try to put herself to sleep.

Sitting there was Frank Hunt, with a bottle of whisky. Elizabeth did not like what little she had seen of Frank Hunt, and she detested circuses. But she had had to be polite while her milk heated. While that happened, however, she had to admit that he was pretty amusing, with his dry comments about The World's Greatest Show, with that Dean Martin twinkle in his eye and his unabashed cowardice. Did Mrs. Mickelfield's little boy want to go in there and try to capture adult lions and tigers? Hell, no.

'Who's Mrs. Mickelfield?'

'My mother,' Frank had said. 'My mother would never have been dumb enough to christen me Frank I. Hunt even if she *had* been Mrs. Hunt. Chuck Worthy figured that "Morris Mickelfield, The

Great Lion Tamer" didn't have quite the right ring about it.'

'Morris? . . .'

He held a finger to his lips. 'Don't tell the press.' Then he added conspiratorily, 'You can call me Mo, but only in private.'

She had accepted a shot of whisky in her hot milk in the hope it would help her to sleep, and she had had to talk to Frank while she drank it. She had kept her distance. But she did want to know about circuses.

'But *is* it a case of you risking your life every day?'

Frank nodded morbidly. 'Unfortunately, yes.'

'But aren't the animals used to you? Tame?'

'Trained, sure. But tame? . . . The lions and tiger?' He sighed. 'You have to watch them all the way. Especially that bitch, Kitty, the young one. Only just got her licked, only bought her a year ago. She'll kill, I'm sure.'

She had a flash of Kitty romping in the glen, and for a moment her eyes burned. 'Would she try to kill the other animals?'

Frank looked grim. 'When she gets hungry. And she's *always* hungry. She'd sure eat me if she got the chance.'

'But surely all the other animals are too big for her to tackle?'

'Your gorillas? That wolf of his? They better watch out. And,' Frank said, 'that male lion, Tommy. Lazy sumbitch, and ornery. And that bull elephant, Rajah. Believe me, when they're defying you to make them do a trick because they're fed up about something, I tell you, Doc, they're very, *very* impressive.'

Which made her indignant. Why were those animals truculent and dangerous? Obviously because they were bullied into submission. She knew that neither lions nor elephants molest human beings in their natural state. But she did not want an argument right now.

'You go into the ring armed, I presume?'

'Isn't a trainer I know who doesn't.'

'What with?'

'A .45. That's only because they don't make a .55. And I've got a $CO_2$ pistol. Knocks them out without killing them.'

'But you've surely never had to kill any?'

'Once. A tiger. Bad brute.'

'What did he do?' she demanded.

'Just tried to kill me. Just suddenly gave this friendly roar and sprang at me. No rhyme or reason. First thing in the morning, as I walked into the ring.'

She was fascinated, despite herself. 'Did he get you?'

'Somebody up there likes me. I got him right between the eyes. And I was a bad shot then. Now I can shoot the eye out of a busy blue-tail fly. Boy, do I practice. But that's the only time. The trick is to dominate the situation.'

'How?'

'By showing no fear. That's the law of the jungle. I've got to show him that I'm a bigger and stronger animal.'

'But you are neither bigger nor stronger than a lion.'

'That's *exactly* how I feel about it, ma'am.'

'Seriously.'

He smiled. 'I'm smarter.'

'But you can't train them with a gun. What else do you use? A whip?'

'Sure. And an electric prodder.'

She grimaced. 'Do you whip them?'

'A school teacher sometimes has to punish his kids.'

'And when the animals *do* what you want, what do you do?'

'Reward them,' Frank said. 'With a tidbit.' He knew what she was getting at, and he didn't care.

'You don't train your animals just after they've been fed, do you? You train them when they're hungry so that they're eager to win the reward. You use a fear-reward system.'

'It sure licks the hell out of them eating *me*.'

She was not amused. She said, 'Davey Jordan—what do you make of him?'

Frank sighed, and puffed on his cigarette.

'That guy . . . Who understands him? Nice guy,' he added. 'Hard worker. But . . .' He shook his head. 'Who can put a finger on it? He's something else.'

'Meaning?'

He sighed. 'Meaning he's crazy, I guess. You've got to be, haven't you, to do the things he does—getting into the lions' cages with them and all that. And the bears. He's sort of . . . like a guru. He *looks* normal, sure. But he just isn't. Not only in the things he does with animals, it's an . . . air about him. Sort of . . .' He waved his hand back and forth. 'Aloof. As if his mind's elsewhere, thinking about something else.'

'On a higher plane?' she heard herself say.

He said, 'Hey, I really dig your accent.'

She was brought back to the present.

'Oh? It's quite ordinary. British.'

'Beautiful . . .' Frank smiled. 'You married?'

She was about to say no, but changed it in her mouth.

'Yes. Yes, I am.'

Frank looked mildly disappointed. To divert from herself she asked, 'You're married? Children?'

'Divorced. One child. But he lives with me.'

'Oh . . . Is he going to join the circus too?'

'Afraid not. He's got polio.'

'Oh. I'm sorry.'

They were silent a moment.

'Your husband English too?'

She did not want to talk about him.

'No. He's Australian.'

And, oh, at that moment she wished with all her heart that he was there. With all her heart she longed just to feel his arms around her, just to lie next to him in their bed, and know that tomorrow when she woke up he was going to be there. Oh, how wonderful, when all this was over, to go back to New York and find him in the apartment waiting for her. How wonderful to get a letter from him telling her he had returned to his senses and wanted her back home in London . . .

Oh, God, her life was a mess . . .


Jonas had made one of his usual censorious remarks this morning. 'Nobody's going to wait for you, my dear, if you can't keep up because you were up all night imbibing.' She felt like death, now, toiling up the mountain. What kept her going was her outrage about that poor elephant, and her furious determination to get this recapture on the road at last.

But she had to admit that Jonas was doing damn well.

In fact, she was amazed. Almost fifty years old, black and blue from being beaten up by an elephant only a few hours ago, yet he was climbing doggedly like a young man. Despite all the criticism, his organization now was good. He seemed to have thought of everything. His knowledge of what animal capture entailed, the experiences of other zoological expeditions, had been encyclopedic, revealed last night when he addressed the recapture team and assigned duties. Also, he had spoken of the animals with a concern for them as individuals, instead of as zoological specimens. He had admitted his mistake in using troops, and for not anticipating the animals' movements down the Appalachian Trail. She had looked at Jonas Ford with new eyes, last night. She could not blame him for the terrible debacle this morning: who could have anticipated that David Jordan would have had the audacity to cross that bridge guarded by all those deputies and risk going through the town?

# twenty-five

David Jordan lay beside the stream while the animals drank. His gut was quivering, his legs spread-eagled. He was trying to squeeze rest out of every moment, trying not to feel grief for Queenie, trying not to worry about Sam and Smoky. There was going to be plenty of time to grieve for Queenie; right now he had to worry about the living.

Sam would find him, he told himself. He had a nose like a bloodhound. And Smoky at least was in black bear country; he was no worse off over there than over here . . .

But, oh, *Queenie* . . . He squeezed his eyes and ruthlessly pushed those thoughts aside, and tried to think constructively.

Hot Springs was eight miles back. The Pigeon River, and the Great Smoky Mountains were only about twenty-three miles on, down the Appalachian Trail.

But now he was not following the trail. He knew that dirt roads wound through the forests, and that the authorities would be hot on their heels today.

Twenty-three miles ... The best man, with a good night's rest behind him, could cover twenty-five miles in a day in these mountains. He did not have a night's rest behind him.

But the animals were surviving. Frightened, tired, sore, but they were okay.

But their feet ... The big cats' pads had covered nothing but a few square yards of sawdust for years, the gorillas the same. Their feet, built for climbing trees, were almost as soft as a city human's.

Davey heaved himself up and looked around. Sultan lay on his side, legs outstretched, eyes closed, big-striped flanks heaving in the sunlight. Davey touched his paw; in an instant his head was up, eyes open; then he saw who it was. 'Velvet paws, Sultan ...'

The tiger drew in his big claws. Davey turned the paw over and looked at it.

The pad was swollen, clean. He had been licking it, to soothe it. Davey examined it closely. Through the soreness he could see a new toughness forming. Sultan was watching him. Davey looked at the big, beautiful face, and gave an exhausted smile, stretched out his hand and stroked the top of the tiger's head. His eyes were burning: for Mama, for Queenie, for Daisy, for the two others left lying dead at Devils Fork, for the horror and heartbreak of it all.

'Down Max Patch Road there're some farms. We must get some chickens. These cats have got to eat. So have we.'

Big Charlie was on his back, eyes closed. He dragged his hands down his face.

'I'll get some. But tomorrow night we cross the Pigeon anyway. Then we'll have the gun.'

Big Charlie knew what Davey was thinking. 'No good worrying about Smoky, Davey. He's more or less where he belongs.'

Davey nodded distractedly. 'But he's wounded.'

'Nothin's broken though. He can live with that lead. Plenty of animals in these woods with lead in them.'

Davey chewed his lip and sighed. It was true.

'Sam's okay too, Davey. He'll track us down.'

'Not if he tries to bring Smoky in. He'll never get a bear through that town now.'

'Maybe at night.'

'Sam won't have the sense to wait for dark. He'll be worried. And excited.'

'He won't bring Smoky in. That bear'll hide or climb a tree or somethin', and Sam'll give up and come on alone. Like you say, he'll be worried. So he'll give up on Smoky.'

'I've never seen him give up before.'

'He's never had a job this big before.'

'I hope you're right . . . I just hope to God you're right.'

But behind his closed eyes Davey saw his Sam trying to herd big black Smoky through Hot Springs, the bear blundering off all over the place, and Sam trying to head him off. And Smoky would panic and go running through people's gardens, there would be a hue and cry, and everybody would grab their guns. He almost heard the hollering and the blasting gunfire, and he could see his brave, faithful Sam lying in the street with the blood running out of him while the townsfolk of Hot Springs gathered around his body, gaping and grinning, prodding him and arguing about which of them had killed him. He screwed his eyes tight shut and prayed. *Please God make him come at night.*

Exhausted, he got to his feet and wiped his wrist across his eyes.

'All right. Let's go.'

Charlie heaved himself up. The big cats were on their feet, the gorillas pent, the chimpanzees staring; the bears were watching him, ready to go, to run, or to flee. Big Charlie said gently: 'Ride Rajah, Davey, you're finished.'

'What about you?'

'I'm all right. I'll see they follow. They'll follow anyway.'

Davey turned and plodded toward Rajah. The elephant watched him, blinking. Davey patted his trunk.

'Lift, Rajah.'

Rajah curled his rough, wrinkled trunk behind Davey's knees and lifted him up onto his neck. He was happier with Davey on his back; he felt safer.

Davey looked down at the animals. Dumbo shuffled solemnly into position behind Rajah and took his tail in his trunk tip; Jamba turned to Clever and gave an imperative grunt that made him shuffle closer to her. Then she picked up his trunk tip in hers, pulled him up to Dumbo's rear, and impatiently wrapped Clever's trunk around Dumbo's tail. Davey gave a soft whistle, and Rajah started plodding.

Off they shuffled through the trees, a big ragged line of animals, with Sally and Big Charlie in the rear.

At that same time, deep in the forest on the other side of French Broad River, Smoky sat on his haunches, trembling, shaggy face averted, but watching Sam out the corner of his eye. Sam stood in front of him, panting, wolf's eyes piercing. The fur on his face was scored with two stripes of blood where Smoky had swiped him.

Sam suddenly whimpered in frustration and darted to Smoky's side and lunged at his rump, but Smoky whirled around, his paw ready to swipe, and Sam jumped backward.

For three hours it had been like this. Sometimes Smoky turned and ran, crashing through the undergrowth, and Sam raced after him to head him off. Then Smoky stopped and swiped at him. Sam had tried to nip his shaggy hindlegs, but Smoky whirled around and swiped. Every time he ran farther and farther away from the river. He understood very well that Sam was trying to chase him back, and he was not going to go. He did not know where he was going; he only knew he had to keep away from the horror of men.

Just then Smoky made another break for it. He lunged sideways suddenly and went galloping through the undergrowth. Sam went bounding after him, and Smoky threw himself at a tree. With an agonized bound, his claws wrapped around the trunk. He started to scramble frantically up it, and Sam got him.

Sam hurled himself at Smoky's rump and got a fierce mouthful of fur just before the bear got out of reach, but Smoky roared and clung on tight. Sam snarled through his mouthful of fur, his forepaws off the ground, hanging on grimly and shaking his head, trying to pull Smoky down out of the tree. Smoky held. Then he began to claw higher, desperately, his claws scrabbling and his wounded shoulder agonizing. Sam still was hanging on, whining. Smoky scrambled another foot higher, dragging Sam behind him. Sam's whine turned to a muffled howl as he felt Smoky getting away from him forever. Smoky heaved himself two inches higher, and Sam came falling down with a thump and a big mouthful of fur.

Smoky scrambled gratefully up the tree. He clawed his way onto a branch and clung. Sam spat out the fur and sneezed, and began to prance around the trunk, looking for a way up it, barking and wagging his tail in anxiety. Smoky glowered down at him. Then Sam remembered he had to keep quiet. He whimpered and laid back his ears, staring up into the boughs again, ears cocked.

Sam did not know what to do. Neither did Smoky.

Through the dense shade of the forest the other animals ran, the big elephant in front with Davey crouched on his neck, his face bruised and bleeding where branches had caught him.

Miles back, Timmons, Milton, and Dawes of the Wildlife Department picked their way through the undergrowth, following the trampled spoor of the herd, and behind them toiled Professor Ford and the rest of the team. In two other locations, other trackers, backed up by troopers, worked slowly up the scattered dirt tracks that wound higgledy-piggledy through the forest. And up through the steep undergrowth crept a number of the sporting men of Appalachia with their hound dogs.

It was three o'clock when a tracker found the remnant of spoor crossing the dirt track. He stared at it, like Robinson Crusoe discovering the footprint on his desert island; his guts turned liquid and he grabbed his walkie-talkie.

'Party One, this is Party Three reporting spoor found on Little Roaring Fork Road. Do you read me, over?'

Jonas Ford snatched the radio from Milton.

'Where's it headed?'

'Southwest, over.'

Ford grabbed the map from Milton. Everybody was staring, astonished that what was meant to happen had actually happened.

'Party One calling Mission base camp—send a helicopter to fetch us immediately.'

# twenty-six

There were still almost two hours of daylight left.

Davey knew he should not stop yet, but they had to. Not so much for the animals, not for Charlie, but for himself. He was exhausted.

Rajah was tired too, now. When he got tired, Rajah began to groan, telling the world he was going to quit, and if pushed, he just sat down in protest. Even Frank Hunt knew he had to stop cracking the whip when Rajah took it into his head to sit down.

Davey lay on his back, chest heaving. His legs were trembling, his gut a sick hollow. He could not feel his hunger through the exhaustion, but he was weakening from not enough food. He badly needed to fuel his lean body. That was probably why Big Charlie could still keep going—he carried fat. Davey could hardly believe the stamina of the man.

Half a mile away down the mountainside was an abandoned homestead. The wilderness had taken it over, but the orchard was still bearing small fruit. Big Charlie was there, collecting anything edible he could find.

Davey lay, trying to rest so he could get up and stand guard, trying not to worry about the animals, not to feel the guilt, trying not to feel grief for Queenie and Smoky, trying not to worry about Sam. What was important now was to rest, to try to store up some strength. The big cats could hold out, they were all strong animals. They were all strong except him and Sally.

Oh, poor old Sally . . .

He did not look at her, but he knew what she was doing—lying in the mud of the stream, taking short groaning breaths, eyes glazed. Sally was almost at the end of her tether.

She would not last more than one more day before she just would have to quit: before she went lame, before her old heart gave in, before her intestines bust. She had hardly eaten. When they stopped, she just collapsed. On the move she stumbled along, head down. Charlie said he had to keep prodding her bumbling haunches. Davey took a deep, trembling breath. He made himself stop thinking about Sally. That would not help her. The only thing that could help her now was for him to get back his strength, so that he could get them all out of here and across that river.

He made his limbs relax. Suddenly, in an instant, he was asleep.

King Kong stood on all shaggy fours, looking anxiously at Davey. He knew that he had fallen asleep. And he knew what that meant, that nobody was watching for the enemies, that they were unprotected. He knew, as clearly as you and I would know it, that that should not be allowed to happen, that the danger had not passed. He stood staring worriedly at Davey, hoping he would wake up. His tension was communicated to the other animals, and they knew the same thing: that their protector was asleep.

King Kong turned and stared across the mountains, the way they had come, brown eyes frowning. He stared into the dense foliage, his nostrils flared, his ears alert. But he could not see very far. For a long moment he hesitated, frightened to leave the place where Davey lay—Davey, his protection and authority. Then he made his mind up as was his natural duty.

He gave a grunt and started warily back up the tracks the animals had made. The chimpanzees stayed near Davey, but the female gorilla, Auntie, started to follow, and he gave another grunt, in a different tone, which meant very clearly that she should stay behind.

King Kong went about fifty cautious yards; then he came to a rock. He peered anxiously over it. He could see a good distance into the late afternoon shadows.

He earnestly weighed up his position. Then he sat down and watched.

King Kong was not the only one watching.

The lions crouched, ears pricked, alert for the first sound of danger, ready to jerk up and flee.

But nothing happened; there were only the heavy breathing of the man, and the twitterings of the forest.

Slowly, a very little at a time, they began to untense. Auntie and the chimpanzees stared disconsolately in King Kong's direction; they they began to feel their hunger and to glance around at the foliage. Slowly, they picked at this and that, still watching.

Through their tension, the lions' hunger was deep rooted and urgent. It gnawed at Kitty's guts, demanding. Crouched there, waiting, watchful, she looked at the chimpanzees.

She knew now that they were made of meat. For on that big bad night when Davey had killed Daisy, Kitty had watched them take that last walk together, off into the darkness. She had not known that Davey killed her, but she had smelled the blood, and after he came back and had thrown himself down, Kitty had crept off, following the scent. She had found Daisy's body, buried under leaves; and Kitty had lain down and eaten her.

Now her blood, nerves, and sinews felt a quickening as she watched the chimpanzees.

On the other side of the French Broad River, Smoky still clung to his branch in the tree. Below, Sam lay on his stomach, his head tilted, staring at Smoky, a whimper never far from his throat.

Sam was at a loss. Every now and again he looked over his shoulder, listening and looking for Davey. Sam understood his duty very well. But he knew that there was no way he was going to get the bear down out of his tree.

The sun was setting. Sam looked up and whined at Smoky in frustration, and in supplication, to come down, to be gone.

All afternoon Smoky had clung to his branch, the infection in his flank thudding and his body aching, just longing for rest and a full belly. But he was afraid of Sam; and he was even more afraid of the darkening forests. Then, as the sun began to lower, Sam became frantic. He whimpered and yowled up at Smoky. And Smoky looked down at him, desperate for him to go away.

Slowly, finally, Sam knew what he had to do. It was no good waiting any more, Smoky was not going to obey, Sam knew. He had to give up now. But he hesitated, reluctant to leave his responsibility. Finally he made up his mind.

He took a last look up, barked once, and waited; then he turned and set off rapidly in the direction of the river. After ten yards he stopped and looked back. Smoky just stared at him. Sam turned and started to run.

Up in his tree, Smoky watched him go. Then he stared at the frightening wilderness about him.

He wanted to scramble down out of the tree and follow Sam, catch up with him and run behind him all the way till he found the other animals.

But he dared not. And his heart was breaking.

Davey slept.

The elephants knew they were unguarded; but after a while they were even more hungry than afraid. Trunks restlessly, nervously, reached out and plucked as they waited. Slowly, one heavy step at a time, they began to move. But they were watchful, aware, alert, and they kept together.

Jamba kept close to Clever; she also watched for Dumbo because, naturally, she was responsible for them both now that Queenie was gone. But neither Dumbo nor Clever needed watching. They both knew about the danger; they both knew about death now.

Nothing happened. The forest was still but for the sighs and slow sounds of their elephantine feeding.

They began to spread out a little in the weary importance of feeding, trunks curling up to their mouths, reaching out, all the time watching.

Then came the sharp bang of the gun.

The forest was rent; the tranquilizer dart smacked into Clever's rump, and he squealed, and whirled around, and he fled.

He went thundering through the undergrowth, hindquarters tucked in, tail curled up, and the other animals fled all about him, blundering down the mountain in a scattered mass. Then they heard Davey's piercing whistle. They saw him running through the trees, shouting for them, and they swerved and ran panic-stricken after him.

Clever ran, galloping behind Jamba, the silver dart bouncing on his big rump, pounding across the dense mountain; for maybe five hundred yards he ran; then suddenly his head reeled.

He lurched and buckled, then jerked his head up and righted himself. He squealed drunkenly and tried to lumber on, trying to catch up, and he staggered straight into a tree. He leaned there, groaning, head reeling, wheezing; then he heaved himself away, and staggered on. He gave a confused grunt as he felt his massive

150

body lurching sideways, and he crashed into another tree headfirst, so that the big tree shook. His hind legs slowly buckled; he sat down with a thump. And the other animals were gone.

For a minute Clever sat on his haunches, groaning, his head swooning; then the drug overwhelmed him, his eyes glazed, and he toppled over onto his side.

The recapture team came panting on tiptoe through the trees, the three Wildlife officers in the lead, then Elizabeth, then Jonas Ford. Way behind them came Frank Hunt and the journalists in a ragged, exhausted line.

Through his grogginess Clever heard the terrible voices. He gave a drunken squeal and scrambled up unsteadily; everybody scattered. He saw the people running, and he flapped out his ears and he tried to trumpet, but it came out as a whoozing snort, and he stumbled backwards. He lurched downhill under his own massive wobbly weight; then he hit another tree. His momentum swiveled him round, and he started plodding unsteadily down the mountainside.

For ten minutes Clever labored through the wilderness with the drug coursing through him. His heart was pounding with the stress of it. He had forgotten why he was running away, but he knew he had to. His eyes were glassy, and the sweat was a sheen on his flanks. Then he blundered head-on into another tree. He leaned there, wheezing; then he gave a Herculean snort to pull himself together, and his brain went black.

In one sudden buckling his legs gave way. His forehead skidded down the tree trunk, and he thumped onto his chest. He was fast asleep.

The recapture team gathered in a wide, panting semicircle around the great fallen animal. The cameraman was busy filming. Ambrose Jones's old face was a mask of regret.

Elizabeth was crouching at Clever's head. The feel of his massive, sweating prehistoric animalness under her hand gave her the same old thrill, of man-beast awe. It was a wonderful feeling: of awe, of love, of respect. She wanted to put her arms around his massive unconscious head and hug it. 'Hello, Clever,' she wanted to say.

But she felt her eyes burn. For she glimpsed the sunlit glen, the chimps romping and cartwheeling for joy, and Kitty chasing them; and the elephants swooshing water over themselves, and Sally wallowing in the beautiful pool. And regret stabbed her breast, for what might have been; for a few days this elephant had been free—a few glorious, heartbreaking, adrenaline-pumping days. Now she was about to return him to his concrete cage. To do what? . . . For the rest of his elephant life.

Jonas Ford came up, blinking behind his glasses. Her throat was suddenly thick.

'Well,' she said abruptly, 'there he is. What are you going to do? The light's almost gone.'

Jomas Ford looked at his massive, immobile prize. What he felt through his exhaustion was enormous relief. Thank God . . . After four, bad days he had at last got one of his exhibits back. After four hectic, embarrassing days he had something to show to the press, to the world.

'I've radioed for the helicopter. We must fell some trees.'

She knew she was being utterly unreasonable—and insubordinate. And she did not care. 'Oh, lovely! It's only taken these trees a hundred years to grow. How long's all this going to take in the dark, before this elephant recovers consciousness?'

Ford was taken by surprise. 'How long will he be out?'

'I told you, I simply don't know! I don't know how much M99 he should have had in that dart, how fast or slow his system absorbs it. He could wake up any moment, he may never wake up!'

She suddenly had tears in her eyes. Jonas Ford stared at her, astonished. She was talking like a shrew. The rest of the recapture team were embarrassed, even Frank Hunt.

'That's a chance we just have to take . . .'

'The point is *time*. We need *daylight* for this business! If this animal wakes up now, we can't even track him! He'll be under stress, he can't see, he could injure himself! You had no business to dart him at this time of day!'

'Doctor, you may be tired, but you will kindly not tell me my business.'

'I'll tell you whatever I think is right!'

'Then get out of here!'

'Like hell I will!'

There was a shocked silence.

Then she dropped her face in her hands and stifled a sob.

Gas lamps hissed bright around the gray hulk of Clever, casting huge shadows. A Wildlife Department jeep had managed to join them.

Dawes and Milton were manning a screaming chainsaw. They knew about forest clearing, and the first tree had come down as intended. Now they were cutting a big triangular wedge out of the second tree.

Elizabeth sat on the ground next to Clever's chest. She had recovered from her emotional outburst, and she was feeling thoroughly ashamed of herself. A stethoscope hung from her neck. From time to time she listened to Clever's heartbeat. The elephant was sweating profusely, dark stains between his legs, and he was making long, groaning noises.

Dawes put down his saw and straightened his back with his wrists. Jonas Ford came over. In the lamplight his eyes were large behind his spectacles. 'What's the trouble?'

'Just taking a rest. Next whirl she comes down. She's going thataway. Everybody way back.'

The television man took up his camera; the troopers scattered. Ambrose Jones was squatting on his haunches beside Elizabeth, his hand on the elephant's flank. Frank Hunt was slumped in the front seat of the jeep, head back, eyes closed, whistling wearily, a flask of whiskey between his thighs. It was nearly finished, and where the hell was he going to get some more before the package store opened in Hot Springs tomorrow? By which time he'd be walking his unfortunate ass off again playing Big Game Hunter for television.

The chainsaw was whirring through the last six inches of the tree's trunk. Then Dawes hollered, '*Timmm—berrr.*'

He moved back from the tree, and everybody tensed, looking upward.

But nothing happened. The tree stood in the hushed, glaring lamplight, with a great bite out of it, held together by a couple of inches of itself.

Everybody waited. Dawes approached it cautiously. He gave it a shove and jumped backward.

Nothing happened. The tree stood firm.

They started up the saw again. They slid the screaming machine back into the trunk, and chips of wood flew. Suddenly the treetrunk creaked; Dawes amd Milton both hollered 'tim-ber' and scrambled back out of the way.

The tree stopped creaking. Everybody was transfixed. Then there was a big rustle of wind up in the treetops, and Dawes' eyes widened in horror.

'Watch out!'

The tree creaked over in the opposite direction with a great rending noise; and Elizabeth yelled, 'The elephant!' There was wild shouting and scrambling, and Frank Hunt opened his eyes.

He saw one hundred feet of tree coming down out of the night on him, in terrible slow motion through the glaring lamplight. He gave a terrified yell and tried to fling open the door, but missed the handle and gargled in horror. Then his scrabbling hand found the door handle, and he flung himself out into the undergrowth, his arms clutching his head. He rolled in a desperate ball. There was a crash and an explosion of metal and flying glass.

Frank Hunt lay on his back, eyes wide, his knees bent up over his stomach. The massive tree lay across the body of the government's jeep. Its wheels were splayed, its axles crushed into the earth.

The tree trunk had missed the elephant by two feet.

# twenty-seven

It was after dark when Sam came to the end of the railway bridge. He stopped and sniffed, then turned and set off down the tracks toward Hot Springs at a fast trot, nose down, bushy tail up. He could smell the animals.

He came around the bend in the river, and ahead were the lights of the town. But Sam was not afraid of the lights, of human habitation. He had lived with humans and in towns most of his life. He understood there was danger from men to the other animals, but he was alone now and did not think of danger to himself. He trotted into the lights without a qualm. There was nobody about.

He went trotting up an empty Main Street for about a hundred yards. Then he smelled food, and his empty stomach ached.

It came from the cafeteria across the road, jampacked with journalists and television men. For only one moment did Sam hesitate. Then he padded purposefully across the road. Sam walked into the cafeteria, his nose up, sniffing the delicious smells, his bushy tail wagging ingratiatingly.

Nobody noticed him. There was a clamor of voices and dishes. Sam walked down the rows of tables hopefully, ears cocked, his eyes appealing, looking for a friendly face. Then he spotted the swing door to the kitchen. He nudged it open and walked in. The smell in there was wonderful.

The cook had her back to him. The first thing Sam saw was the garbage bucket. He stuck his head into a mess of French fries, rolls, ketchup, napkins, and cigarette butts. He got a mouthful of roll, withdrew his head and gulped it; then he saw something else. On the table, behind the cook's back, was a pile of T-bone steaks.

Sam knew it was punishable to steal. Garbage buckets were fair game, meat on tables was not. But Sam was too hungry to care. He glanced nervously at the cook's back, and then he hefted his forepaws up onto the table. The pile of steaks was right in front of him He stretched his neck and twisted his head sideways. But they were just out of reach.

Sam glanced apprehensively at the cook, licked his chops, and stretched his neck for all it was worth, then tried to stretch another fraction; but the steaks were just half an inch beyond his teeth. He slurped out his long pink tongue and tried to hook a steak back toward him; but all he got was a delicious tantalizing taste.

Sam almost whimpered in frustration, and he rolled his eyes nervously at the cook's back; then he gave a desperate little jump, his twisted neck outstretched, and he nipped the edge of a big steak. And the cook turned, and she screamed.

She screamed, fists clenched in front of her bosom; then, as Sam turned to flee, his mouth full of T-bone steak, she wailed, 'Woo-oolf!' Sam dashed for the doors, and a waitress burst through. 'Woo-oolf!' screeched the cook again, and the waitress staggered back through the door, her tray flying, and Sam swerved past her. Still clutching his T-bone, he made for the front door, straight into another laden waitress. She screamed in horror, and threw up her hands, and Sam dashed for cover.

Amid the crashing of crockery, Sam dived under the tables. There were more yells; chairs were being kicked over, people jumped up on tables, and more crockery crashed. Sam scrambled in panic for the back of the cafeteria, and a wave of pandemonium preceded him. He darted between the scattering legs and chairs, his eyes desperate, his T-bone steak slopping out the sides of his mouth. Then the first plate was hurled at him. It walloped his shoulder. He yelped and almost spat out his steak. He collected his wits and turned.

Sam fled underneath the tables the way he had come, scattering all before him again amid more crashing of crockery and yelling, and burst out into the night.

He raced up the sidewalk and disappeared down a lane, making for the dark trees. He scurried under a bush. He gripped the big T-bone between his front paws, and began to work on it.

It was not nearly enough, but it was delicious.

He saw some faraway flashlights, but after a while they receded. The news went through the village like wildfire that a wolf was at large. Everybody figured out it belonged to David Jordan. Everybody who had a gun kept it handy. Everybody kept well indoors.

Sam set out to pick up the scent of the animals.

He trotted jauntily into the middle of Main Street, nose down, oblivious to the consternation he had caused. He picked up the scent straight away, and started following it up toward the Mission, where the Appalachian Trail resumed.

On the other side of the French Broad River, Smoky sat in the undergrowth on the edge of the forest, overlooking the embankment down to the railway tracks. Now he wanted Sam, his only link with the others, to come back. He had followed Sam's scent to this spot, and he knew he had crossed the fearsome bridge. Smoky wanted with all his heart to follow Sam's scent across that bridge. But he dared not, because terrible men were waiting to kill him.

Meanwhile Sam trotted up now-deserted Main Street, nose

down, following the scent. He had forgotten about Smoky; all he had on his mind was finding his master.

He was well off the highway and well into the dark, almost into the black forest, when, on the wind, he smelt a bitch on heat.

Suddenly Sam's nostrils, which had been full of nothing but the pursuit of his duty, were full of the most compelling, irresistible scent, and Davey Jordan and duty went straight out of his mind. He stood poised on the footpath, the blood coursing joyfully to his loins, head up, testing the wind; he isolated the scent, and he started bounding down the hillside, toward the houses in the hollow below.

He came down onto the dark dirt road, heart pumping excitedly, ears and tail up, and went running past fences and gardens with locked, lighted windows. Then he heard an anguished woman's voice.

'Mitzi—come here!'

Sam heard yapping. He went bounding joyfully toward it; then he glimpsed the pack of dogs in the next yard, and in one leap Sam was over the picket fence.

There were a dozen dogs, all shapes and sizes, ears cocked, tongues slopping, tails wagging, all with one purpose. Mitzi was sitting with her tail firmly planted in a flower bed, ears back, whining: she didn't want to have any of these dogs scrambling all over her. But neither did she want to heed her owner and go inside: she was half-enjoying herself.

Mrs. Donnybrook was yelling at her through a window, too scared to venture out because of the wolf scare, when suddenly she saw the terrible animal bounding across the yard at her poor Mitzi, vicious head raised, tail wagging for the kill. Mrs. Donnybrook screamed and ran from the room to telephone the sheriff. Mitzi took fright. She ran across the yard and leaped over the fence, the whole pack of dogs hollering after her, Sam in the middle, trying to bark them aside. He caught up with her in the middle of Main Street. And there and then, after only a few coy protests from Mitzi, he mounted her.

That's how Sam was, happily knotted haunch-to-haunch with Mitzi, his ears back and a smile all over his face, when the lights of the sheriff's car appeared.

The sheriff had not received Mrs. Donnybrook's frantic telephone call, because he was looking for the wolf himself. He was not optimistic about spotting the beast, particularly in the dark, but he wanted to do his duty. He had been driving around fruitlessly for half an hour, and now he was on his way up to the Mission to seek the advice of the circus owner, Mr. Worthy. He considered that a fool's errand too. That is how the sheriff of Hot Springs was feeling as he came around the corner and saw the pack of dogs in his headlights.

He jammed on his brakes, slammed his hand irritably on the horn, and swung his wheel over. Sam looked at him, and licked his chops apologetically. As the sheriff pulled around them he shouted, 'Go home, Mitzi Donnybrook, you brazen hussy, or a wolf'll get ya!'

Then his eyes widened as he realized what he had seen. His car skidded to a halt, and he looked back through his rear window.

All he could see in the red glow of his taillights were Sam's devil eyes. He started to open the door; then slammed it shut and hastily locked himself in. He rolled up his windows urgently and yanked out his revolver. He sat there shakily, wondering what to do. But he could do nothing from inside a locked car. Then he collected his wits and pulled his car into a big U-turn, to get his headlights on his quarry. At that moment Sam finished his copulation and parted company with Mitzi.

He shook himself cheerfully, looked around absently, saw the sheriff's car swinging round, sat down, and had a scratch. He was considering hanging around Mitzi, but saw the car coming straight at him, and decided he had to get out of the way. He got up, shook himself once more, turned and started trotting up the road. He got out of the way of the car as it slammed to a stop, and he trotted past the passenger-side window.

As the sheriff frantically reversed his car around again to get his headlights onto him, Sam stopped. He looked over his shoulder, shook himself energetically, then started up the footpath into the dark forest, his nose to the ground.

And he was gone.

The sun rose, gilding the massive pall of smoke that hung over the Appalachian Mountains.

Eric Bradman stood in front of his television camera. Behind him was the black, smoking forest. He was dishevelled and streaked with ash, weary from a night helping to fight the fire. His voice was hoarse, but he was doggedly doing his own commentary.

'But with this latest catastrophe, which crowns a series of miscalculations, Professor Jonas Ford has officially conceded that he needs expert, outside help. And he is suspending the recapture operation until such assistance arrives. In a brief statement handed to the press a few minutes ago, he announced that the services are being sought of a professional animal catcher from Africa. Who this man is we don't yet know. But, apparently, there are several such people available.'

He gave a sad, genuinely sad sigh.

'But there is a sliver of good news. An hour ago I made contact with Davey Jordan, after a lucky helicopter search. He has agreed to let Dr. Elizabeth Johnson, who is the veterinary surgeon of the Bronx Zoo, join him, to look after the animals' health. We also dropped a pig's carcass for the lions and tigers, and some hard rations for human consumption. However, Jordan refused to answer any questions or send any message to the world, as this clip shows . . .'

Television screens across the world cut to the interior of Bradman's helicopter, hovering above an open patch in the wilderness. The camera showed a large sack falling to the ground, then a medical bag lowered on a rope, then Elizabeth clawing her way down a rope ladder, a knapsack on her back.

Fifty yards away stood David Jordan; the camera zoomed in on his hair flying in the helicopter's downblast, several days' growth of beard on his haggard face.

Dr. Johnson swung off the ladder, and Jordan came toward her. She spoke, and he shook his head. He hefted the sack of meat onto his shoulder, turned hurriedly and led the way toward the trees. Then he stopped and raised his hand to Bradman and gave him a weary smile of gratitude.

The helicopter rose slowly, the camera panning the Appalachian Mountains and the vast forests, resting on the huge mass of smoke in the sky ten miles away.

# twenty-eight

It was three hours since Clever had been darted. Half a dozen big, jagged stumps gleamed white in the lamplight.

A helicopter hovered overhead, roaring, the downblast of its propeller blowing leaves and dirt like grapeshot. Four stout steel cables were snaking down, with a nylon-rope harness flapping from them.

Dawes and Milton grabbed it and wedged it under the elephant's stomach. Then everybody crouched beside Clever, to heave him over into the harness.

'One . . . two . . . *three*.'

They heaved with all their concerted might, and again, and Clever rocked on his great belly; they heaved again, and then he rolled massively over. Dawes, Timmons, and Milton hastily made fast the harness. And Clever was ready to fly.

To fly, fly away, up out of the wilderness to which he had returned, into the night sky and over the moonlit mountaintops, back to Hot Springs; to be put in the steel stockade, then into a truck and hauled back to his cage in the Bronx Zoo, where he belonged.

The helicopter began to lift and take up the slack in the cables.

The great body rose, slowly, saggily, the harness digging into his gray hide, head and trunk hanging. His legs were straightening; then his feet were off the ground. The helicopter roared, and Clever slowly began to lift in the lamplit wilderness—two feet, now four, now eight, rising, rising; when he was twelve feet off the ground, Clever woke up.

He came around with a great wailing snort at the pressure on his guts; he jerked up his head, and all he knew was the earth disappearing below him and the roar of the machine above him and he screamed in absolute terror. He thrashed his legs and lashed his trunk up, trying to grab the harness cable. Four tons of terrified elephant lashed and twisted, and the helicopter lurched. It staggered sideways; the screaming elephant swung like a pendulum, and he smashed into a tree.

The whole tree shook and the helicopter wrenched and keeled, the propeller screaming. The wild-eyed elephant swung the other way, bellowing and twisting, and he crashed into another tree. Branches snapped and blew fifty feet up in the sky, and Clever desperately flung his trunk around the tree.

Clever blindly grabbed the stout treetop, and the helicopter jolted, with a wrenching of its cables. The propeller tried to bite the air, the pilot frantically gunned the engine, and the elephant was wrenched sideways so his trunk tore loose from the tree; the machine staggered upward and sideways again.

The pilot desperately tried to clear the treetops, dragging the terrified elephant through the branches like an anchor, and all Clever knew was the blinding smashing and crashing, and the wrenching of the harness as he was towed twisting through the night sky, wildly trying to catch something. For a hundred yards the helicopter went tearing across the forest-top with Clever bellowing his terror to the night then, just as the machine was almost back under control, Clever crashed into another tree; and he lashed his trunk around it and clung with all his terrified might.

The roaring helicopter was wrenched back in mid-recovery, and Clever clung, desperately trying to lash his legs around the tree like a bear. For a long terrible moment the elephant clung to the tree seventy feet up in the sky, the helicopter tilted madly, and the pilot saw the treetops rushing up at him. The rotor hit the treetops and snapped.

The helicopter dropped, crashing onto the treetops; then it rolled, its engine still screaming, branches snapping, and Clever was suddenly hurtling through the branches. Four tons of elephant went plummeting down, ears and trunk flying and timber tearing. Clever hit the ground at fifty miles an hour, and the earth shook as his great bones snapped with a crack. Fifty feet away the helicopter smashed into the undergrowth, and it burst into flames. A great orange flame exploded out of it like a balloon; giant tongues of fire leaped into the trees to light up the forest. There was another explosion and a bigger balloon erupted, twice as high, throwing a great heat fifty yards wide. Suddenly the pilot appeared, his body contorted, his clothes on fire, his hair and back and arms and legs ablaze. He was clawing at his body, beating and twisting through

the flaming undergrowth in terrible slow motion; then he fell to his knees with a scream that nobody heard, and the flames engulfed him. Then Clever began to try to get up.

The broken elephant came to in the blasting heat, and in his terror he did not feel his shattered bones; he flung his head and staggered halfway up before his crushed body buckled under him. He collapsed with a wail of terror, and his eyes rolled wild. He thrashed his legs again, to try to get away from the dreadful beating of the flames, and the steel cable pulled him back, his shattered ribs jutting through his hide. And he screamed and tried to scramble up again, and the cable wrenched him back again, then a figure was running through the leaping firelight with an ax held high like a madman. It was Ambrose Jones. He bellowed and swiped at the steel cable, to release the elephant. But the ax skidded off it, and he swung again with all his old might. Then Elizabeth wrenched a rifle out of a trooper's hands.

'*Shoot for pity's sake!*'

She floundered wildly through the undergrowth and raised the rifle as Clever tried to get up again, and she fired.

The rifle boomed, again and again, deafening the night. Splotches of blood burst out on the thrashing elephant's head. He collapsed and at last was still. Elizabeth threw down the gun with all her hatred and flung herself against a treetrunk, and she wept.

# twenty-nine

That night there was chaos. The burning mountains lit up the sky above Hot Springs, flames leaping and smoke barreling upward; cars and people descended on the town from all directions; the streets filled with the clanging of fire engines and the flashing lights of ambulances; and the forests resounded with the crackle of flames and shouts as hundreds and then thousands of people toiled to fight the fire.

# part seven

## thirty

In the vast bush of Kenya there is a lot of flat country; on the horizon the bush turns mauve under the mercilessly blue sky and the burning sun. It is beautiful, wild country, and it was very profitable for Stephen Leigh-Forsythe's Animal Kingdom, Inc.

His was a simple, but organized, setup. Animal Kingdom, Inc., had no helicopters, no spotter airplanes, no elaborate long-distance haulage vehicles, no bulldozer. It only had two Land Rovers, a couple of big open-backed trucks, a few tents, a powerful radio-telephone, and a gang of strong, well-trained, lowly paid natives. Timber for his stockades and crates came from the trees, food for his men came from his gun, and if he needed a road they hacked a track with pangas and axes. Down at the Mombasa docks he had one big, hot, corrugated-iron shed where the wild animals were kept, awaiting shipment by sea or air. In New York he had one small office with a telex machine, the furniture covered in leopard skin, the floors in zebra and lion, the walls festooned with photographs of animals he had captured and of his partner, a famous film star.

Stephen Leigh-Forsythe went out and got you the animal you wanted; he put it in a crate, and put the crate on a ship or an airplane, the animal in certified good physical condition. What happened after that—how you collected your animal, what you did with it—was not his affair. His overhead was low, his prices high.

Stephen Leigh-Forsythe was an Englishman born in South

Africa, with a good English accent. He was lean and muscled, with the stamina of a long-distance athlete; he had iron nerves, and an animal's cunning and ability to sense and smell out another animal. He was one of the best hunters Africa has ever seen.

Forsythe's Land Rover was racing across the veldt that bright Friday afternoon. Alongside raced a leopard, bounding through the yellow grass: it was a magnificent animal in superb physical condition, and the bouncing Land Rover was having difficulty keeping up. But a leopard's stamina is low; it cannot race at top speed for long. Forsythe had been chasing it for over ten minutes now, and the terrified animal was beginning to slow. It was heading for the treeline across the plain, and in another few minutes it would be safe. Forsythe was at the back of the vehicle, his free hand clutching a long pole with a noose on the end attached to a coil of nylon rope: This is called a vangstok.

The Land Rover was almost level with the terrified leopard's hindquarters. Forsythe was leaning out over the side, knees bent, taking the bouncing of the vehicle like an expert cowboy, the vangstok stretched out under perfect control. Now the noose was hovering above the animal's ears, then over its forehead, and Forsythe was straining out of the leaping vehicle; in another second he would thrust the noose down over the snout. The leopard swerved.

At forty miles an hour, it streaked off at a tangent, but Animal Kingdom's drivers were expert, and the driver swerved after him. Forsythe took the sudden lurching as easily as a rodeo rider, and within ten seconds the Land Rover was level with the animal again. The leopard swerved again, and now it was running away from the trees that had been its goal. It had slowed to thirty heart-bursting miles an hour, and Forsythe stretched out the vangstok again, another inch, and another, then the noose dropped over the animal's nose.

The leopard was wrenched off its feet and rolled into a roaring mass of jaws and claws. The Land Rover bounced to a halt, and Forsythe leaped down with a net, like a Roman gladiator.

When he got back to his camp, fifteen miles away, his cookboy was speaking on the radio. Forsythe took over the machine.

His blue eyes showed surprise as he listened.

'What kind of animals? Over.'

His voice was surprisingly gentle for a tough man in such an unsentimental business.

'How many of each?'

'What kind of terrain is it?'

Then: 'My fee will be one thousand dollars a day, plus expenses and wages for my boys. I'll be bringing four of my best.'

He looked at the date on his Rolex Oyster wristwatch.

'In five days. Don't try to stop him. Withdraw all troops and police from his path. Keep other people out of the area. If he wants to cross into the Smoky Mountains, let him. Don't try to track him or follow him with helicopters, let him think he's safe. I'll find him.'


# thirty-one


From a long way off Sam smelled the smoke.

He stopped, ears cocked, sniffing the shifting breeze. Sam knew about fire. Then he put down his head and continued urgently up the trail.

The scent of the animals on the ground was still clear that Friday morning, and the smell of smoke came and went. Every now and again Sam lost the scent, and he ferreted around frantically. But then the breeze would shift and he would pick it up again, and trot on.

An hour after sunrise he came over the brow of the slope, and suddenly he got the full sting of the smoke. The scent he was following was gone, and he could see people: dozens of them, standing on the edge of the smoke, beating the flames with sacks.

Sam stared. Then he turned and started creeping through the undergrowth, down the slope of the mountain.

He did not know how far he would have to go, but he knew he had to try to make his way around the fire.

There was nothing else he could do. He knew he could not go back, toward Hot Springs.

All night Smoky had sat on the top of the steep embankment peering into the darkness, waiting, sniffing, hoping for Sam to come back; all night his heart had been breaking for Davey Jordan and the other animals. Several times he had screwed up his courage and clamboured nervously down the embankment, but each time he had turned back.

But with the coming of dawn his fear and anguish had turned to panic; he knew Sam was not coming back, and he knew he could wait no longer. The scent of Sam was still upon the ground, but it was fading.

Smoky came down the embankment, the infection in his flank thudding with each footfall. He started along the railroad tracks, nose down, snuffling like a dog, his heart hammering in fear.

Smoky had a nose as good as a dog's, but he did not know about fire and how it destroys scent.

He began to cross the railroad bridge.

The sun was rising as Smoky came around the bed in the tracks and saw the highway bridge of Hot Springs.

He stopped, his heart quaking. He looked at the embankment, but it was sheer; he looked the other way, at the rocks leading straight down to the river. There was no way to go, except forward. Or backward, the way he had come.

Smoky hesitated. With all his heart he wanted to go forward, following Sam's scent. But he could not bring himself to face the terror of that bridge ahead, and he turned around as if he were chased again, lumbering down the tracks. Then he heard the train.

He did not know what it was. He only heard a distant rumble, then felt the earth vibrating; he ran harder, galloping down the tracks. The rumbling was getting louder and louder. He looked over his shoulder and saw nothing. Then he saw the train coming toward him around the bend from the railway bridge.

A terrible monster was hurtling towards him, three hundred yards away, and Smoky blundered to a terrified halt and he turned around again, and he fled—flat out, fleeing for his life back up the railway tracks toward Hot Springs, the monster thundering after him. The highway bridge was three hundred yards ahead of him now and the train a hundred yards behind. Smoky ran and ran, terrified witless, his heart and his shaggy legs pounding. Now the train was only seventy yards behind him, now sixty, and Smoky ran and ran, then it was only fifty yards behind. Then the engine driver saw him and blew his whistle. The blast of it rent the morning and Smoky's heart leaped in absolute terror, and he tripped and fell.

He crashed onto his chest, and his snout bashed a tie, stunning him right in the middle of the railway tracks. The locomotive blasted down on him with a screeching of brakes and flying sparks. It was only forty yards from him—then thirty—then twenty . . . When the train was five yards away from him Smoky scrambled up wildly and ran from the towering mass of screaming steel. Without looking back, running for his life, he hurled himself off the railway tracks into Main Street.

There was only one way for him to go: straight up the street toward the Jesuit Mission and the Appalachian Trail beyond. Smoky was not thinking of Sam's scent, he was not thinking of Davey Jordan; all he was thinking about was fleeing from the monster that was trying to kill him. He fled up Main Street as fast as his shaggy legs would carry him, past the cafeteria, past the package store, past the houses. The street was deserted at that early hour—except for Mrs. Donnybrook.

Mrs. Donnybrook was emerging from her garden, armed against the wolf with her family shotgun, preparing to look for her Mitzi who had not come home. She had had a sleepless night, and she was in her dressing gown and curlers. Mrs. Donnybrook tiptoed down the dirt road toward Main Street, calling 'Mitzi? Mitzi? . . .' Mrs. Donnybrook peeped around the corner of Main Street, shotgun at the ready, and she screamed.

She screamed at the top of her lungs at the terrible beast thundering toward her; the next moment she was knocked flying by five hundred pounds of galloping bear, and she flew, spread-eagled, over Smoky's back. Her shotgun boomed.

She was still screaming as she scrambled up, and her shotgun pellets rained down on top of the Jesuit Mission like hailstones.

She screamed all the way, as she ran to telephone the sheriff.

Smoky was gone, up the footpath into the forest.

# thirty-two

Davey was at the edge of the treeline, looking down into the valley. Down there, close enough to hurl a stone, was six-laned Highway 40. Beyond the highway, down steep rocky banks, was the wide Pigeon River; beyond that, the Great Smoky Mountains rose up, steep and jumbled and fluted, streaked in the long shadows of the setting sun.

This was it: this very road beside this very river was the place they had been making for last Sunday morning in the circus trucks, a hundred years ago.

He closed his eyes.

If they had made it then ... O God, if only ... Queenie would be alive, Clever, Mama. Daisy, Little. And Sam and Smoky would not be lost.

But they had made it ... A hundred terrible miles, in six terrible days. And, now, there it was; sanctuary, across that river: the Great Smoky Mountains.

Davey had been watching the highway from various vantage points for over an hour. There was no traffic; the road must have been sealed off.

Directly below him was the bridge across the wide river. That was where any ambush would be, if there was to be one: on the other side, in the trees.

A quarter of a mile upriver was shallow drift, stretching across in a curve, the water only a foot or so deep, rushing over smooth stones, swirling away into deep, swift water.

For another half hour he lay there, watching for a sign of life. The Great Smoky Mountains went dark in the flaming sunset.

Smoky smelled the forest fire.

All day the wind had been driving the smoke away from him. Now

# twenty-eight

It was three hours since Clever had been darted. Half a dozen big, jagged stumps gleamed white in the lamplight.

A helicopter hovered overhead, roaring, the downblast of its propeller blowing leaves and dirt like grapeshot. Four stout steel cables were snaking down, with a nylon-rope harness flapping from them.

Dawes and Milton grabbed it and wedged it under the elephant's stomach. Then everybody crouched beside Clever, to heave him over into the harness.

'One ... two ... *three*.'

They heaved with all their concerted might, and again, and Clever rocked on his great belly; they heaved again, and then he rolled massively over. Dawes, Timmons, and Milton hastily made fast the harness. And Clever was ready to fly.

To fly, fly away, up out of the wilderness to which he had returned, into the night sky and over the moonlit mountaintops, back to Hot Springs; to be put in the steel stockade, then into a truck and hauled back to his cage in the Bronx Zoo, where he belonged.

The helicopter began to lift and take up the slack in the cables.

The great body rose, slowly, saggily, the harness digging into his gray hide, head and trunk hanging. His legs were straightening; then his feet were off the ground. The helicopter roared, and Clever slowly began to lift in the lamplit wilderness—two feet, now four, now eight, rising, rising; when he was twelve feet off the ground, Clever woke up.

He came around with a great wailing snort at the pressure on his guts; he jerked up his head, and all he knew was the earth disappearing below him and the roar of the machine above him and he screamed in absolute terror. He thrashed his legs and lashed his trunk up, trying to grab the harness cable. Four tons of terrified elephant lashed and twisted, and the helicopter lurched. It staggered sideways; the screaming elephant swung like a pendulum, and he smashed into a tree.

The whole tree shook and the helicopter wrenched and keeled, the propeller screaming. The wild-eyed elephant swung the other way, bellowing and twisting, and he crashed into another tree. Branches snapped and blew fifty feet up in the sky, and Clever desperately flung his trunk around the tree.

Clever blindly grabbed the stout treetop, and the helicopter jolted, with a wrenching of its cables. The propeller tried to bite the air, the pilot frantically gunned the engine, and the elephant was wrenched sideways so his trunk tore loose from the tree; the machine staggered upward and sideways again.

The pilot desperately tried to·clear the treetops, dragging the terrified elephant. through the branches like an anchor, and all Clever knew was the blinding smashing and crashing, and the wrenching of the harness as he was towed twisting through the night sky, wildly trying to catch something. For a hundred yards the helicopter went tearing across the forest-top with Clever bellowing his terror to the night then, just as the machine was almost back under control, Clever crashed into another tree; and he lashed his trunk around it and clung with all his terrified might.

The roaring helicopter was wrenched back in mid-recovery, and Clever clung, desperately trying to lash his legs around the tree like a bear. For a long terrible moment the elephant clung to the tree seventy feet up in the sky, the helicopter tilted madly, and the pilot saw the treetops rushing up at him. The rotor hit the treetops and snapped.

The helicopter dropped, crashing onto the treetops; then it rolled, its engine still screaming, branches snapping, and Clever was suddenly hurtling through the branches. Four tons of elephant went plummeting down, ears and trunk flying and timber tearing. Clever hit the ground at fifty miles an hour, and the earth shook as his great bones snapped with a crack. Fifty feet away the helicopter smashed into the undergrowth, and it burst into flames. A great orange flame exploded out of it like a balloon; giant tongues of fire leaped into the trees to light up the forest. There was another explosion and a bigger balloon erupted, twice as high, throwing a great heat fifty yards wide. Suddenly the pilot appeared, his body contorted, his clothes on fire, his hair and back and arms and legs ablaze. He was clawing at his body, beating and twisting through the flaming undergrowth in terrible slow motion; then he fell to his knees with a scream that nobody heard, and the flames engulfed him. Then Clever began to try to get up.

The broken elephant came to in the blasting heat, and in his terror he did not feel his shattered bones; he flung his head and staggered halfway up before his crushed body buckled under him. He collapsed with a wail of terror, and his eyes rolled wild. He thrashed his legs again, to try to get away from the dreadful beating of the flames, and the steel cable pulled him back, his shattered ribs jutting through his hide. And he screamed and tried to scramble up again, and the cable wrenched him back again, then a figure was running through the leaping firelight with an ax held high like a madman. It was Ambrose Jones. He bellowed and swiped at the steel cable, to release the elephant. But the ax skidded off it, and he swung again with all his old might. Then Elizabeth wrenched a rifle out of a trooper's hands.

*'Shoot for pity's sake!'*

She floundered wildly through the undergrowth and raised the rifle as Clever tried to get up again, and she fired.

The rifle boomed, again and again, deafening the night. Splotches of blood burst out on the thrashing elephant's head. He collapsed and at last was still. Elizabeth threw down the gun with all her hatred and flung herself against a treetrunk, and she wept.


# twenty-nine


That night there was chaos. The burning mountains lit up the sky above Hot Springs, flames leaping and smoke barreling upward; cars and people descended on the town from all directions; the streets filled with the clanging of fire engines and the flashing lights of ambulances; and the forests resounded with the crackle of flames and shouts as hundreds and then thousands of people toiled to fight the fire.

The sun rose, gilding the massive pall of smoke that hung over the Appalachian Mountains.

Eric Bradman stood in front of his television camera. Behind him was the black, smoking forest. He was dishevelled and streaked with ash, weary from a night helping to fight the fire. His voice was hoarse, but he was doggedly doing his own commentary.

'But with this latest catastrophe, which crowns a series of miscalculations, Professor Jonas Ford has officially conceded that he needs expert, outside help. And he is suspending the recapture operation until such assistance arrives. In a brief statement handed to the press a few minutes ago, he announced that the services are being sought of a professional animal catcher from Africa. Who this man is we don't yet know. But, apparently, there are several such people available.'

He gave a sad, genuinely sad sigh.

'But there is a sliver of good news. An hour ago I made contact with Davey Jordan, after a lucky helicopter search. He has agreed to let Dr. Elizabeth Johnson, who is the veterinary surgeon of the Bronx Zoo, join him, to look after the animals' health. We also dropped a pig's carcass for the lions and tigers, and some hard rations for human consumption. However, Jordan refused to answer any questions or send any message to the world, as this clip shows . . .'

Television screens across the world cut to the interior of Bradman's helicopter, hovering above an open patch in the wilderness. The camera showed a large sack falling to the ground, then a medical bag lowered on a rope, then Elizabeth clawing her way down a rope ladder, a knapsack on her back.

Fifty yards away stood David Jordan; the camera zoomed in on his hair flying in the helicopter's downblast, several days' growth of beard on his haggard face.

Dr. Johnson swung off the ladder, and Jordan came toward her. She spoke, and he shook his head. He hefted the sack of meat onto his shoulder, turned hurriedly and led the way toward the trees. Then he stopped and raised his hand to Bradman and gave him a weary smile of gratitude.

The helicopter rose slowly, the camera panning the Appalachian Mountains and the vast forests, resting on the huge mass of smoke in the sky ten miles away.

he stood, shaggy head up, feeling new fear in his painful chest.

Smoky had never seen fire. But he knew instinctively it was dangerous. He could not feel the heat, but there was a sense of destruction and death in the forest, violence in the sting of that smoke. And now he had lost Sam's scent.

Smoky's instinct was to turn and run away from the smoke, but he stopped: he remembered the monster that had chased him the last time he had turned back. For a long fearful minute he hesitated; then he started slowly forward.

Twenty minutes later he saw the first flames, flickering in the darkness. Smoky stared at them, his heart pounding in new fright. There were flames and embers glowing as far as he could see.

Smoky did not know which way to go. He only knew that he had to find a way around this terrifying thing, because Sam and his keeper were on the other side.

At three o'clock the next morning, Elizabeth lay in her sleeping bag, staring at the stars through the treetops.

Her body was aching from yesterday's march, her muscles were stiff and her feet still sore; she had slept deeply, but not enough. It was worry that had awakened her.

Clever's awful death, coming within days of the slaughter at Devils Fork, was a double nightmare. She blamed Jonas Ford for the horror of it all. She blamed the whole American people. She was certain the British would not have made the botch-up that these bloody Americans had made with their thousands of troops and helicopters and their hordes of bloody journalists, their gum-chewing, gun-slinging sheriffs and 'dooly-sworn' deputies who killed Queenie. As for the helicopter episode and the fire . . . well, it did not help her mood that she could not blame that on America, that even a British pilot might also have crashed. She just thanked God that a Britisher was coming to take over the operation. And she blamed everything, *everything* on David Jordan . . .

She lay there, her mind a turmoil of recrimination and dread of what might be coming. Please God don't let them kill any more of these animals. Please God no gun-crazy hillbillies. Please God we get safely into the Smokies, and let the Englishman get them out without any more blood . . .

*And please please please God talk to David Jordan.*

Yes, and she was afraid of the animals.

She closed her eyes.

For a while she had still been under the spell of that beautiful day in the glen, despite the horror of Devils Gap afterward. The spell of seeing the animals begin to relax, of seeing their dawning joy of space, green things, and sunshine—of them beginning to play. Kitty, the chimpanzees, and King Kong, poor old Sultan up his tree; Sally wallowing in the pool; and the elephants spraying water over themselves; all of them gathering around him. And then the birds ... It had all been so beautiful that for a while she had been unable to shake off its spell, and she had even begun to think it was all going to be possible. Then had come Hot Springs and Queenie's death. Then Clever's, and the fire. Violence and terror were in the air, and the animals knew it; they were hardly the same animals she had last seen in the glen; she was afraid of them.

She felt shame. She was even afraid of the elephants. How many times had she been into their cages? They had never looked as if they might hurt her, but now she was in *their* environment. As for the lions—O God, she was frightened of them. But the worst part of it was that the animals knew she was afraid. She could feel it. She was only tolerated because of him. Like a dog tolerates a stranger only because his master reassures him, or as the master himself now only tolerated her presence because he needed her.

She felt fresh bitterness.

She'd certainly expected a warmer welcome than she'd gotten. He had thanked her for the meat, fed the cats, and without more ado he and the Indian had sat down and ravenously eaten the other food she had brought. Big Charlie had given her an exhausted smile, trying to welcome her, but she had felt his suspicion too.

Gone was the gentle, almost mystical-looking man; Davey's haggard face had been like thunder. She had wisely refrained from any attempt to talk him out of what he was doing. Then, apparently feeling better, he had given her a bleak smile and thanked her again for the food. Then, out of the blue, he had asked permission to search her knapsack and medical bag to see if she had any radio device.

She had been indignant that she was not trusted. But she had let him search. Satisfied that she had nothing more sinister than a pocket tape recorder, he had told her to rest, saying that she could examine the animals in three hours.

It had occurred to her, then, that possibly he blamed her for the killing of Clever, and for the fire, and for Sam and Smoky being missing. She had been about to speak up; then stopped. Why should *she* exculpate herself to *him*—it was all his fault anyway. And he looked in no mood for discussion. He and Charlie had promptly fallen asleep.

And there she had sat, surrounded by terrifying animals. She had been exhausted herself, after helping to fight the fire all night, but she couldn't possibly sleep with all those uncaged animals. Finally, mercifully, the big cats had settled down to sleep, their bellies full for the first time in days. But the bears were still rooting and grunting around. My God, the *size* of them ... those huge, immobile, expressionless furry faces, those giant paws and claws. It was all very different from the glen; now there was shock and violence in the air.

And yes, she was in awe of Davey Jordan—as was the whole world at this moment. She looked at him lying there asleep, almost like some kind of very precious animal himself. Yet his whole bearing, his eyes, spoke of acute sensitivity. She could almost feel it as she sat there: a kind of magnetism. And a composure, self-confidence that made her wonder again if he had not had a very special military training. Three hours exactly after he had lain down he was wide awake, triggered by an inner mechanism.

They had examined the animals together, then. She had felt the raw fear at approaching these massive beasts, but dared not show it: out of pride, and a totally unreasonable anxiety to win David Jordan's approval.

But professional excitement and curiosity had replaced her fear—even when she knelt beside an adult, fully conscious, unfettered lion, its hot breath on her face. Tommy had not liked it, had snarled right in her ear and she had jerked in terror. But David had flicked him on his chin, and Tommy had blinked so injuredly that she had wanted to throw her arms around the magnificent furry neck and hug him. Holding that massive paw, feeling the steely tendons that pushed out so perfectly those inch-long claws, had given her a thrill that almost brought tears to her eyes. How could anybody not believe in God when they saw such a perfect living mechanism? Davey held open Tommy's jaws so she could examine his mouth, lifted his tail (Tommy had *not* liked that) to look for evidence of worms; but he was in excellent condition. A bit on the lean side from all his exertion and spare diet, and his paws were a bit tender, but they were toughening. In fact, all the big cats were fine. They had submitted to her examination with snarling reluctance, tails flicking dangerously, but only because David had ordered them to.

Then Davey had called to the gorillas. Auntie had started to come obediently, but not King Kong. He had given a grunt of prohibition—he recognized Elizabeth; she meant danger, the treacherous world beyond the forest. For a moment Auntie had hesitated. Then Jordan had called her again, impatiently, and she had come. Finally King Kong had lumbered after her dangerously, and taken up position beside them, glowering. Elizabeth could feel his glare while she worked. She was looking for signs of vitamin deficiency, but there were none. Their teeth, gums, nails, eyeballs were all clear. But when she turned to King Kong, he reared up slowly onto his hindlegs and stood, defiantly. Elizabeth stepped backward, her heart knocking. She was *not* going to examine him.

But, just looking at him nervously, she had never seen him look better: his shaggy coat was glossy in the sunshine; he must have lost thirty pounds and his muscles protruded. He had never looked like that in the zoo. Even his dangerous eyes were beautiful. And again she saw him galloping through the glen after Daisy, with Kitty bounding joyfully after him; she thought of the cage that was waiting for him and felt her eyes burn.

'He'll be all right,' she muttered.

The elephants came when he called them, huffing and blinking: first Rajah, Dumbo dutifully following, but not Jamba. Jamba remembered Elizabeth from the zoo, and she didn't want to have anything to do with her. But when she saw Dumbo going, she lumbered after him and stood there protectively.

Her distrust was unmistakable, and Elizabeth was hurt. Animals had always responded to her— she loved them and they loved her. Seeing Jamba again was like seeing an old friend; but Jamba clearly did not think so.

'Hello Rajah,' she had said. 'I'm your friend . . .'

She examined only Rajah, who submitted to her reluctantly. She peered up into his cavernous mouth and under his eyelids. But he was in good condition; they all were. They had all lost weight, and they were tired, but that didn't matter. She had tried to approach Jamba, but the old elephant wasn't having any of that, and Davey had said, 'She's healthy. She associates you with that zoo. It's Sally I want you to look at now—the others can wait till tonight.'

And, oh, poor old Sally . . . She was standing in the stream, head down, absolutely exhausted, her breath coming in wheezing groans, her ribs showing. She submitted to examination without protest.

Elizabeth listened to the old hippo's heart.

'She shouldn't be doing anything like this! It'll kill her, she's an *old* hippo.' Her eyes suddenly flashed. 'How *could* you do this to her?'

'You know what's wrong with her?'

'Yes! She's exhausted. And half-starved.'

'But do you know why? Because her stomach's blocked with tennis balls your public's thrown down her mouth.'

She had turned and stared at him. 'What makes you think people have done that?'

For a moment he looked as if he were about to ignore the question; then anger flickered across his face, and he surprised her with the emotion of his reply.

'Because it's human nature, Doctor. Haven't you found that out yet? That we're the only ones that *enjoy* shedding other animals' blood? For *sport*? Bull fights. Cockfights. Hunting. Even you softhearted British go fox-hunting. One poor fox torn to death by a pack of dogs. And television has that whole series called *Famous American Sportsmen*, and they get guys like Bing Crosby to go to Africa and shoot an innocent elephant or something, just to amuse the public. And what about the 4-H Club? They actually encourage trapping, for kids—as an outdoor sport. Even the U.S. Wildlife Department publishes a little book giving them tips on trapping so they can earn pocket money . . . Long, lingering deaths—hours, *days*. Just to make fur coats for rich ladies. Our national heroes are Daniel Boone and Buffalo Bill, aren't they?'

173

'What's this got to do with Sally?'

He looked at her in amazement that she had not understood. Then he said softly: 'The same mentality, Dr. Johnson. The same ... *mentality* that kill animals for sport, and to make fur coats, thinks ... that it's quite okay to imprison animals in zoos, so they can bring their kids along on Sundays. And laugh at Sally sitting all alone in her cage with her mouth open, and chuck a tennis ball down her throat. And laugh when she swallows it ...' He glared at her, then ended dismissively. 'Can you give her something to make her move her bowels and get rid of the blockage?'

Elizabeth took a deep breath to control her anger. She brought her mind back to science.

'Has she been moving her bowels?'

'Not much. Charlie's been behind her all the way.'

'Normal? The droppings?'

'Liquid.'

She shook her head. 'If I give her a laxative she'll need to rest. If it *is* tennis balls, she could have terrible pain when the laxative works. Complications. If she's lived with that junk all these years most of it's found a home somewhere or other. It could knock the daylights out of her.'

'Then you can give her a shot of vitamins to give her strength.'

It was definitely an order, not a request.


Now Elizabeth lay in her sleeping bag, wide awake at three o'clock that Saturday morning, having spent a full day with the animals, and still afraid of them. And of him.

She hated Davey Jordan. She would give her right arm to be able to do what he could do with animals. The way they loved him. But as an animal lover she also hated him for exposing her animals to this danger, to the incompetence and savagery of fools. O God, how she hated him for that.

And she resented his aloof manner, his reluctance to talk to her, even acknowledge her. 'Why do you talk to me so abruptly,' she had said. 'Why don't you like me, Mr. Jordan? Can't you accept I'm here?'

He had looked embarrassed suddenly, almost shy.

'It's that you don't like me,' he muttered. 'In fact, you hate me. For turning your animals loose.'

'Right,' she said with feeling. 'How very perspicacious.'

He had ignored the sarcasm. 'I don't dislike you. I only hate your screwed-up thinking that causes so much misery. So I'm not going to argue with you, Dr. Johnson, I'm sick of arguing with people like you and Professor Ford. And the animals don't like arguments.'

She was going to fight back, but he had suddenly held out a finger at her in the dark.

'Please listen to me a moment, because this is important.' And then more urgently, he had said, 'Please try to stop hating me, Dr. Johnson, because the animals sense it. They'll get nervous. This thing is working for one reason: *Love*. . . . They love me, Dr. Johnson. And in different ways they're all sort of bound together by that. But if a stranger comes along, full of hate and fear, they sense it. You can't fool animals about things like that.' He looked at her steadily. 'So please try to cool it, Dr. Johnson. The animals have got enough on their minds right now.'

Cool it . . . She had lit a cigarette to compose herself, then had said archly, 'Very well. For the animals' sake, I shall try to put my mind into neutral about what you've done. Though how you can expect that, God alone knows. But I don't want them to be frightened of me.' She added, in self-defense, 'Any more than I want to be afraid of them.'

Then he smiled at her, almost as if making it up to her.

'It comes from here.' He touched his breast. 'You're not afraid of someone you love. It comes from . . . *within*.'

Then he had climbed into his sleeping bag, and across the dark had said, 'I'm sorry I haven't been very polite, Dr. Johnson. I'll be better when we get there and get some proper rest. Now go to sleep, please.'

And, by God, she had. She had shut up and almost immediately exhaustion had claimed her.

Now she lay awake after seven hours of solid but insufficient sleep, churning over what he had said last night. And, clearly, as he himself had said, there was nothing so scientifically remarkable about what she was witnessing, nothing mysterious. Despite all that high-flying talk of love. Any vet knows how tamed animals are emotionally dependent on their keepers—their security blankets. Even the case of poor old Sally, a completely untrained animal, was straightforward enough. He was probably the only friend the poor old thing had ever had. And, actually, hippos are quite bright. She remembered a series of photographs taken in Africa, showing a crocodile grabbing a gazelle as it was drinking. A hippo had come and fought off the crocodile, dragged the gazelle to the bank, and fiercely stood guard over it as the little thing recovered. Lovely pictures. But anyway, as Konrad Lorenz would probably say, Sally probably thought of Davey as some kind of superior hippopotamus or the closest she'd ever got to meeting one.

Well, perhaps not . . . But anyway, there was nothing so scientifically remarkable about it. Except that it had never happened before on such an impressive—*outrageous*—scale.

She had never seen, read of, heard of, anything so extraordinary in her life . . .


Before going to sleep, Davey had told himself he had to wake up at three-thirty A.M. He did.

His body ached, but every muscle was ready to go, run, fight, die.

Elizabeth saw him coming over and for some reason she closed her eyes and pretended to be asleep. Relieved that at least she was not snoring, that her mouth was not open.

'Dr. Johnson? We're going.'

Then something lovely happened. Just then, out of the blackness, came one short bark.

Davey scrambled up, excitement all over his face. '*Sam!*'

And Sam came running through the undergrowth, tail wagging and a laugh on his face. Davey ran to him and dropped to his knees, and Sam bounded his forepaws up onto his shoulders and licked his face, whimpering in joy. Davey hugged him, laughing, 'Oh, Sam— good dog, Sam . . .' Sam whimpered and wagged, beside himself with excitement, then he bounded at Big Charlie and jumped up on him, then back to Davey, wagging and licking. He turned to Elizabeth and came at her excitedly, then he saw who she was and turned and bounded back to Davey.

They were all laughing.

# thirty-three

The six-lane highway lay ahead in the starlight. Beyond it, down a bank of rocks, was the river; then the Great Smoky Mountains loomed up into the sky.

Davey came down the ravine slowly, and stopped at the edge of the highway. He peered across the darkness. Nothing. He whistled, and hurried across the tarmac, looking back at his animals following. He ran across all six lanes to the metal bar on the other side.

Below was the river bank of bulldozed rocks. Five hundred yards downriver was the dim outline of the bridge. He went leaping down the rocks to the water's edge. Rajah followed, clambering over the barrier, ears spread, trunk groping.

The water only reached to Davey's shins; his feet were on firm stone. The animals were scrambling down the rocks in the dark. Rajah sighed as he stopped at the water edge. 'Come, Rajah.' Davey waded deeper into the river. Rajah hesitated, then lumbered into the water.

'Stand!'

Rajah stopped and stood, blinking, awaiting instructions. 'Come, Jamba.' She was poised massively on the water's edge, looking apprehensively at the river, Dumbo beside her. 'Come, Dumbo.' Without hesitation the little elephant stepped into the river and stopped beside Rajah. 'Come, Jamba.' The old zoo elephant gave a groan and lumbered into the water with an elephantine flinch.

The two gorillas were in a bunch, staring fearfully at the dark river. The chimpanzees grouped beside them. Davey splashed back to them. He patted Candy on the shoulder, then patted Rajah's rump. 'Ride, Candy.' The chimpanzee glanced at him, then looked fearfully at the rushing water, measuring the distance; Davey snapped his order again. She jerked, startled at his tone, then she gathered for the spring, and leaped. One arm grabbed for Rajah's tail, and she landed on the elephant's back. In an agile movement she ran down Rajah's spine, and both her hands were suddenly firing imaginary six-guns, just as she did in the circus. Then her legs suddenly shot apart, and she landed astride Rajah's neck like a cowboy. Then Florrie leaped through the air and ran down Rajah's back; but in the circus she was dressed as a Red Indian for this trick, so she beat one hand in front of her gaping mouth, her other wielding her tomahawk. Then Sultan came leaping through the air and landed on Rajah's back behind Florrie, jaws agape and snarling in her ear, just as he did in the circus, with Florrie still doing her Red Indian number. Champ clambered on, too. Davey turned to the two gorillas.

'King Kong. Auntie. Come!'

The gorilla stared. Then he reached up one hand, took Jamba's tail worriedly, and swung onto his back behind the others.

'Good. Now Auntie ...' He took her hand and put it around Jamba's tail. If this did not work he was going to have to take her across the bridge. He slung his arm under her buttocks and heaved. And Auntie clambered up onto the elephant's back apprehensively.

'Good!' Davey grabbed Dumbo's trunk tip. 'Train!' Dumbo grabbed Rajah's tail. 'Forward, Rajah.' The big elephant started plodding into the river, Dumbo earnestly following him. 'Stop.' Rajah stopped. Davey turned to the lions. 'Ride, Kitty.' In one bound Kitty was on Dumbo's back. Then Tommy. Then Princess. Davey swung Champ onto Rajah's back, then took Jamba's trunk and Dumbo's tail and brought the two together. Pooh and Winnie lumbered alongside. Big Charlie shouted, 'Davey.'

Sally could not get over the guard rail, and she gave a big croak of anguish. She had her forefeet on the metal, her hindquarters bunched as she tried to launch herself, jigging in anticipation of the feat. She gave a jump, her forefeet bludgeoned the top rail, and she fell on her rump with a thud. Davey came splashing back toward the rocky bank.

Big Charlie and Elizabeth were trying to heave Sally's hindquarters over the barrier. Sally was grunting in protest, rolling-eyed, her legs beating the barrier.

Davey could see it was no use. He shouted, 'Rajah.' He went bounding back down the rocks to the water's edge, splashed up to the elephants. 'Down, Champ. Sultan—down. Florrie—down. Candy.' All the animals went leaping back to the rocks, bewildered.

'Come, Rajah.'

Rajah turned and lumbered out of the river. He scrambled up the rocks, back onto the dark highway. Davey took his trunk and thrust it under Sally's belly.

'Lift, Rajah.'

Sally wailed in protest, and for a long moment she straddled the top rail, thrashing her legs. Then over she went.

First light was coming from the east, but down in the valley it was still dark. Over the Pigeon River a mist was swirling about Davey, water rushing about his legs. He could not yet see the opposite bank, but he estimated he was nearly halfway across, about where the curve in the rapids began. The water was up to his knees, and he felt cautiously with his feet. Rajah was behind him, Dumbo hanging onto his tail. Davey took another cautious step; then his foot plunged beneath him, he lurched, and he plunged into the swirling water.

He gasped, 'Stop!' and the current swept him backward. He thrashed, and flailed, and kicked with all his might, but his feet were like lead in his sodden sneakers, and the current took him faster and faster, and his feet were not even breaking the water. He thrashed and he flailed, desperately trying to make it back to the rapids, but the rushing water carried him further and further, and already he was exhausted. Then he swung sideways and began to swim across the current, toward the southern bank.

Big Charlie was splashing frantically across the rapids to get in front of the milling animals, upstream to avoid the curve that Davey had fallen into. The animals went stumbling and splashing after Charlie, Sam bounding behind, herding them, and Elizabeth lurching after Sam.

Davey was two hundred yards downstream, the river carrying him faster than the best man can swim; but he was only fifty yards from the south bank now. A hundred yards farther his feet hit rocks. The water still dragged him for another fifty yards. He clung, gasping.

Then, in the dawn, he heard the cars.

# thirty-four

Sheriff Lonnogan and his men had been hiding in the trees at the south end of the bridge. The sheriff was asleep in the back seat of his car when his lookout hollered: 'There they are!'

They scrambled out of their cars, grabbing their guns, and dashed onto the bridge, not knowing what to expect. Jeb Wiggins was pointing upriver. They stared, astonished.

The sonsabitches weren't crossing by the bridge at all. All they could see were the blurred bulks of the elephants. For a long moment they stared, and every man felt the sudden fear in his guts at the confrontation ahead. Then the sheriff recovered and snapped his orders.

Half the men piled into one car, which sped across the bridge to cut off the animals' retreat in case they turned back; the rest piled into the sheriff's car and drove down a track on the south bank. Then they dashed for the cover of the bushes.

Big Charlie splashed to a halt when he heard the car, Lonnogan hollered hoarsely out of the trees: 'Halt or I shoot.'

Charlie was twenty yards from the bank. He shouted desperately, 'I'm stopped.'

Elizabeth came splashing forward, crying, 'Don't shoot.' She stopped beside Big Charlie, soaked from her waist down. 'Don't shoot.'

Lonnogan crouched behind a tree, staring at the river, waiting to see what happened. If they stampeded he was going to blast them. But nothing happened. He stood up, cautiously. He forced himself to full height. He started toward the riverbank, legs trembling. Across his chest he held a shotgun, and from both hips swung his six-guns.

At the edge of the bank he looked down at the extraordinary, frightening scene: the big Indian, the wild-eyed woman, the elephants with their loads of shaggy gorillas, chimps, and big cats. Kid Lonnogan and Jeb Wiggins stood up slowly behind their shrubbery, each with rifles and six-guns. Sheriff Lonnogan took a breath and tilted his cowboy hat, chewing gum.

'Where's the other Wild Man from Cherokee?'

Elizabeth opened her mouth, but Big Charlie jerked his head back at the north bank. 'Back there. In the forest.'

'Oh, yeah? An' you call me sheriff, you hear? What's he doin' back there, Sittin' Bull? Why ain't he with y'all?'

Big Charlie's mind was fumbling for a plan. His eyes darted down the bank. 'Sittin' Bull wasn't a Cherokee. You want to call me anything funny, call me Draggin' Canoe.'

Sheriff Lonnogan paused in his chewing of gum.

'An' none of your lip. Or they'll be callin' you Draggin' Ass, 'cos that's what your ass'll be doin'. Now, where's the Wild Man?'

'Sprained his ankle, bad. Back there in the forest.'

Sheriff Lonnogan looked at Elizabeth. 'You the vet lady I hear about ma'am?'

'I am.'

'You joined sides with these wild guys?'

Elizabeth snapped, 'I am here absolutely officially. To care medically for the animals, until their recapture.'

'You realize you tell me one lie, you become an accomplice to these guys, ma'am?'

'Of course I'm not an accomplice. Don't talk rubbish!'

'Law ain't rubbish, ma'am. Now, if you ain't an accomplice you better come right out of that river in case the bullets start flyin'.'

She cried, 'Professor Ford's orders were strictly no shooting! And I'm here to tell you, Sheriff, that if one shot is fired I personally will see you're prosecuted to the highest court in the United States.'

'Dr. Ford ain't got no jurisdiction over me, ma'am. I happen to be a duly-elected sheriff, and as such I'm responsible under the Constitution of the United States for the maintenance of public safety. Now, get out of that river.'

'I most certainly will not if you're threatening to fire.'

Big Charlie said, to keep him talking, 'I want to see your warrant of arrest.'

Lonnogan looked at him. He smirked. 'Wise guy as well as wild guy, huh? Come on out, Mr. Buffalohorn, an' I'll show you.'

'You come in here, Sheriff, an' show me your warrant—unless you don't want to get your pretty boots wet.'

Sheriff Lonnogan looked at him a long moment in genuine surprise.

'Oh, boy, injun, you sure lookin' to get your ass in a sling.' He said to Jeb Wiggins, without taking his eyes off Charlie, 'Get onto the radio to Ford's bunch and tell him we got 'em nailed down in the Pigeon. Tell him to get some reinforcements pronto, an' them circus trucks. Then call up the television an' tell 'em where the action's at.' He pulled one six-gun out of its holster. He spun it around his finger, then pointed it at Big Charlie, from his hip. 'Okay, come out of that cold river an' get yerself arrested; otherwise you goin' to get more like Sittin' Duck than Sittin' Bull.'

Elizabeth lunged through the water and flung herself in front of Big Charlie. Everybody was astonished.

'Now listen here, Sheriff! You fire one shot, and I'll see you hanged! This man's not trying to escape arrest. One shot and these animals will stampede in all directions.'

Lonnogan stared at her; then waved his gun.

'Out of the way, lady. Or you're an accomplice.'

'Like hell I am! I'm going to stop you scattering these animals to the four winds. Call Professor Ford on your radio and stop playing cowboys and Indians. Because, if you fire, all hell's going to break loose. And you'll never get them back, and half of them'll drown!'

Rajah swung his trunk nervously. At that moment Big Charlie glimpsed Davey. He was creeping through the bushes, silently making for the sheriff's car.

Jeb Wiggins was hunched in the driver's seat, over the two-way radio. Davey slipped into the back seat; one hand slipped over Jeb's mouth. Jeb's eyes bulged, and Davey's other hand came down on the back of his head in a smart chop. Jeb Wiggins slumped. Big Charlie said loudly, 'Okay, I'm coming out . . . Ain't nobody going to start shootin' on my account.'

Lonnogan was surprised.

'Hands on your head. And make those animals stay where they at.'

Davey pulled Wiggin's handcuffs off his belt. He feverishly manacled Jeb's wrists to the wheel. Then he wrenched the transmitter out of the radio. He shoved the ignition keys into his pocket.

Big Charlie came plodding through the water toward the bank. Elizabeth was astonished. Lonnogan had his six-gun trained on the big Indian. Kid Lonnogan had both his pearl-handled six-guns fixed on the animals. Davey slid out of the car, and started tiptoeing through the trees. Big Charlie reached the bank and started clambering up the rocks. Davey was six paces behind the lawmen. He slid behind a tree.

Big Charlie reached the top of the bank. 'Stop there . . . Hold out both your wrists.'

'I got a right to see the warrant,' Big Charlie said.

'When you're good and handcuffed—otherwise the bullets'll start flyin'.'

Big Charlie sighed, and held out his wrists.

Lonnogan put down his shotgun and holstered his six-gun. He took his handcuffs off his hip, snapped them open, and stepped forward.

Davey bounded from behind his tree and sprang at Kid Lonnogan, and at the same moment Charlie seized the sheriff's wrists.

Davey wrenched Kid Lonnogan's guns upward, and they fired, and Elizabeth shrieked, and the animals scrambled around in the water, and they stampeded. Bounding and splashing, wild-eyed, back over the rapids the way they had come and the deputies across the river opened fire. First one wild shot, then they were all firing into the water and the air, to turn the terrible stampede and the animals swung downriver. Lunging and bounding, terrified out of their minds, and they crashed over the edge of the rapids into the rushing water beyond.

Big Charlie yanked Boots Lonnogan onto his knees, and snapped the handcuffs on his wrists. Davey was still wrestling with Kid Lonnogan, one arm around the man's neck in a headlock, the other clutching his wrist; Kid was punching him in the guts, and the gun exploded again. Big Charlie grabbed his wrist and twisted it back until Kid Lonnogan bellowed, and the gun fell. Charlie slapped Kid's handcuffs onto one wrist, then wrenched father and son back-to-back, and handcuffed them together. He snatched the keys off their belts and flung them into the river.

Davey was already chasing flat out after the animals. On the opposite bank the deputies were scrambling back into their car. Charlie snatched up the two lawmen's guns and rifle. He hurled the shotguns into the river and started after Davey. Sheriff Lonnogan wrenched at his manacles and bellowed. *'You got it comin' to you!'*


# thirty-five


Rajah swam, his head half under water, Jamba beside him, their trunks up like periscopes. Dumbo was swimming desperately behind them, his trunk tip clinging to Jamba's tail. The lions swam furiously, ears back, sodden tails streaming behind them, Tommy in the lead, the bears in their midst. The chimpanzees and gorillas were everywhere, wild-eyed, heads up, jaws agape, beating their arms like drowning children. Elizabeth was way ahead, stumbling after Davey, and Charlie was bringing up the rear with his stolen guns, looking feverishly for cover.

There were two good boulders. He threw himself behind them. He could see twenty yards up the track, and he could see the rocky river bank quite clearly. He checked the magazines of the six-guns, then lay on his stomach, panting, the first gun ready.

He had never fired one of these things before.

About fifteen minutes later he heard them coming.

It had only taken the rest of the posse a few minutes to get back across the bridge and find their sheriff. But they had wasted five minutes trying, unsuccessfully, to unmanacle Lonnogan and his son; another five trying equally unsuccessfully, to get Jeb Wiggins free of his steering wheel. They tried to use the radio and found the transmitter ripped out. Then they decided that Jeb Wiggins should try to drive, still lashed to the wheel, with another deputy to change the gears, to fetch reinforcements: only to discover the ignition keys were gone. Then the three unmanacled deputies had set off down the riverbank, with Lonnogan and his co-manacled son staggering behind, twisted back-to-back.

The three deputies ran through the undergrowth, anxiously scanning the river more than where they going. Big Charlie's gun cracked the morning open, and the bark flew off a tree right in front of Fred Wiggins. They all threw themselves flat. Charlie filled his chest, gave a Cherokee war whoop, and let fly with his six-gun for the sheer hell of it.

*Bang-wang! Bang-wang! Bang-wang!*

Bullets ricocheted over the deputies' heads. They went wriggling in all directions, looking for solid rock, and fifty yards back Lonnogan and his son stumbled in their crab-run and crashed into the undergrowth. Big Charlie's bullets cracked and whined overhead, and Lonnogan bellowed furiously, *'Gettem! Just gettem!'*

Rajah's feet hit rock, but the current swept him on; he scrambled and hit more rock, and he heaved; he was half out of the water, flanks heaving, glinting black in the sunrise. Jamba was swept on downriver with Dumbo clinging to her tail. Fifty yards farther, Tommy clawed his way up the steep rocky bank, and twenty yards farther Auntie and King Kong were thrashing toward the bank.

Jamba swam, trunk up, wild-eyed, Dumbo milling behind her. Her hooves flailed rocks, and she tried to anchor herself, but the current swept her on as wind swings a sail, and Dumbo was swung outstream, panic thudding in his chest and water choking his snorting trunk tip. Jamba was swept against a big boulder; she scrambled her hooves frantically, snorting and slipping, and half-heaved herself out of the water, and the current wrenched Dumbo's bulk off her tail, and the river took him.

Dumbo tried to squeal, and it just came out in a gurgle and he thrashed and thrashed, trunk upflung, trying to raise his head out of the water to see, but the current swept him on like an express train, into the middle of a rushing channel. He pounded his hooves and he squealed, and water sprayed up his trunk into the sunrise. Now he was thrashing downriver, and he did not know where anything was anymore, and all he could see was frothing white water.

Jamba lumbered frantically along the riverbank, rocks tumbling beneath her feet, and she gave a scream ordering Dumbo to come back. But Dumbo was thirty yards downstream now, thrashing and spraying, water in his eyes and ears, and the current swept him on, out toward the tumultuous middle. Jamba went blundering back down the rocks like a tank, and she plunged back into the river with a mighty splash. Davey feverishly ripped off his sneakers and slung off his knapsack, and dove in with her.

He broke surface, gasping, and swam flat out with the current. All Dumbo knew was the crashing exhaustion and the dreadful panic of drowning, and he did not know where he was trying to swim to anymore. Ahead, the river curved into a narrow bend, and the water leaped and twisted.

The little elephant was only ten yards ahead of Davey when he was sucked into the bend of the river. He was almost finished now, his head underwater, just his trunk tip sticking up, his legs weakly working. Davey was swept into the bend after him, with Jamba surging ten yards behind him. Exhaustion was seizing Davey's guts, his arms and legs crying out to collapse, but he kicked and kicked toward the little trunk tip twisting above the swirling water. Then he hit it. He grabbed it wildly, and it clasped his hand tight. Then, in a giant rush, they were both gone under the leaping, killer white water, and there was nothing in the world but the terrifying choking in his throat and the tumbling of his body. The trunk tip was wrenched out of his grasp. Davey was pulled underwater with half a strangled gasp of air in his lungs, and the elephant crashed against him. He kicked and fought wildly back to the surface, spitting and gasping, and sucked in a mouthful of choking water; then Jamba hit him. In an invincible mass of hooves her great belly turned barreling over him, and he was knocked to the bottom of the rushing river again without any air. He kicked with the last of his terrified strength and broke surface again, choking—and he saw Jamba's rump and he blindly grabbed at her tail. He got it, and they were swept on downriver. He clung, gasping, coughing, trying to see. But there was nothing of Dumbo to be seen.

Just the swirling, leaping water. Thirty yards ahead the river widened again. On they swept, kicking and spitting; then Jamba's feet hit rock, and the same moment Davey saw the little trunk tip. He let go of Jamba and kicked with all his might, kicked and thrashed and flailed, almost crying, stretching for Dumbo. And the drowning elephant clutched at him.

With all his might, his trunk curling desperately around Davey's arm, trying to heave himself up out of the water, and Davey went under again, shoved under by three tons of drowning elephant trying to climb on top of him. Davey wildly tried to pull his wrist free, and all he knew was the pounding of hooves and the terrified exhaustion and the water strangling in his throat; then his feet hit rock, and at the same moment the trunk was wrenched off his arm, and Jamba was beside him.

She had seized the little elephant's trunk in hers and pulled it up on high, and Davey Jordan was free. Jamba was standing, enormous and snorting and staggering, the water curling off her flanks. Davey grabbed her ear, and he clung. And the feel of it, holding him up out of the water, seemed the sweetest feeling he had ever known.

# part eight

## thirty-six

Before the World was made, all the creatures lived in the sky, on the Sky Rock; and all living things spoke the same language, so they all understood each other. But the creature called Man tried to be too clever, so the Great One punished him by making him deaf to the speech of the other creatures.

Now, the creatures multiplied, and the Sky Rock became more and more crowded; until there was danger that some would be pushed off. So a council was called, of all the creatures, to decide what was to be done about this uncomfortable situation. By this time the Great One had made the World, which was floating around the Sky Rock; but, alas, it was completely covered in water. It seemed to the council that such a place was no solution to their problems, but it was decided to send down the Water Beetle, to see if he could find a single dry place where they all could live.

After many difficulties the little Water Beetle reached the World. He swam and he swam, but he found nothing but water. Finally, in despair, he dived, to see if there was anything down there. And, lo and behold, he found mud.

He brought this mud up to the surface. It grew and grew.

But it was still too wet for anyone to live on. Finally, the sad Water Beetle had to return to the Sky Rock and report that he had found nothing satisfactory.

The council was very upset at the Water Beetle's bad news. But the Grandfather Buzzard, who is the father of all buzzards, announced that he would go down to the World, because with his huge wings he could cover a much greater area than the little Water Beetle. So off he went, down to the World, and around he flew. He found the muddy place the Water Beetle had reported. He flew and he flew over the muddy parts, looking for a suitable place for the creatures to live; he flew until he was so weary that his giant wingtips dipped into the mud, and then his giant breast also. So enormous was he that, where his breast and wingtips touched, great holes were formed that became valleys, and the ridges became mountains. Thus the Great Smoky Mountains were made.

Finally the mud began to dry out, and the Grandfather Buzzard flew back to the Sky Rock and told the council. Soon the mountains were dry enough to live upon, and all the creatures came down from the Sky Rock. All the mammals and birds and the insects and reptiles, and Man, came to live in the Great Smoky Mountains, with the blessing of the Great One; and they were happy, and they multiplied.

That is how the World began.

'This is where the world began? . . .'

It was a beautiful day. They were camped in the valley below Indian Knob, and now that they were actually here, now that they were safely across that Pigeon River, it almost seemed like a holiday to Elizabeth. They were having a day's rest; the spring noon-sun was beautiful, and they did not have to move until tomorrow: at least for today they were safe, and her relief was so intense she felt almost gay. It was wonderful just to let her aching body sit around the little fire with big amiable Charlie and drink whisky. It was also a relief that David Jordan was not here, that she did not have to try to argue with him. She was enthralled with Big Charlie's story about the Sky Rock. 'So Adam and Eve were Cherokees?'

Big Charlie nodded.

'So *this* is the Garden of Eden . . .' She did not want to ask him if he believed it; she did not want to spoil the moment. 'And Adam and Eve were punished by the Great One for trying to be too clever. Were they ever banished from the Garden of Eden, like our Christian Adam and Eve were?'

Charlie looked into the fire, then gave a little smile.

'Yes. But not by the Great One.'

She waited. 'By whom, then?'

'The White Man.'

'Oh . . . I see.'

It changed the whole atmosphere. While he had been telling her the Cherokee legend, with the glow of the whisky and the knowledge that they had arrived at last, it had seemed as it had been back at the glen. But she had no time for this type of thing—zoo-jack in the name of politics.

'I see . . . You'd better tell me what happened.'

Then she had a flashback of the expression in David Jordan's eyes as he had looked at his animals, the birds fluttering about him in the glen. And Big Charlie's deep brown voice held no bitterness; he told her what happened—simply, almost shyly: she wasn't even sure that he wanted to tell her.

'The first white men came with friendliness. And in small parties. So the Indians were friendly too. They were . . . inquisitive. Hospitable. Then the white man came in bigger numbers. More and more . . . by the shipload. With their plows. And axes. And fences. With each shipload they hacked their way deeper and deeper into the wilderness. Into the Indians' hunting grounds. Just taking the land they found. Because it only belonged to . . . savages?'

He glanced at her, the firelight flickering in his brown eyes, then looked away again.

'But they were the Indians' hunting grounds. Where they got their food, because they didn't farm much. The game was retreating, you see. And being shot out. And all this caused all kinds of trouble. They tried to petition the colonialists to hold back to boundaries. But the white men kept breaking their promises. So finally the Indians went on the warpath. Just as they did with neighboring tribes, when there were boundary disputes.'

He glanced up at her and held her eye. She nodded.

'It was pretty bad. The Indians know how to fight. And, of course, the colonists fought back just as fiercely. They were better armed. They even declared a bounty on Indians. To claim the bounty the frontiersman had to have the scalp of the Indian, to prove he killed him.' He paused. 'That's how scalping started. Did you know that?'

She shook her head. 'I thought it was the other way round.'

Big Charlie nodded soberly. 'No, the Indians were shocked. Treating us like ... vermin. So ... they started doing the same thing back.'

He looked back at the fire and took a deep breath.

'Well, there were all kinds of treaties. Establishing new boundaries. They were all broken ... as each shipload of white men arrived from the Old World. Hungry for land. And the Indians were forced back. And fought back. Then ...' He gave a wisp of a smile. 'There came a bit of trouble between the New World and the Old World ... "No Taxation, Without Representation." All that stuff.' He looked at her inquiringly. 'The Boston Tea Party? And the War of Independence?'

Elizabeth nodded. That much American history she knew.

'Well, whose side do you think the Indians were on? The British—or the colonialists, who'd been stealing their land and scalping them for a dollar a head?'

Elizabeth nodded.

'I guess the Indians were delighted,' Big Charlie rumbled. 'And, of course the British were very pleased to have the Indians on their side against the Rebels. The Rebels were as mad as hell.'

Big Charlie's hooded eyes were alive with the story now.

'So, the Red Coats and the Redskins joined. And all around here ...' he waved his hand at the sunset— 'Tennessee ... South Carolina, Georgia ... and the coast, we socked it to 'em, the Cherokees and Red Coats, between us. And of course the Rebels socked it back to us. They got up a big combined army. Then they came at us from four sides, to cut us down to size. And ...' Big Charlie shook his head ruefully, 'they really whammed into us. Whole villages—whole towns were burned to the ground. Women and children. So we retreated. Back to the French Broad River ...' he jerked his thumb over his shoulder 'toward Hot Springs.'

'We met up with some Red Coats there,' Big Charlie continued glumly. 'But we knew we didn't stand a chance. We had to retreat again. So ... the Rebels marched into our territory in Tennessee. We had to abandon everything. And they set fire to the lot. Then the

Cherokees asked for peace. The British were defeated too, after that. And that was the end of the South. The beginning of the United States.' He looked at her. 'But now the Cherokees were at the mercy of the frontiersmen.'

He looked away, then sighed and took a long sip of his whisky. A trace of bitterness entered his deep voice.

'Okay. So we lost a war . . .So, we have to take the consequences. But . . .' He shook his head bitterly. 'We only joined the war because they were stealing our land in the first place. If it's wrong to steal, I don't see why it's lawful to steal at the point of a gun.' He turned to face her. 'Do you, Dr. Johnson?'

She looked him in the eye, and shook her head slightly.

'But what definitely wasn't lawful was what happened after that. Not by anybody's law.'

She waited. 'What did happen?'

'I guess I can't expect you to understand, Dr. Johnson,' he muttered. 'How can you? You see . . . I'm not just talking about all the treaties. The Government made a peace treaty, saying our land is here, then they change their minds and there's another battle and they take our land again and make a new treaty. But, hell, that happened to all the Indian tribes in America, right up to the last Battle of Wounded Knee, when the last tribe was finally wiped out. I mean . . . that was terrible, that was . . . *awful*, a massacre of defenseless people. But, I mean, that's happened, and I don't want to give you the wrong impression.' He looked at her hopelessly. 'I guess what really matters is . . . the Sky Rock. And . . . *life*. The Garden of Eden . . .' He sighed. 'And,' he said, 'the Battle of Horseshoe Bend. A man called Andrew Jackson. And the Trail of Tears.' He looked at her. 'Do you know about that?'

She shook her head. Charlie nodded and took a deep breath.

'Andrew Jackson was the frontiersmen's leader. They made a new treaty with us after they whipped the British. Then they went to war against the Creek Indians. The Cherokees joined forces with the frontiersmen because we were also having trouble with the Creeks. At the famous battle of Horseshoe Bend. And we won . . . but the frontiersmen only won because of the Cherokees. And because one of our Cherokee chiefs, who was called Junaluska, saved Andrew Jackson's life . . . a Creek was about to kill Jackson, and Junaluska drove his tomahawk through the Creek's skull.' Big Charlie looked at her. 'Andrew Jackson eventually got to be president of the United States.'

Big Charlie's hooded eyes widened dramatically. 'Then the white man discovered gold in Cherokee country . . . and you know how important *gold* is.' He stared at her. 'So they decided to annex us . . . the remainder of the Cherokee lands.'

He frowned as if amazed all over again. 'They just sent an army in, and conquered us all over again, Dr. Johnson. Just broke the treaty . . . *all over again* . . .'

He stared at her across the fire, and she looked back, fascinated; then his chest swelled in a sigh, and he looked away. He picked up his tin cup and took a long pull of whisky. Then he continued flatly. 'You know what happened next. The Government wrote a new treaty of surrender again. And that treaty said that the Cherokees surrendered all their lands in exchange for an Indian Reservation in Oklahoma.' His broad face took on a studied frown. 'In *Oklahoma?* Where is Oklahoma?' He waved his hand to the west. 'A thousand miles over *there*. What Cherokee had even *heard* of Oklahoma in those days, let alone *been* there?'

His voice became scornful. 'Of course, the Cherokees refused to sign the treaty. They even refused to go to the powwow. The Government sent their soldiers out to round up the chiefs, but most of them refused, and only a handful turned up. But *those* people'—he shook his head at her—'had no right to make a treaty for the whole Cherokee Nation!' He made a cross in the air with his finger. 'But they made their marks on the treaty. And the Americans got all hotted up to move into the last of the Cherokee lands, to get at all that gold.' He paused, then went on dramatically. 'But the Cherokees got themselves some *lawyers*. They appealed to the Supreme Court of the United States. And,' he ended triumphantly, 'the Supreme Court of the United States ruled in the Cherokee's *favor*.'

She waited. Big Charlie looked at her with big eyes, then said softly, 'And what do you think the president of the United States said? Andrew Jackson, the man whom the Cherokees had fought alongside at the Battle of Horseshoe Bend? The man whose life Chief Junaluska saved?'

'What?' she asked.

Big Charlie took a breath. 'President Andrew Jackson said, "The Court has given its decision. Now let them try to enforce it." '

Charlie stared at her in wonder.

'That was a president of the United States of America speaking, Dr. Johnson ... about the *Supreme* Court. About his own people. All President Nixon did was cover up Watergate. He didn't defy his own courts.' He looked at her, and his eyes seemed to melt. 'And Nixon wasn't stealing a whole nation's land.'

He looked into the fire, and blinked away his tears.

'Chief Junaluska went up to Washington to plead with him. And Andrew Jackson just said: "Sir, your audience is over; there is nothing I can do for you." '

He looked at her, then repeated grimly. ' "There is nothing I can do for you." '

And the Presidential order was given that the Cherokee people were to be removed, on 26 May 1838, so that the white man could have their land. An army of seven thousand men was raised under General Winfield Scott, and the dragnet began through Cherokee country.

They rounded up the people, an entire nation, and herded them into assembly stockades at bayonet point. They were allowed only the possessions they could carry; many were driven out without even a blanket. Children were often separated from their parents, husband from wife, old people from their families, hurried along with prods in the back. Chief Junaluska wept as he saw what was happening to his people. And he lifted his hat and cried up to the sky, 'O God! If I had known at the Battle of Horseshoe what I know now, American history would have been differently written.'

In the assembly stockades the people slept on the ground, under the sky. Many of them became sick from the rations, weak from hunger, and sick from the white man's ailments. Altogether it took four months to round up all the people and herd them into the stockades.

Then, on a cold and rainy October morning, the Cherokee people were herded into six hundred and forty-five wagons. The Chief led his people in prayer. The bugle sounded, and the wagons began to roll, down that long terrible journey, that is called the Trail of Tears.

It was a trail of death. For six long months, through freezing blizzards and rain, the flimsily covered wagons rolled. The Cherokees were without blankets, without fire, without enough to eat. The soldiers and teamsters had blankets and heavy coats, boots and proper food. But not the Cherokees. Every night people died of pneumonia, exposure, malnutrition, exhaustion. In the mornings the soldiers organized burial squads. Then the bugle would sound, the whips would crack, and the terrible cavalcade would start again. From October to March. From Cherokee, down in the foothills of the Great Smoky Mountains, into Tennessee, then to Chattanooga. Then northeast to Athens; then northwest, through Clarksville, and across into Kentucky. And across Kentucky into the state of Illinois, and across the Mississippi, into Missouri. Then in a big arc, into the state of Arkansas. And across the Arkansas Mountains, into Oklahoma ...

Altogether, four thousand Cherokee people died in those six months, between Cherokee and Oklahoma, on that shameful Trail of Tears.

Elizabeth was completely absorbed in the story now.

The whisky had gone to Big Charlie's head, and he had a grim gleam in his eye. But he was enjoying telling her the tale.

'A handful of Cherokees did escape the dragnet. A few managed to hide out in caves and in these forests, right here in the Great Smoky Mountains, while the white man swarmed over our country. First the gold hunters.' He shook his head at her. 'But there was no gold, Dr. Johnson. So the whole Trail of Tears had been for nothing. Then came the lumbermen, chopping down the trees, and the hillbilly homesteaders, hacking clearings and building their log cabins ...' He breathed deep, and his face was flushed. 'Then the Cherokees who had hidden came creeping out. And they began to scratch a living on the few bits and pieces of land which the white men didn't want. And after a while they were sort of allowed to stay.' He smirked bitterly. 'But they had to *buy* those bits of land they squatted on, Dr. Johnson. They had to buy back bits of their *own* land. Eventually even the Government agreed to let us stay, in that small area down there . . .' He pointed through the forest down in the direction of Cherokee. 'They called it the Qualla Boundary Reservation of the *Eastern* Cherokees . . .'

His eyes were suddenly moist; and his face flushed.

'And the white man shot out all the game. The deer . . . the bear . . . the mountain lion.' He waved his hand in appeal. 'These mountains used to be *paradise*, Dr. Johnson . . . full of all the animals. It's . . . where the World began . . .'


# thirty-seven


But this spring there was new life in this Garden of Eden, where once upon a time the World began.

Afterwards Elizabeth had lain on top of her sleeping bag, still in the thrall of the story of the Sky Rock. She had asked him: 'Is this why you're doing this, Charlie—because of that Trail of Tears?' He had looked at her with such weary surprise that she had not understood, that she had said, 'Okay, forget it.' It would have been the wrong moment to argue. He had not told her the story to convert her; he had told her because he wanted to—to make her feel . . . *liked*. And she was too full of relief that they had made it across the river without further bloodshed, that they were safe for the time being, in a National Park where game rangers kept the peace . . .

Where once the World began . . .

When she woke up she no longer felt quite the same.

Lying on top of her sleeping bag, the evening chill waking her at her lowest ebb, half hungover, she woke with the sinking dread: *what happens now?* Gone was the triumph of crossing the river, the euphoria of being safe, the thrall of the Sky Rock and the Grandfather Buzzard. Then suddenly a rifle thudded in the distance. She sat bolt upright, heart pounding.

'It's all right,' Davey's voice said behind her. 'Only Charlie getting some meat for the lions.'

She breathed again. But she was further depressed by the return of the unsmiling David Jordan. He was sitting by the tumbling stream, feeding twigs into a small fire. The lions and Sultan were clustered near him, staring at her, hunched, intent. She felt the old quake of naked fear.

'Did you find Sally?'

'No.'

She stared at him. *He had failed. . . .* Despite everything, she had had complete confidence that he would find her, that there was nothing he could not do in the wilderness.

'She's all right, Dr. Johnson.'

'Rubbish! She's a sitting duck for hunters.'

He said quietly, 'She's in the sort of place she should be, Dr. Johnson. She's in the Smokies, by a river. But I'll probably go back and find her—after we get there and settle down.'

'Get *where*? I thought we *were* there. I thought this'—she waved her hand dramatically—'was the Garden of Eden.'

He ignored her tone. 'The place I'm heading for is only a few more days.'

She stared at him. 'Only a few more days to Eden, huh? Then we all settle down happily? Excuse me.' She grabbed her towel and soap and strode away through the undergrowth.

Davey did not look up. He was sorry for her, but he could not dwell on it; all he could think about was Sally. She *was* all right. She was exhausted, and she was better off back there at the Pigeon than battling her way over the Great Smoky Mountains, straining her old heart and guts. *She had made it to the country where he had been taking her, she had survived.* She could rest now. Lumber into some quiet eddy and just let the water take the weight off her weary hooves, and wallow and huff and puff; she did not have to run any more. No more exhausted, pitiful trailing along behind everybody else, trying to keep up: now she could swim all day as a hippopotamus should, wallowing along the bottom of the river in her underwater world as comfortably as the old sea cow she was. And there was plenty for her to eat along the banks; that's probably what she was doing right now. Tonight she would sleep as nature made her to do, at the bottom of the river, slowly rising unconsciously when she needed to breathe. And in the morning the whole Pigeon would be hers.

Davey sat, staring into the fire, trying to convince himself of all those things. But all he could see in the fire was poor, old Sally stumbling along the riverbanks all alone in the gathering darkness, with the fear of the night closing in on her, wondering where they had all gone. She wouldn't be eating like a lawnmower because her guts were clogged, and her old heart would be breaking.

Elizabeth had regretted her outburst almost immediately. Flouncing off with sarcasm was not going to put David Jordan in the mood to listen to reason. And it was true that Sally *was* better off back in the Pigeon River than straining herself over these mountains for the next few days—that is why she had not been unduly alarmed when the poor old thing had gotten lost. And she would probably be easier to recapture there.

Elizabeth felt better after her bath. She had intended washing only her face and throbbing feet, but that had felt so good she had stripped off in sections and washed the whole of her, finally sitting in the water for a freezing moment and scrubbing herself frantically as if Sheriff Lonnogan's posse were about to descend and catch her bare-assed. Afterward her whole body tingled, and, by God, she was going to have another drink.

The lions tensed as she came back up the mountainside, and she felt her stomach quake again. But she did not let herself hesitate.

'I've got a bottle of whisky. Would you like some?'

Davey looked up from the fire. 'You better keep it for yourself, Dr. Johnson.'

'Very well.' She sloshed a big shot of Scotch into her tin mug, added a dash of water. She could feel the lions watching her every move. She did not want to sit down, she wanted to be ready to run. But she made herself sit, on the other side of the fire. She lit a cigarette and inhaled, and took another swallow of whisky.

Then he astonished her by saying, self-consciously, 'I want to thank you for coming with us, Dr. Johnson. It's a great relief to know you're here. And I . . . admire your guts.'

It almost bowled her over; she felt her eyes burn for an instant in near-gratitude at being acknowledged at last. Then she wanted to blurt, *Oh, Davey, give it up now.*

'Won't you have a drink? And let's . . . talk?'

'I don't want to use up your whisky.'

'There's not going to be much left after tonight anyway. Unfortunately.'

He smiled. His face softened, and his eyes were the most beautiful she had ever seen. 'Okay. Thanks.' He held out his cup.

Pleased, she poured a shot into it, though she suspected he was only taking it to be polite. He filled his cup with water and took a sip.

'You don't drink much?'

'No. I like whisky, though.' He nodded at the wilderness and said affectionately, 'Old Charlie's had a few, hasn't he?'

'Yes. Over lunch.'

'He loves it. Save a bit for him.'

She smiled and nodded. 'He's an awfully nice man. He hasn't got a girl?' This was going better than she'd hoped.

'He's always working on it.' He thought, then dropped his voice a few octaves and quoted: ' "But it's not always too easy for a three-hundred-pound Jewish Indian." That's his favorite joke about himself.'

'Charlie's *Jewish?*'

Davey smiled. 'He fell for a Jewish girl and converted. Very kosher, he became. They were going to go to a kibbutz and everything.'

'What happened to her?'

'She flew off with somebody else.'

She smiled. 'Poor Charlie. Is he still Jewish?'

'No.'

She was anxious to keep him talking. She ferreted in her knapsack and pulled out a bar of chocolate. 'Would you like some?'

'No thanks.'

She broke off a piece and put it in her mouth, putting the bar in her top pocket. Suddenly, out of the corner of her eye, she saw Kitty get to her feet. Elizabeth jerked her head around and froze, wordless; then Kitty came padding straight for her, menacing, purposeful. '*David*.'

'Keep still,' he commanded. 'Stop, Kitty.' Then he said, 'Open your eyes.'

Cringing, she opened her eyes, heart pounding. Kitty was standing in front of her, her neck stretched as far as she could, her nose trying to reach the mug of whisky clutching in her trembling hand. Elizabeth wanted to cry *Call her off please*. But she heard herself croak with hollow playfulness: 'Lions don't like whisky, Kitty . . .'

Kitty was encouraged and took another step forward. Elizabeth jerked back, one hand in front of her eyes. Kitty stopped, poised. Elizabeth opened her eyes, and looked straight into the huge face of the lioness. She jerked again, and Kitty blinked as if she were expecting to be hit; then she sat down and looked at Elizabeth reproachfully.

The hurt look on her big lion face pulled Elizabeth out of her terror, and suddenly she wanted to laugh and throw her arms around Kitty. 'Oh, poor Kitty!' And poor Kitty seized her advantage. In one big, invincible movement she suddenly swarmed all over Elizabeth and bowled her over.

One moment Elizabeth was half laughing at Kitty, the next she had four hundred furry pounds of lioness knocking her off balance; head down, purring like a tractor, huge shoulder wiping against her, splashing her whisky over her bosom, and she gave a strangled gasp as Kitty found her chocolate. In one cunning movement Kitty zapped it out of her pocket, and she was gone. She bounded five paces away, then crouched and gripped the chocolate between her front paws, and proceeded to get into it.

Elizabeth was sprawled, one arm curled over her head, her bosom soaked with whisky and her heart pounding. Davey was standing.

'It's okay, it's okay, Dr. Johnson.'

'I'm all right . . .' Elizabeth gasped.

Kitty tried to nip at the wrapping, couldn't get a grip on the flimsy stuff, then gulped the chocolate down, silver paper and all.

She crouched, ears half back, deciding about the taste; then she looked back at Elizabeth hopefully. She got up and came padding straight back at her.

Elizabeth cringed in dread; then Kitty arched her back, raised her tail, and wiped her massive self against Elizabeth. Then she turned and rubbed herself the other way, nuzzling Elizabeth's bosom for more chocolate and almost bulldozing her off balance again. Kitty coughed up a piece of silver paper; then nuzzled her neck and ear. Elizabeth's ears were full of the terrifying ticklishness of slobbering lion, the enormous purring, and the huge rough tongue licking; she cringed, giggled, and wriggled in a mixture of terror and pleasure. For five seconds the delightful agony went on; then Kitty gave up on more chocolate and turned and sauntered off back to the others.

Elizabeth crouched in a state of delighted shock.

'Oh,' she gasped, 'that was *wonderful.*'

She had another stiff whisky after that. So, to her surprise, did Davey. She felt on a warm, lovely cloud. She could not stop thinking about being cupboard-loved by a beautiful lion in the wilderness. She wanted to throw her arms wide and tell the animals she loved them all. She could hardly believe the things that were happening to her; it was the sort of dream-come-true she had had as a little girl when she thought she wanted to marry a game ranger in Africa when she grew up. She did not want to spoil it all by arguing with Davey right now. She just wished it were day, and he could call the birds down again.

'Have you worked with animals all your life, Davey?'

'Yes. Pretty much.'

She looked at him. He seemed almost shy at being asked a personal question. It was a sweet face, even an angelic face—but controlled.

'Have you ever been in the army, Davey?'

He looked surprised, even uncomfortable.

'The Navy. I was drafted.'

The Navy? A million miles from the wilderness and and animals. 'What, in the Navy?'

'The SEALS.'

'What's that?'

He shifted. 'It stands for "Sea, Air, Land." They're sort of commandos, I guess you'd call it,' he explained reluctantly.

She stared at him. The SEALS, yes, she had heard of them. The crack troops. Underwater sabotage. Espionage. All that derring-do Clint Eastwood stuff. It was the complete opposite of what she imagined him to be. Yet she had been right; she had felt his military-like competence, the can-do-anything confidence he inspired.

'But have you ever killed anybody?'

'No.'

'Where did you serve?'

He smiled uncomfortably. 'That's classified. I'm sorry.'

'But . . . did you enjoy it?'

'No.'

She heard herself blurt, 'Is that why you're doing this? To somehow make up for what you did in the SEALS?'

He looked at her in genuine surprise.

'No, Dr. Johnson. You know why I'm doing this. Please, let's not argue about that any more, Dr. Johnson.'

She had blown it, dragging that last question in by the scruff of its neck.

'Please call me Elizabeth.'

He looked shy. 'Okay.'

She took a sip of whisky. 'Tell me about birds, Davey. How do you explain that? Can you call them out of the trees every time?'

He looked relieved at the change of subject. 'Provided there's nothing unhappy or dangerous happening on the ground. But I've never tried to train birds. Let them be birds. They're quite hard to train. They've got very small brains. They've never evolved a very high degree of intelligence because they could always fly away from their problems.'

She muttered, 'Maybe the same applies to airline pilots.'

He was puzzled. 'Why?'

'I married one. He was always flying away from his problems.'

He looked amused.

'I'm sorry,' he said.

'Don't be. I'm over it.' She added wryly, 'Can't you tell?'

He smiled, then ventured: 'Were you his problem?'

'Me? No. I mean, I suppose I must have been, or he wouldn't have left me. But I adored the man, let him do as he liked.

Except I didn't know he was bedding everything in sight on his stopovers. That shows what a dumb-dumb I am.'

He straightened his face apologetically. 'Where is he now?'

'Back home in England. London.' She added, 'Living with a nice blonde with black roots. In *our* house.'

'Shouldn't you have gotten the house?'

She took a sip of her drink and stubbed out her cigarette vigorously. 'I could have. All kinds of alimony too.'

'And you don't?'

She lit another cigarette.

'If he doesn't want me anymore, I don't want his money, Davey. I'm not going to be bought off; I earn my own living.'

He nodded sympathetically. 'Do you have any children?'

She felt the sadness sweep over her all over again. 'No. I really wanted to, but . . .' She stopped. 'Just as well, I suppose.' She tried to be brightly philosophical. 'Besides, there're enough mouths on the Earth, aren't there?'

'Right,' he said.

She stared into the fire, then sighed and pulled herself firmly back out of the past. 'How did we get into this? Let's get back to the birds.' She ran her hand through her hair. 'How do you account for it—people like you?' She sloshed some more whisky into her cup.

'It's a gift,' he said finally. He shrugged slightly. 'You've got to have love. And confidence.'

'What about magnetism?'

He smiled shyly. 'Okay. I guess that's the gift. But I mean it's also an . . . intellectual thing . . . to be able to *think* like that little bird. To . . . almost be a bird yourself, for the time being. But you've got to work at that.'

'Go on. Please.'

He sighed uncomfortably. 'You've got to *know* birds . . . study them. Then you begin to understand what's going on in their little heads. Then you can think the same way.' He smiled at her. 'But you're better at it than them, aren't you, because you've got a better brain. So, because you're superior, the birds are attracted to you even more. But first you've got to really *love* that little bird. Really want his love. And be confident you'll get it . . .'

She nodded earnestly. 'And with higher animals?'

He fed a twig into the fire. 'The same. Except that it's easier, because they're much more intelligent. And with these animals here, especially the circus ones, it's very easy, really. They understand complicated commands. But you've got to be able to get inside Rajah's *head*, to understand what's going on in there. Then you can think like an elephant.' He paused and sighed. 'But *confidence* . . .' He clenched his fist in emphasis. 'That's so important. People make such a mystery about it. Even you,' he glanced at her apologetically, 'a vet . . . You've got no confidence in yourself to do the same thing.' He looked at her. 'Have you?'

She felt like a student again. Yet there was nothing professional in his manner. She was just in the presence of . . . a maestro. He was simply telling her, because he knew she really wanted to know.

He spoke to the fire. 'So you've got to think positively. It's . . . will power. To reach into that animal's mind. His heart. To communicate with him.'

'Telepathy?'

He nodded absently. 'Yes . . . two people can do it together. Especially if it's someone you love. But our minds are stronger than animals', aren't they? So you've got to use it . . . projecting your thoughts. Most animals are very sensitive to this kind of thing.'

She nodded earnestly. He fiddled with a twig.

'They've got extra senses that we hardly know about, haven't they? Like how migratory birds navigate across continents and oceans to the same spot every year. How dolphins and whales echo-locate. They can tell each other's emotions with a kind of x-ray. Can hear each other hundreds of miles away. We haven't begun to understand these extra senses, because we haven't got them. But you've got to have confidence in yourself. And you've got to have love.'

She breathed deep. 'And the gift.'

She was fascinated. But she believed he was underestimating his gift. She could almost feel his gentle, simple magnetism as he talked. He went on quietly, almost as if to himself. 'Animals are usually very willing to cooperate with you. *If* they understand. If you're trustworthy. It's not so difficult to understand them. We're very alike.' Then he shook his head. 'No. It's us who are like *them*. We're all part of the same animal kingdom, aren't we?'

She nodded.

'So we have many of the same characteristics. Like trust. Cooperation. When you trust someone, you'll follow them, take their advice. People think animals are entirely different. But most animals are quite prepared to be cooperative if you give them the chance.'

She almost felt foolish asking, but she had to put it to him. 'But can you ... I mean, you can't actually *talk* to them, can you? As such.'

He smiled at the fire. He had often been asked that question.

'Not talk. I can only make some of their own noises they understand. And signals, and some words they've learned. But people and animals can understand each other well if they try. I was up in Canada once. Right up in the tundra. Some of the Eskimos there could understand wolf wails. They'd hear a wolf howl, and say to me, "Three caribou are coming." And sure enough, three would come. Not two. Or four. But three.' He glanced at her. 'Or they would listen to the wolf and then say. "A man and a woman are coming this way." And they would come. Not two men—a man and a woman.'

She was rapt.

'Could you understand the wolves?'

'Eventually. The Eskimos taught me.'

'Is that where you got Sam?'

Sam pricked up his ears at his name. Davey put his hand on his head affectionately. 'Yes. His mother was a Huskie. They let her mate with a wolf.'

'He's beautiful.' She asked, 'What were you doing up there?'

'Just looking around. The Canadian Government was poisoning the wolves.'

'Why?'

'Because they said that the wolves were hunting the caribou, and the Eskimos need the caribou for food.' He snorted softly. 'Wolves don't. They eat mice and rabbits. I watched them. They only occasionally killed a caribou that was sick. Or old.'

Though he spoke softly his tone was bitter, and she felt for a moment that he regarded her as one of the heartless foolish establishment that drove him to despair.

'Man will think up every excuse to justify killing every creature he possibly can. Even the American wild mustang, Dr. Johnson. Even the poor old black bear who grubs around our rubbish dumps. The day the season opens the hunters are there in their cars, with their wives and kiddies and picnic lunches. Waiting for the Game Ranger to officially declare the season open at the stroke of noon. Do you know that?'

She shook her head. She was put out a bit by his change of tone, but she was not going to argue.

'Go up to Copper Arbor in Michigan, and you'll see the hunters at the rubbish dumps every year. Men *enjoy* killing ... Bullfights. Cockfights. The Bunny Hop, in Harmony, North Carolina—have you heard of that? Every year the whole town turns out to club a dozen rabbits to death in a field. And all these American ranches where hunters hide behind a blind with their whisky bottles and kill a lion or a buck that was sold by zoos as "surplus stock." And it's legal. Haven't you heard of "coon-on-a-log"? That's a famous American sport. A poor little raccoon is chained to a log and set out into a pond? Then hunting dogs are sent after it, to see how many dogs the raccoon can beat off before the dogs kill it?'

He sat back and stared into the fire. Then he spread his hands. 'If a friendly little thing like a raccoon can expect no mercy, what chance has the wolf got?' He sighed sadly. 'As a result there are only about five hundred wolves left in the whole of America.' He added bitterly, 'But the agriculture department will tell you they're a threat to the whole sheep industry and should be destroyed too.'

Yes ... she felt the same impotent anger at the selfishness and cruelty of her fellow man. But she wanted to get the happy mood back.

'Please don't think I approve, Davey.' She added, 'Please carry on. About talking to animals.'

But the mood was broken. He seemed to have retreated into his private self. He muttered. 'I'm the only friend those animals had in that circus. And in the zoo.'

She had to argue that one. 'In the zoo they had plenty of friendly treatment, Davey. Especially from the keepers.'

'Are you kidding?'

'I am not.'

He shook his head. 'That's not what I mean, Dr. Johnson. The keepers didn't maltreat them. Sure. But the keepers weren't *friendly* in the way the animals want a friend. They didn't go into the cages and play with them and pet them; the keepers weren't ... fellow creatures. Just jail guards.'

She took a breath. Then she decided to let the remark go. 'And the circus animals? Was Frank Hunt cruel?'

'You know how they train animals. That's why he's afraid of them. He doesn't dare go into that ring without somebody riding shotgun for him.'

'Would the lions attack him?'

'What would you do if you were one of those lions, Dr. Johnson? Kept in a cage all your life. Only let out to do your tricks. By a man who cracks the whip at you. And you're frightened of him all the time. And you know he's terrified of you. And that's the way you live. *For the rest of your life.*'

He looked at her for a long moment. Then he frowned. 'And it's just as bad for your zoo animals, Dr. Johnson. I know you disagree, but ...' He gave up and sat back, and stirred the fire. 'I'm sorry, Dr. Johnson, but ... that's why I can't understand you. You're a real animal lover, I can tell. So how can you want these animals to be put back in their cages?'

Elizabeth suddenly felt completely sober. She was also seething with indignation because he equated her animals' conditions to a circus. But, this was good—he had opened up the subject he had declared closed. She lit a cigarette.

'Davey,' she said, 'I won't debate the obvious merits of zoos. Except to say that they're *vital* ... to educate the public. And to conserve endangered species. Though I agree there is a great deal of room for improvement in most. But'—she looked at him earnestly, her eyes imploring—'to release these animals in the Great Smoky Mountains of the United States of America is *wrong*. For three basic reasons ... One'—she held up a finger—'because they won't be able to fend for themselves. And second, because they'll be hunted. And thirdly because these are dangerous animals, Davey ... They *are!* The Smokies have ten million tourists every year. There're a dozen towns sprinkled all around it.' She clenched her fist. 'The Great Smoky Mountains, in the heart of America, is simply *not* a suitable place for lions, tigers, grizzly bears, and elephants!' She closed her eyes. 'Oh, Davey, there're better ways of getting the animals' conditions improved. Legal ways . . .' She ended ardently. 'I *beg* you to use your wonderful talents *legally*. Correctly . . .'

He had listened to her, patiently staring at the fire.

'You're wrong about those three things, Dr. Johnson. The Great Smoky Mountains is a beautiful place for all these animals. There's plenty of food. The climate is fine for all of them. There're different climates here, from subtropical to Canadian. There used to be all kinds of animals in the Smokies a hundred years ago—including the mountain lion and the grizzly bear. There used to be lions in Europe—*and* elephants. The climate's fine. And they will *not* be dangerous to people, unless people interfere with them.' He spread his hands. 'The game parks aren't fenced in Africa, Dr. Johnson. Millions of tourists go through them every year. . . . People aren't allowed to hunt in the Smokies anyway; so why should they be allowed to now?' He held up his hand to silence her. 'The rangers will stop them, once the Government has to accept that the animals are here to stay and that they can't get them out without killing them. There will be a public outcry against *that*.' She opened her mouth again to argue, but he went on resolutely. 'All these animals will survive perfectly well, Dr. Johnson. The lions will learn to hunt when they're hungry.'

She said fervently, 'I wish I believed all that, Davey Jordan . . . I could forgive you everything if I believed all that.'

'I'm not asking anybody's forgiveness, Dr. Johnson.'

She cried, 'But how the *hell* do you think you're going to get away with it? That's what I'm begging you to consider. The government just won't stand for it. Let alone the American public. They'll be terrified to think of lions and tigers in their midst. Let alone Jonas Ford wanting his animals back—and the bloody circus. Let alone the gleeful American hunters dying to blood their guns.'

'Dr. Johnson, there'll be a public outcry *for* the animals staying here, I'm convinced of that. That's why I wrote to Eric Bradman and *The New York Times*. It's started working already, you've told me. And I can outwit the government for weeks . . . By the time Jonas Ford gets organized, the public's going to be rooting for us. Writing to their newspapers and congressmen.' He took a deep breath. 'But we won't be alone in the Smokies, Dr. Johnson. We'll have help.'

She stared at him. 'Who?'

'This is my home territory.'

There was a pause. Then she lowered her head. She could feel her dread-filled frustration mounting. She wanted to raise her voice and use her hands.

'I want to say something else, Dr. Johnson. Before we finish ... This is the *only* way to do it, Dr. Johnson, I promise you. You tell me to use my talents legally. How? Write more letters? ...' He shook his head impatiently. 'The only way to end the suffering, to ... do what is right, is to *act*. ... Get into those cages and do what I did. Because all the letters to the newspapers, all the books, all the questions asked in Congress—won't even get those poor animals bigger cages, let alone their freedom. Why? Because Man is lazy, Dr. Johnson. We're so ... self-centred that even if we care about animals we forget about them.' He waved his hand. 'Because animals are remote. We've cut ourselves off from them, with our civilization. We'll forget about them after we've read the letter in the paper because we'll be too busy making money, catching subways, and going to the supermarket and the movies.'

She started to speak but he went on. 'So the only thing to do to stop the cruelty is to *act*, Dr. Johnson. Do it, and face the world. Face the consequences. Because otherwise there'll be all talk and no do. And those animals will live on in their terrible cages forever.' He clenched his fist in frustration. 'Like the only way to stop those Norwegians and Canadians killing the seal pups on the Saint Lawrence every year is to drive them off the ice with a whip. Because talking and pleading has achieved *nothing* to stop the killing, has it? The only way to stop those Russian and Japanese from killing the last of the whales is to sink their factory ships. Because all the United Nations resolutions and boycotts won't stop them. Because they're heartless. The rest of the world won't force them to stop. Man will forget about the whales, because he'll be thinking about himself again. He won't care long enough to do anything.'

He sat back with a frustrated sigh. He went on quietly, bitterly. 'We put up with Idi Amin. Didn't we? Did we *act* to get rid of him?

No . . . we just shook our heads, let his people die. As we tolerated Papa Doc Duvalier in Haiti. We just shook our heads and let him get on with his terrorizing. As the German people tolerated Hitler. As we tolerate the Russians with their . . . Gulag Archipelago it's called, isn't it? We just say isn't it awful, and forget about those people.'

He looked at her, and his eyes narrowed a moment. 'We forget about the horrors of the fur trade—even though we see the fur coats in the store windows every day. Don't we, Dr. Johnson? We know about the agony the animal suffers in the trap . . . taking days to die, wrenching and wrenching at its broken leg. Sometimes even chewing their own legs off, to try to escape. Their hunger and their thirst. Their terror. We know, and some people have campaigns to raise public awareness, as you said. "Real People Wear Fake Furs," et cetera. The government bans the import of the skins of certain animals in danger of extinction. But do we *do* anything to stop the cruelty of the fur trade?'

He shook his head.

'No. We still put on our backs the sufferings of little creatures, that took so long to die.'

He shook his head in wonder.

'Why are we so cruel? We claim to be Christians . . . "And the Lord gave Man dominion over the whole earth." Maybe we'd have been better off as Muslims. If it hadn't been that the Romans were ruling Judea at the time of Christ, maybe we would be. Maybe guys like Marco Polo would have brought back some of the reverence for life of the eastern religions. But the Lord gave us dominion, so we have the right to put every other creature on earth to our use.' His eyes were bright with contempt. 'Women even wear their fur coats to church on Sundays. Do you ever hear a priest preaching about the sin of that?'

Then he astonished her by beginning to recite softly:

'Tis strange how women kneel in Church and pray to God above,
Confess small sins and chant in praise and sing that He is love,
While coats of softly furred things upon their shoulders lie
Of timid things, of tortured things that take so long to die.

She stared, moved.

'Do you hear our churches speaking out against the fur trade?

The most *sinful* trade of all? And you tell me to do my work legally? The law protects the *trappers*. Have you seen their traps?'

She nodded.

'But can you imagine what it feels like? Those steel teeth suddenly cracking through your leg and holding you by your muscles? Can you imagine the agony? And you know what happens after that?'

She closed her eyes and nodded.

'No, you don't, Dr. Johnson. You've never seen the animals in those traps. The bears, the lynx, the foxes, racoons, and otters, with their legs broken through, tugging and wrenching and twisting, have you? Trying to gnaw their legs off to get free . . . for days, until they die of exhaustion and agony and thirst. Can you imagine that kind of death?'

She closed her eyes. He continued remorselessly.

'Every year over twenty-five *million* animals die like that in the United States. And the government encourages it, Dr. Johnson. Publishes a book on trapping hints for youngsters! What chance have animals got when even our wildlife department doesn't see anything wrong with trapping and furs? But *you* tell me to do things *legally*, Dr. Johnson?'

There was nothing in this that Elizabeth could deny. Then he began to recite again:

> The steel jaws clamped and held him fast,
> None marked his fright, none heard his cries,
> His struggles ceased; he lay at last
> With wide, uncomprehending eyes;
> And saw the sky grow dark above,
> And saw the sunset turn to gray,
> And quailed in anguish while he strove
> To gnaw his prisoned leg away.
> Then at last day came from the east.
> But still the steel jaws kept their hold,
> And no one watched the prisoned beast
> But Fear, and Hunger, Thirst and Cold . . .
> Then through the gloom that night came One
> Who set the timid spirit free;
> I know thine anguish, little son;
> So once men held and tortured Me.

He turned to her in the firelight. 'Do we ever hear priests telling us that?'

'No,' she whispered.

'Some people try, and they campaign. Like Eric Bradman. Guys like Cleveland Amory start the Fund for Animals, and even film stars like Doris Day stand up and say that wearing fur coats is awful, and people write to their congressmen. But what happens? Does the government ban furs? No. Because the fur trade is big—a lot of voters. It's much better for twenty-five million animals to be put to a long, slow death every year than for congressmen to lose votes. But do they even ban the leg-hold trap, the cruelest trap ever made? No. Over half of the states in America don't even have laws that say the trapper must visit his traps every forty-eight hours, to put the animal out of its agony. Do you know that, Dr. Johnson? They don't even say *that much* for the animals. And this is *America!*'

His eyes were bright. He sighed, then went on simply.

'It's the same with zoos, Dr. Johnson. Lord—why is it that human beings take pleasure in imprisoning animals? *Pleasure! ...*' he looked at her in wonder ... 'in catching a wild animal, taking it away from its home where it was happy, and shutting it up in a small iron cage where it's miserable. So that other human beings can come to look at it in its awful prison. Why?' He appealed to her, hands spread. 'We're supposed to have laws against cruelty to animals. What could be more cruel? In solitary confinement! We *know* that one of the worst punishments for a prisoner is solitary confinement—because after a few days it drives him up the wall. He goes crazy.' He dropped his hands. '*Why* do we do it, Dr. Johnson? It's like the olden days, when people could pay to go into the lunatic asylums to have fun watching the inmates.'

She started to say something, but he went on.

'The Bronx Zoo ... the famous New York Zoological Society. Two hundred and fifty acres, Dr. Johnson—and the elephants' cage is the size of your bedroom! Because it would cost the Bronx Zoo money to be kind to their prisoners. They spend a fortune building a skyway cable car so people can ride through the air over the zoo, but it's cheaper to let the animals suffer. And besides,' he ended bitterly, 'it's easier for the people if the cages are small, so they haven't got too far to walk to the next one.

'What chance have the animals *got* legally, Dr. Johnson?' He paused, then leaned forward. 'How long will the animals have to wait for us to change the laws?' He shook his head in despair. 'It's taken us two thousand years to work out a . . . *half*-decent Man-to-Man system. How long will it take us to work out a decent Man-to-Animal system?'

He sat back and took a big, weary breath.

'It's got to be done, Dr. Johnson,' he said quietly.

She stared at him and felt her eyes begin to fill. She looked over at the animals, gathered in a big scattered circle about the fire. They were all staring at her, the firelight flickering on their faces, as if they were waiting for her to reply, as if their fate lay in her hands, as if they knew Davey had spoken on behalf of all of them. She felt her heart swell, and she wanted to drop her head and sob, for all the terribly true things that he had said, for all the misery and heart-break of these beautiful animals in their cages: how they were going to feel when they were put back in there after their short, glorious burst of freedom; and the terror of the recapture, the running and the crashing and the dust, the screams, and the blood, and the heartbreak. She saw those beautiful animals clustered anxiously around, and she dreaded what was going to happen. She clenched her fist and cried, 'But Davey—what's going to *happen?*'

Davey's weary face was calm and gentle again, and it seemed that the whole forest was waiting, the animals attentive. When he spoke it was with a soothing firmness that seemed to hang softly in the air, a sweet vision.

'We are going to a valley I know. It's a lovely place, not far from here, in the Smokies, maybe sixty or seventy miles. It's completely remote and self-contained; there're not even any foot trails. The sides are steep, with the most beautiful trees, vines, and ferns, and there're glades and glens. A beautiful little river tumbles down, and there are waterfalls, rapids, pools; the water is crystal clear, and it's full of trout. But at the bottom of the valley is a big lake, and it spreads for miles. The mountains rise up, up . . . And the flowers, and all the time there's the song of birds. Nobody ever goes there, not even the rangers. There's absolutely everything there for the animals to eat. It's a Garden of Eden.'

The tears were running down her face. She wanted to throw her arms wide and take each animal in her arms and tell it that it was beautiful and that she loved it; and that she was sorry. O God, so sorry that they would not have the life in the valley that he was promising them, in the sunshine and the flowers by the rumbling river, but that they had to go back to their cages again, never to smell and feel and see the beautiful wilderness, never to romp and play and rejoice again, and never to see their beloved Davey Jordan again. That men could not allow them to live free, that they were so terrified of them they would not let them live uncaged, that these mountains were set aside by men for people to enjoy, not for elephants, lions, tigers, chimps, and gorillas, and grizzly bears, not even one old hippopotamus; and besides they had no right to be free because they were all the property of other people. O God, God, she was so sorry, and so ashamed, and her heart was breaking and her mind was torn with confusion.

She wanted to spread her hands in appeal and cry it out loud; but she only whispered, 'They're coming for you, Davey. For *all* of you. For God's sake, Davey, I've seen the hunters. I've seen the type of brutes they are. At Devils Fork and in Erwin . . . And what about those other men who descended at Devils Fork? O God!' She stared at him, tear stained. 'Where do you think they are now? How long before *they* come back? . . .'

# thirty-eight

Dawn spread across the mountainous treetopped horizon, making silhouettes of the animals shuffling along the high Appalachian Trail. And coming in the opposite direction were the silhouettes of two men.

Both carried bedrolls and knapsacks. The first was about fifty years old, gray haired, with hooded eyes in a square, intelligent face, and he strode along the trail with the confidence of a man in his own element. His name was Thomas Underwood, and he was partly

Indian. Down in the pretty little Indian town of Cherokee he owned a prosperous store called The Medicine Man.

The man behind him was almost seventy years old, but he too walked easily along the high rough trail. He was tall and carried himself with dignity. He had a hooked nose, and the skin was stretched tight across his broad-boned face; his eyes were wise. His name was Nathaniel Owle, and he was the elected chief of the Eastern Cherokees.

Davey Jordan and Tom Underwood each lengthened their stride when they saw each other, and they hugged when they met.

'There he is,' Tom Underwood was beaming. 'There you are, Davey!'

The sun was tinging the bulbous clouds, shafting between the mountaintops down into the misty valley. A little fire had been built in the middle of the trail on the ridge of the Great Smoky Mountains, a tin can simmered. A hundred yards away the animals rested in a long ragged line, and Elizabeth sat beyond them. The four men were cross-legged around the small fire. They were waiting for Chief Owle to speak.

When he did, it was with a slow judicial clarity and the dignity of a wise man who was accustomed to being listened to. He spoke in English.

'I would prefer to speak in Cherokee—not because it's more expressive, but because of the remarkable occasion. After all, it is the language of these mountains. Not enough of our people speak it today. Nor even know the alphabet that Sequoyah gave us. This is a grave pity. Our language is about the only heritage left to us.' He paused a long moment, then said regretfully, 'We have taken the white man's ways as thoroughly as he took our lands—and our lives, and finally our dignity.' He paused. 'It's important to recall these things this morning, when considering this remarkable request. I am not harking back unnecessarily when I repeat, *The white man stole our lands and our lives. And finally our dignity as well.*'

He stared out over the cloud tops. After a moment he went on. 'But history is written. Four thousand of our people died on that dreadful Trail of Tears. Only a handful of our grandparents managed to hide so deep in these mountains that the troops could not find them. Only that little tract of land down there is what remains to us of our vast domain.' He turned his head and looked at them. 'And this, my friends, was only yesterday: only in my grandfather's day. Yet all across this mighty land of America, there are white men who owe their wealth to their inheritance from their fathers, and from their fathers' fathers, and even fron *their* fathers before them. The right of ownership is sacred under American laws; why is it that they did not apply the same sacred laws to us? I find this very puzzling.'

No one moved.

'So, now I am chief over a handful of people who have no birthrights as white Americans do, as do members of every other race of man who has been allowed under American laws to descend upon our shores and seek their fortunes, and to pass those fortunes on to their sons, since the days of the Pilgrim fathers. A tiny nation of store owners is what we have become. We cannot enter our own mountains except as tourists. And now, to my astonishment, a white man has come to us, bringing magnificent animals—but as a fugitive from the very American laws that stole our land, that impoverished us ... that made *us* fugitives in our own mountains. And you ask me for help.'

He turned slowly to Davey, and for an instant a twinkle entered his eye.

'You're a clever man, Davey Jordan. I remember you, better than you remember me, I'm sure. I remember you as a boy, riding that pony of yours over from Bryson to Cherokee, barefoot and without even a bridle. We all marveled at that, how you could control a pony without even a bridle. It used to follow you around like a dog when you dismounted at Charlie Buffalohorn's house. And that pony used to gallop like the wind. You were asked how you did it, and you said that the pony was your friend. You always had a dozen dogs following you.

'And I remember the way you could handle snakes, and birds.' He smiled. 'Once there was a black bear kept in a cage for the tourists to see, you remember?' His old eyes twinkled again. 'So one night you and Charlie snipped the wires and let it free. And there was a great deal of trouble, and you finally had to pay twenty-five dollars compensation to old Eberhard Ross for his bear, plus you had to ride your pony bareback and bridleless in front of his store every weekend for a whole summer to attract the tourists. We all thought you were a funny boy, but then your father was Birdie Jordan, and we said, "like father, like son." We said he had the gift of tongues of the animals.' He smiled. 'We had a joke about your family, in Cherokee: One day your mother complained to your father about the smell all the animals caused in her house. Your father said, "Why don't you open the windows?" And your mother replied. "What? And let all those birds come in?" '

All four men smiled, and Davey felt his eyes burn, remembering his father.

'So you have inherited your father's gifts. And more. But that is not why I say you are clever.' He paused and looked at him. 'You are clever because you did not come to me first, before you stole these animals, to ask for my help. If you had, I would have thought that you were crazy, and told you so. I would not have believed that you could do it, anyway. And as a chief, I would have told you not to break the law ... Instead you told only Tom Underwood, knowing what a trouble-shooter he is, a born daredevil and woodsman from way back who would gleefully plead your cause.' He smiled. 'And he has done so, with great eloquence. He has got the whole of Cherokee on your side—as Eric Bradman seems to have got half of America on your side. You seem to have captured the heart of the world.' He looked at him, with amusement. 'Now you have presented me with this extraordinary feat before you ask for help.'

He paused. They waited.

'You have asked for men, to help you foil the government's attempts at recapturing these animals.' He looked out over the mountains. 'I cannot do this for you, Davey.'

They all stared at him. He turned slowly back to Davey.

'As chief of the Eastern Cherokee Nation I cannot be an accomplice to your crime. I must abide by the laws. Nor do I have a mandate from our Council of Representatives to help you.' He looked at him wisely. 'That is the chief of the Eastern Cherokees speaking. Remember I said that.'

Davey nodded earnestly.

'But as Nathaniel Owle, store keeper in Cherokee, I say this: you shall have all the help I can muster as an individual.'

A smile twitched at the corners of his mouth. The others were smiling widely.

'And, as chief, I promise you this: I shall raise my voice loud. I shall go myself to Washington, if necessary, to plead with the president to let those animals be . . . to re-create, in this small corner of the world, something of the glorious freedom that these magnificent mountains used to have.' He paused, then shook his head. 'It would be a wonderful symbol! A gesture . . . of generosity of spirit. Of compassion. Of human kindness. I think it would be wonderful to have these animals living in our mountains. And in some way it would partially compensate us for the rights we were denied. . . .'

# part nine

## thirty-nine

The British Airways terminal at John F. Kennedy airport was jammed with thousands of people. Journalists and television men from all over the world had come to witness the arrival of Stephen Leigh-Forsythe from Africa. Crowds overflowed onto the sidewalk and the road; there was chanting and singing; a roar of voices and a mass of placards bobbed above the heads. The atmosphere was electric with a kind of derisive festivity.

People seemed divided into two main camps: the antizooers who were hostile to the man coming from Africa, and the other camp equally hostile to them. Both sides carried posters—'Zoos are Concentration Camps,' 'Put the People in the Zoos,' 'God, not Man, made the World,' 'Davey Jordan the Liberator'; and 'Releasing Zoo Animals is Cruel,' 'Everything in its Proper Place,' 'Davey Jordan is a Monster,' 'People and Animals Make Bad Bedfellows,' and even 'God gave Man Dominion over the Animals, *Genesis*, Chapter One.'

These two public tempers had spread across America. Street demonstrations had spread like a rash: outside zoos; outside pet shops that sold imported animals; outside animal dealers' offices, hunting-equipment stores; outside offices of magazines such as *Fur Age Weekly*, *Shooting Times*, and *Field & Stream*; and particularly outside stores that sold furs. Indeed, a fur fashion parade held at Saks had been interrupted by egg-throwing demonstrators, and as a consequence another show was canceled at Bloomingdale's. Bricks were thrown through the windows of the two largest furriers in New York. In Washington there had been renewed demonstrations outside the Japanese and Russian embassies, protesting against their whaling, and outside the Canadian and Norwegian embassies, protesting their annual slaughter of seal pups.

There were guitars, and singing swelled through the crowded concourse of JFK, and the rhythmic clapping of hands to a new popular ballad called 'The Great Free Smoky Mountains.'

Stephen Leigh-Forsythe came into the crowded VIP lounge where Professor Jonas Ford was waiting for him, and a barrage of cameras flashed.

Whatever the newsmen had been expecting they were surprised. For instead of a Stewart Granger figure in a leopard-skin banded hat, or perhaps a hard-bitten John Wayne type, they saw a fresh-faced man in his mid-thirties, with unruly blond hair. His face was tanned, but not etched with signs of a rugged life. It was almost boyish. Altogether he looked disarmingly charming. He was slightly above average height, dressed in a neat but functional khaki safari suit. He did indeed have a leopard-skin banded hat, but he carried it politely and it looked functional and well-worn. He was followed by four Africans in their best go-to-town clothes. Beside Forsythe walked a portly, gray-haired American in a sober business suit, who had obviously taken control. The press were held back a few yards by a rope cordon.

'Professor Ford? How do you do?' He grasped the bewildered Ford's hand. 'I'm Marvin Isaacs of the Trans-Continental Literary Agency here in New York, and I represent Mr. Stephen Leigh-Forsythe. Mr. Forsythe, this is Professor Jonas Ford.'

Forsythe shook hands with an open smile. 'How do you do?' Ford shoved his glasses up on his nose.

'I'm afraid I don't understand. Why does Mr. Forsythe have a literary agent?'

'I flew out to Kenya to offer Mr. Forsythe my services,' Isaacs explained. 'I will be negotiating all his literary, film, television and related contracts arising out of his agreement with the government to recapture these animals ...'

222

Ford was astonished. 'Now look here,' he began, 'we're not turning this thing into a circus . . .'

'Of course not,' Forsythe said quietly.

'Of course not,' Isaacs confirmed soothingly. 'But Mr. Forsythe is perfectly entitled to write a book afterwards, and I have persuaded him to do so.'

Ford was incredulous.

'Now look here! I'll have you know that I've been approached by half a dozen newspapers and publishers, offering me large sums of money to write books and stories about this—and I've sent them all packing! I refused to profiteer in this tragedy. And I'm damned if I'll let you turn it into some kind of Hollywood spectacular . . .'

'After the operation is finished,' Marvin Isaacs broke in, 'my client is perfectly entitled to write a perfectly honest historical account, Professor Ford. *Afterwards* . . .'

Ford glared at Isaacs. Forsythe looked above the dispute, but he was embarrassed.

'Well,' Ford said gruffly, 'until then he has a very important and demanding job to do—for which he is being exceedingly well paid.'

'And quite properly so,' Marvin Isaacs said coolly.

'Well . . .' Ford cleared his throat. 'Welcome to America. Let's get out of here. We've got a conference with the wildlife department tonight. After that we fly straight on to the Smokies. I've already set up a camp on the edge of the mountains. I want to start work first thing tomorrow morning.'

'I would like,' Forsythe said quietly, 'a decent night's sleep. So would my men.'

Ford blinked. 'All right,' he conceded. 'Of course. We'll get the briefing with the wildlife people over with straight away.' He switched subject. 'Can you tell us how many helicopters you'll want?'

'Helicopters?' Forsythe smiled. 'One. Just for lifting.'

'Very well. We've arranged for three.'

'Send the others back.'

'Anything else? Guns, for instance?'

'I've brought my own.'

'Very well.' Ford patted his hip pocket. 'Let's go . . .'

'May I introduce you to my men?' Forsythe suggested.

223

'Can that wait? All these damn press people here . . .' He glanced at his watch.

Forsythe said quietly, 'My men would appreciate it. Professor. They're rather formal with strangers, and they've come a long way.'

Ford cleared his throat again.

'Of course. How do you do?' He nodded at the black men.

Forsythe turned and spoke in Swahili. The first African came forward, beaming shyly.

'Jambo, America.'

The cameras flashed.

'He says, "Greetings, America." ' Forsythe was determined to take his time. He spoke Swahili again, and the African beamed shyly. 'My name is Ben-i Majuju. I am-i the chief tracker.'

'Ben Majuju is one of the best trackers in the world, in my opinion, Professor. He has eyes like the proverbial eagle, and he can smell animals long before he sees them.'

'How do you do?' Ford said. Another African stepped forward grinning from ear to ear. 'This is Mr. Mpondo, or Sixpence. He is also a first-class tracker. He is a "Flanker," which means that he is a sharp-shooter—he walks on my flank, to protect us from ambush by dangerous animals.'

'How do you do?' Ford said again.

The third African stepped forward. He was six feet and eight inches tall, and he was unsmiling. He spoke in Swahili and Forsythe translated: ' "Jambo. I do not speak English. My name is Samson. I am a flanker too. I am Maasai." ' Samson nodded curtly, then stepped backward. Forsythe explained. 'The Maasai are a nation of cattle herders and warriors. A Maasai boy has to kill a lion, with a spear, single-handed, before he is elevated into manhood.' Marvin Isaacs whispered something; Forsythe nodded and said, 'Samson has killed seven lions with a spear.'

'How do you do?'

There was a murmur from the reporters who heard. The last African stepped up to Ford. He was tubby, round-faced and beaming.

'Jambo! My name is-i Gasoline Ndhlovu. I am-i the cooker-boy, but-i I can also do everything-i.' He burst into giggles.

Forsythe grinned. 'Gasoline *can* do everybody else's job, too,

Professor. But an army marches on its stomach and a good cook's important.'

'How do you do?' Ford was becoming impatient. 'Well, let's go, we've lots to do . . .'

'Professor,' Isaacs said, 'I think that the ladies and gentlemen of the press would like to meet Mr. Forsythe . . .'

Ford glared at him and touched his glasses irritably.

'Look,' he said, 'there're plenty of pressmen down in Cherokee, if that's what you want, too damn many for my liking!' He tapped his watch. 'This is the taxpayers' money we're spending . . .'

Then I think,' Isaacs said firmly, 'that the taxpayer would like to see the man they're getting for their money.'


# forty


Sheriff Lonnogan did keep his county clean, as his election posters said. The out-of-town rowdies passed through pretty damn quick, and if they stopped for longer than it takes to fill up with gas they had Sheriff Lonnogan chewing gum in their ears. The sheriff had a favorite line for them, which was also one of his election slogans: *'Man hunting is the best sport I know.'*

Which had not sounded too good when they had unmanacled him on the banks of the river. Sheriff Lonnogan had been shaking with outrage when he met the folks of Hawkstown in his office. 'I had them all trapped right there in the river, cut off on both sides, under the gun!—Which is a hell of a lot more than Professor Ford with the whole goddamn national guard ever managed to do, ain't it? And I could have shot that injun in the leg for resistin' lawful arrest, but I ain't no cold-blooded gunslinger. And then he attacks me, and still I would've got him, except that sumbitch Jordan comes sneakin' up and clubs me from behind. That can happen to *anybody*. I ain't got eyes at the back of my head!'

The local newspapers printed it sympathetically, but there had been a lot of sniggering. Worst of all had been Eric Bradman's television footage of the episode: the famous Bradman, tongue in cheek, earnestly questioning the sheriff who was uncomfortably lashed back-to-back with his fat son while somebody laboriously cut through his handcuffs with a hacksaw. And now, to add insult to injury, he had to watch Stephen Leigh-Forsythe on television. Lonnogan sat in silence with a face like thunder while his posse heckled the screen.

'Whatya mean, everybody got to keep out the Smokies?' Jeb Wiggins demanded. 'Who the hell is this guy? Is he a duly-sworn law-enforcement officer? Has he suddenly been sworn-in as a deputy?'

They were gathered in Fred Wiggins's *You-Bust-'em-We-Buy-'em Scrapyard*.

'Well, we are,' Jeb tapped his chest. 'And until I'm constitution-ally suspended from my duties I'm here to tell y'all that I'm going to do my duty of keeping this county clean. And that means I'm going to arrest and bring to trial all people who steal animals and firearms, and assault officers of the law. Has this kid'—he jabbed his finger at Stephen Leigh-Forsythe on the screen—'got a warrant of arrest?'

Lonnogan said nothing.

'He don't say so,' Deputy Sheriff Kid Lonnogan said.

Jeb exploded: 'But he says he's gonna capture Davey Jordan! Who the hell is he to tell the police to keep out of the case when he ain't even got a warrant? What does he think he's going to do? Make a citizen's arrest? He ain't even a citizen! He's a goddamn English-man or somethin'. Or has he suddenly gotten himself deputized all in the five minutes he's been in the USA?'

'Look at him.' Jeb glared at the screen. 'Fifteen years old. Look at that grinning kid, can't hardly even speak his own language, like his mouth's full of doughnut or somethin'. Listen to him!' He listened aggressively, then exploded. 'Niggers! A bunch of illiterate niggers—and he's tellin' us to keep outa our own goddamn case!'

'Switch that thing off,' Lonnogan said.

Fred Wiggins hastily snapped the switch. Sixpence Mpondo disappeared with a gurgle. Lonnogan stared at the blank screen. His men waited. They had never seen him so quiet. At last he said softly, 'A kid from South Africa an' a bunch of niggers going to tell

226

me to keep out of my own case in my own terri-tory?' He stood up slowly and looked at them; then he wagged his big finger. 'Well, I'm tellin' y'all that I'm goin' in there. And y'all comin' with me as my posse. I don' care what the president himself says, *I'm* not havin' officers of the law assaulted, or lions and tigers and then grizzly bears terrorizin' the folks near *my* county.'

There was a loud murmur of agreement.

'But this time,' he said grimly, 'we's goin' to be organized. Deputize more men. ... Fred—you go'n get Bert Waller an' Turkey-George and tell 'em we hittin' the trail day after tomorrow, sunrise. Jeb—get your ass over to Cherokee and tell that Chief Owle we want a couple of his Injun trackers chop-chop.'

'What about dogs, Pa?' Kid Lonnogan said excitedly.

'No, son,' Sheriff Lonnogan said, 'hound dogs'll go yappin' and barkin' when they pick up the scent an' have Davey Jordan runnin' for dear life.'

He breathed murderously deep. 'Man huntin' is the best sport I know ...'


That night three men met in Sylva, North Carolina.

The meeting was held in the den of one of their houses. It was opulently furnished in leather. A gun rack held a dozen rifles, and more rifles and pistols were mounted on the walls. There were also framed photographs, all of hunting scenes: a man leaning out of a low-flying helicopter aiming at a pack of fleeing wolves; the same man standing beside a slain lion, his foot on the animal's head; a polar bear floating in an icy pond, blood flooding from its head. The lion's head was mounted on the wall above the bar; the wolf and bear stood in the corner. There were also two big elephant tusks; a hollowed-out elephant's foot served as a wastebasket; another stood upon the bar, fashioned into an ice-bucket. Next to the ice-bucket stood a glass jar of neat alcohol, and in it lay a human finger. There were many other trophies, including a zebra's head, a buffalo's, half a dozen species of buck, and zebra and lion skins on the floor. Resting on top of the skins was a large wooden frame, and stretched tight across it, treated with chemicals and still drying, was the striped skin of Mama, the zoo tigress. Her head rested on a piece of plastic, and there were several tubes of plastic filler, with which the men had been carefully patching up her bullet holes. But now they were watching the video tape of Forsythe's television interview.

When it ended, one man said, 'Well . . . what d'you think? . . .'

Their host poured more whiskey into his glass. He began to pace the floor.

'This ain't Africa,' he said quietly. 'He doesn't know those mountains. It'll take him months. It's not going to be nearly as easy for that guy as he thinks. It'll take him a long time. Meanwhile, all those animals are up for grabs. With every fool and his dog going in there with their goddamn guns.'

'So? When do you reckon we go in?'

The first man clasped his hands behind his back as he paced.

'Not yet. If we get caught the judge could be tough right now. There's a lot of starry-eyed nonsense going on. And business could suffer too. I say we let this guy Forsythe fail first. *And* he will.'

'But if we wait, every one else will go in, like you said, and get them before us. Then we'll miss out. Or all the best ones, anyway.'

'No, let him make a few mistakes. Then the public will be more on our side if we're caught. We could say that we only went in to protect the public because this guy's screwing it up. *We'd* be the do-gooders then. That would even be good for business.'

'But all the best ones may be gone by then!'

'None of these local hicks have got the experience we've got.' He smirked and jerked his head at the finger in the jar. 'Like this fink, here.' He smiled, picked up the jar and admired its contents. 'If Forsythe's not going to find those critters in a hurry, those slobs won't either.'

'An accident might happen,' the third man mused. 'Somebody gets gored. Or attacked by a lion. Then we'd be goddamn heroes.'

'*That* would be very good for business . . .' The first man smiled.

'Aw . . .' The second man sighed in exasperation. 'Business, business, is that all you guys worry about? We all got good businesses, goddammit, that's why we can go to Africa for hunting—so why we so worried about a little bit of bad publicity in town—*if* we're caught . . . huh? Why should we get caught, anyways? Look, every year we spend a goddamn fortune going places, but this year it comes to our goddamn doorstep. And what do we do? We worry about business and let these local hicks have the fun?

The government's failed, ain't it? And those are dangerous critters.'

'Goddamn dangerous. And they're here illegally.'

'I say give him a week first.'

The second man shook his head. He got up and walked slowly across to Mama, and prodded her snout with his foot.

'She don't really count; we didn't kill her,' he muttered. Then he said 'God-*damn*, I'd like a tiger. . . . Always wanted to go to India. Look good in my bar, huh?'

'They'd all look good. How about a grizzly? To keep this guy company?' The first man indicated the polar bear.

'Listen, we got to be fair about this. We got to throw dice or somethin', to decide who gets what, otherwise it could work out unfair.'

'Sure,' the first man said. 'I'll buy that.'

'And a gorilla,' the second man continued. 'Never even *seen* a gorilla. He'd look good, huh? Goddammit—it must be just like shooting a man . . .'

# forty-one

The Appalachian Trail winds down the very spine of the high ridges of the jumbled mass of the Great Smoky Mountains, through the same tall timber that grows in Canada, through birch forests, lofty hardwoods, and evergreen pines, rhododendron and laurel, and around rocky peaks and crags, and across grassy balds. Sometimes the trail is only a few feet wide, a knife-edge six thousand feet high. Below, way down there, are the vast masses of green blue valleys, mountaintops climbing up out of the smoky haze, vast, stretching on and on, all the way to the horizon.

To Elizabeth those were heartbreakingly beautiful days—because she knew they would end soon. Soon the man from Kenya would arrive, and the terror and the stampeding would start again. This paradise, this fool's paradise, would be over. But right now it was wonderful to know that for today there was going to be no fleeing, no fear. It was wonderful to be walking, unafraid for today at least, across the Great Smoky Mountains heading for the valley that was the Garden of Eden.

The animals knew it too. She could see it in their eyes, in the way they held their bodies. Before crossing the Pigeon she had sensed a common fear among them, a need to stick together and close to Davey Jordan. That was gone now, and from Davey Jordan too. He was as he had been that first day back in the glen, ten days ago: serene, unobtrusive, but *there*, leading them as they ambled along the beautiful Appalachian Trail. Sam had a jauntiness about him she had not seen. Before, he had padded along like a sheepdog, head low, ready to charge off to do his job; now he trotted along, bushy tail high, cheerfully sniffing this and that. When she spoke to him he put his ears back and smiled at her like any other happy dog.

Sometimes a gorilla stopped to grab a handful of greenery and sample it thoughtfully, and Sam did not worry it. Elizabeth could see the elephants' trunks snaking out to feed as they shuffled baggily along, and Dumbo carried all their knapsacks and her doctor's bag as if they were garlands.

He had wanted to carry her again too; he had curled his trunk around the back of her legs and clumsily tried to lift her. He had dumped her on top of the knapsacks, and she had toppled with a shriek to the ground. Dumbo had looked very taken aback, and blinked his eyes rapidly when Davey had rebuked him. 'Oh, don't,' she had laughed, hastening to reassure Dumbo that it was quite all right, that she quite understood.

After that she had insisted on riding him, at least until her bottom and thighs hurt. Riding along the Appalachian Trail astride Dumbo's bristly neck, she could feel his pleasure, that he was no longer a frightened baby elephant. And she could tell that Rajah and Jamba were happy too, just by their huffing gait; she could feel it in the air about her. When she had finally dismounted because her legs were sore, Dumbo had looked crestfallen, frequently looking back at her over his shoulder.

'He's got a crush on you, Doctor,' Big Charlie rumbled.

She knew that was true: it often happened with young male elephants and women. Male elephants are very pampered by their mothers and aunts; Jamba had not yet quite replaced Queenie as his foster-mother, and Dumbo had latched onto her. That was why he was proud to carry the knapsacks: he was showing off, to ingratiate himself with her. And, O God, no, she did not want Dumbo to go back into his cage . . .

She was getting to know all the animals as individuals, and she felt sure most were starting to accept her. Perhaps not the bears, or Jamba. Jamba was clearly still nervous of her, and did not like her being with Dumbo. Similarly, King Kong did not like her approaching Auntie. He glowered at her every time she went near. Tommy looked dangerous too. And poor old Sultan was just plain shy of everybody.

But Kitty . . . Oh, how she loved Kitty! Oh, the thrill of having a lion as a friend!

Well, not exactly a friend, because Kitty was mostly after chocolate: sloping seductively up to her at the campfire with her steamroller blandishments, purring like a lawnmower and trying to look sweet. And when Elizabeth jerked back, Kitty blinked her eyes as if expecting to be smacked on the nose—but the nose was busily twitching, trying to zero in on the whereabouts of goodies; the blinking was an act. Kitty wasn't afraid of anything except missing out on something to eat. Elizabeth would hold out a piece of chocolate, and Kitty's big, rough tongue would slurp it out of her fingers like a vacuum cleaner, with one big lick of the chops afterward. Then, forbidden by Davey, she sat down, curled her tail neatly around her paws, fixed Elizabeth with a penetrating stare, and prepared to wait it out.

One night, Princess got in on the act. Suddenly she came padding purposefully over at her, glowering hopefully, spat at Kitty, then sat down to join the siege. Kitty ignored the intruder, and started purring louder. Then Tommy followed Princess. On the other side of the fire, Sam shot bolt upright, aghast at missing out on any chocolate, but not daring to muscle in. The thrill of it, of having three lions clustered around her expectantly; but the most wonderful part was that Elizabeth had not felt afraid. It was the most liberating of feelings. She was in love with the world. She wanted to hug each one, and feel their furry warmth against her face.

She tossed a piece of chocolate to each lion, and each dashed off in different directions to gobble it. Even though she had made it clear she had no more, Kitty came slinking back and delighted Elizabeth by lying down beside her.

Elizabeth was afraid to move in case she disturbed her. Then Kitty rolled her stomach to the fire and stretched her legs languidly, closed her eyes and began to purr. Quite naturally, Elizabeth placed her hand on Kitty's head and stroked it. Kitty purred and rolled onto her back, paws in the air, and Elizabeth scratched her whiskery chin. And she was unable to resist it any longer, and she lowered her face against the lion's chest, listened to her heart beating, hugged her, and whispered joyfully: 'Oh, Kitty Topcat, I love you ...'

# forty-two

That day Smoky arrived at the Pigeon River.

In the late afternoon he stood on the edge of the forest, looking down onto Highway 40 and the river. His wounded flank was a long swollen lump now, but for the moment he did not feel the pain, in his anxiety.

Smoky's heart sank. He saw how wide was the highway, and beyond it the strong, frothing river, and the bridge. Smoky was not afraid of water itself; but this was the same sort of place where the monster had tried to kill him.

He had not found Sam's scent again after the forest fire, nor the scent of any of the other animals. But he had found the Appalachian Trail, and he had doggedly followed it, only because it was the sort of trail his keeper had been following.

Now, for the same reason, Smoky knew he had to cross the highway and this wide river. Smoky stood there, his big round furry face staring worriedly out of the undergrowth. He knew he had to wait until it was dark, when monsters and men would not see him easily.

At dusk he came down the steep bank toward the highway, the gravel cascading beneath his paws. For one long moment he paused on the edge of the tarmac, his round face raised, nose twitching, and eyes wide; then he rushed.

Smoky galloped across the lanes as fast as his legs would carry him, his claws biting into the surface. He burst onto the bridge and ran and ran; head down, as if hounds were chasing him, and every moment he was expecting the terrible scream of the monster. He did not feel the pain in his side.

Beyond was the steep, black forested mountain. Smoky hurled himself into it and went scrambling, clawing desperately up its side, and his heart was pounding in exhaustion. But he did not stop. On and on Smoky went until he was over a mile up the mountain; then threw himself down to rest.

If Smoky had crossed the river where Davey Jordan had, he would probably have heard Sally croaking in the dark. For that is where she was—staying on the riverbank where she had last seen the animals, hoping and waiting for David Jordan to come back. Maybe, if Smoky had crossed the rapids, she would have seen him and recognized him, and maybe she would have blundered out of the water and followed him. Maybe.

The next morning Smoky found the Appalachian Trail again on the crest of the mountains. He limped painfully up and down the steep and winding footpath, knowing only that perhaps his keeper was at the end of it.

That day Smoky came across a pile of elephant dung on the Trail. He stopped and smelled it. His heart surged.

At about noon that day, Sam suddenly dived off the Trail.

One moment he was happily trotting along; the next he was bounding furiously down the mountainside, the hair standing up on his back. He hurled himself into a bush, then sprang out of it, and his jaws was a possum. He shook his head to kill the little animal; then he flung it into the air so that the brown bundle cartwheeled; then it hit the ground with a thud. Elizabeth came pounding down the slope yelling, 'No, Sam!' Sam crouched over his prey, growling a low warning, looking at her out of the corner of his eye.

The whole caravan of animals had stopped, all surveying the drama below.

'Leave him,' Davey called. 'It's his.'

Sam gulped a better grip on his quarry at the sound of his master's voice.

'But,' she yelled, 'it's a possum! It probably isn't even dead. They just faint from fright.'

'He's dead,' Davey said quietly. 'His neck's snapped.'

'You of all people! What harm's that possum done? It's his wilderness—not Sam's. And this'—she jabbed her finger at the trees—'is a national park. Everything's protected, that's why we're all here, isn't it?'

He said, 'It's Nature, Dr. Johnson.'

'She cried, 'Is Nature always right?'

'Yes, Dr. Johnson, it's pretty much always right.'

'Then hunting's right. And zoos. Because might is right—that's Nature too.'

He said patiently, 'Hunting's only right to fill your belly, not for pleasure. And zoos are for pleasure.'

She yelled, *'Come and save this possum!'*

But Kitty came instead, bounding down the slope, and Sam, who had had his attention on Elizabeth, was taken off guard.

He saw Kitty descending on him, and he spun around with a snarl that came out as a muffled yelp with his mouth full of possum. Kitty bounded to a stop two paces from him, tail flicking, eyes piercing. Sam crouched, heart pounding, trying to snarl convincingly. For a long moment (from Sam's point of view) the two adversaries faced each other dangerously; then, slowly, Sam began to walk backward. Purely out of sensible preservation of his possum against the slings and arrows of outrageous fortune—without surrendering an inch of his dignity—Sam retreated one, two, three, stiff-legged steps, his hair bristling, his wolf eyes bright, and his dog's heart quaking, snarling unsuccessfully through the four pounds of densely furred possum hanging from either side of his face. Kitty stood poised, glaring. Now Sam had widened the distance between them where it would have been only prudent and in no way undignified to consolidate his gains and retreat rapidly with his prize to a place of safety. He was about to turn and bolt for his life when Kitty sprang with an awful roar. Sam fell over himself in mid-turnabout, and he spat out the possum, to face his terrible adversary. Kitty tried to grab the possum, and Sam hurled himself suicidally onto the back of her neck. She was knocked off balance, and they rolled.

They rolled down the mountainside in a furious mess of jaws and fur, amid the yells of Elizabeth, Davey, and Charlie. Mercifully Sam still was on top of Kitty's neck, out of the way of her slashing feet, then he let go and fled. Sam went bounding flat out, back up the mountain, snatched up his possum, and fled across the mountainside, crashing through the undergrowth, his tail between his legs. He took one look over his shoulder, saw Kitty's gaping fangs just behind him, and ran for all his terrified worth—slap bang into a hole. Suddenly his forelegs disappeared, his hindlegs twisted in mid-air, and he lost the possum. Kitty dived for it, Sam picked himself up and hurled himself onto her neck again, and the possum suddenly took to its feet and tottered off.

For he had only fainted, as Elizabeth had suggested; he come around with a terrible headache and sore ribs, and his ears full of the most deafening din. He staggered off under a nearby bush to collect his wits and looked back at the frightful melee taking place over his flesh, remembered what had happened, and took to his heels. He scuttled down the mountain and got the hell out of it.

Meanwhile, back up the mountain, Sam still clung to Kitty's neck with all his desperate might, too terrified to let go because then she would be onto him. Kitty roared and twisted in fury, then Davey was on them both. He flailed his lumber jacket, grabbed Sam by the scruff of his neck, and threw him; he walloped Kitty across the head with the jacket.

Sam landed in the undergrowth, wild-eyed, gave a winded half-bark of defiance and took gratefully to his heels. Kitty dodged around Davey and started after him. But she had lost heart in the battle. Sam was too far ahead, and her bounds turned to a few half-hearted prances; then she gave up.

Elizabeth was holding onto a tree, laughing.

'If Nature's always right, why didn't you let Kitty clean up this possum-eater here? . . .'

That night they crossed the Newfound Gap road, the highway that cuts the Great Smoky Mountains and connects the town of Cherokee, in North Carolina, with the town of Gatlinburg, in Tennessee.

Six Cherokees, friends of Chief Owle, were waiting for them in the forest. They told Davey that the coast was clear; the highway had been sealed off by the government. They had a big knapsack of food supplies and a pig's carcass—plus a bottle of Scotch whisky which Davey had asked Tom Underwood to send as a treat for the doctor.

To Elizabeth, it was a wonderful feeling to cross that highway unafraid, knowing that the Cherokees were protecting them, that no rifle shots were going to crack out. Two Cherokees remained at Newfound Gap to cover their rear and to obliterate their spoor in the morning. Davey and the four other Cherokees led the animals down the short tourist road along the mountains' edge to the Clingmans Dome tower. It was the first time Elizabeth had seen him in such good spirits.

That night, deep in the forest, they had a feast.

The big cats slavered over their pig's carcass, Sam chomped on his share of it (well away from Kitty), a leg of pork roasted over the fire, the elephants rumbled and sighed around, feeding, the bears rooted, and the gorillas scratched their nests together. While the pork spat and sizzled, Davey ceremoniously presented the Scotch to Elizabeth. The grinning Cherokees all applauded her, and for the first time she almost felt like an accomplice.

# forty-three

When she woke up just before dawn, her body telling her that she had drunk too much, the anxiety had come back: *O God, what happens now?* And when?

So, they had made it: extraordinary. Wonderful. But the ghastly fact was that if these animals weren't recaptured immediately they were going to be butchered by the great American hunter, or have war declared on them by the local citizenry such as Sheriff Boots Whatisname in the righteous claim of protecting hearth and home. O God, the blood, and the suffering! The stark fact was, the sooner Mr. Forsythe got himself down here the better, for the animals own sake.

And, oh how awful it was going to be for them . . . having tasted the wilderness. How awful it was going to be just to stand behind bars for the rest of their lives, confused, wondering, with nothing to do but remember and yearn and wait. For what? For death. For Davey Jordan to come back. But he would never come back for them. Because he was going to go to prison for a long, long time . . .

At first light they were on the move again. The four Cherokees stayed behind, painstakingly collecting the animals' dung and putting it into separate plastic bags.

'Are they trying to obliterate our spoor?'

'No,' Big Charlie rumbled. 'Our spoor here is too big.'

'What are they doing, then?'

The big Indian did not answer.

'Charlie?'

'Forget it,' he said apologetically.

'Charlie? . . .'

He kept walking. 'Yes, Dr. Johnson?'

'Please stop a moment.'

He stopped reluctantly and turned to face her.

'Look. You either trust me, or you don't.'

She waited for some response, but there was none.

'Do you trust me or do you not?' she demanded.

He looked at her embarrassed. 'No,' he said at last.

She stared up at him. 'Then all that jolliness around the campfire last night was phoney?'

'Of course we appreciate you, Dr. Johnson. You're our vet.'

'But?'

He took an uneasy breath. 'But you still want those animals back in their cages, don't you?' Before she could answer he put his hand

237

gently on her shoulder. 'That's what you've got to decide, Dr. Johnson.'

He turned away, embarrassed, and hurried to catch up with the animals.

She stared after him. But after ten paces he stopped. He turned around uncertainly and looked back at her.

'They're going to make phony spoor with that dung, Dr. Johnson. They're going to take it back to the other side of New-found Gap, way down into the valley, and spread it around some. Then tell this guy from South Africa where it's at. Then he'll follow a false trail. It probably won't fool him for long, but he'll waste time checking it out. Okay?'

'Thank you,' she said tersely.

He walked on, hurt. Then he tried to make her feel good.

'What we need now is a real good rain. To wash out *all* our spoor.'

After a while, she rode Rajah. The going was difficult, crossing the mountain; she did not ride Dumbo because in his enthusiasm he would not be smart enough to watch out for overhanging branches. Rolling along on Rajah's neck, she could tell he was pleased—maybe it was because he was showing Jamba what he could do. He had curled up his trunk and felt her gently, in a kind of reassuring greeting, and he watched carefully for overhanging branches, maneuvering ponderously around them; she could tell he liked her riding on him and that he was happy with the whole world. Dumbo was jealous and came huffing alongside with his load of knapsacks, to make her pay attention to him, and Elizabeth smiled at him. She did not want to think about what Big Charlie had said, about whether she deserved their trust; if it were true, it was only because of her dread of what lay ahead.

Then the sun came up over the Great Smoky Mountains, and, oh, she did not want to think about the expert from Africa. The sun flamed red across the sky, setting the mountaintops on fire and turning the oceans of cloud mauvy gold; the air was crisp and clean, and the whole world was young and free. She looked at the big broad backs of the animals lumbering so earnestly and trustingly after their shepherd, and she could only think about those lovable creatures and what it must be like to have all the magnificent space after their awful cages. The words kept recurring to her: their Promised Land . . .

*Their Promised Land.* This is how it was in the beginning, before Man came and murdered and raped and plundered. Now new life coming back where life belonged . . .

Maybe she was becoming emotional, but it made her feel young again, strong and full of determination to be fully alive, appreciate to the full these days when life was coming back to the wilderness of America. Her head felt light; her blood was zinging. The whole world was clean and clearly etched.

And *free.* She prayed fiercely to the omniscient, omnipotent, omnipresent God she truly believed in, prayed with all her might— for what? That the man from Africa would fail, that the animals not get caught? For rain, to wash out their spoor? Oh, she didn't even know what she was praying for any more! For peace? For no more blood. For no more terror. That only the right thing would happen? She looked at the beautiful animals lumbering along; they were God's perfect creations, and she knew what was the right thing to happen. He had made them to live free . . .

> *The Lord is my shepherd; I shall not want.*
> *He maketh me to lie down in green pastures . . .*
> *Yea, though I walk through the valley of the shadow of death,*
> *I will fear no evil; for Thou art with me.*

When she prayed she could almost believe that somehow they would escape the skills of the man from Africa, that finally the world would cry out, 'Enough!—let them be!'

And she wanted to pray for rain, to wash out the spoor.

Late the following afternoon Big Charlie pointed it out to her in the distance: a mountain called Thunderhead. Way below it was the valley they called the Garden of Eden.

There was not a cloud in the sky.

# forty-four

The sun began to come up again, lighting up the tips of the multi-fluted mountains and the silent crests of the ocean of cloud, and glinting into Elizabeth's exhausted eyes.

She sat slumped against a tree on the slopes of Thunderhead Mountain, her heart singing. *They had made it.* Way down there, beneath that gold-tipped ocean, was the magic jumble of valleys that David Jordan had promised them.

She sat, her limbs aching. They had been on the march most of the night, and her body wanted to collapse on her back and feel the exhaustion pouring out of her into her mother earth, and sleep. But she also wanted just to sit here and marvel, revel in the wonderful feeling of being at the end of the trail.

Big Charlie came and crouched down beside her.

'Dr. Johnson? It's all downhill from now on . . .'

She heaved up to her feet. She stood for a moment, watching her beautiful animals loping down the slope in the misty sunrise, following the man they trusted into the promised land. Then she started after them, into the early morning shadows of the wilderness, down into the clouds.

She swung down through the steep forest, and she was laughing inside because they had made it. She looked at the animals lumbering down the mountain, blindly trusting and following Davey, and she wanted to throw her arms around their great big animalness and tell them that a beautiful country lay just ahead below those clouds, a wonderful country for an elephant to be an elephant in, and a lion a lion and a bear a bear. She wanted to fling her arms wide to the sky and cry out: *Please keep helping us now. In the name of Love and Pity!*

Then she felt the first drops of rain on her flushed face.

Then, as suddenly, down it came.

The rain came sweeping up the Great Smoky Mountains in great curls and furls, up through the forest to the high rugged crests, obliterating the spoor and washing away their scent.

Elizabeth stood in the rain, her arms held wide and her head tilted back, a laughing smile all over her face.

*O thank God!*

Davey and Big Charlie were plastered wet and grinning. They looked back up at her standing there with her arms outstretched, and they laughed. She looked at them and she laughed too, and there were tears in her eyes.

Sultan and the lions had scattered to shelter beneath the trees; the elephants and the bears stood still, enduring the water beating down on them; the gorillas and chimpanzees all crouched together under one tree, horrified, rain dripping off their miserable faces, soaked, trying to squeeze under each other, quarrelling for the notional shelter. Davey tried not to laugh at them.

'Come.'

The chimpanzees came scrambling, but King Kong and Auntie stared out miserably.

'Come!' He held out his hand.

They didn't move. He had to turn away to smother his smile. He called, 'Sorry, Dr. Johnson, we got to keep going.'

'Where're the lions?'

'They're in the forest, they're all right.'

'But will they follow us through the rain?'

'It doesn't matter if they don't. We're here now. But they'll follow; they're hungry.' He turned to Rajah, standing forlornly behind him. 'This is called rain, Rajah—rain. It's good for you. Makes things grow green.' He gave him a big pat, and started striding on down the mountain, singing as he went.

The elephants and the bears lumbered hurriedly after him, but the gorillas huddled doggedly under their tree, sodden.

They did not want to walk in the rain, but neither did they want to be left behind. Elizabeth was swinging down the mountainside. They clutched each other wetly, wracked by indecision. Then Elizabeth passed out of sight, and King Kong gave a decisive grunt. He started galloping down the steep mountain, the rain beating on his screwed-up face.

Out of the forest came the big cats, springing distastefully through the mud and rain. First big, grumpy Tommy, his tawny hide like a sodden old carpet and his mane bedraggled, trying to dodge the wet bushes and shaking his paws. Then Kitty, as if discharged from a catapult, then Princess, hot after her, and finally Sultan, looking as miserable as sin, soggy and discommoded.

But it was downhill all the way.

Thirty miles beyond Newfound Gap highway, the rain beat down on Smoky bear.

He stood in the middle of the trail, the rain flattening his fur, making him almost look skinny; his brown eyes were gaunt, his black nose twitched desperately at the mud. He couldn't smell the scent any more, only the sharp fresh rain. His left foreleg was bent, and his head pounded with the pain that swelled down his shoulder.

Smoky sniffed at the mud, then slowly, painfully, sat down. He sat, at a loss, enduring the throbbing: then, with a grunt, he painfully shoved himself off the ground, and reared up onto his hindlegs.

He could see nothing but the gray mist of rain, and he could smell nothing.

There was nothing he knew to do, except carry on the way he was going.

Seventy miles away Sheriff Lonnogan and his posse slogged through the rain, heading in completely the wrong direction, collars turned up, doggedly following the Cherokee tracker whom Chief Nathaniel Owle had provided.

They had been following this tracker for almost forty-eight hours, and it was mostly uphill all the way. Lonnogan had dark bags under his red-rimmed eyes and his stubbled face was etched with exhaustion; he could feel the grandfather of all colds coming on.

# forty-five

The bottom of the valley was like a cupped hand, the steep mountain ridges, the fingers, and the valleys the spaces between. A dozen streams came tumbling down, cascading over rocks, bubbling and tinkling, and wandered into a river, crystal clear, with little waterfalls, deep pools, sparkling rapids, and smooth boulders. Along the banks grew ferns and vines, heavy rhododendron, and thick green grass. At the bottom of it all lay blue Fontana Lake, long and jagged, spread-eagled along the edge of the Great Smoky Mountains, with hundreds of bays and inlets reaching into the steep, mountainous forests.

The clouds had disappeared, the sky was blue again, and the sun shone through the treetops in dapples and patches, sparkling on the gurgling water. The earth smelled rich and clean, and the boulders by the rivers felt warm.

An abandoned homesteader's cabin stood a quarter mile up a gentle little valley. It had only one room, with a loft above it. The walls were made of logs, mud stuffed between them, and the roof was made of wood-chip shingles. The door was almost gone, and one corner of the roof had collapsed, but the loft's wooden floor and the fireplace, made of stone and mud, still stood. A stream ran by the cabin and the hillbilly had cleared a pasture, a couple of acres, on both sides of the river. But the forest was reclaiming it, and now thick vegetation grew along the river again. There were the remnants of a wormwood fence paddock, and some hogsties of stone. Once upon a time, there had been a path from the pasture to the cabin, but now trees grew right up to the rotting porch. There had been scrawny chickens scratching about the yard, a barefoot woman to serve the tough hillbilly, and smoke spiraling from the chimney. And now there was smoke again.

She would remember the rest of that day as a dream.

She wanted to sleep, to throw herself down on the friendly earth, but she was too happy to sleep. She wanted to glory in earthiness, feel it between her fingers, feel the grass and the leaves, the sun and crisp warm air on her skin. She wanted to kick off her boots and go running and skipping over the cool green grass, dance through the forest, and sing. She wanted to throw her arms around the animals, and rub her face against theirs and tell them that they were here at last.

But she just had to lie down.

She threw herself down on top of her sleeping bag in the sun outside the cabin, on her stomach, her arms outspread, reveling in the feeling of being at the end of the trail.

She slept.

When she woke, the Garden of Eden was in deep shadow. Smoke was curling from the chimney, and there was the smell of roasting meat. Davey was smiling down at her.

'I'm going to feed the lions, Dr. Johnson. Do you want to come?'

She sat up. She felt groggy, rested, stiff, sore and dirty.

'Where did you get the meat?'

'Charlie shot a boar.'

'Where does he get the strength?'

The boar's carcass was suspended from a rope in a tree near the river. The big cats had found it: they were prowling under the tree, sniffing and licking its dripping blood. Kitty had climbed the tree in desperation and pawed at the carcass, while Princess moaned below, but all Kitty had reached was the rope so the carcass was swinging like a pendulum, while feline heads were turning to and fro, salivating.

Kitty clawed her way down the tree when she saw Davey and Elizabeth, and came bounding excitedly toward them, tail up straight. Sam, who had been following jauntily, turned when he saw her, and retreated to a safe distance to watch. But Kitty only had eyes for Davey and the boar's carcass. Tommy and Princess were pacing about in anticipation, and even Sultan perked up when he saw Davey and came stalking out of the undergrowth, looking moderately optimistic.

Davey unlashed the rope and the carcass thumped to the ground. The lions fell upon it. There was a short sharp roar, and Tommy swiped at Kitty. The lionesses scattered. Tommy got down on his belly, his long tail flicking, put one paw onto the ribs, and sank his teeth. Kitty and Princess slunk back to the carcass, snarling and cringing, and he roared at them again, and they stopped in their tracks, crouched.

After a minute of solitary feeding, Tommy allowed them in to share. They fell on the carcass, snarling for position, and tore into it. But Sultan sat forlornly on the fringe, his eyes intent and saliva drooling. From bitter experience he knew better than to try to muscle his way in yet.

'Let's cut a chunk off for him.'

Davey shook his head absently, watching them. 'He's got to learn.'

'But he's famished.'

'Maybe tomorrow he'll do something about it. Go off and try to fill his gut.'

It seemed so unfair. She watched the tiger sitting hopefully.

'There's nothing unfair about Nature, Elizabeth.'

It was the first time he had called her by her Christian name. And how had he known that she was thinking it was unfair?

'I'll stop feeding them tomorrow. Let them get so hungry they'll want to go out and hunt.'

'But they won't know how.'

'I'll teach them. I'll go tracking some wild boar with them.'

'Supposing they start hunting our other animals?'

'All our animals can look after themselves against a lion.'

'And if they can't the laws of Nature apply? Unless it happens to be Sam who's getting the thin end of the wedge?'

Davey smiled. 'Let's go back to the cabin.'

Elizabeth could see a change in Davey since they had left the Appalachian Trail. Or since the rain. Since they had laughed at each other laughing in the downpour—sharing the relief that their spoor was being obliterated. His face had lost the gauntness. And now, when they got back to the cabin, he almost bowled her over with another act of kindness. He went to his knapsack and came out with a small wrapped box. He looked embarrassed and said, 'I asked Tom Underwood to get you this. Charlie and me. You haven't got many comforts on this job. It was all we could think of.'

She was astonished. He had been carrying this surprise for her for two days, while he treated her so distantly?

She was overwhelmed. She tore off the paper. It was a bottle of lavender water. A bottle of *perfume!* And he had thought to get it especially for her and had carried it as a present for the end of the trail?

'Oh—that's so kind of you!'

'At least it's something you can carry easily to make you feel better.'

'I feel better already.'

'And this . . . to celebrate the end of the trail.'

It was another bottle of whisky.

'Oh, wonderful, Davey. Thank you!' The thoughtfulness brought a burn to her eyes.

He whispered, 'Thank Big Charlie nicely . . .' Then he called, 'Firewater's flowing, Rainmaker . . .'

Wisps of mist were filtering through the trees; the air was soft and still.

They sat in a row on the crumbling porch, Elizabeth in the middle, and solemnly sipped the whisky, watching the gathering dusk and feeling the glow of the liquor, Elizabeth still feeling the glow of their gifts. Yet she felt strangely formal—yet conspiratorial. Or comradely. Big Charlie sat hunched, looking self-consciously inscrutable. Davey sat cross-legged, as serene as a guru, but his eyes were embarrassed when she glanced at him.

The animals were gathering uncertainly around the cabin, getting ready for the night, or ready to move on again, whichever they were told to do, waiting for leadership. The chimpanzees sat about aimlessly. The elephants were shuffling and sighing, trunks wearily plucking leaves, but always with an eye on Davey. The two gorillas sat together, anxiously watching for a signal. Then, at last, they began to scrape leaves into a circle around themselves. 'That's right,' Davey muttered. 'But what's wrong with the trees? That's where gorillas like to make their nests.' King Kong looked at him, hoping for direction. But Davey just smiled. But the most delightful thing about it all was that it no longer seemed extraordinary to Elizabeth to be sitting in the wilderness surrounded by animals. It seemed all perfectly natural. Familiar. She felt she knew them all, what they were thinking and feeling, like a big family. Her body was rested, and there was the delicious knowledge that tomorrow she did not have to run anymore. An end to running . . . And the glow of the whisky in her empty stomach. She almost believed that everything was going to be all right from now on, that Davey Jordan's sweet vision was going to come true. Had it not come true already? ...

Just then the two bears appeared out of the dusk, enormous, shuffling to the security of their keeper, and Davey smiled gently at their big brown eyes and furry dish-faces.

'Hello, bears ...'

He patted them, and then they came snuffling toward Elizabeth, eyes hesitant, ready to back off at the slightest warning. Maybe they could feel the happiness emanating from her, or maybe they thought she might have some chocolate, or maybe it was the lavender water she had dabbed behind her ears, but it was the first time they had shown any friendliness toward her. She sat rock-still, smiling, her heart hammering, and whispered, 'Hello, Winnie. Hello, beautiful Pooh. Come on ...'

Winnie's nose touched her hand, investigating her, then jerked back, then touched it again. She dared make no movement, just continued to beam. Then Pooh heaved his massive shaggy forelegs up onto the porch, tentatively stretched out his great head, and hesitantly sniffed at her neck. Then Winnie also hefted herself up on her other side, in case she was missing out on something. Elizabeth sat rigid, trying not to burst into terrified giggles under the animals towering over her, with their warm snuffling tickling both her ears—but she couldn't control herself any longer, burst out laughing, and jerked backward. She put a hand on a furry paw of each to reassure them and gasped: 'Dance? Shall we dance?' She turned to Davey. 'Would they dance for us?'

He was smiling. 'If you want, they'll even dance with you. They enjoy that.'

'Oh, yes! How?—what have I got to do?' She looked at the great shaggy faces looking down at her, disappointed that she had pulled away from them. 'Dance?' she appealed. 'Will you dance with me?'

'They understand that word,' Davey grinned. 'But they're puzzled that you're just sitting there, with no music.'

'What shall I sing?'

'Try "The Teddy Bears' Picnic." '

Before her nerve should fail her, she slid off the porch and stood between the two bears, eyes shining. They looked at her, digesting this development. Then Pooh heaved himself up onto his hindlegs.

Then Winnie did the same. They stood expectantly, towering over her like thunderclouds.

'What do I do now?' she said breathlessly.

'Take a paw each.'

She took a huge paw in each hand. She had never felt so little in her life.

'Now sing.'

She took a nervous breath.

> If you go down to the woods today
> You better not go alone . . .

She gently jigged each paw, and the bears responded uncertainly; they began to shuffle on their hind legs, their paws held up in her tiny hands, and she felt her heart turn over. She began to shuffle in tune, and the two great bears began to dance with her.

Her eyes were sparkling, and she wanted to whoop and shout. Davey and Big Charlie were smiling and singing along with her. Winnie and Pooh went dancing off with her, one each side, through the trees, shuffling amiably in the twilight, heads bobbing, their free paws waving to the crowds they were accustomed to, their shaggy backsides daintily shaking as she sang:

> Today's the day
> The teddy bears have their pic . . . nic . . .

# part ten

# forty-six

Overnight, new green things started to appear a little higher up the steep wilderness slopes, and the whole forest smelled young after the rains. At three o'clock that afternoon, through the trees, Smoky bear saw the Newfound Gap highway. He stopped.

There it was again, another man-made place. Smoky stared at the highway; then he turned and lumbered hurriedly off the trail for cover. He crouched in the undergrowth, ears pricked.

For an hour Smoky sat, peering, waiting for a sign of dreaded man. He only knew that he had to cross yet another terrifying road which lay across his trail. Finally he screwed up his courage and came out of his hiding place.

He crept cautiously through the undergrowth, peering and sniffing, stopping twenty paces from the highway. His heart was pounding harder, as he summoned the courage for the dash.

He hit the parking area with a grunt of pain, and he started running. He hobbled desperately across the parking area and onto the road beyond. Then he heard the helicopter.

He heard its drone, and, frightened, he turned and started galloping back across the road. Then he saw it was farther back than to cross, so he swung around and went galloping back again toward the far embankment. At the last moment he saw that it was vertical.

A high stone wall supported the embankment. Smoky leaped panic-stricken. He hit the wall, fore legs upflung and his hind legs frantically clawing; for a long second he clung there scrabbling,

then he crashed back to the tar with a thud. He scrambled up
desperately and looked up the road for another escape. The road
and its embankment curved out of sight. He turned to run back
across the road again; then suddenly Smoky saw the helicopter.

.The huge flying monster, the most terrible sight he had ever seen,
was coming over the Appalachian Trail from the direction of the
Pigeon River, and Smoky swerved again. He went galloping up the
road, following the bend, the machine roaring louder and louder;
then he saw the tourist road that led to Clingmans Dome, he fled
wildly down it for a hundred yards, the machine thudding above
him; the wall ended and he plunged up the embankment into the
dark forest beyond.

The helicopter turned in a tight circle and hovered above the
parking area at the Newfound Gap lookout. Stephen Leigh-
Forsythe looked around at the vast blue mountains stretching all the
way to the horizon. He had just finished a four-hour airborne
inspection of the Smoky Mountains, accompanied by his trackers
and Professor Ford, Frank Hunt, and a journalist. His face showed
no emotion at that massive beauty—no awe, no doubt. But his
African trackers were wonderstruck at the experience.

"Put us down on that parking area.'

Forsythe spoke quietly to his trackers in Swahili; the four black
men climbed out and headed separately for the forest on both sides
of the road, each carrying a walkie-talkie radio.

'They looking for that bear?' asked Jonas Ford.

'No. There's nothing to suggest that's one of the animals we're
looking for. This area's full of black bears. My men are having a
quick check for spoor. But even if Jordan has crossed over here, the
rain yesterday will have washed everything out. Still, we may be
lucky and find a bit of jumbo dung.'

The reporter was scribbling.

Forsythe climbed out of the helicopter, walked slowly to the edge
of parking area and looked around. Then he inspected his map.
After ten minutes he spoke into his walkie-talkie radio. A few
minutes later his men emerged from the forest and made their
reports in Swahili.

'Nothing,' he reported to Ford. 'Back to the camp.'

*

The Oconaluftee Visitor Center is on the edge of the Great Smoky Mountains, outside the little Indian town of Cherokee, surrounded by forest. There is a big pasture with a log barn, and in the modern visitors' center there is a museum. No tourists are allowed to camp there.

This was Operation Noah's camp, and there were cars and tents everywhere, belonging to the scores of reporters and television crews. Jonas Ford had wanted to refuse the reporters admission but Forsythe had tactfully dissuaded him.

There were the trucks of The World's Greatest Show, the caravan trailers of Charles Worthy and Frank I. Hunt, and numerous national parks vehicles. There were several military vehicles, even a bulldozer, and several helicopters. The newsmen had clubbed together to hire a caterer from Cherokee to run a fastfood service, and permission had been obtained for a temporary bar. This had scandalized Ford, but once again Forsythe had overruled him, if only because many reporters seemed to be rooting for David Jordan. Equally reluctantly, Ford had consented to allowing Bell Telephone Company to install temporary lines.

The national parks department had provided a large, air-conditioned trailer for Forsythe, but he had declined it. He was more accustomed to living in tents, he had said with his fresh-faced smile. He had insisted that Jonas Ford use it, but he had felt he had to decline too. He also preferred to camp, he said—didn't get enough outdoors in his job. And—although he didn't say so—it wouldn't look good for the director of the Bronx Zoo to be living in luxury while the hardy expert from Africa slept under canvas. Forsythe was amused. All this hoo-hah. All their souped-up gear, bulldozers and helicopters, troop trucks, caravans, and telephone lines. Even a first-aid station. The resources of the entire United States at his disposal, just to recapture a handful of animals—tame ones at that. Trust the Yanks.

Forsythe had three tents, pitched well away from everybody else. Outside his dining tent a log fire was smoldering, attended by Gasoline. On the other side of the fire was Forsythe's sleeping tent. It had a canvas floor and contained a stretcher, two canvas chairs, a pressure lamp, and a pole for his clothes. The third was the 'operations tent.' It held several large trestle tables, two covered with maps. On the other was a large, plaster-relief plan of the Great Smoky Mountains, showing every detail.

At the other end of the pasture a stockade was being constructed of stout builders' scaffolding, bolted together.

Beyond the pasture, in the forest on the outskirts of Cherokee, another tented village was springing up. Its residents were mostly young people who had come from all over America and Canada to protest the recapture operation. Many of them were members of Greenpeace and Friends of the Earth.

Forsythe sprang out of the helicopter and started striding toward his own tents. Jonas Ford hurried after him, shoving his glasses up the bridge of his nose. A dozen television crews were filming their return. Frank Hunt gave the cameras a cheery wave and his conspiratorial Dean Martin smile.

The recapture team crowded into the operations tent after Forsythe. 'Ben?' he asked quietly.

'Mambo?'

Forsythe spoke quietly in Swahili to his men, pointing to the relief map.

'I'm sending my trackers out at first light in the morning,' Forsythe said to Ford. 'In the helicopter. Dropping one of them at each of these points.' He pointed at the map. 'They'll start looking for spoor in this direction.' He swept his hand southward. 'I'm also putting one man down *on* the Appalachian Trail, on the crest, about here.' He indicated a point about five miles from the Pigeon River.

Ford nodded. It irritated him that young Forsythe had hardly consulted him.

'It's bad luck about that heavy rain yesterday,' Forsythe continued. 'We have to start from scratch searching for spoor. However, some signs will remain. Such as broken branches where an elephant has been feeding, the odd bit of dung. But it's going to be hard to estimate its age. When a tracker finds spoor he will radio back to me here at the camp. He'll then shoot off a flare, and I'll proceed to where he is by helicopter. I'll estimate the age of the spoor, and if it is suitable, follow it. And Operation Noah proper will begin.'

Ford didn't like that—'Operation Noah *proper*.' But Frank

Hunt smiled. 'Won't Jordan also see the flare, and start running?' asked Ford curtly.

'It doesn't matter if he does. The spoor must lead me to him. He can't run forever.'

'He's done a pretty good job of it so far.'

'Yes, he has,' Forsythe agreed mildly. 'My guess is he's moving in this direction.' He indicated.

Ford was irritated by Forsythe's demeanor.

'Why do you think he's still on the move? Now that he's reached his objective. One part of those mountains looks as vast and impenetrable as another.'

'Well, we'll see if I'm right.'

Chuck Worthy said with a trace of triumph, 'Do you think you know where he's headed?'

'Yes,' Forsythe said quietly, 'I think I do.'

'Where?' Ford demanded.

'Let's wait for my trackers to find some evidence before I say any more, gentlemen.'

Then Chuck Worthy announced, 'While you were out there today, some Indian gents from Cherokee came here and told us they had found spoor. *They* know where the animals are . . .'

For the first time Forsythe looked taken aback. Then anger flickered across his face.

'Excellent. Where are they?'

'Waiting patiently outside to speak to you.'

Frank Hunt scratched his cheek to smother his smile.

'Well,' Forsythe said, 'obviously we'll check out their story at first light tomorrow. Thank you,' he said to everybody with polite dismissal.

He turned to the national parks man who had been assigned to him as liaison officer.

'Will you please telephone your head warden and tell him that I saw an injured black bear today. Something wrong with his leg. If I have the opportunity—and I'll probably cross his tracks in the next few weeks—I'll shoot him. He should obviously be destroyed. But I'd like the skin for my Nairobi office. Just get the okay from the head warden, as a courtesy.'

# forty-seven

The elephants felt abandoned. It was the first day Davey had left them alone.

They had tried to follow him when he set out this morning with the lions, but he had firmly ordered them back. They had pretended to obey, looking forlorn, plucking leaves in displacement, but as soon as he was out of sight they furtively followed, trying to keep out of sight, which is difficult for three worried elephants to do. Davey ordered them back again, clearly showing his displeasure, and they looked at him as if they had been whipped. Rajah turned around guiltily; Jamba was less accustomed to discipline and stood her ground doggedly, flapping her ears and sighing until Davey had to show anger. She turned with monumental reluctance. After ten yards she stopped and looked back at him over her shoulder. He did not smile. She sighed and lumbered back toward the cabin.

It was another beautiful day. It was like the first day that God made.

That is what Elizabeth thought as she followed Davey, creeping up a little valley below Paw Paw Ridge. The lions padded silently through the undergrowth ahead. Sam trotted behind. She watched for signs of the hunter instinct in the lions, but all they seemed to show was feline caution, alertness bordering on nervousness, bewilderment bordering on distaste. The kings of the jungle were pussyfooting along. They had not been fed since the day before yesterday, but instead of showing any inclination to hunt they had just hung about Davey. Only Kitty had shown any initiative by sneaking into the cabin and stealing the remnants of their roast dinner.

Davey was following the spoor of wild boar. It was fresh. Now the pigs should be resting in the noon sun. The wind was in his favor.

He crept noiselessly up to an outcropping of rock and peered over it.

The boar were about thirty yards away, in a little clearing. Some were lying down, some rooting around, bustling, their curly tails shaking. Davey looked back at the lions.

254

They were standing around aimlessly. Tommy looked at Davey with stern cat's eyes, then blinked and looked away. Princess scratched herself. Kitty looked bored. Only Sam seemed to know what was going on.

Elizabeth thought: Can't you smell them?

Davey shook his ash bag. The ash drifted away from them: they could not smell the wild pigs.

Elizabeth lifted her eyebrows inquiringly. He shook his head: he would wait and see if the wind changed.

Elizabeth crouched on her haunches, willing the cats to act—to peer over the rocks or wander around and sight the pigs by accident. But no. Tommy was just sitting; Princess was grooming herself.

The wind did not change. Davey signaled to Sam to stay, then gave a soft hiss to the lions. He started creeping round the side of the rocks; the lions began to slink after him.

Then a boar squealed.

The lions froze.

They stood, ears pricked, absolutely motionless, staring.

Davey's heart was hammering, willing them to act. For a full twenty seconds the lions stood, pent; then a boar gave another angry squeal.

Kitty took a hesitant step; then another. And another. She moved noiselessly, head up, eyes intent. Princess took three quick paces after her. Then Kitty dropped her stance, paused, then she started slinking quickly through the undergrowth. Princess watched intently, ears up, motionless: then she too dropped into a crouch, and followed Kitty fast.

Davey crouched, excited, looking around for Tommy.

Tommy's head was up, ears pricked, every beautiful muscle bulging. Davey willed him; *Go, Tommy, go!* He took one silent, determined step forward. Then another.

Then he put his ears back, and sat down. He blinked, lifted up his forepaw, uncurled his big, red, rasping tongue, and proceeded to wash his face.

Kitty crept through the undergrowth, head down, muscles quivering. She had smelled the wild pigs. She heard their grunting loud and clear, and she knew by an age-old instinct that she was doing the right thing; she felt the cunning in her heart and guts and

255

in the way she placed her silent paws. The she glimpsed the wild boar.

The nearest was ten paces away, lying on its side, back towards her, grunting in hoggish doze. The others were scattered about the clearing. Kitty stared at them a long murderous moment, then crouched onto her stomach, her legs bunched under her. She felt surge through her the instinctual knowledge of being a lion. For a moment she crouched there, every fiber in her tensing up, up, up, her eyes fixed murderously on the sleeping pig; then she sprang.

She gave a mighty roar as her muscles uncoiled, and the boar woke up and fled.

All the pigs went squealing and scampering through the forest as fast as their legs would carry them. Kitty landed on the sleeping pig's spot half a second after it had been vacated. She went after him, bounding high over the undergrowth for twenty yards, then came to a disappointed halt.

Davey closed his eyes and groaned.

'No, no, *no*,' he muttered, 'you roar *after*wards ...' Then he called, 'Sam!'

Sam came running from behind the rocks. 'Away,' Davey ordered.

Sam swerved and went streaking through the undergrowth to herd the wild boar back.

Sixty miles away, on the other side of the Great Smoky Mountains, Stephen Leigh-Forsythe crouched with his chief tracker, Ben Majuju, and examined the spoor to which the two Cherokees had taken them. They had been following it for several hours, with the whole recapture team, plus two jounalists, struggling along behind them.

Forsythe was puzzled. The dung he was examining could be two days old because it had obviously not been rained on, but it must have been dropped shortly after the rains when the earth was soft. Yet there were few footmarks to go with the dung. Quite a lot of scuffs, but with the ground as soft as it must have been, it was surprising that there were no clear footprints. There were other signs, certainly—the odd broken branch, fallen leaves, uprooted grass. But not one clear footprint.

Except human.

Doubtless they were Jordan's or the Indian's. But if they had left discernible footprints, why had not the animals?

Mind you, the light was difficult, and the forest floor was mostly in deep shadow, dappled in shifting sunlight, and the undergrowth was thick.

'What do you think, Ben?'

Ben's surly eyes flicked over the surrounding undergrowth.

'It is noon.'

Yes, it was the most difficult time to track because of the angle of the sun.

'But in the morning this side is in the shadow of the mountain until quite late.'

'And in the shadows of the trees. And in the afternoon it will be in more shadow,' Ben said. 'It is difficult country, when one is in doubt. And we have been going fast.'

Yes, probably too fast. He had been impatient with the Indians. First, they had shown up late at the camp, a good hour after sunrise. Then they had had difficulty recognizing the terrain from the helicopter. Finally they had indicated a place, but it had proved to be a good mile out of the way. It had taken them two hours just to find the first spoor. Gorilla dung. Plus their nests, leaves scraped into crude circles. But no elephant spoor, nor bear, nor lion. Evidently the animals had already split up. That was to be expected, sooner or later. But there were the odd human footprints, so Jordan was with the gorillas. Forsythe had felt that he should follow the spoor, even though it was two days old, because gorillas do not roam rapidly. They could be quite near. For two hours they had followed a clear trail of broken twigs and depressed undergrowth. Then it had petered out, at a stream. Ben and the other trackers had been unable to pick it up again.

Strange. Gorillas don't like water. Could they have jumped from rock to rock? It was a possibility. They were trained animals and Jordan was leading them.

Thereafter, Forsythe had ordered the Cherokees to show him the other spoor they had found.

It had taken another hour to reach the elephant dung.

'Why are there no hoofprints, Ben?'

'It is possible.'

Ben stood up creakily, his old felt hat flopping over his eyes. He lit his pipe. 'We follow? Spoor is spoor.'

Forsythe straightened up. His blue eyes seemed pale in this light. He pulled a map out of his pocket.

He didn't like following spoor that old, but it was the only spoor they had. Where would Jordan be heading from here? Why should he head anywhere? Maybe he was just the other side of the next ridge.

'We follow. Take your time, now, Ben.'

At a thousand dollars a day, he need not worry if he lost a bit of time following old spoor—but that was beside the point. Stephen Leigh-Forsythe was not only an expert, but an Englishman who gave value for money. Furthermore, the eyes of the world were upon him.


# forty-eight


On the western side, where Forsythe was, the sun was still shining, but on the eastern side, the valleys were in deep shadow. For tracking purposes, the light was finished.

Davey crouched in the undergrowth, stalking a wild boar. He was tired, but the lions were bored. They had been plodding along after him all day, obediently, and he had tracked down no less than three pigs for them. But apart from Kitty, they had shown very little savvy. They were very hungry, but it seemed they did not associate the interest they had shown in the wild animals with their stomachs; it was the playful killer interest which a house cat displays with a cockroach. Each time the boar had galloped off, suffering no more than a mild heart attack.

Elizabeth was in despair. Tiptoeing around the forest all day, hardly daring to breathe, was exhausting. She was convinced the lions would never learn. What she had been feeling recently seemed unrealistic euphoria. After seeing Kitty fight Sam for that possum a week ago she had though that Davey had been right, that the lions would learn. But how long did the man imagine he had to teach them before Forsythe caught up with him? How long could he keep this up? With the log cabin as a focal point, they were becoming like house cats—wanting to come indoors, hanging around the smell of cooking, three bloody great lions lounging around the porch, squabbling, waiting for a handout. Every time Kitty moved, Princess hissed and moaned. Kitty had taken to stealing: shadowing anybody who was cooking, purring voluminously, nose twitching; nothing edible was safe from her enormous darting paw.

Now Davey trained his rifle on the busily oblivious boar, about to kill it for the lions. He hated what he had to do, and above all he wanted to make a clean kill. The boar wasn't making it any easier for him, bustling around. For the sixth time, his finger whitened on the trigger. The shot rang out, and he stood up with a sad sigh.

It was about five o'clock when they got back to the log cabin. Davey cut enough off the boar's carcass for themselves, and suspended the rest of it from a tree for the cats. He was not going to feed them until they were really hungry: he had other plans.

Big Charlie started to roast the boar's leg with some edible roots he swore were better than potatoes. Elizabeth sat on the porch. She badly wanted a drink; there was still some whisky left, but she was denying herself. She did not want to induce any euphoria. She also wanted to lose weight. She had lost a lot already in the nine days since they crossed the Pigeon—she could feel it; the hard exercise accounted for most of it, plus her lower intake of alcohol, and she wanted to keep up the good work and get her old curvy figure back. But the real reason for not having a drink was that she wanted to have a no-nonsense talk with Davey, try to persuade him to give this whole thing up. She was very worried.

Elizabeth sat, absently watching the gorillas beginning to make their nests. She felt sorry for Champ. He was imitating King Kong, scraping the leaves into a circle about him, but chimpanzees do not build nests like that, as far as she knew; he was simply imitating the gorillas. He did not seem to like the two other chimps. But at least he seemed to have reduced his dependence on Davey and no longer insisted on holding his hand. Elizabeth still felt he was a colorless little creature. Would he ever be a real chimpanzee?

Kitty had been banished from the aromatic cabin by Charlie, and was now watching the gorillas making their nests. Kitty's stomach was hollow with hunger, and though she had not yet tumbled to the fact that wild boar were made of meat, she knew chimpanzees were, because she had eaten Daisy's flesh. Gorillas were too big for her; but chimpanzees . . .

Out of the corner of her eye Elizabeth saw a sudden tawny flash. One moment little Champ was earnestly scraping leaves around himself, and the next a terrible lion was flying at him through the dusk. Gaping jaws, vicious cat's eyes and great clawed paws extended, and, as Elizabeth yelled, Champ scrambled. He threw himself aside, screaming, horrified, and raced toward Elizabeth for protection. He flung himself into her arms. Kitty bounded after him with a snarl, and Elizabeth staggered back; Champ threw himself at a tree and bounded up into its branches, and Kitty leaped up the trunk.

Kitty clawed up the tree, ears back, and Champ jumped wildly higher, screaming. Elizabeth yelled at Kitty—then Davey was at her side.

'She won't catch him, Dr. Johnson,' he said calmly.

'She might. Call her down!'

Champ had clambered out onto the very end of a high branch; there was nowhere else for him to go unless he leaped through thin air to the next tree. Now Kitty was creeping out along the branch at him, head down, leg muscles bulging, paws groping cautiously, eyes fixed on little Champ. Champ crouched on the end of the branch, his black face creased in terror, trying to show his fangs, his eyes rolling as he looked about for escape. Then the branch creaked, Champ screamed, and he had no choice.

He flew through the air, caught a branch of the neighbouring tree and clawed up into it while Kitty clung to her breaking branch. She tried desperately to turn around, but lost her footing. In a flash of legs and tail, Kitty was hanging upside down, yowling.

Davey was grinning. Elizabeth fumed, 'You and your Laws of Nature!'

Kitty was trying to get one hind paw onto the branch again, but the other hind leg lost its grip, and then she was hanging by her forepaws, moaning. Then the branch broke, and down she came. Her yowl was cut off as she thudded to the ground, the branch crashing on top of her, and Kitty disappeared in a pile of leaves. The pile of greenery erupted, and she burst out, fleeing into the forest as if pursued by demons.

Elizabeth snapped, 'You'd have stopped her if it was Sam she was chasing!'

'Sam isn't going to return to the wild, Dr. Johnson.'

He walked over to the tree where the boar's carcass hung. He lowered it to the ground, and hefted it up onto his shoulder. He whistled for the lions.

'Where are you going?' she demanded.

'I'm taking them to a place I know.'

A stream tumbled down the steep valley below Paw Paw Ridge. An old mineshaft, hewn into a cliff, abutted the stream. The excavated rocks had been thrown into the stream, so they formed a steep jumbled bank and a broad rubble terrace outside the mouth of the mine. Bushes and creepers had grown over the rocky platform, and the mine's mouth was almost entirely obscured.

But the most important feature of this valley was that the stream ran right down its middle: it was possible to climb up the stream, from rock to rock, right to the mouth itself without leaving any signs for a tracker, nor scent for a dog to follow.

Davey toiled up the stream, the boar across his shoulders, the lions following. He walked into the mouth of the mine, and slung down the carcass. The lions fell upon it.

'Why are you feeding them here?' asked Elizabeth.

'I was going to bring them here tomorrow anyway. It's a good den for them. I don't want them to settle down at the cabin, or they'll get territorial about it. By the time they're finished feeding we'll be over a mile away. They won't be able to follow our scent because we'll follow the stream.'

'But they'll try to follow and get lost.'

'The whole forest is their home now, Dr. Johnson. They won't be lost for long.'

'But they can't *hunt* yet.'

'I thought you were complaining about Kitty hunting a little while ago?' He smiled. 'I'll come back the day after tomorrow and take them hunting again.'

'But what if you can't find them?'

'I don't think they'll be lost, Dr. Johnson. They'll hang around here: the last place they saw me and got fed. Anyway, I'll find them, don't worry.'

She looked back at the lions crouched around the carcass, snarling and feeding. And dear Sultan anxiously hovering, awaiting a break in the ranks.

It seemed awful to sneak away and leave them. Knowing that when they were finished they were going to start looking for their keeper. Afraid. How far would they look? . . .

Twenty minutes later they reached the bottom of the stream.

'Don't worry about them, Dr. Johnson.'

'Of course I'm worried.'

'They've got to start looking after themselves.'

He suddenly looked formal, and a little embarrassed. He said, 'Dr. Johnson, I'm very grateful for everything you've done. But . . . we're here now.' He looked her in the eye. 'If you want to quit now, okay. No hard feelings.'

She stared at him. 'Why should I quit *now?*'

'To get back to your job. And this is a pretty rugged life for a woman.'

'This *is* my job. I'm still a salaried employee of the zoo, you know. I'm just on temporary assignment.'

'But all this is going to be upsetting for you.'

'Oh! Because I'm upset about abandoning tamed lions in the wilderness, I'm being a nuisance, am I? And because I made a fuss about Kitty trying to murder Champ? Well, of course I'm upset— any sane person would be. And so should *you* be, laws of Nature or not. Tell me,' she demanded, 'would you have stopped Kitty if she close to killing Champ?'

He was not going to argue. He said quietly, 'A lot of things are going to start happening soon, Dr. Johnson. I'm going to start splitting up the animals. They can't keep living in a circus group any longer.'

She was staring at him with a sinking heart. She started to speak, but he went on. 'We're going to be moving about some. We may get separated. Especially in an emergency.' He looked at her. 'Do you know how to find your way out of here?'

She blinked. 'Yes. I think so. The Appalachian Trail's somewhere up there.'

'But there're no foot trails to get to it. And it would be at least four or five nights alone in the wilderness getting out.' He added, 'I can get you escorted out now, if you want.'

'What are you *talking* about, Davey? Do you *want* me to quit? Aren't I an asset? Or am I just another responsibility?'

He didn't answer her question.

'I think you *should* quit now. Think about it, Dr. Johnson. Because things are going to start happening soon.'

'I've thought about it! And I'm *not* quitting. And what's going to start happening soon?'

He turned and started walking.

'You still don't trust me, do you?'

He didn't answer. She called after him: 'I don't get it, Davey! If you don't trust me, I could go and tell Jonas Ford where you are, if I quit now, couldn't I?'

He stopped. 'If you did that, I'd soon know. And we'd be gone.' He shook his head slightly. 'I can run circles around those people for weeks, Dr. Johnson.'

He started to turn away, then he said, 'Yes, I would have stopped Kitty. There's plenty for her to eat here apart from chimpanzees. But Champ learned something today.'

'What, pray?'

'Not to trust lions. Or even me, any more.'


At that moment, high up on the crest of the mountains, the furry silhouette of Smoky bear was hobbling along the Appalachian Trail. Before him loomed the mountain called Thunderhead.

The pain in his side was very bad. His whole flank throbbed, and with each step his head thudded from the yellow poison in his body. He was exhausted from running, hobbling, going he knew not where; he only knew he had to keep going, to find his keeper, keep running from the terrors that lay behind him.

Near Thunderhead, he stopped on a small rise, to test the wind again, searching for a familiar smell. He stood, his head slowly turning, his black nose pointed, the wind ruffling his fur; then his heart contracted with excitement.

It was gone on the shifting evening breeze, but he had definitely caught it once: the faint but familiar whiff of elephant dung, coming up the mountainside in the dusk.

That night the three men from Sylva sat around the bar in the den. Large-scale surveyors' maps of the Great Smoky Mountains were spread across the floor. On one wall was Mama's tiger skin, freshly hung. She was too good to have on the floor as a mat. Her bullet holes had been patched up nicely, and two glass tiger eyes, sent from New York, had been mounted in her sockets. Her snarling jaws were agape. She looked good. Three knapsacks with bedrolls were stacked neatly against the wall. The three men were drinking whisky. A leather cup of poker dice stood on the bar between their glasses. The first man was behind the bar, and he was reading slowly from a list.

'Three elephants, two grizzlies, one black bear, two gorillas, three lions, one tiger, three or four chimps, one wolf. Okay? . . . That's it, far as we know from the press. Anything else is a bonus. Now, how're we going to organize this? Do we play straight poker dice—winner chooses his kill? Or lie dice? Or what?'

The third man said emphatically, 'Not lie dice. That ain't the purpose, to kid each other. The purpose is just to be fair, so each has a decent chance.'

'Right,' the second man said. 'There's three lions, so we each have one of them: all we play dice for is the male 'cos he's the best trophy. Same with the elephants. Same with the bears.'

'Except one's a goddamn black bear,' the third man said. 'They're a dime a dozen.'

'Still makes a good trophy,' the second man insisted. 'The gorillas we dice for. What's the male supposed to be called?—King Kong. Hey, how about that? Having the actual King Kong in your den!'

'And the tiger?' the first man asked. 'There's only one of him.'

'Well,' the second man said reasonably. 'I vote that with the tiger it's first come first served. We don't dice—whoever has the chance

264

slowly laid the rifle across her lap. She felt for her cigarettes, lit one with trembling fingers, inhaled deep.

Now, think this through, Johnson . . . there are no such things as fiends and goblins. *You're safer here than in the streets of New York* . . .

Then the doorway darkened as a dreadful fiend blocked out the light; her eyes widened in terror, a scream welled up, and she grabbed up the gun.

Smoky bear stared at her a petrified instant, then he whirled about and plunged out of the doorway.

He bounded off the porch and went galloping into the undergrowth, and Elizabeth yelled, 'Smoky! . . .'

He blundered on into the trees; then stopped when he heard his name. Flanks heaving, he looked back fearfully over his shoulder.

'Oh clever Smoky! How did you *find* us?' Her heart was still hammering.

She could just see him in the shadows. But she had seen his limp.

'Poor Smoky. What's happened to you?' It was like seeing an old friend—and she wasn't alone anymore. 'Come here, Smoky. Come . . .'

Smoky stood, listening to her reassuring voice, wanting to trust her, but not daring to. He remembered her from the first day in the glen: he could smell the other animals; he knew his keeper must be near, and he was too sore to run any farther.

Elizabeth withdrew from the window, and reached for her medical bag. Perhaps it was crazy, but she was going to do it: she was about to approach a wounded animal four times her size and try to treat him—alone. Without iron bars, straitjackets, assistants. In the zoo she would have half a dozen people helping her. Her heart was hammering again. But she knew, without hesitation, that she was going to do her duty: this was what she was [t]here for.

[Sh]e pulled out the tranquilizer pistol, and shakily slotted in a [car]tridge. She took a deep breath and stepped slowly through the [doorw]ay.

['Up], Smoky,' she smiled.

to swat him, good luck. Otherwise it's unfair; one of us gets the best trophy and the other two just got to watch him have the fun.'

'Supposing we all see him at the same time?'

'Fine. We all have a crack at him.'

'And the skin?'

'In that case we dice for the skin, like we did for this bitch.' He jerked his head at Mama. 'Same deal with the wolf.'

'We should try to knock that wolf off first of all,' the first man said. 'He'll make trouble.'

'Sure. Get the bastard out of the way.' He added, with a smirk, 'Be kind of good to get that Indian and Jordan out the way too . . .'

They all smiled. 'Wouldn't that be something?'

The second man thought, then said, 'Say, you know where I reckon we should go next year? Brazil.'

'Why the hell Brazil?'

'Because,' the second man said, 'I hear it's about the last place left where you can bag yourself a real live Indian.'

# forty-nine

At sunrise, Elizabeth was suddenly wide awake.

She lay in her sleeping bag, tensed, listening. There was complete silence. Then she realized that was what it was: the silence. Suddenly she knew, with awful certainty, that she was alone.

She scrambled out of her sleeping bag, wearing only her bra and panties, dashed to the door of the cabin and looked out. Her heart sank. She stared into the wilderness morning: they were gone.

There was not a sign of anybody. The porch, where Big Charlie and Davey slept, was empty. Their bedrolls and knapsacks were gone. There was not an animal in sight. She felt the panic rising. She spun around, and her eyes darted about the cabin. All that remained was their rifle and their stewing pot.

She stood there, her mind fumbling over what he had said

yesterday. 'Things are going to start happening.' 'Do you know your way out of here?' And now, because she had refused, he had just left her to it. She looked feverishly around again, for a note, perhaps.

But there was nothing.

Panic. She pulled on her sweater, jeans, sneakers. Then she rolled up her sleeping bag and shakily strapped it to her knapsack. Then stopped.

To go where? . . .

Where was she going with her knapsack? Cherokee? To look for the animals? How was she going to find them if Davey could run rings round the experts, as he said? She stood, collecting her wits. The she dashed outside.

She crouched and examined the ground for spoor.

There was spoor everywhere. It all looked fresh. She hurried toward the pasture for twenty paces: more spoor. Elephants'. Gorillas'. Bears'. It could be today's or yesterday's

She felt helpless. What spoor to follow? She knew the only thing to do, but she had no confidence in herself doing it: 'a three-sixty.' Walk a big circle around the cabin, decide on the freshest spoor, and follow it. That was the scientific way she had learned on zoological expeditions, but she had not been good. She would follow the wrong spoor. How would she even *see* the spoor in that shadowed forest? She could get hopelessly lost. *Lost* . . . Then came the primitive fear of being alone in the dark wilderness. *Pull yourself together. There is nothing to be afraid of. You are not lost yet. You know how to get out of here.* Now, *think* . . .

Why did she assume that Davey had just abandoned her? Or Charlie? He had said he was going to split up the animals—that was what he was doing, just taking the animals out, to resettle them. Would Davey be so cruel as to leave her alone in the wilderness after all she had done for him? Or Big Charlie? . . .

She closed her eyes. The answer was yes.

A man who had the audacity to rob a zoo and a circus to return his beloved animals to the wild was just the sort of man to abandon you if it became necessary. All he cared about was those animals. And what *had* she done for him? Nothing but try to argue him out of it. She had not even had to use her medical skills yet. And he had

266

warned her, loud and clear, last night, that he wanted her out. And if he was just taking the animals out, why had he taken his sleeping bag? He obviously didn't intend returning tonight. He had left her the gun, for protection. He did not need the gun because he wasn't going to feed the lions again—and Charlie had one of the sheriff's guns.

The panic surged back—she felt the eerie fear of discovering herself completely alone. Of the ringing quiet of the wilderness, as if everything was watching her. The primeval menace of it. And Elizabeth wanted the rifle. She dashed back to the cabin. She picked up the gun, her eyes darting from the window to the door. She sidled into the corner; then looked at the gun in her shaking hands. Was it loaded? No—Davey would never leave a loaded gun around. How did it work? She was looking at a simple Winchester, with a silencer and telescopic sights. She identified the bolt action, and pulled it open recklessly, half expecting the thing to explode. It opened with a business-like click. The chamber was empty.

She looked for the cartridges, found a small box. She hastily slid one into the chamber and closed the bolt.

The thing was ready to fire . . .

And, definitely, she felt safer with the gun in her hands. And, suddenly, she also felt foolish.

What was the gun going to protect her against? From hillbilly murderers? From Sheriff Lonnogan and his posse?

She took a deep, quivering breath.

No, realistically, she was not afraid of them. It was th wilderness she was afraid of. Like that first night in b car in the mountains outside Erwin. The primitive forest, the dark unknown, the *menace* of goblins dreadful fiends and evil spirits, lurking in low p anything else she wanted to run for her life u menacing low-lying darkness into the sunli God, how thin the veneer of civilization stood the human need for the cave fearsome Nature—and for woman t wanted Davey Jordan around no

She made her muscles unte

Smoky had turned to face her, but he had moved farther into the forest. Elizabeth walked slowly, nervously, out onto the porch, the pistol held against her thigh, smiling reassuringly, repeating his name. Smoky backed off a little farther.

Elizabeth slowly sat down on the end of the porch, holding the tranqu-pistol between her legs, smiling at him. Smoky was trembling. 'Come on, Smoky ...' For another minute he stood there, trying to make up his mind; then slowly, painfully, he sat down. Elizabeth estimated the distance between them behind her smile.

Fourteen, fifteen paces ...

It was the maximum distance she felt she could use the pistol on such dense fur. But, oh, everything else was wrong: he was in deep shadow and she needed light. He was in thick undergrowth and she needed space. She needed water. But if she waited till she had everything, this bear would never get treated. If she so much as coughed now he would run. She slowly raised the pistol, her heart thumping.

Smoky jerked when he saw the movement, ready to run for his life. Elizabeth whimpered, *Please God he falls the right way*—and she squeezed the trigger.

There was a popping noise, and Smoky jerked at the stab of pain, terrified at this treachery. He blundered five frantic paces before he fell.

Elizabeth lashed the rope around his paws. 'Oh, Smoky, why did you fall on the wrong side?'

She looped his forepaws together, then ran the rope to his hindlegs and bound them too. She jumped over the furry body, and heaved on the rope, gritting, *Please* God ...

Smoky's legs came up saggily; she took the strain with all her weight, and Smoky was nearly halfway over. She heaved again, her heels digging in and her hands starting to slip, and Smoky was almost about to thud back; then over he came, with a thump.

She dropped to her knees, and parted his fur.

'Poor Smoky ...'

His flank was matted with dried blood and pus, and she could feel the long hump of swollen flesh beneath. 'Poor baby ...' She ran her fingers through his fur, measuring the size of the lump. Then she grabbed up her medical bag and hurried to the stream to scrub her hands in the ice cold water.

First, she snipped with the scissors, cutting off big chunks of matted fur, exposing the swollen stripe of inflamed flesh. She changed to the clippers, plowing away the fur on both sides of the wound. She sloshed soapy water onto the swollen flesh, and began to shave it with a razor. She swabbed away the soap and thickly painted the whole area with strong disinfectant. Then she pulled on a pair of surgical gloves and picked up a scalpel.

Where to start? Which way to cut? A long courageous incision which would let out more poison but require lots of stitches; or a short deep one where that bullet was lodged, and let the poison drain gradually? She studied her site, juggling alternatives: time available, stitches, antibiotics, aftercare, tomorrow, the next day, next week—what was going to happen to this bear? He wasn't going to be waiting in a cage. And what else was she going to find after she'd opened him up?

She made up her mind, and leaned forward. She sank her knife carefully into his flesh. The blood welled up around the shining blade; then, with a firm hand, she began to cut.

Through the blood it came: the yellow, red-streaked pus, welling out of Smoky bear, yellow poison flooding out over his sleeping flank; and Elizabeth could almost feel the relief of the awful pressure. She was glad with all her heart that she was a vet.

She put down the knife and pressed the sides of the big incision, and more yellow-red poison oozed out. The flesh was wrinkling like a deflating balloon; then began to flow the surgeon's enemy—blood.

She cursed and swabbed it away, and cut farther, probing for the bullet. Elizabeth knelt beside Smoky, working on him, making him better, and she had forgotten about demons.

It was almost noon when she finished.

She slumped on the porch, reeking of disinfectant and blood, her jeans smeared. Her leg muscles ached from working on her haunches, but she felt elated. She had done it, by herself.

Smoky lay on his side fifteen paces away, breathing stertorously, his wound an ugly swathe of bleeding stitches. But to Elizabeth it was beautiful. She had done a beautiful job, if she said so herself: she had removed the bullet, the chips of ribs, arrested the infection. Smoky bear was going to live happily ever after.

Though he wasn't going to feel too clever when he came around. For a while, the pain would be worse, and the wound exposed to scratches from the undergrowth. He wasn't going to have the sense to keep still; he was going to go blundering around, trying to escape the pain—and that was going to be agony. And he would probably go charging off, so she would never get near enough to bang another dart into him to treat him further.

But she had packed that wound and shot him full of enough antibiotics to last him a good few days. After that, his big bear body had an excellent chance of fighting off infection. He was young. He was in bad shape, run down and undernourished but he was young.

And, oh, he was so beautiful. She looked at Smoky's shaggy body, his killer paws lying harmless, his furry face outflung, red tongue slopping out, half-closed eyes glazed, his sculptured nose vibrating and his tufty ears so fluffily defenseless. He was her friend.

It was no good keeping his legs tied. How could she untie them when he woke? Would he run away? He probably would, looking for Davey. From here he would be able to track him like a bloodhound. She would never keep up. She had considered keeping him tied by one leg, but it would frighten him; he would struggle and run, the rope dragging behind, which could kill him if it caught.

'Oh, Smoky, don't leave me. Stay and let me fix you up properly. Then we'll find him together.'

But she was too happy to let herself worry about that yet. She had to stay where she was until Smoky woke up. Maybe six hours. Maybe twelve. The longer the better. There was nothing more she could do today; she could not leave. She just had to sit here and look at her splendid work.

She sighed. She deserved just one whisky.

Then the fear returned. She tried to push it aside ruthlessly.

*What's the worst that can happen?* She held her breath a long moment, to get herself under control. At worst she had four days'

271

slog to get out of here! So what? She knew perfectly well where she was. Then she closed her eyes.

Because, despite her ruthlessness, she could see herself picking through the deeply shadowed wilderness, the sky blotted out, the very branches leaning out to grab her; and lying in her bedroll at night, too terrified to sleep. O God . . .

Oh, why, oh why had he left her?. . .

*It was because he still did not trust her.*

Because she might move out and go tell Jonas Ford where they were. That was why he had stolen away, to a new hiding place. So this was not the Garden of Eden after all—was coming here just a trick so she would mislead Jonas? Maybe they weren't even going to stay in the Great Smoky Mountains! Maybe he was going to bundle them all into more trucks and hurtle them on to the Everglades, while the expert beat his brains out here.

Then she felt a thrill of excitement, and a smile was dawning.

Is that what he had done? *Gone and fooled us all again, Davey?*. . . And her heart was beating with a new hope that made her almost want to laugh.

Then she shook her head to herself.

No. He would not risk that again. They had gone through hell to get here. This was Cherokee country, where once the world began. *This* was the Garden of Eden . . .

Then she felt it well up from her heart, and she wanted to drop her head and sob.

For grief. Not for primitive fear. She was big enough to make her own way out of these mountains. It was heartbreak, at being left behind. Like the little crippled boy in the Pied Piper story who got there just too late, who only glimpsed the paradise beyond the door. Grief for not being with her beloved animals anymore: no more to see the look in their faces as they returned to their wilderness, real earth and sun and sky and smells. No more would she see and feel their growing joy as they began to learn to play again. Instead she was going to make her way out of here courageously, and be on hand to care for them as they came back one by one from their wilderness, back into their cages . . . And she would write her scientific paper which would be internationally acclaimed, and even her personal story—and she would be rich and famous . . .

And in a flash she saw herself back in the concrete jungle of New York, going to work every day with locked-up animals: pathetic, neurotic creatures who could not see the sun and the sky, who looked at her with dulled eyes, who did not know how to play. How could she go back to that life after experiencing this? . . .

How could she go to that zoo each day while her heart and soul were here? How could she enter that abominable Elephant House and her heart not break for Dumbo, for his happiness because she rode on him, and for Rajah and Jamba? How could she enter that Big Cat House and not feel her heartbreak for Kitty, bounding after Sam for that possum, cupboard-loving her for chocolate, sniffing round the cooking pot with her heart set on theft? How could she ever look at the Ape House again with its bloody awful concrete tree? . . .

And suddenly Elizabeth knew crystal clear what the result of all this would be. Davey had been right not to trust her until now. Now she *knew* that she did not want these animals back in their cages. She never wanted any animal in a cage ever again. And she was going to stay and find her animals, come hell or high water, and use the last breath in her body to get them the right to be free.

Then, as suddenly, she knew how to find Davey Jordan and her animals: at the lions' den, in the mineshaft. Sooner or later he would go there to see them!

Her heart was singing. She wanted to jump up and shout it to the skies so even Jonas Ford would hear. And then a further fact dawned on her, and she was grinning with the simple joy of it. *She was not afraid of the lions!*

She was not afraid to go alone into their den, and sit down with them and wait for him. Sleep among them, defenseless—she was not afraid. It seemed the most natural thing in the world.

And it was such a liberating feeling she wanted to shout it—how wonderful to be free, to walk unafraid in the world with the fellow creatures God made!

Then Smoky began to wake up.

# fifty

With a groan, his head jerked up; then he collapsed. Elizabeth dashed to him. She dropped to her knees and put her hand on his head. 'Smoky?' He groaned again, then struggled.

He made it groggily to his feet. He stood, head down, the pain thudding back into his side, unaware of Elizabeth standing beside him. She had looped the rope once around his neck. Then his brain cleared for a moment, and he remembered her—the one who had caused the pain. He lurched to get away before she struck him again, and the rope pulled on his neck. Elizabeth stumbled after him, holding the rope and calling his name. He wrenched harder, panicked, and Elizabeth let go. The rope slid from his neck, and he was gone, blundering off into the undergrowth.

But Elizabeth was smiling. Smoky bear was going to be okay.

He had made it here all by himself. He would find Davey. He was free.

In the late afternoon she made her weary way up the stream. Fifty yards ahead was the rocky embankment outside the mineshaft. Only then did she hesitate.

'Kitty?'

She felt the age-old man-lion fear turn her intestines to water. Then, lest her nerve fail her, she started climbing again. 'Kitty,' she called. 'Tommy? Princess?' She peered upward into the gloom as she climbed.

But no frightening feline heads appeared. Then she felt a new fear well up—they were already gone! Davey had already fetched them and she would never find them.

'Kitty!' she yelled.

She started bounding up the rocks. Then one big furry head peeped nervously over the embankment.

'Kitty,' she gasped. 'Oh, thank God, baby . . .'

She sat in the mouth of the mine, her back to the rockface. Kitty lay beside her, one huge paw in the air, eyes closed, chin extended, purring voluminously as Elizabeth scratched her throat. Her other hand held her second whisky in three days.

It was tasting marvelous, and she felt marvelous. She wanted Jonas Ford to see this; she wanted every zoo in the world to see this. She wanted to tell the world. She would.

For was not this what mankind had always thought of as paradise? Where animals gamboled and lived happily together, and Man lived unafraid among them with his children. Was not that paradise envisioned in Christianity, in the story of Adam and Eve, and in so much folklore of every country? Was it not the story of the Pied Piper in almost every language in the world; was it not what the little crippled boy saw as the mountain closed in front of him? And have we not cut ourselves off from it by our insatiable civilization, which is born of our fear of the wild because we are furless and clawless and fangless and need to compensate, gird ourselves? And did we not evolve into furless and fangless creatures because we were so afraid that we huddled together for protection against Nature and resolved to cooperate to beat Her? Have we not now become like the fat aldermen in the Pied Piper story who cut themselves off from the joys of our birthright, worrying about the price? And Davey knew that we will always be like the aldermen, only interested in money and talk talk talk, afraid to *act*.

Afraid to do what is right because it is too costly. Afraid to stop polluting the very air we breathe because of the price. Afraid to stop polluting the oceans that make the oxygen and rain that feed us. Afraid to stop the extinction of beautiful animals like whales because they are too valuable to be allowed to live. Afraid to stop murderous megalomaniacs because it is too costly . . .

But Davey was one of that unique brand of men who finally despaired of the endless talk and who jumped up and *did* . . . because he knew that all the letters to the newspapers and all the questions asked by congressmen and all the societies would never get anything done, with all their talk and good intentions; and year after year of misery would pass, until even the last place for an Eden was cut down, plowed under, and polluted; until like the aldermen, we only had the grief of the loss of our birthright . . .

And she was glad with all her heart for what she was doing, and she wanted to spread her arms wide and shout, 'Come back . . . I'm with you . . .'

She heard a stone fall, and her heart was suddenly pounding. The lions' heads jerked up, ears pricked, ready to run; then Princess darted deeper into the blackness of the mine. Elizabeth scrambled up and peered out. Suddenly Kitty bounded forward, tail straight up. Elizabeth shouted joyfully, 'Davey!'

There he was, climbing the steep embankment. Behind him labored the black shaggy form of Smoky. Elizabeth came stumbling out of the mine, laughing, almost crying, and she just wanted to throw herself into his arms and hug him in welcome. But Kitty got there ahead of her and flung her paws up onto his shoulders. Elizabeth stood, hands on her hips, and she laughed.

'Well—I'm still here!!!'


# fifty-one


Sixty miles away, on the other side of the mountains, Stephen Leigh-Forsythe was furious. It was the second day he had been following elephant spoor shown to him by the Cherokees. They had come to the stream called Middle Prong. But once again, the spoor disappeared, just as the gorilla spoor had done yesterday. Again, circular sweeps on both sides had failed to turn up any continuation. Forsythe was convinced the spoor was a hoax. Here was elephant dung, but no footprints. All right, the ground was stony, but before that? Had this elephant jumped into the stream? As the clever gorillas who hate water had done?

He considered his position while his trackers searched. The rest of the team were still toiling through the undergrowth to catch up with him. He was not going to admit that he had been hoaxed, but he had to explain why he was going to abandon this spoor. He hated being made a fool of.

Professor Ford came tramping along, drooping under his knapsack. He propped his glasses up. 'Well? What's happening?'

'I'm abandoning this spoor. And looking for new.'

'Where?'

'Where I first decided, night before last.'

'But if this spoor is only a day or two old, shouldn't we continue? Otherwise it's like looking for a needle in a haystack.'

'No. It's over two days old.'

Ford looked at him. 'But that's not bad, in my experience. There's no reason for these animals to keep moving now, except to feed.'

Forsythe was about to lose his cool with a client. 'You must trust my judgement, Professor.'

'I insist upon knowing why . . .'

Frank Hunt came plodding up. 'Hello, Professor, I suppose you're wondering why I asked you to meet me here today? . . .'

'Please shut up,' Ford snapped.

At that moment Forsythe's walkie-talkie radio rasped in Swahili. He listened, then hissed, 'Stay here!'

He leaped over the stream and disappeared. A minute later he was examining the very fresh footprints of Sheriff Lonnogan and his posse.

Sheriff Lonnogan was exhausted, and he had a filthy cold. So had most of his posse. He was furious. For almost five days he had been foot-slogging behind his Cherokee guide with elaborate caution. Every hour the Cherokee had pronounced they were getting warmer. Lonnogan was getting very warm indeed, his cold reaching fever proportions, when Forsythe suddenly appeared from nowhere, striding through the trees.

'*What the devil's the meaning of this?*'

Lonnogan whirled around, astonished, his shotgun at his hip. He recognized Forsythe from television, and his mind was suddenly fumbling with his options.

'Have you been laying phony spoor?'

Lonnogan didn't understand. 'Phony spoor?' He looked around for his Cherokee tracker. The man had vanished. His face creased in genuine bewilderment, and he scowled. 'Now where's that sumbitch at?'

He did not have a chance to ponder. Forsythe grabbed him by the shirtfront.

'You've been laying false trails, and I'm arresting you!'

Lonnogan could not believe it. Nobody had ever done that to him! Putting *him* under arrest? In an awful flash he saw the ultimate indignity coming hot after the debacle of the Pigeon River, the gleeful headlines of Sheriff Lonnogan manacled again. For a moment he stood bunched up under the smaller.man's grasp, nose to nose; then he recovered.

His fist swung at Forsythe's guts, and the next instant his head exploded in stars as Forsythe savagely butted his forehead onto his nose. And the next moment he was flying through the air. Lonnogan didn't know what had hit him, as Forsythe twisted and flung him over his shoulder, head over heels. He crashed onto his back, winded, blood streaming from his nose. Suddenly three black men appeared. His posse had scattered into the trees. Lonnogan stared, shocked.

'I'm taking you all back to basecamp.'

The Kid Lonnogan shouted hoarsely, 'One false move an' I fires!'

Forsythe turned his angry blue eyes on him, and Sheriff Lonnogan scrambled up and lunged. Forsythe staggered backward and fell, and Lonnogan sprawled on top of him, punching blindly. Then the whole posse was coming running, Kid Lonnogan was yelling, and suddenly the sheriff was rising through the air.

One moment Boots Lonnogan was pounding away with both fists as Forsythe's fingers gouged his face, the next he was wrenched vertically upward as Samson seized him by the hair in one big heave, and he bellowed in pain; then Samson threw him—straight into Kid Lonnogan, who was charging to his father's aid. Kid Lonnogan sprawled on top of his father, and Forsythe scrambled up, wild-eyed. *You-Wreck-'em-We-Fetch-'em* Jeb Wiggins slugged him in the chest and sent him sprawling again, and the next moment Ben Majuju got Jeb slap-bang in the groin with his hiking boot. Fred Wiggins was charging furiously to his brother's defense and Gasoline Ndhlovu was thundering into the fray, and Lonnogan's fist collected him right in the guts with an explosive gasp; then both Boots and Kid Lonnogan were furiously onto Forsythe again, wildly punching. Forsythe was slugging as he staggered backward,

278

and then Fred Wiggins was in there too, and then Ben and Sixpence, a mad mass of incompetent punching, kicking, and hollering in Swahili and English in the knee-deep undergrowth, while Jeb Wiggins reeled about clutching his testicles and then Samson reentered the melee, and Sheriff Lonnogan swung his boot at his groin. The huge black man doubled up, *hors de combat*, and the sheriff yelled, '*Run y'all.*'

The posse fled into the dense forest in different directions, crashing through the bushes.

Samson half-straightened, bulging-eyed, murderous. He rasped something in Swahili.

Forsythe panted, 'No ... we've got enough to do. They won't give us any more trouble.'


# fifty-two


Elizabeth and Davey did not go back to the cabin that night because the other animals would go there and Davey did not want them to get used to finding him there. He had left them scattered in the valleys. They had left the big cats at the den, with some meat he had brought for them. Davey and Elizabeth camped at the lake. He built a little fire between some boulders.

Maybe, she realized, it was just the calm that precedes the storm, but to Elizabeth it was a peaceful night—with her decisions made. She did not want to talk about it—it was enough that he believed her. It was lovely just to sit. At one time she said, 'Do you believe in God, Davey?'

He smiled. 'Oh, yes. Don't you?'

'Yes. Definitely.'

He was quiet a long moment, then he said: 'How can anybody see the wonders of the world and not believe in God? How can they know about a whale and not believe in God? The wonderful things it can do. A dolphin? A lion?' He paused, thinking. 'How can you hold a pigeon in your hands, look into its beautiful little eye, and know that it can find its way home across a continent it has never seen. Of course there is a God.'

'Exactly,' she agreed fervently. She sloshed more whisky into both mugs, as if to celebrate.

'Where's Big Charlie?'

'In Cherokee.'

That took her by surprise.

'Cherokee? Why?'

'He'll be back tomorrow.' He added, mysteriously, 'I think you'll be pleased when you see him.'

'What do you mean?'

'Let's see if it happens first.'

She was content to let it go, and wait.

'He's a lovely man, Charlie. But very quiet.'

'He's just shy with you.' He added, with a small smile. 'He thinks you're terrific.'

For a moment she wondered what that meant. Then Davey said, 'He'll be pleased you didn't quit.'

She stared at him. She thought: Oh no—just my luck! An ageing teetotaling zoologist, and now a three-hundred pound ex-Jewish Cherokee outlaw. Johnson, you really pick 'em good. Then Davey said, 'I'm very pleased too.'

She was suddenly blushing. She could hardly believe her ears. She had never even thought about him that way . . .

She got up and climbed into her sleeping bag, to cover her embarrassment. 'Good night,' she said.

'Good night.'

Or was that true, that she had never thought about him in that way? She had thought he looked beautiful at times . . . but that was his—inner beauty. His gentleness. His eyes when he looked at his animals. His sweet vision. His love.

Yes, but hadn't there been some of the other thing too? Hadn't she marveled at his body—his stamina, his strength? Hadn't she reacted? And when he smiled, didn't she think he looked absolutely charming? Wasn't this whole thing he had done wrapped up in love? And she was only feeling that same kind of love herself now.

She closed her eyes. Right now she did not want to know. She did not want to demean her decision with other questions.

It was nonsense anyway—he had not exactly made a pass at her. She hardly believed he knew how.

She closed her eyes tighter, and tried to force the thoughts from her mind.

But her body was talking to her now. Aroused by her thoughts.

And her body felt wonderful. She had lost so much weight. She could feel it in the slackness of her waistband, the new roominess in the seat of her jeans. In the ease with which she could run and climb. Her whole body felt lighter and lither, the chubbiness almost all gone from her hips, tummy, and arms; she wished she had a full-length mirror! The only parts of her that didn't feel slimmer were her calf muscles. They had grown with all this foot-slogging; she could feel their new fullness. Which was good! Her legs were getting shapely at last. No longer were they just the 'sexy carrots' Bernard used to joke about.

Then suddenly the chilling dread came back. She tried to stifle it; then had to say it. She whispered, 'Davey? What are we going to do? The man from South Africa must track us down soon.'

He answered quietly from beyond the fire. .

'Wait till tomorrow, Dr. Johnson. You won't have confidence until you see things happen.'

'What? Tell me. I won't betray you.'

'It's often easier to be the hunted than the hunter. A lot of things are about to start happening. You'll see tomorrow.'

She lay still, trying to dispel the old cold fear. Then, out of the darkness came the thought, *Before the cock crows twice, you will deny me thrice . . .*

She was amazed at herself for thinking it. Why did she think of him in Biblical terms?

'Davey?'

'Yes?'

She took a breath.

'Will you please, please call me Elizabeth?'

# fifty-three

Before first light he knelt beside her and shook her shoulder. 'We've got to go now. Back to the cabin.'

It was still dark when they arrived. He told her to stay there, and he disappeared down the path to the old pasture.

With the first light a canoe came slipping silently across the water, with three men in it. As it nosed into the shore, Davey stepped into the water and held the bows steady.

'Good morning, Mr. Bradman!'

As the sun came up they sat inside the cabin, drinking coffee and munching Eric Bradman's biscuits. Elizabeth's spirits were soaring, bubbling over with relief. She was stunned at the public relations job Davey Jordan had pulled off: Eric Bradman could topple kings!

'How long will you need?' Davey asked.

Bradman looked at the forest outside, his handsome old face enthusiastic. The early mist was hanging in the first golden rays shafting between the trees, and out of this beauty had emerged three very relieved elephants and two huge bears who sat like dogs in the undergrowth, never taking their eyes off the door. Eric Bradman shook his head in delight.

'I wish I could stay forever. But I must get back by tomorrow night. To capitalize on Forsythe's debacle yesterday. My wife's filming some important sequences around Cherokee today. I want to splice those in tomorrow night, for screening the next day.' He shook his head enthusiastically. 'It's going to have the whole world weeping.' His wise eyes were moist for a moment. 'Can you show me everything in a day and a half?'

'I think so.'

He turned to Elizabeth. 'And you, Doctor? Will you help?'

She stared at him. She could still hardly believe that the great Eric Bradman was actually here.

'What do you want me to say?'

'Only the truth.'

Only for a moment did she hesitate. For a moment she wanted to clutch at the shreds of the establishment she belonged to, the professional rules and truths she was steeped in. But she knew what the truth was now.

'Yes.'

Davey and Big Charlie were smiling at her, Eric Bradman too, and her spirits soared. With Davey Jordan and Eric Bradman together, anything was possible.

It was not till they were about to set out that Bradman suddenly stopped, remembering something. He pulled a letter from his pocket and handed it to Elizabeth.

'This arrived for you, addressed care of my office in New York. I guess it's a fan-letter.' He added jovially, 'You've got a multitude of fans out there, now, Doctor.'

She stared at the letter. The familiar handwriting on the envelope made her heart turn over. It was postmarked Sydney, Australia, and the writing was her husband's.

Her heart was hammering, she felt a contraction in her stomach, and suddenly her face was throbbing with the old emotion. She was afraid to open it.

She tore it open slowly as the others filed out of the cabin into the beautiful morning.

*My darling Liz, I have read all about your fantastic experiences and I'm kind of basking in reflected glory wherever I go, both in England and Aussie . . .*

It went on to tell her that his admiration for her was unbounded, that his affair with the blonde was over, and that he wanted to come back to her.

# part eleven

## fifty-four

The president of the United States was a conscientious man to whom years in office had not yet really taught the art of delegation of responsibility. He was also deeply religious. This made him a little too ready to drive a softer bargain, to welcome reconciliation. He had come to power on a platform of human rights, and this had proved a two-edged sword. Both by temperament and policy, he often sacrificed practicalities at home and abroad on the altar of vague, emotionally charged principle.

Now he had a new problem, emotively called humane rights. It was unprecedented, and it had become a national issue. Indeed the whole world seemed up in arms. The White House was daily inundated with thousands of telegrams and letters, either urging him to let the stolen animals stay free, or urging him to use all his resources to get them safely back behind bars. Normally such missives would receive scant presidential notice, but elections were around the corner. There were numerous demonstrations, and now, in Washington, hordes of young people with banners. A petition had been delivered to the very gates of the White House and had received wide television and newspaper coverage. It purported to come from the entire Cherokee Nation, and it was headed: 'The Trail of Tears started and ends here.' It was delivered by a band of Indians in full war paint.

Now the president of the United States sat pensively with his First Lady and watched a worrisome television program made by the venerable Eric Bradman and his nationally popular wife.

The forest was flickering with campfires; there was a sea of faces; singing swelled and banners were raised. Barbara Bradman was speaking.

'This is the atmosphere that greeted Stephen Leigh-Forsythe on his return last night from his expedition into the mountains. Boos went up as his helicopter landed, and when word got out that he and his trackers were battered and bruised from a fight they had had with trespassers, quote, unquote, there was loud cheering, and some fireworks were let off . . .'

The screen cut to Forsythe painfully climbing out of his helicopter. His cheek was swollen; he had a limp which he failed to conceal. But he smiled bleakly for the cameras. The same could not be said for his team. Samson walked only with difficulty, his legs well apart and his face like thunder. Sixpence had a swollen eye, and Ben was limping too. Only Frank Hunt looked in good humor, if somewhat footsore, with a cheery smile for all.

Barbara Bradman continued. 'But nobody was able to tell us what really happened in the woods today that brought them home all tattered and torn, as this clip shows.'

Professor Ford snapped, 'I don't know because Mr. Forsythe chooses to give me no details. Ask him yourself. Now, please excuse me.'

'Are you going to use troops again to guard against more trespassers?'

'No. It would take half a million soldiers to encircle the Smokies effectively. Now, will you kindly excuse me.'

With that the campers' fireworks went off. The president smiled, despite himself. He was quite sure that Bradman had edited his film that way, but it was funny. And worrying.

'This morning, Mr. Forsythe and one of his trackers were unable to go out, due to their injuries. This left Professor Ford in charge again. He and a diminished party left at dawn to start their renewed search for spoor. Meanwhile, Mr. Forsythe went to pay a visit to Chief Nathaniel Owle of the Cherokees . . .'

The road through Cherokee was lined with hostile faces and masses of banners. There were a good number of black faces too.

The president paid close attention. Where had they sprung from? Barbara Bradman supplied the answer.

'Several busloads of blacks arrived this morning from neighbouring cities to join the demonstrators of Cherokee. A spokesman for them, Mr. Cunningham, a school teacher, had this to say.'

An elderly black face appeared. 'In our school we had been following this drama closely, and after considering all the pros and cons we held a vote; the unanimous verdict was we want these animals to be free. Freedom is something we blacks understand better than whites. Like these animals, our ancestors came to this country as slaves, and that memory is not so distant. My grandfather was a slave. Most of these children have heard tales from *their* grandparents about *his* father, and so on. We are aware of those days, far more than whites. And, when all is said and done, most of us still find ourselves living in conditions . . . er . . . reminiscent of our unhappy origins, despite election promises. We have a feeling of comradeship with the Cherokee people—and with all the Indians. They are an underprivileged minority, just as we are. Let's not mince words. They had their lands stolen. We feel for them. They had their birth rights stolen, just as we did. And so did these animals. And the Cherokee people. By rights they own these Great Smoky Mountains. They want the animals to stay—perhaps to them it is a kind of emotional restocking . . .'

Then an angelic black girl took his place.

'We never thought much about them until this happened. Now we've all got class projects; we get books from the libraries and make scrapbooks. We really want to study Nature now. And the whole environmental crisis too, about pollution and overpopulation and the energy crisis and all that. It's *very* interesting.'

'What do you want the government to do about these animals?'

'Oh,' the girl gushed, 'we want them to be *free!*'

'What do your mother and father think?'

'The same. Every night they're glued to the televison; they're all rootin' for the animals. Everybody!'

'How do you think the animals feel, now they're free?'

'Oh! . . .' the girl clasped her hands. 'They so *happy!*'

The beatific black girl's smile faded into the puffed-up black eye of Stephen Leigh-Forsythe as he climbed out of the US government vehicle outside Chief Nathaniel Owle's office. People stood both sides of the entrance in silent rebuke. Forsythe winced as he put his weight on his injured leg. Barbara Bradman reappeared on the screen.

'The media were not admitted to the meeting, but we do know what happened *out*side. When Mr. Forsythe emerged he found this.'

All the tires on his vehicle were as flat as pancakes. Forsythe glared with his good eye. Then he limped furiously, climbed in and slammed the door. The wildlife liaison officer gaped, then hurried after him. Forsythe gunned the engine and, before the liaison officer had closed the door, the vehicle roared flatly away.

Then the screen faded, and the dignified, twinkling smile of Chief Nathaniel Owle formed. He was seated in his office beneath two portraits: one of Junaluska, the other of the president of the United States.

'The meeting was more or less polite, I think, in the curious way of foreigners. We Indians have considerable experience of colonialists; we understand their little ways, from reading our history books.'

'What did he want?'

'Apart from my scalp?' the old chief twinkled. 'Well, now, there's another curious thing. You see, I had invited Mr. Forsythe, as a matter of courtesy, to visit me some days ago. But when he arrived today he seemed to come not as a visitor, but as if he was a kind of detective. But I guess this is just a curious colonialist characteristic and should not be taken too seriously. I must say I thought it was a good thing he was not addressing one of our black citizens like that, or he might have gotten his other eye blackened.' The old man smiled indulgently at the camera, and went on brightly. 'I suppose that in the unsentimental business the government is bent on, diplomacy is not a priority. After all, we Indians do not add up to many voters.'

The president of the United States groaned.

'What transpired between the two of you?' Barbara Bradman said.

'Well,' the old chief said, 'he made a rather blunt suggestion that two of my fellow tribesmen, who assisted him, deliberately misled him. He was rather emphatic about that. I asked him how an expert such as he could possibly be misled by anybody. After the huge sums the government is paying him, one expects him *not* to be misled, doesn't one? My goodness! With what this young man is costing us, could not the government compensate the owners of these animals and leave the poor creatures in peace? Still, government moves in curious ways ... And the president is a law-abiding man, I believe.' He sighed with the patience of old age. 'However, Mr. Forsythe went on to request that I ban the people who are presently visiting our little town. He said they were disturbing the peace and being less than friendly.' The old man spread his hands. 'What right have I to do that? American citizens are free to go anywhere. The campgrounds are private property. They seem perfectly decent people, as far as I can see. If they wish to express their views, they are free to do so in Cherokee. No, no, no, Mr. Forsythe, I said, you may be able to clamp down on public sentiment in Africa, but not in Cherokee. And I'm sure the president'—he indicated the portrait—'would agree with me.'

Barbara Bradman was smiling. 'What else?'

'Well; finally he rather changed his tune. He really can be a charming young man, and he is very lucky because he seems to be able to turn this on and off like a faucet, which must be a great convenience. He asked me to "provide" him with a number of "honest" and "reliable" trackers. The area is so huge that finding the spoor may take some time, even for an expert such as him.'

Chief Owle sighed. 'Well, I had to tactfully explain.' He spread his hands. 'Of course, if any of my people *want* to work for Mr. Forsythe, they are free to do so. But every Cherokee *wants* these animals to stay! Even today we delivered a petition to the White House. I believe there will be more. Indian chiefs from all over America have cabled me expressing their solidarity. It seems the whole Indian population wants these animals to stay in the Great Smoky Mountains. As do a great many other people of goodwill, all over the world ...'

His eyes took on a faraway look. He had his audience the world over enraptured, even the president, waiting for wisdom.

'You see, to us humble Indians, this a *spiritual* issue. Apart from the fact that we like animals, that we now realize just how inhumane

289

zoos are, and circuses, apart from the fact that now they have tasted freedom in our mountains and it is heartless to send them back to their miserable cages—apart from all that, this crisis has a very special significance to our tribe.' He paused. 'For it is right here, in these very mountains, that the notorious Trail of Tears began—when the president of America, Andrew Jackson *himself*, defied his own Supreme Court and stole the last of our lands, dragged our women and children from their homes, and herded us Cherokees into stockades like cattle; then deported us to Oklahoma, through a terrible winter journey lasting six months that claimed four thousand Cherokee lives. It was in these very mountains that Chief Junaluska'—he pointed at the portrait above him—'who had saved the life of President Jackson at the Battle of Horseshoe Bend, raised his eyes heavenward and cried, "O God, if I had known at the Battle of Horseshoe what I know now, American history would have been differently written." '

The old chieftain slowly lowered his fist and looked at the camera with tears in his eyes.

'And it was in these Smoky Mountains that a handful of our grandparents hid and escaped that shameful round-up of our people. And from that pathetic handful we Cherokees of today are descended. So those mountains out there are also the place which gave *re*birth to our present-day people. It is also our *re*birthplace . . .' He looked at his audience with old, strong eyes. 'And now *another* Trail of Tears has ended in our Great Smoky Mountains. But a Trail of Freedom! A valiant fight for life that brings tears to the eyes. And once again our mountains have given sanctuary! There is new life again in our sacred Smokies.'

He paused, his eyes shining.

'And those mountains *are* sacred to us, for yet another reason . . .' He wagged his finger gently. 'Because, according to our Cherokee legends, it is in the mountains that the very first life on earth began.' He paused to let that weighty notion sink in. 'For when the earth was covered in water and only a little mud, the Grandfather Buzzard was sent down from the great Sky Rock, where all the animals lived. To look for dry land, and finally he came to this place. And then all the animals on the Sky Rock came down to live here. They were the fathers and mothers of every creature in the world! *Including* Man . . .'

He looked at his audience solemnly, then gave his lovely smile.

'Think about that a moment, please. Isn't that a beautiful thought? It is the Garden of Eden. Isn't that a thought to be cherished? To rejoice in? So you see how spiritually exciting it is that these animals have come to our sacred mountains.' He spread his hands eloquently. 'Our Garden of Eden is created again. The animals have come back—as they did tens of thousand of years ago. To start a new world, afresh. And to multiply . . .' He looked at the world earnestly, then his old eyes twinkled, inviting his audience to share another delightful thought. 'And, perhaps, did not the Great One send them? Did He not send Davey Jordan as once long ago He sent the Grandfather Buzzard?'

He let that thought dangle, his fine old face wise and kind, then he sat back unhappily.

'And we Cherokees look about us with joy and wonder. But then what do we see?' He looked grim suddenly, and said slowly, sadly, 'We see the White Man descend upon us, all over again. To spoil it all again. Ruthlessly, thoughtlessly determined to start a new Trail of Tears all over again . . .'

# fifty-five

Elizabeth went down to the lake through the early morning mist, peeled off her clothes, and dove in.

The water was like glass, and it was icy cold. She struck out from the bank for two hundred strokes, whirled around, and came splashing back. She scrambled out, gasping and goosefleshed—but she felt wonderful. As she dried herself she looked down at her legs: they were firm, the dimples gone from her thighs, her whole leg shapely. She gripped a handful of buttock, and it too was hard; and

291

the spare tire was gone from her stomach; she could feel flat muscle underneath.

She combed out her wet hair, feeling the glow of her new body, the joy of a beautiful day. She dressed in fresh clothes, and began to head back through the forest.

Eric Bradman had left last night, after two intensive days. She had been impressed by how hard he had worked, how fast, how ingeniously. She had also been very impressed with Davey. He had been highly anxious that Bradman make a good film, and he was nervous; but when he had to speak he had been astonished at his fluency; he had spoken with a confidence that was both so intense and gentle that it reached out and took your heart; he had projected his strength of character beautifully—his goodness. And when he smiled he had touched her so, that she just wanted to love him.

Yes, love him. Not in a man-woman, romantic way, but as a person, for his warmth and justness. And dear, sweet Big Charlie. In his gentle-giant manner he had come across beautifully too. He had been horrified to learn he too was going to appear on film. But he had done it. Eric Bradman himself had been excellent, the born preacher, eloquent, with such clever powers of persuasion; they could not have had a better advocate!

And Bradman had thoroughly enjoyed himself. He had wanted much longer to do them full justice, but he had to get back to develop his film. His confidence had been infectious: By God, he was going to jerk tears from every eye in the world. Did not every man still yearn for paradise? And it had seemed as if Nature and the animals had gotten together and resolved to put their best foot forward: with the early morning mists and the sunrises glinting in tiny spectrums on the dewdrops, and the spring buds and flowers, and the buzzing of the bees and the singing of the birds.

When the sun came up, King Kong and Auntie still were lying in their nests, stretching, yawning, scratching. For a while they had hung around the cabin, eyes soulful, waiting for Davey to tell them what to do. Then they began to melt into the forest, to feed, and the chimpanzees went with them.

They were still cautious. But they began to relax in the warming sunshine, in the pleasure of feeding on the lush abundance, in

292

experimenting, examining new morsels between forefinger and thumb, thoughtfully tasting. They browsed across the open pasture and into the forest, getting bolder and bolder, losing sight of each other but communicating by grunts.

King Kong was always on the alert. For now, back in the wilderness, his dimmed memory had returned of that terrible day a decade ago when men had murdered his clan to capture him; the shattering gunfire, the screams, the terror, and the clubs. And King Kong knew now that he was naturally the leader, even of the chimpanzees, for might is right in the kingdom of apes. Even Florrie, who used to be the boss of the chimps in the circus, accepted that now.

So big King Kong stalked warily through his new kingdom on his knuckles, and even when he stopped to eat he was watchful. When he lost sight of Auntie or of one of the chimps for too long, he gave a short bark, and they came back; when it was time to move he gave an imperative grunt and stared in the direction he wanted them to go, and they went.

So when Eric Bradman had come stalking up with his camera, Auntie bobbed out of sight, then promptly bobbed up again—but King Kong ripped up foliage, threw it in the air, and beat his black chest as his troupe fled. Then he spotted Davey, and stopped in mid-roar. He stared, blinked, and slowly lowered himself.

Davey approached him, smiling and congratulating him, and Bradman filmed. The chimpanzees and Auntie came creeping back when he called, and, when they were quite reassured, they went up to the camera and stared inquisitively into it, almost poking their fingers into the audience's eye. But not King Kong. He stood back, like a great dangerous dog, and glowered and grunted, and made it clear that only because Davey was there did he tolerate such foolishness.

But with patience and Davey's conspicuous presence even King Kong reluctantly settled down to Bradman. He filmed them feeding, and then playing, climbing trees. Elizabeth had stood in front of the camera and said, 'This is probably the first time in their lives that these two gorillas have actually *played*. This is the most mind-blowing cruelty that most zoos commit—and all circuses: nothing for their animals to play with. Including, I'm sorry to admit, the famous Bronx Zoo. We have a very modern Ape House, but our huge gorillas have only one small cell and one concrete tree. The London Zoo is no better. Even human prisoners have recreation. It is a scientific fact that all animals need to play, just as we do—for exercise, to give vent to natural feelings. But these animals are still experimenting. Now that the desperate business of survival is over, they're learning. In fact, they're overdoing it. They're eating until the edge is off their appetite, then off they go to romp, then they get a bit confused and stop. That's because they're run out of ideas. These natural playthings are new to them. Then the chimpanzees tumble and roll—that's probably a circus trick, but now they're doing it for fun. They're having a lovely time . . .'

She had committed herself. And she was glad. It was definitely a breach of her contract of employment. It probably even made her an accomplice. She did not care.

But when she came walking up to the cabin after her swim, her towel over her shoulder, she sensed something was different, and immediately she spotted it. Davey's knapsack was packed, and Big Charlie's was gone.

'Where's Charlie?' Her heart was sinking.

Davey had water boiling. 'Up to the top,' he said. 'Thunderhead.'

'What for?'

'To keep a lookout.' He poured water into her cup for coffee.

'And you?'

'I'm going to look after the lions for a while. Teach them to hunt.'

She stared at him. 'Am I going with you?'

He looked at her apologetically.

'No, Dr. Johnson. I need to be alone to teach them. It's getting urgent now.'

She sat down slowly. 'Yes. Of course . . .' She felt for her cigarettes. 'And?'What am I—what do you want me to do?'

'Will you be afraid to stay here by yourself?'

Of course she would be afraid. 'Can I keep Sam?'

Sam cocked his ears at hearing his name. 'I need Sam to herd the wild boar.'

She nodded distractedly. 'Of course ... no. No, I won't be afraid.' And she wouldn't be. She would have the animals for company at night.

'You don't need Sam to protect you. I wouldn't leave you alone if I thought that.'

'No, I know.' She fumbled mentally. 'What do you want me to do?'

'Stop the animals hanging around the cabin. Take them away each day. Then leave them.'

She stared at him. 'Will they follow me?'

'If I'm not here. In fact, they'll start going off by themselves. It's important that I'm not here. That they don't see me.'

She nodded. 'Yes. I understand ... When are you leaving?'

'Right now. I'm going to slip out the back door so they don't see me go.'

'Oh. Right ... What do I do if I need help? Come up to the lions' den?'

'Only if it's an emergency.' He smiled. 'Try not to worry, Dr. Johnson. Big Charlie's up there. With a whole lot of Cherokees dotted all along that trail. They'll know when anybody's coming.'

Thank God for that.

'Then what'll Charlie do?'

'Those guys know what to do. They're pretty smart about these woods.' Yes, of course. Thank God for Big Charlie.

'Okay.' She forced a smile. 'When do I see you again?'

'I'll need as long as it takes, Dr. Johnson. It's not us that matters. It's the animals.'

She nodded.

His face filled with optimism.

'But I don't think it'll be very long—before Operation Noah is cancelled. Mr. Bradman's film will go out on television tonight.'

She looked at his strong, gentle face, alight with enthusiasm, and she felt her spirits rise.

'Good.' She smiled a little wryly. 'So that's why you left me alone four days ago. To test me. See if I could take it.'

'To give you a chance to think about all of it. You can still leave now, if you want.'

'Don't be silly.'

He smiled, 'Okay.'

He stood up. 'So long, Dr. Johnson.'

She wanted to close her eyes and whisper, *Just hold me, Davey . . . just hold me once tight*. She looked at him.

'So long. Pardner . . .' She smiled tightly. 'Please give my love to the lions. And lots to poor old Sultan.'

He picked up his knapsack, slung it across one shoulder, and picked up the rifle.

He looked at her; he hesitated; then, gently, he put his hand on top of her head.

She closed her eyes. There was nothing amorous about his touching her. But she could almost feel a balm coming out of his hand that made her want to stretch up her arms to him. For a moment they were completely still. She opened her eyes. He looked down at her and gave her the most gentle, affectionate smile. Then he turned and silently slipped out the back door.

She whispered, to herself: 'And please call me *Elizabeth*.'

For five minutes she sat. Examining how she felt.

Davey Jordan had just touched her, for the first time. And she understood a little better his sweet magnetism. She had glimpsed, in that moment, how the animals felt when he touched them.

Now he was gone, and she felt lost. Not afraid. Bereft. When Bradman had left, some of her confidence had gone with him. But now Davey had gone, and she felt bereft. If she never saw him again, she would feel grief. She would want to search the world for him; and if she never saw him again, she would cherish her memory of him and rejoice in the vision she had glimpsed and shared with him: a man with the strength and the sweetness to recreate paradise.

*Out of the strong came forth sweetness . . .*

Then, out of nowhere, she remembered the letter in her pocket. She had read it a dozen times; each time it had put her emotions in a whirl, she had put it back, and put off making the decision.

She slowly opened the letter again.

*My darling Liz . . .*

She stopped there. She knew what her decision was.

But for another long moment she hesitated. Then she slowly

reached out and dropped the letter into the fire, and watched the flames eat it.

*There . . . She* was free, too, now . . .

# fifty-six

The town of Gatlinburg nestles in the Tennessee foothills of the Smokies. It is a pretty town, one broad main street sweeping right out of the wilderness, lined with shops and restaurants and woodsy motels with rustic fences. It is a prosperous little place, for every year eight million tourists pass through. The folk are decent and friendly. But they were not so friendly tonight.

A meeting was being held in the Civic Center. Almost every man and his wife were there, plus many of the press contingent from the Operation Noah camp, and a large group from the campgrounds of Cherokee. Sheriff Lonnogan from neighbouring Hawker County was there, complete with fractured ribs sustained in his fight with Forsythe, accompanied by his son and Jeb Wiggins. The meeting was presided over by an elected chairman, and its purpose was to discuss The Situation. Gatlinburg should have been starting to enjoy its annual tourist boom, yet the Great Smoky Mountains National Park was sealed tighter than a drum. The Rod and Gun Club had formed themselves into a Home Guard to protect Gatlinburg from the predations of the animals suddenly infesting this neck of the woods, and this gave the town an air of siege. It was a stormy meeting, and it was being televised.

The first image to appear on the screen was of an angry man saying, 'Where's the tourists? Locked out! Our motels empty. Our shops empty. Even the hippie-types and journalists are all over at Cherokee where the action is! The Chamber of Commerce says trade is down ninety percent on last year. We're losing money hand over fist while this hired gun from South Africa sits in his tent with his sprained ankle at a thousand bucks a day!'

Loud cheers. The Chairman said, 'What is your proposal, Mr. Dickson?'

'I say we give the government an ultimatum: get those animals out in seven days or we go in and get 'em ourselves.'

'How?'

'Why're we pussyfooting round with Big Apple zookeepers and English schoolboys from Africa? Gatlinburg has a proud mountain tradition; we're quite capable of looking after ourselves!'

There were loud cheers, and a woman's voice shouted, 'What about our children?'

'One at a time, please—this is a democratic meeting.'

Freda Jackson stood up defiantly. 'All we hear about is the Chamber of Commerce. I say, what about our children while all these dangerous animals are loose? Lions and tigers and grizzly bears! Not to mention elephants that could smash that barricade down in one thump and come charging right through the town. How can we let our children go out? Even to Sunday School. Just go down to the drugstore for a soda? Even let them drive their cars in case they get charged by an elephant! Now that isn't farfetched, Mr. Chairman; we saw what happened in Hot Springs.'

Cheers and jeers, and the Chairman shouted, 'Order, please. Mr. Dickson, what is your proposal exactly? This meeting will be a failure if we don't come up with a constructive proposal to put to the authorities.'

'Well,' Hank Dickson started, 'if this hired gun from South Africa hasn't succeeded with his fancy drugs in seven days—or five days—I say we are the authorities.' (Cheers and boos.) 'These mountains aren't meant for wild animals—they're ours. We got plenty of good hunters offering to do their civic duty!'

There was loud jeering and shouts of 'shame,' and a bunch of young people started derisively singing, 'Davey Crockett, King of the Wild Frontier.'

Another voice made itself heard: 'With these exotic animals, our tourist traffic would double. What a story! People will come from far and wide to see our elephants and lions and gorillas. Especially if we encourage them to live in an open area like Cades Cove. We'll have wall-to-wall tourists. We'll become famous as the American town that set itself up as a miniature Africa. I say we should get *more* animals. Let them breed. And as for the animals attacking us, that's *really* rubbish. Animals know where they're safe, and they stick there; they don't come out of the game reserves in Africa, or attack the tourists in their cars.'

'Once is enough,' somebody shouted.

'But this is not Africa,' the chairman said. 'The point is these mountains are for hikers; the people of Gatlinburg go for picnics, eight million tourists a year pass through.'

A woman stood up. 'Good God! Is this what we Americans have come to? The wilderness is just for picnics? Is this all that's left of the American frontier spirit—tourists in their automobiles? What's happened to us? We've got black bears up there now, haven't we? They don't spoil our precious picnics.'

'Lions and tigers are a bit different from black bears, Mrs. Munday.'

'Exactly!' somebody shouted.

· 'But Bill Abrams is right; animals in game reserves don't give problems! There're grizzlies in the Rocky Mountains, and they don't eat the tourists.'

'There's always a first time,' somebody shouted, and there were shouts of 'Yeah, yeah.'

Miss Williams, the schoolteacher, stood up with authority. 'Mr. Chairman, ladies and gentlemen.' She glared around. 'I am *appalled* at most of the arguments we've heard tonight. Do you realize what we've been talking about? Nothing but money! I am *ashamed* to be a Gatlinburger tonight. We're so-called mountain men! Yet we're dismayed to find a few animals in the wilderness God made. We sound like a bunch of sissies. The people of Cherokee put us to shame.'

Barbara Bradman took over the screen again.

'Meanwhile, what has the Operation Noah team been doing? For the last two days, Mr. Forsythe has been confined to camp with his sprained ankle, but every day Professor Ford and Mr. Hunt have flown off with the African trackers. Earlier tonight Mr. Forsythe gave this brief conference.'

On the screen the campfire's light leaped. Forsythe stood at the table outside his operations tent, flanked by a grim-looking Jonas Ford. Forsythe smiled reassuringly.

'The going *has* proved slow because two of us have been out of action, but there's nothing to be depressed about. It's a huge area, very steep, with thousands of valleys, and visibility is about twenty-five yards at best. Also, the heavy foliage cuts out a lot of light and makes tracking difficult. Searching for spoor is often, of necessity, a process of elimination—which is a positive process.'

'How much have you eliminated?'

'We have covered most of the area from Newfound Gap back to the Pigeon River. We are satisfied now that they're not in that half of the Smokies.'

'But that's a huge area. How can you have covered all that in five days?'

'Of course,' Forsythe said reasonably, 'our handful of men could not cover every nook and cranny. But my trackers are the best, and in five days they've got a pretty good idea of what's been around. However, in view of the huge area, we do need more trackers. Three experienced Cherokees have now offered their services. So . . .' he smiled reassuringly again, 'I think business will go a bit brisker.'

'When will *you* be back in business?'

'As soon as spoor is found, gentlemen.'

'But do you think you know where they are?'

Forsythe knew better than to answer that one directly.

'A good hunter plays his hunches, but he also covers the field.'

On that note Stephen Leigh-Forsythe was faded out, to the music of the new smash-hit ballad, 'The Great Free Smoky Mountains,' and then Eric Bradman appeared on screen, a triumphant expression on his face.

'But *here* are the hunted animals . . . alive and well . . .'

The music swelled; the sun was rising, and through the mist loomed the benign massiveness of Rajah, his wise eye contentedly blinking as his trunk curled up to his mouth with a clump of grass; then he faded, and there was King Kong stretching his shaggy arms and yawning cavernously right into the camera; the sun came through the trees, and there was the fat furry face of Pooh snuffling happily; as the ballad swelled there followed a series of montages: the chimpanzees romping, rolling and tumbling; Jamba rolling happily on her back, all four massive hooves waving in the air; Tommy lying on his back in the sun with his eyes closed; Davey

300

Jordan playing in the grass with Kitty. Then Bradman's story began.

It was a stunningly good program, and it certainly stunned Forsythe. The liaison officer had come running to his tent. 'Eric Bradman has found the animals, sir!' He could not believe his ears. His expanded tracker force had just returned from their first day with still nothing to report.

Forsythe stared at the television screen, his anger rising like gall. He stayed long enough to see Davey Jordan romping with Kitty, then he turned and limped away. He was so angry he did not hear the suppressed laughter from the reporters.

'Call Professor Ford! I want Bradman found. If he's not around, get the police. I don't care a damn about journalists' privilege of secrecy. He's an accomplice.'

But Eric Bradman was nowhere to be found.

The president of the United States did not see the program, but the First Lady sure did, and he heard all about it for two solid hours when he got to bed; and he knew the White House was in for a new deluge of telegrams. In Gatlinburg everybody saw it, and whether they were for or against the animals they were delighted that the hired gun from South Africa had been made a fool of. Every person in Cherokee saw it, and there were roars of applause and singing until late, around the campfires.

One hell of a party sprang up at the press bar that night; the journalists had been bored stiff for days, and Eric Bradman's scoop had given them plenty to write about, with many a horselaugh between the lines, and many a lofty phrase for the animals.

Close by, another party developed. Ambrose Jones presented two bottles of corn whiskey to Forsythe's four African trackers, for all of whom alcohol ruthlessly had been banned by their boss. It contained a tasteless additive which induces a monumental hangover and acute nausea for several days.

In Hawkstown, another party developed in Fred Wiggins's *You Bust-'em-We-Buy-'em Scrapyard*, as Lonnogan's posse watched Bradman's program and guffawed at the snotnose hired gun from

Africa. Lonnogan watched with a grim, dangerous smile. He banged his fist into his palm.

'Goddamit, *now's* the time to go back in and get that Jordan, an' really laugh that Englishman out of town.' He looked around. 'Anybody think they recognized any part of that forest on that film?'

In Sylva, the three men watched the television set in the den. Their rifles were cleaned and ready.

'Well? Recognized anything?'

They all shook their heads.

'He was careful not to film anything conspicuous.'

The first man went to the television, pushed a button, and the video cassette rewound. Eric Bradman's face reappeared on the screen. 'But *here* are the hunted animals. Alive and well . . .'

'Watch carefully. For anything . . . and we'll keep playing this video until we're sure to recognize places when we come to them.'

'Dogs,' the second man said. 'I still say we use the dogs.'

'Perhaps,' the first man said. 'But those are good dogs; I don't want mine being murdered by lions and tigers.'

'There he is . . .' the second man breathed, looking at Rajah. 'Oh, boy, you're mine . . .' He raised his arms like a rifle and squinted down the imaginary sights. 'Bang. Right between your eyes' boy . . .'


# fifty-seven

The next day two long caravans of Indians set out from Cherokee and Oklahoma, in rented trucks, buses, and old automobiles. They were carrying four thousand wooden crosses, one for each Indian who had died on the Trail of Tears, and they were headed for Washington to deliver a petition to the president.

Forsythe left camp at sunrise. He was even more furious than he had been the night before because the Cherokee trackers had not shown up and his African trackers were almost blind with hangovers. They sat in the helicopter, bloodshot eyes closed, suffering the din of the engine, stomachs heaving.

Frank Hunt did not look too well either. He too had a monumental hangover. He had had one hell of a night at the press bar, tickled pink that Horsemeat Ford's protégé had been made a horse's ass.

Sitting beside him, Professor Ford was still appalled at Bradman's film. Its cheap, sentimental sensationalism would give the world quite the wrong impression! And the criticisms of his zoo had infuriated him. The sheer ignorance of it! Whipping up public emotion, absolute bias, total suppression of the simple truth that animals get used to captivity—even like it.

And as regards Elizabeth—well, he was absolutely *appalled* at her unprofessional conduct! She was in clear breach of her contract. Had she taken leave of her senses? Had she gone temporarily off her rocker? Lord—that was a beautiful Ape House! Almost brand new . . .

Forsythe ordered the pilot to hover near Clingmans Dome. They climbed down the ladders. Then Forsythe let rip at his woebegone Africans in Swahili.

'Are you men? No—you are children! Are you worthy of my trust? No—you are *tsotsis!* You are *skellums!* Today you will suffer, my *tsotsi* children! Today you will work until the blood comes out your pores! Today you will work until your excrement drops!'

For another two minutes he heaped traditional curses. His trackers stood stoically, eyes downcast. Then he turned and pointed angrily in the direction of Thunderhead Mountain.

'They are somewhere over there—*children!* It is no good searching for spoor on the Appalachian Trail because the rain will have washed it out—*children!* So get down into those valleys and look! And may your heads throb right down to your toes!'

He assigned them their areas. Half on the North Carolina side, half on the Tennessee side.

Then it was discovered that the batteries in their radios had been stolen, and so had the flares for the flare guns.

The helicopter had gone, and there was no way of calling it back.

It took Frank Hunt the rest of that day to walk back to the camp, to tell the pilot to bring new batteries. Forsythe refused to release his trackers for the mission. But none of them did any tracking that day. Once out of his sight, each lay down and nursed his nausea. They were incapable of doing their job.

It was late afternoon when Frank Hunt reached the camp, sorely in need of a drink, his feet aching. He gave the pilot Forsythe's orders, gave Chuck Worthy's caravan a wide berth, and gratefully repaired to the press bar with another good story for his new buddies about what happened out there in the woods today.

The sun was setting when the helicopter touched down near Clingmans Dome, with the news that there were no batteries to be found at the camp; they had all been stolen. But the liaison officer was fetching more from Nashville.

That night, Forsythe summoned a meeting in the warden's office at Oconaluftee. Only Jonas Ford and the warden were present, and Forsythe did all the talking. Sometimes his voice quivered, but he looked murderously calm.

'We're going to put an end to this Cherokee sabotage, gentlemen. Complete secrecy. That's what we're going to have from now on. Nobody will speak to the press, except Professor Ford. And I will tell him what to say . . . There're spies in this camp. And up in those mountains there are plenty more spies—waiting to jump on us, or to warn Jordan. Or to try to mislead us with more false spoor. But we're going to play them at their own game, gentlemen.'

He looked at his small audience.

'First, we're going to move our tents from that pasture right into this visitors' center. That includes the trackers and Hunt. *Nobody* else will be allowed in here. All they'll know is when they see our helicopter come and go. Until we bring the first animal in. Understood?'

The warden nodded. Ford looked at him grimly. Forsythe turned to the warden.

'Now, I want four trustworthy black men found immediately. They must be the same size as my trackers. Get them from the armed services, or the police. They must be absolutely trustworthy and sworn to secrecy.'

The warden and Jonas Ford were staring at him.

'And,' Forsythe continued, 'I want one white man. Also from the services. He must be my size. . .'

# part twelve

## fifty-eight

But in the Garden of Eden, there was peace. With each day, Elizabeth's hopes rose higher.

Maybe it was an unreal peace, but she fiercely closed her mind and trusted—in the God in whom she ardently believed, in Eric Bradman's powers of persuasion, in Davey Jordan, in Big Charlie and his Cherokees. *Is this not how You intended it, God? Then stand by us now!*

When she prayed, she almost believed that this was part of His Grand Design, to restore the world. Had not the world gone mad? Was not Man overrunning it—such an evolutionary success that he was destroying it as if he were a plague? How much longer could the earth's resources last? And now we even had acid rain—acidified by industrial pollution of faraway countries and blown across oceans to fall on lakes and rivers, killing the fish. How much longer before the whole system broke down? How much longer could wild animals survive with the jungles being cut back every year? How long before all animals were kept in skyscraper batteries just for men to eat?

*Is that how You intended it all to end, God?*

When she thought of it like this, she was almost positive that Davey Jordan was part of a Grand Design. And Eric Bradman—one of the most powerful voices in America! Wasn't it succeeding? Hadn't Bradman said that the world was up in arms? O God, did You not also send Eric Bradman?

But from time to time the dread returned, the feeling of unreality:

that soon the terror and stampeding, the blood and thunder would come back and break this happiness wide open—that they were going to be hunted down one by one, taken back to their cages ... Then she prayed fiercely all over again.

Every morning she was gone with the sunrise to do her medical rounds, making notes for the scientific paper she was going to write, determined to wring every moment out of the day. Every morning was like the first day God made, the mist rising from tumbling streams, the eastern sky flaming red, the whole world young and beautiful. And she felt young and almost beautiful too.

She was not even worried about the lions any more. Davey was teaching them to hunt. Davey could do anything: make fire, find food and shelter, hunt, fix, fight, find his way, lead them to safety. Davey could run from Athens to Sparta.

The lions stayed around the mineshaft, waiting for him to return.

Davey slept there as little as possible, to break their dependence on him. Every day he took them out hunting; every time they failed. At the end of every second day he shot a boar. He fed it to them back at the mine, and disappeared. When the meat was finished, when even Sultan had been allowed his share, they would venture forth to try to follow him. They followed the stream, hesitantly, slinking, sniffing, but after half a mile they would turn back. They went back to the familiar mineshaft, where they knew he would return.

For the first few days there had been a complete breakdown in law and order, squabbles between Princess and Kitty about who should lie where, who could come back into the mineshaft, and when. But now order was returning. Tommy had put a stop to their quarrels with a snarl and a swat of his big paw. Old Tommy didn't know what was happening either, but he was biggest and he wasn't going to put up with too much nonsense. Mostly he dominated the mouth of the mine, watching the wilderness, waiting for Davey to come back and feed them.

But Kitty was starting to learn something about the wilderness, now. For the first few days she had not dared go far out of sight. But then, one day, she got bolder—cautiously, slinking through the undergrowth, ready to whirl and run back to the protection of the mine. But she only saw things to interest her: the scuttling of insects, the fluttering of birds. She froze when she saw them, crouched, gathered for the spring, and pounced: but it was all in play. Then one day she scented a black bear cub.

Kitty froze. Her blood quickened. She stood absolutely still, cat's eyes wide, scenting his position; then her lithe body lowered a fraction. She started, soundlessly following its scent, as faultlessly as if she had been born in these mountains.

The cub was one-third grown. He was glossy and black and fat, and it was a beautiful morning for a bear cub to be out, rooting around by himself. His black nose was buried in a hole, his shaggy backside stuck up happily to the sunny morning, completely oblivious.

Kitty crouched, watching him, fifteen yards away, every nerve tuned, hunting instinct pumping through her. Then she did something she just naturally knew: she tested the shifting breeze, and began to creep downwind of the cub.

She moved through the undergrowth without a sound, every muscle taut, her killer heart pounding, never taking her murderous eyes off the bustling black backside.

Kitty stalked five crouched steps, then she stopped. Her sharp claws dug into the earth; for a long blood-thrilled moment she gathered herself; then her muscles unleashed and she sprang.

One moment the little bear cub had his snout happily full of roots, the next he was hit by a roaring monster. Kitty hit him a full charge, jaws agape, claws outstretched. He was knocked flat into the grub hole, the air knocked out of him, then the terrible creature's jaws were fast around his gullet, shaking him, strangling him, and the little bear twisted and kicked and screamed; his sharp claws slashed into Kitty's hide. She crouched furiously over him, joyfully killing him, shaking and snarling. Now she could taste blood, and suddenly Kitty knew why she was killing this bear. The lust to kill and eat was suddenly a frenzy, and she shook and shook her head so the bear was wrenched back and forth.

Then something hit her senseless. Like a ton of bricks, as big mommy black bear came thundering onto the scene. One moment Kitty was minding her own business killing a bear; the next it seemed her head was knocked off. She reeled, stunned, astonished, and all she saw were these huge black jaws and outraged eyes and giant paws swinging. Kitty dodged, shocked, almost falling over herself, and then tried to go bounding after the scampering cub again, but Big Mommy was after her like an avalanche with murder in her heart. Her great clawed paw swiped Kitty on her rump so her whole backside swung around in mid-bound, and Kitty decided to quit.

She turned and fled three hundred panicked yards, with a still-stunned head, then she slowed. She stopped, flanks heaving, and looked back, her tail swishing. Her chest was stinging from the scratches. She glared, smarting with the injustice of it all. For a long, mean moment she considered going back; then she decided she had had enough, and started back toward the mineshaft.

After five hundred yards she sat down on a warm rock and began to lick her wounds. Her cuts were hurting, but Kitty had had a good morning. She had learned something more about the wilderness, how to stalk and hunt, and best of all she had discovered the thrill of it all—and that all animals are made of meat.

# fifty-nine

When the sun went down, the elephants reappeared out of the forest, but they did not hang around close to the cabin any more; they just liked to know she was not too far.

Elizabeth slept outside now. During the night, she could glimpse them through the trees, great, silver-dappled wraiths; it was lovely to know that they were there. Sometimes one would come toward her and stand right next to her, feeding and sighing, huge bodies looming over her; but she was not afraid. They knew she was there, and they stepped carefully around her.

But with the dawn they did not go back into the wilderness; they stayed near the cabin, in case Davey came back. Every morning Elizabeth spoke to Rajah, as the leader, telling him to take them away.

'Go, Rajah. Go!'

But Rajah, though he understood perfectly, just stood there, blinking at her soulfully and curling his trunk apologetically.

So finally she had to take them into the forest. They followed her solemnly, in a slow, lumbering line, wondering where Davey was. The bears followed too. She took them way over the ridge into the valleys beyond; then she ordered them to stay.

Rajah looked at her mournfully. He understood. Their trunks hung dejectedly; they were hurt by her tone. She had to suppress a smile. She gave them each a no-nonsense, reassuring pat and walked away. They watched her go. They knew better than to try to follow her, but at sunset they came home.

Finally, one morning, Elizabeth refused to lead them out. She ordered them away with a theatrical show of anger, hands on hips, and they understood her tone.

'Now look, Rajah! You too, Jamba. And you, too, pay attention, Dumbo! And stop looking at me like that. I've had enough of wet-nursing you lot! The boss isn't here any more. You're your *own* bosses now. Now, get out there and behave like it. We've gone to a great deal of trouble and *enormous* expense to get you here. Now push off! Go on—push off, Rajah. Go!' She pointed dramatically.

Slowly, Rajah turned, with a sigh. He walked slowly toward the pasture, his ears sadly flapping; Jamba and Dumbo followed, looking rebuked.

Elizabeth felt so sorry she wanted to run after them to apologize.

That night they came back. But in the morning they did not wait to be scolded. Rajah led them off somberly without being ordered.

Elizabeth was not worried about them re-adapting. But she was sad that, in the new regime, Dumbo no longer had a crush on her.

In fact, for all his hangdog expression, Dumbo had not lost his crush on Dr. Johnson: he was just too happy to think about her for long. When Elizabeth visited them, he wanted to go with her, but Jamba called him back with a snort, bossing him. All of which was all right with Dumbo, for if ever there is a mother's boy it is a young male elephant. Jamba still did not trust Elizabeth. Wherever Jamba went, Dumbo went, trundling through the forest together; he watched what Jamba ate and ate the same; when she found something new that she considered suitable for an elephant she broke off a bunch and stuffed it into his mouth; if she saw him about to eat something unsuitable, her trunk snaked out and took it away from him; if he persisted she gave him a whack. If he wandered too far she called him back impressively. And in the middle of the day they stood side by side, napping, rocking gently. At the end of the day, when elephants want to take their bath, they headed down to the lake, and that was great fun. They waded out into the water and ponderously sucked up great trunkfuls; when each had drunk about thirty slow gallons, they curled up their trunks and squirted the water over their backs in huge sprayings and gushings so rainbows sparkled. Then they wallowed—ponderously getting down onto their knees, and toppling enormously over; wallowing and thrashing with great elephantine sighing and gratification.

And Dumbo, who had only had a bucket to drink from, thought all this water was wonderful; he wallowed and squirted, full of joy, and every evening he could not resist doing what he had learned in the circus: he filled his trunk, stuck it out like a firehose, and jetted it straight at Rajah's ponderous backside. Then, glinting black, they set off slowly to the cabin.

Then, one evening, they did not come home—for something else began to happen in those beautiful days: Jamba went into estrus, and in her giant belly there began the same urgent feelings that used to make her trumpet to the stone walls of her cage in New York for a bull elephant to hear. But this time Rajah was the first to know about it.

And Rajah could hardly believe his luck. Old Rajah had never been allowed a female, but he knew what to do, and the giant courtship began. Suddenly he was not interested in feeding any more—all he could think of was the wonderful smell of Jamba. He lumbered after her wherever she went, bumping winningly against her and curling his trunk to embrace her. But Jamba was not yet ready, and she moved away provocatively. He plucked up big tidbits of foliage and popped them into her cavernous mouth, then slopped his trunk amorously over her neck and squeezed her. Encouraged, he entwined his trunk in hers and tried to heave back her great head and kiss her, and she twisted away, her tail held down coyly. And he blundered hopefully after her, slinging his trunk

310

between her baggy hind legs and fondling her teats. She let him do that, huffing and sighing, sniffing at him; then he tried to mount her.

Suddenly, without proper permission Rajah bunched up his massive hindquarters and crashed his forelegs down on Jamba's back. Jamba scrambled away, crashing bushes flat, and Rajah hurried desperately after her on his hind legs, his fore legs trying to grip her retreating bulk and his baggy hindquarters hopefully thrusting. Jamba twisted her rump, and he skidded off with a thump. She moved off sweetly, trunk swinging, hindquarters tucked in; then she began to feed with a massive display of feminine indifference. Rajah went after her again, penis slopping through the undergrowth. He did not care what he dragged his penis through, just so long as he could get his forelegs up onto her beautiful back again.

But Jamba was having none of that yet. She was feeding elaborately, her hindquarters demurely away from him. So Rajah fed elaborately too, with masculine snorts, breaking off high and difficult foliage and stuffing it tastelessly into his mouth, watching Jamba out of the corner of his eye, ready to pounce on her the first off-guard moment, trying to edge unobservedly closer as she chomped.

For a whole day the elephantine courtship continued: two great gray beasts milling through the forest, huffing and puffing, amorous intertwining of trunks, cuddling. And Dumbo trundled along behind, bewildered, trying to keep out of the way of the huge preoccupied bodies. The next morning the huge copulation took place.

With the early sun shafting through the forest, the two elephantine lovers intertwined their trunks and tilted back their great heads and kissed, and Rajah's trunk was groping urgently between her hind legs, all the time huffing and working his way down her flank towards the desperately important position. Then in one invincible mass of hooves he bunched up his hindquarters and sort of leaped up onto Jamba's squirming back. Thrusting urgently, his spine hunched, but he kept on missing and banging his penis against her rump. Of course he could not see what he was doing way back there; and Jamba was squirming her willing hindquarters around, and all in all it was a very difficult but happy-making business.

Finally he got it right. With Jamba on her foreknees, Rajah's legs splayed over her, gripping with all his bulging might, frantically thrusting and their trunks intertwined, grunting and squeaking.

With the first sunlight Elizabeth had gone out to look for them. Now she hid in the bushes, whispering breathlessly into her tape recorder. She wanted to go running through the forest and throw herself into Davey's arms and tell him the beautiful thing that had happened.

# sixty

But on the mountaintops each morning was tense.

Big Charlie sat with his Cherokee partner, as still as a statue, scanning the blue vastness below; two dozen more Cherokees were spread along the crests at strategic intervals. They were watching for the helicopter, listening for gunshots. On the other side of Fontana lake, more Cherokees were watching for canoes. Tom Underwood had supplied radios. If anyone saw or heard anything they would radio up to Big Charlie, and he would contact Davey.

Charlie did not trust the radios. To be entirely reliable they needed to be much stronger. The men on the lakeside and along the crests could talk to each other easily, but once down into the valleys contact was lost. And, by nature, Big Charlie did not like mechanical things, fully expecting them not to work for him. Furthermore, despite his Cherokee friends, there were still places where Forsythe or hunters could slip through without being seen. Not likely, but possible.

So Big Charlie relied on his eyes and ears, and he anxiously listened to his radio for news that Operation Noah had been cancelled.

But no such news came. Each day Charlie's tension mounted. But every morning Forsythe had lost another day. Everyday his helicopter went in quite the wrong direction. Every day lost gave the animals a better chance of survival, and Eric Bradman's stories and the Cherokees' petitions a better chance of success.

The helicopter rose from its new site beside the offices of Oconaluftee and went chopping off into the sunrise. It finally hovered just above the treetops in the valley below Mount Le Conte, on the other side of Newfound Gap road. The first three members of the tracking team began to clamber down the ladders: Forsythe, Samson, then Frank Hunt.

Frank waited with a pained expression until the noise of the departing helicopter had ebbed, then pulled out a magazine, and sat down wearily against a comfortable tree. He started to read. The other two looked around restlessly.

'Excuse me, sir?'

Frank did not look up from his *Newsweek*. 'Yes, Mr. Forsythe, sir?' he said pleasantly enough.

'Do you mind,' he said, 'if I go off and ... actually, well, look around?'

Frank sighed wearily. 'You do what you like, son. You're the boss, ain'tcha?'

'I mean,' he said, 'you never know, there may actually *be* spoor around here. They may have come back.'

Frank looked up slowly.

'Look, sergeant. You don't even know what spoor *looks* like. But if there *is* any around here, you want to keep well away from it, son. You stick with the marines, and you'll live long and happy.'

The black man was grinning.

'Besides, these woods are full of fierce Cherokees. *Red*skins, son. They see you, you're a goner. They'll pounce on you and steal all your radio batteries.'

The black marine gave a laugh. The white sergeant was grinning now too. Frank said, 'But I don't care if you screw up this operation. Sure beats lion-taming. But you take my advice and lay low, son, like Professor Ford said, until he comes back for you tonight in his nice helicopter. You let the real Mr. Forsythe and his darkies look for spoor.' He glanced up. 'All you go to do is *look* like the sonofabitch, son.'

Elizabeth did not know what was happening out there in the world. Big Charlie and his Cherokees were protecting them; Eric Bradman was campaigning for them; Davey Jordan was looking after them all. And there was God. She placed her trust in God and Eric Bradman and Davey Jordan and Big Charlie—not always in that order. Any day now the news would arrive that Operation Noah had been cancelled.

Meanwhile, she looked for work. There was little for her to do—and yet there were not enough hours in the day. Every morning she had to take the bears out and lose them; then, she tracked down the other animals.

She carried out a daily medical examination of each. It was unnecessary, but she wanted to revel in the privilege of working like this. The animals were quite unafraid of her now, as they let her pull down their eyelids and peer into their ears and lift their tails. The joy of being the recipient of such animal trust! Of being quite unafraid. She wished that Jonas Ford could see her. *How could anybody want these animals back in cages if they could see them now?*

And she sat and unobtrusively observed them, her tape recorder ready, watching the behaviour of animals returned to the wild. She was going to write a book for the housewives and schoolchildren of the world. It would make them weep and laugh and fall in love with Nature. Then they wouldn't want to lock up animals in cages any more.

With each passing day King Kong began to relax more—with the feeling of being able to move in any direction, no iron bars or sheet of glass to stop him. There was no end to the trees and the valleys, and all the green things to smell and touch and climb and explore, and the sun and the breezes. His body had become hard and strong, and he could run, jump and climb as much as he liked. Slowly, King Kong began to learn to play. Then he hardly knew what to do with his gorillaness.

Suddenly he was sized with a desire to run, and he went galloping through the undergrowth on his black knuckles, pounding and

314

crashing, and Auntie, Florrie and Champ took off after him, jumping and cavorting for the sheer infectious joy of it. King Kong leaped up onto his shaggy hindlegs and ran like a man; then Candy, Florrie, and Champ began to do tricks—throwing themselves and tumbling as they did in the circus. King Kong did not know these tricks so he beat his chest. Champ leaped up and beat his little furry chest imitating King Kong, charging at Auntie in mock battle. And as suddenly as the outburst of *joie de vivre* began, it stopped.

King Kong and Auntie and the chimpanzees rambled through the wilderness, plucking this and that and munching contentedly under the wide, tree-topped sky. Then one of the chimpanzees would feel frolicsome again, and they would play hide-and-seek and king-of-the-castle and follow-the-leader, racing through the trees for the sheer joy of it.

But even though King Kong began to relax, he was also very much the boss, and the chimpanzees accepted that. Although he let Champ pretend to threaten him, one bark, one glare, was enough to put an end to any boisterous mess that he didn't feel like. And at the end of the day, when it was time for gorillas to start thinking of nesting, he gave his long significant stare in the direction of the cabin, and home they started, four hairy humanoids walking purposefully in a shaggy line.

Elizabeth dictated into her tape recorder: 'Health perfect. Much leaner, coats getting glossy. No evidence of dietary deficiency. But despite daily-growing confidence, when I first arrive the gorillas duck out of sight, then peep for quite a long time. Have to avert my eyes and shake my head to show nonaggression. But after a while they settle down and let me examine them. King Kong is still suspicious. But others submit philosophically. Wonderful to receive such trust.

'But they still huddle around the cabin indecisively at sunset. Gorillas have made no attempt yet at building tree nests, despite profusion of suitable thickets . . .'

Then, one late afternoon, King Kong stopped near the cabin and looked up into the boughs and studied them. Auntie dutifully followed his gaze. So did the chimpanzees. And from deep in his ancestral memory, King Kong was told that he should sleep above ground. He hesitated; then he reached up and began to climb.

He climbed slowly for fifteen feet, then he stopped in a fork. He tentatively took hold of a branch, and bent it toward him. He wedged it into the fork, and looked at it dubiously. It held. He reached out for another. And another. He painstakingly wedged them into position. Finally he had a rough-and-ready platform. Auntie was watching intently. Carefully, experimentally, King Kong climbed onto the nest and lay down his big body.

Then, slowly, Auntie began to climb, and she started bending branches too.

Elizabeth wanted to applaud.

With the wilderness all about him, King Kong's thoughts began to turn to fancy—which was something he knew much about, having been lord of the Ape House for many years.

Auntie recognized the urgent feelings that came and lingered, and she knew exactly what she wanted to do about it when she began to ovulate. One day King Kong's sober senses were invaded by a musk that took his mind off everything else, and Auntie suddenly became the most beautiful gorilla in the world. Absolutely irresistible, she knew it, knew just how to exhibit her shaggy rump: it worked like a charm.

There was no courtship, no seductive jostling and popping of tidbits into each other's mouths. Auntie had asked for it, and she promptly got it. King Kong lumbered purposefully up behind her with a gleam in his eye, reared up, grabbed her hips in his big black hands, and wrenched her on to him; he threw back his head and thrust.

And thrust and thrust, his mouth open and his eyes closed; Auntie thrust back at him on all fours, her head hanging. For ten blissful seconds they thrust and ground; then King Kong, the experienced lover, changed position. He heaved her around roughly to face him, sat down with a thump, and pulled her onto his lap. Auntie sat down on him, and they clutched each other.

King Kong thrust upward, and Auntie bounced and ground downward, both hugging each other, heads back, eyes closed, grunting and groaning. Then King Kong took a shuddering breath so his chest swelled, opened his mouth, and gave a roar as he juddered; Auntie gave a groan-bark at the same time. Then they both went limp.

After a few moments she climbed off him, a little unsteadily. King Kong sat there, staring at nothing; Auntie sat down beside him. She took his big black hand in hers.


# sixty-one

Every time she saw any interesting behaviour, she thought, I must tell Davey this, and she made a note on her recorder. Every time she saw something beautiful she wished that he was there because he would think it was beautiful too.

In the evenings, back at the old log cabin, she missed him badly. He understood much that other people did not, even sensitive, educated people like her. It amazed her how much he seemed to have read, how articulate he could be when he opened up.

She wanted to ask him, what's going to happen to the world, Davey? How do we stop our own environmental suicide? What about the forests which make the oxygen and which we're destroying at the rate of thousands of acres a day? What about acid rain, Davey—how on earth do we stop the sulfurous pollution from Japan blowing across the Pacific and dissolving in American clouds? And the industrial smoke from England blowing across to Scandinavia and making acid rain there? How do we *make* those people stop it? And how do we stop them killing the oceans, Davey? How long before the oceans rot, and greenhouse effect causes the icebergs to melt and flood the coastlines with rotting sewage, and we all die on mountaintops gasping for air? How do we stop people killing us like *that?* What about the fish, the dolphins, and the whales, Davey?...

She thought she knew what his answer would be.

It is no good talking any more, Elizabeth. Politicians won't listen because it costs money, and votes. It is our last chance, now. We must *do*. What is right.

In fact, if she had looked for signs, she would have known that Davey Jordan *did* come back to the log cabin from time to time.

He came whenever he could, to see if there were any signs that she was in any distress. But there were none. Each time, her sleeping bag was neatly rolled up, her cooking utensils washed, her underwear hanging out to dry, and the level was unchanged in the bottle of whisky Eric Bradman had brought her.

If Elizabeth had been a better tracker, she would have seen from the spoor that sometimes he had been there with the animals just hours before she arrived; if she had had eyes for anything other than the animals maybe she would have glimpsed him watching her, standing in the forest, with Sam sitting silently beside him.

Every day he climbed a high ridge and spoke to Big Charlie on his radio. They did not know what to make of Forsythe.

Every day Davey took the big cats hunting. Each day he was more encouraged, particularly by Kitty. But it was slow work.

Something always went wrong: either the wind changed and the pigs smelled them before they were close enough to strike; or a noise startled them, and they fled. But each day they got a little closer to a kill. Except Tommy.

Old Tommy seemed to understand perfectly well that, when pigs were sighted, a hunt was about to begin; and he got excited, looked mean. He even began to stalk; then, when he got into a favourable position, he sat down ponderously, and watched the scene with interest. Like a general, he watched Kitty and Princess go on his behalf. When they failed yet again, he looked mildly disappointed, then bored.

And Davey almost despaired of Sultan.

The tiger trailed at the back of the line, looking as if he expected to be chased off at any moment. Sultan understood that the pigs were to be stalked and pounced upon, but he would never have dared interfere. He would not have dreamed of trying to muscle in on what Kitty and Princess and Tommy were up to. When Tommy sat down to watch his troops, Sultan sat down too, at a sensible distance, and watched Kitty and Princess have the fun.

Davey tried to encourage him, make him take the lead, be the first to see the pigs, to get him excited. But as soon as Davey was not looking, Kitty and Princess balefully overtook him. He tried to take Sultan out hunting by himself, but the others always followed,

318

despite his orders. The breakdown in discipline was something that Davey did not want to interfere with, in the same way as he did not want to interfere with Tommy sitting down with centurian dignity when Kitty and Princess went into action—because in the wild, male lions mostly let their lionesses do the killing.

When he came back to the mineshaft after visiting the other animals, their huge tawny heads peered out, ears pricked; then in a mass they would come bounding down the embankment, muscled killers with piercing eyes. They would be all over him, on their hindlegs, paws on his shoulders, growling and licking, squabbling for position, slurping in his ears and rubbing against his legs. But poor old Sultan hung back, sitting at the top of the embankment, looking disdainfully away, feeling entirely out of it. Davey thought bitterly of Mama lying dead in the car headlights at Devils Fork; how wonderful it would be if she were here now, Mama and Sultan together. Sultan stuck with the lions because they were the only family he had. And they didn't want him. Davey worried about him.

But Davey did not worry about Kitty. He had seen the clawmarks on her belly from her encounter with the bear, and he was delighted. She would make the first kill; she would show the others how it was done. There was an intensity about her, a hungriness: Kitty was a killer.

Then, one day, she was not at the mineshaft.

That day Kitty caught her first pig.

Admittedly it was a very unlucky pig, and only a piglet at that. The breeze was blowing toward Kitty as she crouched, just her eyes peeping above the grass, as the mother boar and her brood rooted and bustled closer and closer in the dappled sunshine. It had all the makings of a walkover. But it was the big, tusked female boar that cautioned Kitty. She knew something about mothers now.

The sow was oblivious, her litter scattered, and the biggest of them was grubbing his way straight toward Kitty's nose, his tail curled up over his back. Closer and closer the little boar came, grunting and chomping. If Kitty had just opened her mouth he would probably have gone bustling straight into it. Kitty watched him, eyes bright with excitement, heart hammering joyfully. Now he was only five yards away—stop, grub, bustle—now only four—stop, grub, root. When he was three paces off, Kitty's quivering muscles unleashed, and she sprang.

Massive paws crashed down on the little pig; then his head was inside terrible jaws, and he was squealing frantically.

Kitty ran, carrying the screaming piglet in her mouth, and the sow and her litter fled. Kitty ran for several hundred yards before she was satisfied she was safe from the mother boar. Then she stopped and dropped the piglet.

He took to his heels, but Kitty's great paw swatted him flat. He lay gasping under Kitty's claws, his eye rolling in terror and Kitty's tail flicked happily. Then she playfully lifted her paw, and the battered little pig scrambled up and made his dash again. Leaping joyfully, Kitty swiped him across the head in full run, and over he rolled, shocked witless. Kitty leapt up onto her hind legs and boxed the little pig with both paws, to shock some life back into him, but he just slopped around. So she grabbed him in her mouth and tossed him high.

He went cartwheeling up into the trees, and came hurtling down. Kitty pounced and tried to box some life into him, but the little pig just lay there. Kitty sat down, disappointed. But he was a tough little pig and still alive. Kitty sat, waiting for him to revive, looking disdainfully around at the forest.

The pig opened his dazed eyes. Then he staggered to his feet and began to totter off. Kitty began to wash her face elaborately. She let him stagger off for six paces, and with each tottering step his hope fluttered. Then he tried to run, and Kitty bounded after him.

For another five minutes the great cat played with him, thoroughly enjoying herself, but by now the pig was dead of multiple internal injuries and, finally, heart failure induced by terror.

Then she settled down to eat him. It was her instinct to take him back to the den, to show him to the other cats; but she realized they would want to eat him too. And there simply was not enough of him.

She took him between her paws and began to crunch. She ate every bit of him, head, hooves and all, and he was delicious.

It was a good day, and an important one. But it was the last of the good times.

# sixty-two

That day, soon after sunrise, Elizabeth led the bears out as usual.

She was satisfied with Smoky's recovery. *By God, you did a wonderful job there, Johnson.* She was also pleased how he was returning to the wild; he showed much more independence than the grizzlies. Smoky no longer thought he was just a puny grizzly bear, and although he still hung around the cabin at night, come daylight he wandered off by himself.

She had to discourage the grizzlies firmly, or they would have followed her around all day like two huge dogs. They were good company at night, especially after the gorillas took to nesting farther away, and the elephants had not reappeared. She loved the big, furry, cuddly beasts with their sniffling noses and their fat, waddling backsides and stubby tails; and when they reared up onto their hindlegs, towering nine feet high over her, she wanted to take their great paws in her hands and ask them to dance with her. But they had to forget the past. They had to go off into the mountains, steamrollering through the wilderness like the natural monarchs they were. Furthermore, she wanted them to go off separately, for grizzlies are meant to be solitary creatures. But Winnie and Pooh wanted to be with her, and they were devoted to each other.

That day she took them much farther than usual, with Smoky following. When she was to look back on it, she would wonder whether Smoky sensed something wrong that day: something afoot. For did she not feel it herself? She was very anxious to get these bears really moving today—as if there was not much time left.

She led them over Welsh Ridge, into the valley below, and addressed them sternly.

'Sit,' she commanded.

Smoky sat. But Winnie and Pooh just looked. They had got wise to her now; they knew she was going to abandon them again.

'Sit!' She was angry at their disobedience. But on the other hand she badly wanted them to forget all about commands.

At last they sat, with monumental reluctance.

'Stay!' She glared at them, then muttered, 'And don't come back tonight,' and she disappeared into the wilderness.

Smoky did not go off by himself that day. For a while they all sat on their haunches, pessimistically waiting for her to come back. From time to time they stood up and sniffed the breeze for her. Finally they began to start sniffing around, looking for breakfast.

In truth, they were not disconsolate for long. After a while Smoky forgot his nervousness because, if there's one thing that's uppermost in a bear's mind it is breakfast, lunch and dinner. After a while they forgot about seeing her again before tonight. There was plenty to eat, and they were happy enough. But they stuck close together: the two future monarchs of the wilderness, big Pooh following Winnie, and Smoky following both of them. They knew which way was home.

Then, in the middle of that afternoon, it happened. Suddenly, amid the sounds of feeding, Smoky heard a human voice. So did Winnie. Only Pooh, a bear of rather little brain, missed it.

Slowly, Smoky and Winnie rose onto their hindlegs. They stood there, hearts pounding, noses twitching, absolutely tense; then simultaneously they smelt the dreaded scent of man. They both crashed to the earth, and turned and fled—Smoky one way and Winnie the other, with Pooh blundering after Winnie.

It was almost dusk when Winnie and Pooh came running up through the Garden of Eden. Elizabeth had not yet come back. They reached the log cabin and stopped, looking back the way they had come, flanks heaving and their eyes full of fear.

That sunset, when Jonas Ford returned to the camp in the helicopter, the warden informed him that Sally had been sighted along the Pigeon River.

There had been complete radio silence from Forsythe and his trackers for five days; and Ford was thoroughly fed up with the lack of results. For all he knew Forsythe had been kidnapped in those forests by the very Cherokees he thought he was duping.

# part thirteen

## sixty-three

On the banks of the Pigeon there were eddies and still places among the rocks, with weeds, fish, and salamanders.

In the daytime Sally trundled along the banks, the sun on her back, her big square mouth munching through the rich greenery, and earthy smells. She lumbered herself into the clean, cool water and sank to the bottom, and plodded around down there, experimentally nudging this and taking a mouthful of that; then she took off like a ponderous submarine, her fat body suddenly streamlined, her stubby legs expertly churning, and her eyes wide.

She swam like a submersible tank, maneuvering around rocks, diving into dark hollows, and surging up the other side, in and out of the gullies, grazing the bottom of the river like the old sea cow she was. In the middle of the day she slept at the bottom of a tranquil pool, and when she needed to breathe she rose to the surface naturally, without waking, took a long sighing breath, and sank down to the bottom again.

But, for all those good things, old Sally was not happy. Despite all the space to be a hippopotamus in and the real mud beneath her feet—and even though she did not have to run for her life any more—she yearned for Davey Jordan and for the company and security of the other animals.

In those first few days, following the crossing of the Pigeon, she had been terrified, croaking for Davey to come back. But he had not, no matter how hard and long she had called. Now she almost accepted that he was not going to fetch her, though she still had hope. She still sometimes croaked; then listened. She was still afraid of being alone, of the long dark nights.

Her old heart and soul yearned for another hippopotamus just to be with. In the night when hippopotamuses like to play, in their herds, barking at each other, Sally swam disconsolately all by herself, and she made her long, lonesome noises, then listened, her eyes staring in the darkness. But no answer ever came back.

Then, one afternoon, she heard a hippopotamus croak.

She jerked up her head, her heart pounding. She stared, ears pricked, her whole body suddenly quivering with excitement; and she barked and lumbered forward. She stopped, listening, nostrils eagerly sniffing the breeze. She turned around and stared in the other direction. Then she heard the bark again.

She spun around and went lumbering along the bank, haunches bouncing, and gave a long desperate croak in excitement. She came to a lumbering stop and listened again. She could smell nothing; she turned and stared the other way. She gave a long, heart-rending croak from the bottom of her belly, and she heard the answer. That time she could identify where it came from; she gave an excited answer and went lumbering through the bushes away from the river. She blundered excitedly up a narrow ravine for twenty yards; then suddenly she smelled man.

The dreaded scent. She whirled around to charge back to the river and saw a line of men blocking the ravine with a net. Sally snorted in terror, whirled around and went thundering up the ravine again; then she crashed headlong into another net.

Slapbang crash, and the net was all over her, and ropes entangled her thrashing legs. Sally croaked and thrashed her hooves; she scrambled up and fell onto her chin. She tried to scramble up again, and she crashed. Again and again. And all the time the men were shouting and wrenching the ropes tight, and all the time she bellowed in terror. For ten minutes Sally fought, and the ropes got tighter and tighter. Now her struggles were just grunting wrestles. Then her entangled hind legs were lashed together, her jaws pulled shut by the net. Then her forelegs were tied together.

She lay in a tangled mess of nets, flanks heaving, eyes rolling, groaning in fear. Professor Ford surveyed his first capture with intense relief. He had done it. Without Forsythe. The panting marines and wildlife officers were grinning.

For another fifteen minutes Sally lay trussed, quivering. Then a new terrifying noise began—a drone that got louder and nearer; the air vibrated and Sally kicked and wrenched. Then the roar reached its crescendo and dust was flying, and she screamed in her throat as she saw the helicopter, huge and roaring, coming down at her.

Sally went berserk, wrenching and thrashing, her heart almost bursting, and she crashed her head up and down on the stones and kicked and jerked; and the terrible roaring monster descended on her, and the men were swarming all round her as she screamed and thrashed, heaving on the ropes. Then her legs were being heaved up so she was writhing on her spine, and all the time the monster was blasting above her. Suddenly she felt her body begin to lift off the ground, the ropes biting into her. The earth was disappearing beneath her, the trees and river falling away, and Sally was filled with the purest terror. She screamed and twisted in the deafening downblast, and her neck swelled; her stomach was bulging around the ropes as the helicopter roared over the mountaintops, the valleys yawning below. Sally kicked and twisted all the way, terrified out of her mind. Then she was suddenly dropping, down, down, down, the mountain and valleys rushing up at her, crowds running toward her, and new terror leaped on top of the old. Sally screamed, and she bumped to the ground.

Dirt flew and the monster roared; men were dashing all about, and Sally screamed so her eyes bulged bloodshot. Ford cast off the helicopter's ropes, the pressure left her guts, and Sally tried to scramble up. But she was still in the net and she crashed. Ford cut the ropes binding her legs, Sally bellowed, and all the television cameras were rolling. Ford could not disentangle the nets. His only hope was to pile ten men on top of her, and he did not like to do that because she was an old specimen. For another five minutes Sally tried to get up; then all of a sudden she sort of froze.

Quivering, her hobbled backside stuck up, her chin on the

ground, her chest was wracked with pain; she crouched for a long instant as the agony streaked through her. Then she gave a big groan and toppled over onto her side.

Sally had suffered a heart attack, and she was dead.


# sixty-four


Elizabeth hardly slept, worrying about Smoky's disappearance. She had noticed the tension in Winnie and Pooh when she got back last night. She lay inside the cabin, listening. Finally, she had fallen into a fitful doze, but before dawn she was awake again. The bears were gone.

With the first light she was hurrying through the forest with a sense of foreboding, going to look for Smoky's spoor where she had left him yesterday. Maybe she had not done such a fantastic job on him after all. She had been working alone, against time; there had been all that blood and pus . . .

But no . . . that was not why she was running through the forest with dread in her heart. She wanted to find Smoky, then go plunging off to look for the elephants, and then the gorillas: to reassure herself. In fact she wanted to herd them all together, guard them. For the second time in her life, Elizabeth wished she had a gun. She felt fierce enough to shoot somebody.

It was eleven o'clock when she reached the place where she had left the bears. She found the initial spoor easily.

It was difficult tracking, because the bears had wandered all over the place. There was no sound but her own panting and rustling in the stillness of the forest. It was noon when she saw it. She stopped, her heart knocking, the color drained from her face: it was an unmistakable human footprint . . .

She stared at it. Her first reaction was to sink down like an animal. She forced herself to stand still and think; she made herself look around for more. Her fear rose like bile. She could make out three different sets of feet. None of them was Davey's, Big Charlie's or her own. She crouched in the silence, eyes wide. Then she turned to go and warn Davey.

She started striding through the forest, the way she had come. For two hundred yards she controlled her panic; then she started to run.

It was nearly three o'clock when Elizabeth came stumbling down out of the forest into the pasture below the log cabin. She was exhausted: hair in her eyes, sweating, gasping, lugging her medical bag. She splashed across the river, through the trees, and out into the other half of the pasture.

She slowed to a stumbling walk up the path through the trees to the cabin. She was halfway up when a rough hand slammed over her mouth from behind.

She struggled and kicked, horrified, but her screams were stifled. Another set of hands grabbed her ankles. She was carried up the path, kicking and wrenching, and into the cabin. They thumped her down. Somebody pulled her hands behind her back and tied them. She was gargling into the hand that gagged her mouth.

'Sorry about this, ma'am.' Sheriff Lonnogan gave his big fleshy smile and raised his Stetson. 'But as a duly-sworn officer of the law I'm required to take certain steps which may inconvenience law-bidin' folk, for the greatest good of other folk. Now, I know you ain't no criminal, ma'am, though you came precious close at the Pigeon River, but in order to carry out my duty today, I find it necessary to restrain you for the time bein'. Now, I don' want to put no gag in your mouth, ma'am, but if you were to holler when he comes, I just got to do it. Now, what do you say?'

The sheriff nodded, and the Kid lifted his hand off her mouth. Elizabeth was outraged, but her mind was racing desperately. She hissed, 'Unhand me at once!'

Lonnogan's smile creased into a puzzled frown. 'Come again?'

'If you don't let me go this instant, I'll sue you to the highest court in the land!'

Courts were something Lonnogan knew all about. 'Now I'm here to tell you, ma'am, that I can see you goin' to obstruct a duly-sworn sheriff in the execution of his duty. Gag her,' he said to his son.

She started to holler, and Kid Lonnogan clamped her mouth. She wrestled her shoulders and sank her teeth into his finger with all her might. Kid Lonnogan hollered and let go, and she yelled '*Help!*' Kid Lonnogan hopped around nursing his finger, and Jeb Wiggins and Fred and the sheriff lunged at her.

Lonnogan pulled out a handkerchief. She clamped her jaws shut and ducked and twisted, and Jeb grabbed her hair and wrenched her head back; she screamed, and Lonnogan jammed the handkerchief into her mouth. He tied a knot at the back of her neck. Then they let her go. Lonnogan stood over her.

'Now listen here, ma'am! You just committed your first offense!' He glared at her. 'How's your hand, son?'

Kid pulled his finger out of his mouth. 'Sore, Pah.'

'She done drawn blood?'

'Sure has, Pah.'

Lonnogan cocked his fleshy scowl, and his big finger trembled at Elizabeth.

'*No*body—but *nobody* bites an officer of the law around here and gets away with it, d'you hear?' His voice shook. 'But I don't want to make no trouble for you, ma'am. So I give you one more chance. Behave yourself, and we'll forget about that bite. But make one false move . . . and I'll tie you up like a *hog* and *drag* you in front of the judge.'

He gave her a bulging-eyed stare, then he barked his orders. He sent Fred Wiggins and Freddie Bushel into the trees at the back and side of the cabin. Lonnogan himself and Jeb stayed inside the cabin. He sent Kid Lonnogan down to the trees along the river that divided the pasture. He reckoned that would be the safest place for the boy.

They settled down to wait; guns ready.


# sixty-five


The honeymoon was not quite over.

Jamba's great womb had ceased to ovulate, and now she no longer wanted Rajah's loving bulk scrambling up her rump all day, crashing joyfully down on her and his huge hooves splayed amorously around her gut. But Rajah was still very much in love, and still optimistic. He hung about, plucking tidbits and stuffing them into her mouth, even when her mouth was full, and trying to intertwine trunks in passing. He squeezed and fondled her and though Jamba's belly already was working on her first-ever calf, she was affectionate and she went along with most of it.

And Dumbo, who had felt rather neglected the last few days, began to claim her attention again. They were all happy, even if Rajah was feeling restlessly wistful for the glories of the past few days; now there was an elephantine togetherness, a family feeling. That is how the elephants were that afternoon when the sharp crack of Forsythe's dart gun shattered the forest.

The elephants stampeded down the mountain, horrified, thundering through the trees, trunks swinging, tails curled up; Dumbo galloped between Rajah and Jamba with the silver dart flashing on his rump.

Dumbo ran for his life, desperate to keep up with the big elephants who would protect him; he ran and he ran, his hindquarters trying to tuck themselves in from his pursuers. Then suddenly the drug hit him; he lurched, and his legs buckled. He crashed onto his chest, his rump in the air, his trunk outflung. The air was knocked out of him; he tried to get up, and he squealed to the other elephants, and he collapsed onto his side.

Jamba and Rajah came thundering back, great ears out. Dumbo's hooves beat the air, and Jamba grabbed his trunk with hers, and heaved. He groaned, and made it halfway up; Jamba squealed at him and wrenched, and Dumbo staggered to his feet, groaning, wheezing. He started forward; then he thumped onto his haunches in a heap. He got up again, and Jamba grunted furiously and lumbered her flank against his to support him, and she threw her trunk tight round his neck. Rajah heaved his flank against Dumbo's other side. They started to run again, stumbling and lurching. For two hundred yards they blundered downhill through the undergrowth; then Dumbo lurched headfirst into another tree. His head reeled, and his forelegs crumpled; he toppled over onto his side.

329

And Jamba squealed and swiped his rump with her trunk to wake him, but he just lay there, groaning. Then she got her trunk around his foreleg and heaved backward, with all her desperate weight, and Rajah grabbed his trunk and heaved also, and Dumbo began to plow through the undergrowth.

The elephants went struggling down the mountain, great anguished animals reversing with all their might, trying to drag Dumbo to safety. Then a second shot rang out and Forsythe's dart smacked into Jamba's forehead.

She shied back, ears out, and Rajah saw the men. He gave a mighty trumpet and flapped out his ears, curled his trunk under, and he charged.

Rajah charged; enormous and furious. The earth shook, and the recapture party turned and ran—each man for himself, running and stumbling in all directions. Rajah charged for a hundred yards, scattering all before him, then he was about to give up and go running back to Jamba when Gasoline looked over his shoulder, and tripped, and sprawled, headlong into a laurel bush. He scrambled up wildly, and Rajah saw him and swerved.

He gave a furious scream and went thundering straight at Gasoline, his trunk curled under like a battering ram. Gasoline hollered to the sky and ran, as fast as his legs could carry him, terrified that this elephant was now concentrating his murderous attention exclusively on his backside. He looked wildly over his shoulder, and all he saw were terrible ears and tusks as Rajah lowered his head in full thunderous charge to ram him down and pick him up and beat him back to the earth like a club and hurl him over the treetops—that is what Rajah was about to do to Gasoline, when another shot rang out.

It thudded into Rajah's head exactly where Forsythe intended, to stun without killing. Rajah stumbled in mid-killer charge, and he almost fell; then he righted himself; he turned around blindly and ran back down the mountain, blundering, trying to shake the pain out of his head. He ran past Dumbo without even seeing him, and on down the mountain, making for the safety of the cabin.

Jamba was nowhere to be seen.

Dumbo lay all alone, wheezing, dizzily fighting the drug; he tried to lift his head, but he could not, because he was lying on his ear. He was pinned to the earth by his own ear, and he slumped back. Then, out of the corner of his groggy eye, he saw the men and he went berserk.

He squealed and scrambled his hooves, but his ear wrenched him down. He twisted, trying to see the terrifying men. His hooves ploughed up the earth, and now he was pushing his body around, thrashing and squealing around and around. Then the scream of a chainsaw filled the air, cutting down the trees to make space for the helicopter.

For another five minutes the little elephant thrashed and ploughed, his terror fighting the drug; but his struggling grew slower and weaker; then he just lay, groaning; suddenly his eyes glazed over.

They tied his hooves together, and the slings came down from the roaring helicopter to lift him out of the forest and fly him back over the beautiful mountains to his cage, where he belonged.

# sixty-six

None of Lonnogan's posse had heard Forsythe's shots. They only heard the distant trumpet of an elephant, an ancient, terrifying scream rising up out of the forest.

Crouched in the riverine foliage in the pasture, Kid Lonnogan went pale and his sphincter muscles winced. Up in the cabin the sheriff and Jeb Wiggins both stiffened, and they paled also; Lonnogan stuck his head over the window sill, and Jeb peeped around the door.

They waited, clutching their guns. Another furious scream rose up, louder. Then came the distant sound of crashing bushes, a smashing noise that got louder and louder; then, the sound of great hooves pounding the earth, and out of the forest came the beast.

Furious, in terrified stampede, his head covered in blood, his great ears out, and his trunk swinging, Rajah came thundering into the pasture; and in the forest, Fred Wiggins and Freddie Bushel broke cover and ran, flat out in the opposite direction, running for their lives; inside the cabin Lonnogan shouted, 'Close the door!'

Two hundred yards away, Kid Lonnogan lay absolutely flat in the undergrowth, gripping his gun. His stomach turned liquid. Through the tips of the undergrowth he saw the terrible sight thundering across the pasture, huge face covered in blood, heading straight toward where he lay. Kid Lonnogan's mind stuttered, and his sphincter muscles let go. Kid fouled his pants and scrambled up with a gargle of terror, his gun upflung; he fired one wild shot, turned blindly to run, and tripped. The bullet smacked into Rajah's skull, and he staggered; Kid Lonnogan scrambled up, and Rajah saw him. He shook his great head and bellowed his fury, and he charged, trumpeting and pounding through the riverine trees. Kid Lonnogan came bursting out of the undergrowth into the pasture, arms swinging. He looked back and saw the terrible bloodied head thundering right down on top of him; he hollered and tried to swerve, and Rajah hit him at full killer-charge.

With a swipe of his trunk, and Kid Lonnogan was hurled sideways, crashing head over heels. He hit the earth and rolled, and Rajah thundered down on him. Kid Lonnogan tried to scramble, and Rajah lashed his trunk around him and wrenched him up. He heaved him high over his head, and all Kid Lonnogan knew was the terrible trunk around him, the forest whirling about upside down. Then Rajah smashed him down like a club, and gunfire cracked out.

Sheriff Lonnogan was running down from the cabin, blasting above Rajah's screams. The bullets smashed into the elephant's back and ribs, but Rajah just kep on clubbing Kid Lonnogan up and down. Then Davey burst out of the forest with Sam.

Davey came running out of the trees screaming, 'No, Rajah!' and brandishing a branch. He ran through the gunfire at the screaming elephant, and Sam went for the sheriff, bounding furiously, hair standing up, his jaws agape and his eyes flashing. Lonnogan scattered backward and opened up on him with both six-guns. The bullets shot up the earth, but Sam kept coming, and Lonnogan began to run. Davey bellowed, 'No, Sam!' and Sam turned. Davey charged at Rajah and swiped him across his bloody face, bellowing, 'No, Rajah! No!'

And Sheriff Lonnogan recovered. He opened up wildly on the

elephant again, and Davey's blows suddenly penetrated Rajah's crazed brain. He scrambled backward under the barrage, dropped Kid Lonnogan's body, and turned and ran, shocked, the bullets thudding into his bloodied body.

Davey was yelling, 'Stop shooting—stop shooting!'

He ran to Kid Lonnogan. A bullet whined past his ear, and he threw himself flat. The bullets tore all about him, and the sheriff was charging at him with both six-guns. Davey scrambled up and dived headlong into the undergrowth, bullets crashing all around him. He scrambled up again and hurled himself into the river, up the opposite bank, and he ran.

Lonnogan and Jeb were blasting across the river, and the sheriff bellowed, 'Shoot to kill!'

Jeb splashed across the river as Davey raced across the open pasture beyond, the bullets whamming into the earth, then he threw himself into the forest.

Back on the other side of the river, the sheriff crouched over the dead body of Kid Lonnogan, weeping. Then he threw back his head and howled above the cacophony of the gunfire, '*You'll all hang for this! If I don't shoot you full of lead first!*'

Big Charlie burst into the cabin. He whipped out his knife, slashed the ropes around Elizabeth's ankles and wrists, and pulled off her gag. He snatched up her medical bag and her knapsack, grabbed her wrist, and plunged out of the cabin. They stumbled up the mountain for half a mile. Then Charlie stopped, chest heaving.

'Go the mineshaft . . . Davey'll find you there . . .'

'Supposing he's been hit? . . .'

'I'm going to look for his spoor now . . . Go to the mine and wait for him . . . Up the stream, so you leave no spoor . . . Are you afraid of the lions?'

She shook her panting head. 'Are you going to come . . . afterward?'

'If he's been hit, I'll bring him to you . . . Otherwise I got work to do . . . Tomorrow the trouble starts . . .'

Twenty miles away, the helicopter was roaring over the mountains, carrying Dumbo. The freezing wind brought him back to consciousness, to the terrifying sights and sensations of flying, and the terrifying noise. He kicked and screamed, three thousand pounds of terrified young elephant bucking in the sky, and the sling swung; the helicopter lurched and keeled. As they began their descent, Dumbo began to wail from the bottom of his lungs, as he felt himself falling through the icy blast and saw the forest rushing up. He wailed all the way to the ground inside the stockade, as the television men filmed him. Outside the camp the mob of young people chanted, 'Shame! . . . Shame! . . . Shame! . . .'

Dumbo kicked, and wailed, and tried to get up, and crashed over, again and again, until Forsythe decided he had to dart him again, to knock him unconscious so he could be disentangled.

When Dumbo awoke it was the middle of the night. He was all alone. He lumbered around and around, trying to find a way out of the stockade, his trunk groping. He trumpeted for the other elephants, and for Davey Jordan, and he listened desperately for their answer, flanks trembling, his big ears out.

The television men came back when they heard him, and he backed away and curled his trunk over his head in supplication, as Frank Hunt had taught him. He cried all night.

# part fourteen

## sixty-seven

The sunlight was going when Elizabeth came toiling up to the mine, splashing and clambering, her heart thudding and her legs trembling. Before she could see it she caught the sharp musty smell of lions. Fear and death were in the air, and all animals sense it and trust nothing, and she was but an animal. For a moment she hesitated, feeling fear in her bowels and down to the roots of her hair; then she took a breath and clambered on. Then she heard a snarl.

Her heart stabbed, and she froze. 'Kitty?...'

Silence.

Then four heads appeared above the embankment, four pairs of eyes staring down, and she looked up with a frozen, white-faced smile. Suddenly, slowly Tommy stood up; then the others. She smiled up at them, her heart pounding and her guts watery; then Kitty suddenly took a slow step forward, head low, shoulders bulging. One after another the lions started down, staring fixedly, one muscle-bound step at a time, killer paws stalking. Elizabeth stood petrified, and every fiber cried out: Davey!

Kitty stopped, staring hungrily; suddenly she crouched six inches lower, poised. Elizabeth felt the scream of pure terror well up from her loins; then Kitty came padding up to her, arched her back and rubbed her head against Elizabeth's leg. Elizabeth closed her eyes.

'Hello, Kitty ... Hello, everybody...'

She sat outside the mineshaft, her back to the cliff, her knapsack on her knees as a shield, and she tried not to give off fear waves, to stop her heart hammering. She prayed for Davey to come—that he had not been hit.

Darkness came.

An hour passed. Two.

Then, suddenly, she heard a stone knock, and her heart leapt. She got to her knees and peered. She was about to cry, 'Davey!'—then she saw the other human shapes.

She strangled a cry and dashed for the mine's mouth, fleeing from Lonnogan and his posse, and a voice called out, 'Dr. Johnson?'

She stopped in mid-turn, and her heart soared. 'Davey!'

She went stumbling over the platform. There he was, with the gorillas, the chimpanzees, Winnie and Pooh, and Sam, and she flung her arms around him.

'Oh, thank God! Are you all right?'

Davey ordered the lions to stay at the mouth, and left Sam on guard outside. The gorillas and chimpanzees huddled together away from the fire he built, their brown eyes staring anxiously. Winnie and Pooh sat, enormous, furry, watching Davey. King Kong's eyes shifted between him and the dark tunnel.

They knew that the terror had returned, that they were on the run again, and they were waiting for him to tell them what to do. Elizabeth sat with her eyes closed, in a turmoil of shock at what he had told her about Kid Lonnogan and of dread for tomorrow. She tried to pray, for the Lonnogan boy, for the animals, and to thank God that Davey was unhurt and back to lead them.

But a man's life had been taken, an animal of hers had done it, and she was horrified and grief stricken. Through her shock surged the dread: no matter whose fault it was, Rajah would not be allowed to live; no animal that has killed a man is allowed to live. *Particularly* in a national park. On top of that, Sheriff Lonnogan would pursue them with all his hatred, especially Davey. And she wanted to cry out at him, Oh, run now, Davey—before they gun you down! Run for your life and let Forsythe get the animals back where at least they're safe from mindless savagery . . .

Davey was shocked too. His eyes were narrowed, staring at the fire. She had seen the suffering when he had told her about the Lonnogan boy. But she could also tell that, in his way, he had put his suffering to one side. He would come back to it later. Now he had put it aside grimly, and his mind was feverishly dealing with the living.

'How did you find the gorillas?'

'They were running from the gunfire. When they saw me they followed. The same with the bears.'

She kept her eyes closed. 'How come you were so close when the shooting started?'

'Charlie and I were having a meeting up the mountain.'

Through her distraction she thought: A meeting? A mile or so from where she was, and they hadn't been to see her?

'And Dumbo, and Jamba? Do you think Forsythe got them both?'

'He got one of them. I heard the helicopter come. But it couldn't have taken both of them. One's loose.' He added with a quiet tension, 'Stop worrying about it. Charlie's gone to find the spoor and figure out what's happened. He'll know what to do.'

'How badly is Rajah hit?'

'Badly, Elizabeth.' Tomorrow Rajah was her job.

It came out in a fierce whisper. 'What happens tomorrow?'

'Tomorrow we find Rajah. And you get those bullets out of him.'

She closed her eyes in dread-filled frustration. 'I know that. But what about Lonnogan? And Forsythe?'

He did not lift his eyes from the fire.

'Lonnogan won't be around much longer, Elizabeth. He's not allowed in here. Eric Bradman will see he's kicked out. And Forsythe doesn't want him in here either. Everything's loaded against Lonnogan. This place will be safe again in a couple of days, Dr. Johnson.'

She stared at him incredulously. She could not believe he thought that. And God knew she wanted to believe him . . .

'And Forsythe? What are you going to do about *him?*'

'We needn't worry about Forsythe for the time being, Dr. Johnson. Charlie and his Cherokees will be there in the morning, waiting for him when he comes back to pick up the spoor of the elephants.'

Of course . . . Forsythe would have to come back to where he left off. For a moment she felt her bludgeoned hopes rise.

'But you can't keep that up forever . . .'

He looked at her in the flickering firelight. The animals were sitting attentively; they could tell from their tones and the tension in the air that their fates were being discussed.

'I won't have to keep it up forever. Operation Noah is going to stop.' Then he gave her a grim smile. 'Now stop worrying. I'll do the worrying; you go to sleep. We've got a long way to go tomorrow.'

She sat there rigidly, eyes closed. And she wanted to cry it:

*Oh hold me. Please just hold me.*

# sixty-eight

Before dawn Big Charlie and his men were near Hazel Creek, where Dumbo had been darted, waiting for Forsythe to come back to pick up Jamba's spoor.

The self-appointed liberation team from Cherokee was also ready. When the first pink came into the east, and the Operation Noah helicopter rose slowly over the dark foothills, navigational lights getting smaller, over the fence they swarmed.

They raced silently between the tents toward the stockade. Ambrose Jones was waiting for them. In six breathless minutes Dumbo was free. He went lumbering down the avenue of tents, gleefully herded toward the big hole in the fence that had been cut in the night. Dumbo was out into the wilderness before anybody knew it.

That dawn, the four thousand Indians from Cherokee and Oklahoma arrived in Washington, D.C. They left their vehicles outside the city, and they began to walk into the capital. They formed a column over two miles long, dressed in tatters, holding four thousand crosses aloft. They were singing the new American ballad, 'The Trail of Tears,' and they were being herded along by men cracking whips and dressed up as soldiers.

Television men were everywhere. Marlon Brando was there and a dozen other celebrities who had rallied to Eric Bradman's call. They marched on Capitol Hill where Chief Nathaniel Owle made his speech. It was the best speech of his life, bringing tears to the eyes and shame to the breast, and his huge audience roared their applause.

Then they marched on the White House.

Twenty thousand people marched, led by Chief Owle and Eric Bradman, singing 'The Great Free Smoky Mountains.' They marched up Pennsylvania Avenue like an army and formed up around the iron railings of the White House until the presidential compound was completely surrounded. Then began a chant that rose up over the city: *The President . . . the President . . . We want to see the President!*


Two hours before first light, Davey and Elizabeth left the mine to go back to Rajah's spoor. Davey had shot a boar the day before and hung it in a tree. He fed it to the lions to make them stay behind—they were safer around their den. But the other animals followed Davey and Elizabeth.

They were half a mile downstream when Davey noticed Sultan following them. He sighed, but decided to do nothing until it was light.

It was still before dawn when Davey stopped, two miles above the cabin.

'Rajah ran up this way.'

She looked about in the darkness, 'How can you tell we're there?'

'I know.' He sat down, crosslegged; she slumped against a tree. The gorillas huddled together. Sultan lurked in the darkness, pretending he wasn't there.

'We'll hear Forsythe's helicopter as soon as it gets light. Other side that ridge.'

'And we'll have Lonnogan and his men here at first light too.'

'I don't think so.'

'Why not?'

'Because there's only one way for Lonnogan to find me, and that's

339

to follow my spoor which I left yesterday when I ran away from him. That'll lead him all over the place. Back to the stream below the mine. Then he'll lose it. We're a full day ahead of Lonnogan. We can keep a day ahead of him forever.'

Elizabeth prayed that he was right. That Lonnogan wouldn't follow Rajah's spoor too.

At last it began to get light. Davey walked over to Sultan. The tiger was behind a bush, looking studiously away, with one ear cocked. When he heard Davey approaching he feigned intense interest in the middle distance. Davey put his hand on his head. 'Sultan? Back. Go back.'

Sultan looked glassily ahead, ears slanted.

'Sultan. Go back.'

Not Sultan. He sat there, with a severe attack of deafness. He wasn't going to go back to those lions if he had a chance of sticking with his keeper. Davey crouched and turned the big striped face toward him. Sultan looked away out of the corners of his eyes.

'Sultan, I can't worry about you today. You're much better off with Tommy and Kitty and Princess. Now . . . go back.'

Sultan didn't move.

Davey stood up with a sigh and walked back to Elizabeth. 'I'm losing my touch.' He said softly to Sam: 'Sultan . . . see him off, Sam!'

Sam looked up, as if his master had gone out of his mind. Then he glanced apprehensively in Sultan's direction.

'See him off!'

Sam stood up reluctantly, looked at Davey again, saw no reprieve, uttered a nervous huff to get himself warmed up for the formidable task, glanced at Davey once more, then worriedly threw himself into ferocity. The hair stood up on his neck, and he bounded at Sultan's bush, giving tongue. Sultan whirled around with a snarl, ears back, claws ready. Sam nearly fell over himself in braking, then Sultan turned and ran. He went bounding through the undergrowth, and Sam went after him at a safe distance, barking furiously. After fifty yards Sultan slowed down to a lope, and Sam slowed too, listening hopefully for his master's recall.

Within ten minutes Davey had found Rajah's spoor. He whistled for Sam.

He started up the steep mountain, followed by Elizabeth and the animals. The spoor was as easy as a trolley track to follow, blundering footprints and plenty of blood.

# sixty-nine

With the sunrise Big Charlie heard the helicopter.

Three hundred yards away was the place where Dumbo had finally collapsed. In the undergrowth, on both sides, hid five Cherokee men. The helicopter droned closer and closer; finally it was chopping overhead in an arc.

The rope ladders unfurled, and Forsythe climbed out, followed by his black trackers. Frank Hunt, Jonas Ford, and some television men followed.

Within a minute the black men had found the spoor. Forsythe examined it, and they set off, Ben and Samson leading the way. Big Charlie and his Cherokees crept after them.

Forsythe was following Jamba's spoor, not Rajah's. She had been darted and would therefore have moved more slowly, and she would have collapsed for several hours in the night. Rajah had been wounded, and he would have run, probably all night.

They followed her spoor for half a mile, down the mountain; then it turned drunkenly and headed back up the mountain.

So Forsythe and his trackers did not cross the ridge into the Garden of Eden; they did not see where Rajah had killed Kid Lonnogan. They followed Jamba's drunken spoor for over two miles up the mountain; then they noticed a change. The spoor became firmer, but it still headed resolutely up the mountain.

'Ben?'

Ben looked at his master and nodded at the spoor. 'This elephant is recovering.'

'This elephant'—Forsythe pointed to the top of the Great Smoky

Mountains—'has run up this valley to the Appalachian Trail and over the other side.'

Forsythe turned to Jonas Ford.

'If we fly to the top in the helicopter, we'll find the spoor up there, where it crosses the trail. It'll save us a whole day. If we don't find it, we can always come back here and continue.' He called for his radio.

Big Charlie and his men were left standing. Charlie did not understand what was happening until the helicopter was hovering overhead again, and Forsythe and his men were already on the ladder. It was too late. He beckoned to his Cherokees feverishly.

'They're going to look for the female's spoor at the top of the mountains. One of us must stay here in case they fail and come back. Two must go back to the male elephant's spoor. Forsythe will return there to start tracking Rajah, either later today, or tomorrow. The rest of us must follow Jamba's spoor on foot . . .'

Rajah had four bullets embedded in his skull, seven lodged in his ribs. The agony thudded with each step, but he kept on, wheezing and snorting, fleeing from the men who had tried to kill him. It had been after midnight when he came toiling up Thunderhead Mountain. His exhaustion was as bad as his pain now, and he was very thirsty.

He stood in the steep forest, his trunk up, trying to smell water, blood oozing out of the bullet holes, waiting for the thudding agony in his head to settle. Then he curled back his trunk and sniffed at his head, touching the bullet holes one by one.

He groped at the forest floor and sucked up some soil. He curled up his trunk and sprayed it over the bullet holes. Again and again he did it until he had covered his wounds. Then he could do nothing more than just stand there, and endure. He was afraid of the black night forest. He wanted to raise his trunk and trumpet to Jamba, but he dared not, lest the men hear him.

With the dawn he had reached the top of Thunderhead. Below him were the valleys down to Cades Cove. He was afraid of the unknown. But he had to hide, and find water, and let his wounds heal.

In the afternoon, Davey reached the place where Rajah had tried to rest in the night.

He examined the ground, examined the foilage. Elizabeth came toiling up.

'He stopped here for a long time,' he said. 'But he didn't eat. He didn't lie down. He hasn't been near water yet. That's what he'd have started looking for from here. Are you very tired?'

'O God, yes . . .'

'Okay, we'll take a rest.'

'Have we got time?'

'Lonnogan's well behind us. He's only getting to Paw Paw Ridge now.'

But he was wrong. Lonnogan and his posse were also following the spoor of the wounded elephant. They had reasoned that that was where David Jordan would be.

Ten miles away, Forsythe had found that he was right.

Within half a mile of where his helicopter had dropped him on the Appalachian Trail, he had found Jamba's spoor. It crossed the crest of the Great Smoky Mountains, then headed down into the wilderness of Tennessee below.

The helicopter pilot had told him of Dumbo's escape. Jonas Ford had been incredulous, outraged. Forsythe had let go a flood of invective against America in general and the Cherokee nation in particular; then he had withdrawn into seething silence.

Now Forsythe stood on Jamba's spoor at the top of the mountains, and he was furiously determined that by tonight there would be another elephant in that stockade at Oconaluftee.

Jamba did not know where she was.

She had blundered to the top of the mountains during the night, and when the drug had worn off she did not even know that she had crossed.

She had waited: for daylight, for Davey Jordan, for Rajah. When she had heard the helicopter, she had blundered farther down the mountain into Tennessee. After five miles she stopped, frightened of going deeper into strange territory. For a long time she stood in the deep shade, nervously sniffing the air. Eventually she began to relax.

Then the dartgun barked.

The dart smacked into her rump, and she whirled about and ran down the steep mountainside, smashing bushes flat. Then the drug hit her, and she was fighting dizziness, stumbling and straining. She crashed into a tree, but she struggled up again; she stumbled on, and on, then she collapsed into a stream.

The shock of the water brought Jamba round. She struggled up again. She labored on down the stream bed, falling, but the repeated shock of the icy water fought off the drug. She climbed out of the stream and into the forest again; she bumped into many trees, but she did not collapse again.

For two hours Forsythe followed her spoor. Then he called a halt.

'The damn animal's recovered! Look at that spoor.' He turned to Ford and snapped. 'It's afternoon already. We might not catch up all day. She'll be on the alert now. Samson—bring the radio.'

He crouched down and called the camp, ordering the helicopter to come back. Then he turned to Ford.

'We're going to split up. I'm leaving you here to follow this spoor, with Ben and Sixpence. When it gets too dark to track, camp right there and follow the spoor in the morning.'

'Where're you going?' Ford demanded.

'Back to where I shot the male elephant yesterday. While there's still light left to track him.'

# seventy

Big Charlie and his two men had been toiling up the mountain for only twenty minutes, following Jamba's spoor and the helicopter, when they heard the dogs.

Big Charlie halted, panting, aghast. Then he heard it again, the faraway baying of a whole pack.

'You guys carry on following this spoor!'

He turned and went running back down the valley, leaping and swerving around the trees.

Sultan had not gone back to the mine. He didn't want any more to do with the lions than he had to. He had recognized where he was,

344

and he made his way disconsolately toward the log cabin.

Sultan smelled the dogs before he heard them. For a moment he thought it was Sam again, that Davey had come back for him. Then he crouched; it was not Sam's scent. He whirled and fled, leaping through the undergrowth; then all the dogs were in full cry after him, the three men from Sylva excitedly running after them.

Sultan ran flat out, head low, across the steep mount in the direction of the mine, the terror pounding in his chest. The dogs were used to this rough country, and they were gaining on him, then he threw himself at a tree trunk. He started scrambling upward, and a dog got his tail.

Sultan clawed for all his might against the wrench, and he roared down at the furious mass of leaping jaws. Then another dog got his hind paw. His leg skidded, and he scrambled with all his strength, dragging the dogs with him; then he came crashing down into the furious mass of dogs. They leaped all over him, onto his back and hindquarters. Sultan roared, twisted, swiped, and tore off the side of a dog's face; another dog leaped on his back, and Sultan twisted again and swiped and missed; then he spun on another dog and clawed his head open, bounded up, and threw himself at the nearest tree trunk. He scrambled desperately, and was just out of reach. He clung with all his might, his heart thudding and ears back, with a howling moan of terror. His legs trembled, and he tried to claw up higher; then his way was blocked by a branch. Old Sultan just clung, fangs bared, trying to rest, his legs frantically wrapped around the trunk, blood all over him; and the dogs leaped up at him frenziedly. Then he saw the three men coming.

For a wild moment he thought it was Davey Jordan; then he heard them. He looked desperately up the tree for escape, and the dogs barked and leaped with redoubled excitement at the arrival of their masters.

'Don't spoil his head.'

The first shot rang out above the cacophony; then the gunfire opened up from three sides, as the hunters dashed to get a shot in. The bullets smashed into him and all about him, and Sultan tried to scramble up around the branch. Then a shot shattered his spine, and down he came.

With a terrified roar, into the mass of dogs, trying to twist around in mid-air to face them, scattering them in all directions. He hit the earth and tried to run, and he crashed over, and they hit him from behind, in a furious melee. Sultan tried to twist and swipe at them, but his spine was broken, and he crashed onto his side. He roared and lunged his shoulders around, trying to bite at the dogs on his back. Again and again Sultan tried, and all the time there was the barking, the jumping, the biting, the shouting, and the blood, and his heart was thudding in exhaustion. Then he could fight no more, and he just tried to drag himself across the forest floor: on his chest, ear back, moaning, his hindquarters sprawled, dragging with his forepaws, trying to heave himself toward the next tree. The dogs hurled themselves at him again, savaging with all their might; Sultan snarled and heaved himself through the undergrowth, dragging the dogs, and the hunters were shouting encouragement at them. Then his forepaws reached a tree, and he tried to haul himself up to it, and the dogs went crazy. The first man shouted, 'See how far he gets!'

The old tiger moaned and heaved, his paws upstretched, then his exhausted forelegs could claw no more, and he just clung, howling deep in his throat, with the dogs wrenching and savaging gleefully; then there was a bellow.

'*You murdering bastards!*'

A shot rang out, and Charlie's merciful bullet smashed through Sultan's head. Then Big Charlie was swinging his rifle furiously like a club, and astonished hunters and dogs scattered, shocked, yelping. Charlie swiped the first man across the ribs with his rifle with all his might; he bounded after the next one and swiped him across the back. The men were running, and Big Charlie fired furiously at their feet, and then over their heads as they went stumbling through the trees, and he bellowed, '*Get out murdering bastards!*'

Then the first man turned and fired, and Big Charlie jerked.

He clutched his stomach, and blood welled up between his fingers and he turned and staggered away.

It was early afternoon when Forsythe reached the Garden of Eden. Three Cherokee men were still furtively following them.

Forsythe saw all the signs as clear as a book: where Kid Lonnogan had hidden in the trees, his cartridge shell, the place where Rajah

346

had clubbed him to death; they found the bloodstained branch with which Davey had beaten off Rajah, saw his footprints fleeing across the river and back into the forest, and Rajah's spoor; they found the footprints of Lonnogan and his posse, all their cartridge shells, saw their spoor following Rajah's—and Forsythe seethed; they found the spoor of Elizabeth and Big Charlie fleeing the cabin, until they separated, where Elizabeth's spoor headed alone over Paw Paw Ridge toward the mineshaft.

Forsythe was murderous with rage: that Dumbo had been released, that Jamba had got away, that somebody else had found David Jordan's hideout before him, that Rajah had been shot.

It was mid-afternoon. There was no time to lose. There were two important spoors to follow. He divided his team yet again.

He ordered Frank Hunt and Gasoline to follow Elizabeth's spoor over Paw Paw Ridge. He took Samson and the rest back to the pasture, and grimly started following Rajah's spoor, up the mountain toward Thunderhead.

The Cherokees followed Forsythe.

# part fifteen

## seventy-one

The infection had set into Rajah's wounds, throbbing around the lumps of lead embedded in his head and all down one flank, stiff, swollen humps, oozing.

He rested against a tree trunk, blinking slowly at the pain. He badly wanted to lie down, to take his great weight off his legs, but he dared not, for the agony when he got up again. So he just leaned there, trying to rest. He curled up his trunk with a groan and gently sniffed the wounds, and he tested the wind for the dreaded scent of man.

He caught the faraway scent of the green pastures of Cades Cove, down in the valleys of Tennessee, and he knew that was where he had to go: he was very hungry, and he could not feed properly up here in the high places because of the pain when he lifted his head to pull the leaves off the trees. He had to get down into the grassy low lands, to feed and to rest.

It was early afternoon when Jamba crossed Rajah's spoor, but she did not notice it. She passed within half a mile of where Rajah was resting, but she did not smell him.

It was late afternoon when Davey spotted Jamba's spoor, crossing Rajah's. He examined it excitedly. It was still fresh. He closed his eyes and smiled. He waited for Elizabeth to catch up.

'Jamba's here. She's fine.'

Her eyes widened, and she smiled. 'Oh, thank God . . .'

Davey did not follow Jamba's spoor. He had to find Rajah before it got dark and get those bullets out of him.

Half a mile farther they saw him, standing beside the stream, rocking slowing, his trunk hanging, fast asleep.

Davey pulled out his ashbag and tested the wind.

It was blowing away from Rajah. He beckoned to Elizabeth. 'How long will your $CO_2$ gun take to pull him down? There're only a couple of hours of daylight left.'

'Could be half an hour. Depends on his condition.'

'Can you operate in the dark with your flashlight?'

'If the batteries last.'

It was no good. She might be able to operate by flashlight, but he could not track in the dark if the elephant ran. 'Get behind a tree so he can't see you.'

He crept silently down the slope toward the sleeping elephant and quickly past him for another twenty paces. He shook his ashbag and took a few paces to one side, positioning himself so that the elephant would both smell him and hear him at the same time.

'Hello, Rajah!'

Rajah woke up with a lurch, flapping out his ears. He shied backward and turned to flee. Davey called cheerfully, 'Stop, Rajah. Stop.'

The familiar voice penetrated Rajah's panicked mind, and the same instant the familiar smell registered; he came lumbering to a stop, turned around and stared, flanks heaving.

Davey was coming toward him, smiling, and calling his name, holding out his hands to show him he held nothing.

'Hello, Rajah. Hello, old man . . .'

Davey stopped in front of him. The tears were stinging his eyes, for the swollen bullet wounds on his old friend's face, and the blood.

'Oh, I'm sorry, Rajah . . .'

He went forward, arms outstretched, and the frightened elephant extended his gnarled trunk and wrapped it about him, and they hugged.

Tears were burning in Elizabeth's eyes too as she tried to examine his wounds.

'Yes, I think I can fix him. But it'll have to be by daylight. And not here either, with all the moving shadows. It must be open, and with plenty of water. And a fire.'

'I know a place.'

He took the tip of the elephant's trunk in his hand.

'Come, Rajah.'

Less than twenty minutes later, Professor Ford's trackers, following Jamba, crossed Rajah's spoor.

Ford examined the tracks with excitement. They had been searching for almost two weeks for any reliable spoor of any one animal, and now, in one swoop, he had hit almost the whole lot—elephant, gorillas, chimps, bear, the wolf, Jordan's—and even Elizabeth's!

He excitedly ordered his trackers to abandon Jamba's spoor and to follow the others', as fast as possible.

# seventy-two

They trundled down the mountain slowly, so as to keep to Rajah's groaning pace. Davey held his trunk tip; Elizabeth walked at his flank. The animals were strung out in a line. But at the very back was King Kong, not Sam.

For King Kong did not like Sam behind him any more. He did not like Sam at all, let alone growling up his backside if he stepped out of line. Now Sam frequently glanced back uncomfortably, at the glowering gorilla breathing up *his* backside.

In the last hour of daylight Ben spotted them, strung out in their long line, heading across a glade just a hundred yards ahead. Ford was just in time to see King Kong disappearing into the trees.

Ben shook his ashbag. The wind was in their favor.

Five minutes later the gun banged, and the dart smacked into

Auntie's rump. Suddenly there was pandemonium, animals stampeding everywhere. Davey shouted, 'Herd, Sam!' and he ran beside the panic-stricken Rajah. Auntie fled, the dart flashing on her rump, and King Kong went galloping after her. Then he thundered to a stop and turned around. He sprang up onto his hindlegs and gave a roar to terrify his enemy with his size and ferocity, to give his troupe time to escape. He tore up foliage and threw it in the air and beat his chest. But he could see nobody, and he turned and went galloping after his troupe again. Then suddenly Auntie collapsed.

In less than a hundred yards Auntie crashed as if she had been pole-axed, and King Kong tripped over her. He scrambled up frantically and barked at her to run, and he grabbed her arm, but Auntie was a dead weight. He barked at the others to wait, but they were gone, crashing through the forest. Then he flung his arm around Auntie's middle, heaved her up onto his hip, and started to run again.

Auntie hung, head down and arms dragging, the silver dart sticking up out of her rump. King Kong staggered down the mountain, grunting, his eyes flashing, stumbling into trees under the saggy weight of Auntie. Then he fell on top of her, got up, heaved her up again, and staggered on. Then he could carry her no longer, and he let her fall.

He grabbed both her hairy wrists and started dragging her, looking over his shoulder, heaving Auntie on her stomach, over roots and logs and bushes, the silver dart waggling on her rump like a flag; then he tripped and fell. He barked in fury and burrowed both arms under her big belly, and he heaved her up.

He ran for fifty yards, rasping and lurching through bushes, desperately following the vanished animals. Then he crashed again. He started dragging her. For nearly a mile King Kong dragged and carried Auntie down the mountain; then he fell for the last time, and he could carry her no more.

King Kong crouched beside her, rasping, frightened. Auntie lay on her back, face and chest bleeding from scratches, uttering long wheezing groans. His instinct was to give up, to run for his life after the rest of the animals; his instinct was never to give up, to stay with her and fight to the death. He stared fiercely at the forest, but he could see nobody. He knew Auntie was not dead. He lifted her eyelid with his big black thumb and forefinger. All he saw was white. He gripped her neck and shook her. He slapped her face. Auntie just kept on groaning. He put his mouth right next to her ear and barked.

King Kong sat in exhausted despair. Then, suddenly, he saw Ben and Jonas Ford through the trees.

He gave a roar, jaws flashing white in furious black face, and he leaped to his full height, and tore up foliage and threw it in the air, and he smashed his hand on the earth, and the men turned and ran.

King Kong charged on his shaggy hind legs, his eyes flashing, roaring and crashing. Ford looked frantically over his shoulder at the black beast six feet tall with the gaping jaws just ten yards behind, and his long legs bounded as fast as they could, and his glasses bounced off his nose. Then King Kong dropped to all fours like a giant dog, and he galloped. He hurled himself at Ford's fleeing buttocks and got him in the ankle; his jaws ripped through his boot, and Ford crashed onto his side, wildly kicking and hollering and grabbing for his tranquilizer pistol—and King Kong let go. He could have killed Ford, bounded at his throat and ripped it out in one wrench, but he had routed his enemy and now he had to get Auntie out of here. He let go and turned, and Ben hit him across the head with the rifle butt.

The gorilla reeled sideways, stunned, his arms up over his head protectively; then he tried to start running again, and Ben hit him again across his shoulders, and King Kong sprawled onto his face. He tried to clamber up, one arm still curled across his head, and Ben swung the rifle again. A voice bellowed 'No!' Ford was holding the tranqu-pistol in both hands, his eyes screwed up without his glasses, and he fired.

The dart smacked into King Kong's back; he stiffened, then shuddered. He dropped to his four feet, the dart sticking out of his hide, and he tried to run. He ran two hobbling strides and fell. Then he did something that Jonas Ford had never heard of.

King Kong got up quite quickly, like a man embarrassed by falling down at a party, and he turned to face them; then he began to walk backward on his hind legs—like a cowboy in a bad western, it occured to Jonas Ford—just like a man. He walked backwards ten paces like that, menacing and defiant; then he tripped and crashed onto his buttocks.

He sat there in a lump for a long moment, his mind swimming; then laboriously he got up, as if he had forgotten about his enemies, grunting like an elderly man getting off a park bench. He turned his back, showing the dart again, and began to plod off the way he had come. Ford and Ben and Sixpence tiptoed after him. One arm reached absently behind King Kong's back. He groped for the dart, plucked it out. He examined it cursorily, then tossed it aside. He dropped to all fours and headed purposefully in the direction of Auntie.

Suddenly King Kong's clouded mind cleared at the sight of his mate, and he remembered everything clearly. He reared onto his hind legs again, whirled around, and saw the men scattering. He stood glowering after them, his chest heaving in fury, and for good measure he gave another bark and beat his chest. Then he turned back to Auntie, and heaved her up to his hip again, almost effortlessly.

Altogether King Kong dragged and carried Auntie nearly half a mile, grunting and whimpering. He only knew he had to keep going, but he did not know where he was going.

Finally he crashed for the last time. He sat in a heap, Auntie's head on his feet; he grunted, and slumped over her body.

# seventy-three

Davey kept them running until it was dark, until it was impossible for anybody to track them.

Elizabeth struggled behind Rajah in the dark, her face and arms scratched, lugging her medical bag. She was not feeling the anguish for the missing gorillas any more, nor even hunger, only her exhaustion. She had been walking since long before dawn. It was after nine o'clock when they came into open starlight, into an overgrown orchard. She could make out a log barn beyond and hear the rushing of a stream.

'This is it,' he said. 'Used to be called Judd's Place. Cades Cove is a mile down there.'

The barn was big enough for Rajah, but he stayed under the stars, feeding on the grass.

Davey built a fire, and Sam stretched out in front of it. Davey took Elizabeth's flashlight.

'Where are you going?' she demanded.

'To get us something to eat.'

'But we've got enough.'

'Your hands must be steady tomorrow.'

She sat by the fire, clutching her knees.

O God, tomorrow . . . The operation was the least of it. What else was going to happen tomorrow? She closed her eyes tight, trying to shut out the dread.

Where did he get the stamina? And where was he going to find something to eat? But he would. Of that she had no doubt.

Twenty minutes later he came back. His shirt was a sodden bundle containing four trout. 'How on earth?' she said.

'Netted them. Pulled them with your flashlight.'

'God, you're clever.' She wrung out his shirt and put it close to the fire. He pulled a sweater out of his knapsack, and they hunched around the flames while they roasted the trout, skewered on green sticks.

She looked at him across the fire: sitting on his haunches. He looked gaunt. Yet, somehow, relaxed. And indestructible. Like a . . . completely philosophical gladiator. Why did she think that? He was the most ungladiatorial man she had ever known. But how could he have been through what he had today and still look so completely self-controlled? And, oh, she wanted a drink. But she wouldn't. She hadn't had a drink for a week. Her hand had to be steady tomorrow. He smiled at her gently. 'Are you starving?'

She almost gushed like a girl. 'Aren't *you* tired?'

'I'm okay.'

She felt his shirt impulsively. It was still damp. She held it out to the fire.

They ate biscuits and dried beef, then the hot trout. First, she nibbled frustratedly, worried about the bones; then she could be cautious no longer, and the juices smeared all over her mouth and ran down her chin. He gave half of his to Sam.

She wiped her mouth and got up stiffly. 'I'm going to have a wash.'

She picked her way out to the stream. She scooped up water and washed her face vigorously. She had left her towel, soap, and toothbrush in the Garden of Eden.

When she got back to the barn he was scooping some earth out of the floor with his knife.

'For your hip,' he explained. He unrolled her sleeping bag, over the indentation.

She was touched that he had thought about her comfort. 'Thank you.'

'You're very tired. And you've got a lot to do tomorrow.'

She eased herself down, then lay back, exhausted.

She turned her head to him. He was staring at the fire, absolutely still. She wanted to cry out: What's going to happen tomorrow? Then she realized she was not thinking about the animals—Forsythe was going to get them sooner or later, and probably sooner. Thinking of them living free had been but a short-lived dream. Now she was thinking of him. And dear, sweet Big Charlie. What was going to happen to *them*? She whispered, 'Davey?. . .'

He turned his head and looked at her. She closed her eyes to control her anguish.

'Tomorrow they're going to catch up with you, Davey. Forsythe was right behind us this afternoon. And Lonnogan's not far behind!'

He said quietly, 'I can outrun them, Elizabeth. Until the job is done.'

Her eyes were full of tears. 'Oh, Davey! The job is done! It was beautiful. It was the most wonderful notion I've ever known! But it's over! They're catching the animals, one by one.'

'They've only caught Dumbo.' He did not know about Sally's fate. 'And he won't stay locked up in that stockade for long.'

'What do you mean?'

'Somebody will let him out again, Elizabeth.'

She stared. For a moment she felt her hopes rise. Then she blurted: 'You mean the Cherokees? . . . But you can only pull that trick once, Davey. They'll be watching a second time. What about Auntie today? And where's King Kong? Forsythe probably got him too!'

'Don't be too sure. Big Charlie and his braves are out there. I don't think any of those circus trucks will get very far when they leave Cherokee with any animals. They'll be hijacked. And the animals released all over again.'

She stared. He made it sound so simple. And maybe it was . . . If Eric Bradman was correct, they were only playing for time. But that was before a man was killed! The animals would never be allowed to stay now that one had killed a man.

She cried, 'Davey, you've done your best! But they're hot after you now. You're a criminal! Lonnogan's going to keep after you until he gets you. If he doesn't catch you alive he's going to gun you down.'

'Give myself up?' he asked.

She cried, 'No! *Run*, for God's sake.' Her eyes were bright. 'Get out of the mountains. Get right out of America! Keep running until you get to the Andes. Go to Africa and do your wonderful things . . .' The tears were glistening on her cheeks. 'But *run*. For God's sake don't let them gun you down . . . Don't let them stick you in prison like an animal yourself.'

He was looking at her steadily. Then he gently reached out and squeezed her shoulder. He smiled and shook his head.

She stared at him, her eyes wet; then she slumped back. She lay in the flickering firelight, her arm across her eyes. She took a deep breath and whispered fiercely, 'Hold me, Davey.'

There was a moment's silence. Then she heard him get up.

He came uncertainly. He knelt down beside her. She lay rigid. Then he gently lifted her arm off her face.

She looked up at him in the firelight, neither of them knowing what to do. Then she slowly raised one hand, and she tremblingly touched his face. She looked at him, brimming with new tears. Then she stifled a sob, he awkwardly scooped his arms around her, and they held each other tight.

'There, there, Elizabeth . . .'

'Oh, beautiful Davey . . . I don't want anything to happen to you . . .'

He held her against him, her wet cheek pressed against his, and he hesitantly kissed her face. She sobbed, 'Lie with me . . .'

She let go of him and shifted over on the sleeping bag and patted the place beside her. He came down beside her awkwardly. They took each other in their arms again, her tears shining in the firelight; she closed her eyes and parted her lips, and they kissed.

Tremblingly, nervously, lips and teeth pressed together, every muscle tense. Then she sobbed; her mouth and the rest of her body went soft and she held him tight. She broke the kiss and looked at him, and he looked down at her, not knowing what to expect. She gave a little sob, and she yielded completely and kissed him—again and again, short, tearful, nibbling kisses, on his mouth, his chin, his cheeks, his nose, his eyes, and he held her tight and kissed her tearful face. Then, just naturally, one of his hands fumbled for her breast, and she sob-moaned and clutched him tighter; and she cried into his shoulder, 'I won't let anything happen to you . . .' She kissed him fiercely, her whole body pressed against him.

Sam got up from the fire elaborately and went and lay down with his back to them; afterward, lying in Davey's arms, Elizabeth's face was beautiful.


# seventy-four


A lot of other things happened that night. Jonas Ford, hobbling on his bitten ankle, peering without his glasses, surveyed the two fallen gorillas. He ordered Ben and Sixpence to tie their feet and hands securely, back to back, while he called the Oconaluftee camp on his radio. Apart from the pain in his savaged ankle, he was full of grim self-satisfaction, but he announced his success tersely, gave the liaison officer a rough map reference, instructed him to dispatch a helicopter with a tree-felling crew, plus antitetanus serum for his ankle, and finally told him to radio his news to Forsythe. Then he lit a big fire and settled down to wait, while the trackers bound his captives. Five minutes later Charlie's two Cherokees came upon the scene.

They had doggedly followed Jamba's spoor since that morning. They had found Forsythe's spoor on the way, then followed Ford's when the party split up. One minute Jonas Ford was grimly congratulating himself and nursing his ankle, the next a hand clamped over his mouth, and his hands were wrenched behind him. In a moment he was gagged and bound. Ben and Sixpence were tying the gorillas; the next moment they were tied hand and foot themselves. The Cherokees stamped out the fire. One tipped out Ford's knapsack and found his flare gun; the other sat down with the radio.

'This is Professor Ford calling basecamp. Cancel helicopter; the gorillas escaped. Repeat cancel helicopter. I will sleep on the spoor and follow them in the morning. Over and out.'

Then he lifted the radio above his head and smashed it on the ground. The other Cherokee took Ford's tranqu-pistol, and the darts. Ford was goggle-eyed. They took the gag out of his mouth. 'Sorry about all this, sir.'

Ford spluttered, 'What's the meaning of this?!'

They were busy untying the unconscious gorillas. 'We'll untie y'all when they woken up and gone, sir. Then you'll be free to go. Nearest place is Gatlinburg, that way. It'll only take you three days. Four at the outside.'

The other side of the mountains, Forsythe made camp on Rajah's spoor, so as to get going again at first light. Every minute was going to count tomorrow. It was clear from the spoor that not only was Jordan tracking Rajah, but so were the gunmen who had shot the elephant near the cabin. Forsythe's heart was black with fury.

The three Cherokees waited until everybody was in his sleeping bag, until it sounded as if everybody was asleep.

Enormous Samson had to be the first to go, He woke up with a hand slammed on his mouth, a Cherokee on his chest and another on his feet, hastily binding him up in his sleeping bag, while the other Cherokee sat upon a bucking, muzzled Forsythe till the other two could come and help. The three television men were easy after that. The Cherokees apologized for the rough treatment. They regretfully smashed the radio and the dartguns. Then, with assurances that they were not going to hurt anybody, they cut open the ends of the sleeping bags. One by one, they put on their captive's boots for them, helped them to their feet, and politely told them to start down the mountain. Two of the Cherokees stayed behind to start following Rajah's spoor with the sunrise.

Forsythe and his men went down the mountain like resuscitated mummies, bound in the sleeping bags, the ends trailing like bridal trains, stumbling through the undergrowth, the third Cherokee herding them politely. Many times the captives fell and had to be helped up. It took over six hours to retrace their steps to the Garden of Eden. Then the Cherokee asked them to lie down in a line.

'Anybody who wants a pee just say, and I'll untie you enough. I'm gonna keep you here until noon, then you're free. Your best way back is up the mountains, along the Appalachian back to Newfound Gap. Take you about three days, four at the outside. Now everybody please go back to sleep.'

# seventy-five

It was a lovely morning. The sun was just coming up, riotously golden red; a light mist was hanging, and the world was young and alive.

Elizabeth sterilized her instruments while Davey led Rajah by his trunk down to the stream.

'Kneel, Rajah,' he said gently. The last thing Rajah wanted to do was kneel because of the pain, and he looked at Davey imploringly. But he insisted. 'Kneel, Rajah, please.'

Rajah wanted to obey, so he tried, and he grunted at the pain and straightened up again. 'Kneel, Rajah.' Finally the elephant painfully made it down.

Davey held his trunk, stroked it and praised him, while Elizabeth went quickly to his hindquarters. She shoved the big syringe of anesthetic into his hide, and heaved down the plunger. Rajah squealed and began to scramble up, but Davey leaned on his trunk and shouted, 'Kneel, Rajah.' Elizabeth heaved down on his haunch and kept pressing the plunger. Rajah complained and flinched; then she yanked out the needle.

'*There* you are, Rajah.'

They knelt at his head and thanked him for being good, stroking him, and Rajah knelt there, blinking, not understanding what all this agonizing kneeling was about but knowing they were sympathizing, so he continued to suffer for their sake, enjoying their affection and praise. Then, suddenly, the pain began to dull, and a drowsiness came into his great thudding head.

Elizabeth tied her hair in a knot, washed her hands vigorously in the stream, pulled on new rubber gloves, and set to work. Her instruments were laid out on a piece of cloth. She was not sure how long the anesthetic would last, how deep Rajah's unconsciousness, so she had a booster shot ready.

She cut into the lump of swollen, infected flesh on his shoulder. A mass of pus and blood welled out. She pressed on the sides of the wound, and it bubbled out. She pressed until clean blood came; then she probed deep into the wound.

Davey was pale, watching her face intently.

'Gotcha!'

She snatched up a pair of forceps and buried them into the blood. She bit her lip as she probed, then she triumphantly withdrew the forceps. Clutched in them was the bloody, distorted bullet. She flung it aside and sprinkled a big dash of antibiotic into the wound.

Then she took up a large needle, threaded with thick catgut. She shoved the point into his thick hide, and grimaced as she pressed hard. The curved needle slid in, reappeared inside the open wound, disappeared into the other side of it, finally coming slowly up out of the hide. She repeated the sewing process three more times, and tied knots.

'That'll have to do.'

Then she opened up the first wound on his flank. More blood and pus gushed out. She probed, frowning.

'It hit the rib. We're having luck.'

She eased the bullet out with the forceps. She packed the wound in antibiotic, and stitched it. Then the next wound. Then the next.

'We're having luck, Rajah. We're hàving luck, boy. All these are pretty superficial.'

Davey said, 'They're all forty-fives so far. A forty-five doesn't have much range.'

'Think positively, Davey.'

'I am. Don't worry.'

It took her well over an hour to attend to all the wounds on his flank. But all of them were shallow.

Then she started on his head. Some of these wounds had been made with a long-range rifle.

Grimacing, she sliced hard into the heavy, gristly hide. Rajah groaned, and his trunk twitched in protest, even in sleep, and Davey held him tight. She sucked in a breath angrily.

Elizabeth knelt back, her hands dripping blood. 'I'll never get this one out like this. It's gone right into the skull, at least an inch.'

'Can you feel the bullet?'

'Come here.'

He knelt beside her. 'Spread the wound open like that. Wait, I'll enlarge it.' She buried the knife again and sawed downward into the bloody hide.

He pressed his hands on both sides and forced open the lips. She muttered, 'How can I see with this blood?' She probed, peering. 'Blood, the surgeon's curse . . . Aha!'

She picked up the forceps and buried them, squinting; she pulled out a chip of bone. She flicked it away. She probed again, and out came two chips.

'I may be lucky. I really need to chisel away the sides of the hole, so I can get the forceps around the bullet, but how can I see what I'm doing with this blood?'

She picked up a thin instrument, slid it into the hole, and wriggled the top, her tongue clenched between her teeth.

'Eureka! I've turned it over. Oh *yessir!*'

She probed triumphantly, picked and flicked, and a bloody lump of lead came tumbling out.

'This is some surgery, Johnson,' she muttered. 'You're winning no prizes. If my professors could see me now.'

'They'd be very proud of you,' Davey said fervently.

An hour later she slumped on her haunches. Her hair hung over one eye, blood smeared her cheeks, her hands wet with blood. Rajah still knelt, fast asleep. Eleven wounds were all cleaned and stitched. She looked at Davey wearily, and smiled.

'You're fantastic,' Davey said.

'Oh, all in a day's work.'

He sighed in relief and gratitude. 'How long will he be unconscious?'

'A couple of hours. I don't know.'

He glanced up at the sun. 'Is it bad to give him an antidote to wake him up?'

She was too drained to think about anybody following; she was just filled with professional happiness and love for this poor elephant she had saved. She shook her head firmly. 'He needs his strength. He's going to be in pain when he wakes, anyway. It's good to let him sleep for a while.'

At about the same time that beautiful morning, a pale Frank Hunt urgently radioed the basecamp to tell them about the lions' den.

The lions had fled into the blackness of the mine when they saw him, and now Gasoline stood guard at a safe distance with the rifle. Frank wanted Forsythe to get his ass over here pronto because there was no way he was going to handle this little lot by himself without a Sherman tank.

The liaison officer at the camp replied that he would report to Forsythe on the radio next time he called. Then Charles Worthy came on the air and excitedly congratulated Frank, telling him to stay where he was until help arrived.

'Remember this is our show, Morris! Over and out.'

Deep in the mine, Big Charlie lay with a bullet in his guts.

# seventy-six

Fifty yards up from the barn was a little waterfall. From there they could see Rajah lying asleep.

The sun was shafting through the trees, sparkling on the stream. Below them the wilderness stretched on and on in the mist, silent and still.

The waterfall cascaded over a sheer rock, white and rainbowed, into a pool that was crystal clear and deep. Elizabeth crouched at the edge and washed the dried blood off her arms and face, while the chimpanzees, the bears, and Sam all solemnly watched her. Then she stood up and began to undo her shirt. She did not feel shy, but she noticed the animals all staring. 'Do you mind?' she smiled. She gave Davey an embarrassed grin, hastily unhitched her bra, unzipped her jeans and peeled them off, hopping on one leg, then the other, muttering, 'Damn—how unromantic.' In one reckless bound she sprang into a dive, every muscle tense, and crashed into the pool in a rigid bellyflop.

She broke surface, gasping, her hair plastered, and looked around for Davey, then screeched as he came up underneath her. He burst up beside her, grinning and splashing, and she laughed, twisted out of his arms, and struck out for the waterfall. She climbed out and plonked herself onto the rock beneath the cascade, grinning and gasping, the white freezing water falling onto her head; she scrubbed her fingers thoroughly through her hair.

Then, lying in the warm sunshine, she let him make love to her.

She watched him approaching, smiling nervously up at him; he knelt down beside her, too shy to look at her nakedness yet: he put his hand on her soft flat belly. Tremblingly he stroked her, then he looked at her: her breasts, her thighs, the drops of water sparkling on her body. She lay still while he stroked her, feeling her woman-smoothness, the bliss in his hands, and her eyes were bright and happy. 'You're beautiful . . .'

She smiled, closed her eyes, and held out her arms; he came down onto the grass beside her, and kissed her.

And the sun made a little rainbow in the waterfall, and the birds sang in the trees.

Afterward, lying in his arms, she said, 'Davey . . . when this is all over, what are you going to do with your wonderful life?'

He looked at the sky and smiled.

'There's so much to do . . .' Then he turned his head to her. 'Will you come with me? Please.'

She smiled at him with all her heart.

'Yes. I'll come with you.'

And she knew with absolute certainty that he was indestructible.


He could see Judd's Place through the trees. Automatically he noted how the wind was blowing: gently downhill, from behind them. Sam trotted beside him, quite relaxed. He could see Rajah still fast asleep.

They crouched at his head. He was taking long, groaning breaths. 'Rajah?' she said gently.

He did not stir. 'Rajah?'

Rajah just gave a long snoring sigh.

'Water,' she said. 'What can we fill?'

He emptied his knapsack, and scooped it full of water. He carried it to the good side of Rajah's head.

'Stand clear.'

He got ready to toss the water over Rajah. Then suddenly Sam barked. Davey spun around, and Lonnogan's voice bellowed from the trees, *'We've got you covered, Jordan.'*

The animals turned and galloped back into the forest, and Sam was bounding across the barnyard furiously barking. 'Sam!' Davey shouted and he dashed the water over Rajah. The elephant lurched, trunk upflung, trying to scramble up, and a shot rang out.

Sam yelped in midbark and twisted and crashed. Then Davey was running flat out across the barnyard to Sam, bellowing *'Don't shoot!'* He fell onto his knees beside his writhing dog, and in one desperate movement scooped him up, and turned. He ran, staggering under Sam's weight, lurching for the cover of the trees; Elizabeth was running wildly to help him, screaming, 'Don't shoot,' and two more shots rang out.

Davey lurched and blood splats appeared on his back. But

somehow he righted his fall, and he staggered on, lurching for the trees, with Elizabeth running beside him, yelling, trying to support him. Then he fell onto his knees and elbows, still clutching Sam. Elizabeth shrieked, grabbed his arm wildly, and wrenched him up. He made it to his feet, and he tried to run again, still holding Sam to his chest; then the shots rang out again from all sides, shattering and terrible.

The shots that pulled down Davey Jordan, 'in the course of resisting arrest,' smashed through his back, and he let go of Sam and flung up his arms. For an instant he seemed to hang in the air before her horrified eyes, his face contorted. Then he fell on top of Sam, his arms spread wide. Elizabeth screamed and collapsed onto her knees beside him; she flung her arms around him and tried to lift him, crying his name. She crouched over him, gasping and shaking him, crying, 'You're not dead—you're not dead!'

Then a strangled howl wracked up from her belly, and her mouth contorted open, her face wet with his blood; she clutched him fiercely to her bosom, and she threw back her head, and out it came, a wailing cry of grief, grief, grief.

# part sixteen

## seventy-seven

By three o'clock that afternoon Charles Worthy could wait no longer. Neither Forsythe nor Ford had radioed, which, Worthy figured, left him in charge. How long would those lions stay put in that mine? It was a golden opportunity, never to be repeated.

He commandeered a big press helicopter, lashed the lions' portable cage to the sling, plus the barrels they used in their pyramid trick. Plus a lot of fresh meat. Plus Frank's scarlet ringmaster outfit. Plus a bottle of whisky. Plus as many television men as he could cram into the helicopter.

Forty minutes later the helicopter hovered over the mine and deposited the circus gear on the rocky platform outside; then it shifted to a safer place, and the people clambered down. A few minutes later, Frank's intense relief at the arrival of help and a stiff snort of whiskey changed to incredulity as Worthy explained the idea.

'You've go to be joking.'

But Chuck Worthy was deadly serious, and he made a few promises which added up to an offer Frank couldn't refuse, not least of which was that he would leave Frank right here tonight, all alone if he didn't like it.

So while Frank fortified himself with the whiskey and changed into his ringmaster's outfit, the circus barrels were arranged in tiers outside the mineshaft next to the lions' cage, and the television cameramen hid up trees and behind rocks. Then, after a long last pull on the bottle, Frank reluctantly took up his position beside the cage, his .45 very handy, the fresh meat ready, while Worthy kept him covered with a rifle from behind a tree. Frank took a deep breath, put on his cavalier smile glassily, cracked his whip, said 'Wuzza, wuzza, wuzza,' and threw a chunk of meat into the black mineshaft.

Cowering in the darkness, the hungry lions smelled it, and heard the familiar voice of authority. Big Charlie whispered hoarsely, 'No, no' but Tommy could not bear it. He darted forward to grab the meat, and scurried back and gobbled it. Frank threw another piece into the darkness, and this time both Tommy and Princess scrambled for it, snarling at each other. Big Charlie rasped 'No.' Frank threw another, and another, closer to the mouth each time, and now he could just make out the two lions. Only Kitty held back.

They were crouched just inside the mineshaft, waiting to pounce on the next piece. They could see their ringmaster clearly and their barrels. They knew what they had to do to get the reward. Frank Hunt was smiling, dangling meat and saying, 'Wuzza-wuzza . . . Wuzza-wuzza . . .'

It took them a long time to get up the courage. Finally Tommy could stand it no longer, and out he came, slinking low, trembling, ready to whirl around and flee back. He hesitated, ears back, fangs bared; then he bounded for his barrel and leaped onto it. He cowered up there and roared for his reward, as he did in the circus. Frank tossed him a piece of meat, and Tommy snapped at it. Frank held up his hand to the television viewers, smiling, and the cameras rolled.

Then he tossed a big hunk of meat into the cage, cracked the whip and said, 'In, Tommy.' And Tommy jumped off his barrel, slunk hungrily in, and fell ravenously upon the meat. Frank slammed the door.

He raised his hat to the television cameras and gave his smile. He was almost enjoying himself now. He began to seduce Princess out of the mine.

Crouched in the blackness was Kitty. She was drooling, and she knew what she had to do. Big Charlie lay, one hand clutching his bloody stomach, the other trying to reach Kitty.

'No, Kitty. No. Don't go.'

Kitty crouched, tail sweeping, her stomach growling in hunger. Big Charlie whispered, 'No, Kitty . . . they'll go away and you'll be free . . .'

Then Princess went slinking out and bounding up onto her barrel for her reward, and Kitty jerked. Big Charlie's hand grabbed her swishing tail, and she moaned in protest, her eyes fixed on Frank Hunt tossing Princess her reward. 'No, Kitty!' Then Frank tossed another piece of meat into the black mouth, and it was more than Kitty could stand.

She scrambled for it, and Charlie clutched her tail. Kitty snarled over her shoulder and wrenched, and she was gone. She fell upon the meat. Then she looked out to Frank Hunt for more. Frank dangled a big hunk and said, 'Wuzza-wuzza . . .' and waved it at the barrels. Kitty hesitated, then she went dashing low out of the mine for her reward, and leaped up onto the barrels—and Big Charlie bellowed '*No.*'

He scrambled up, clutching his gut, his dirty face contorted, and he stumbled fiercely through the blackness, doubled-up, bellowing 'No, Kitty.' Frank jerked backward, astonished. Big Charlie burst out of the mineshaft, lurching, wild-eyed, and he screamed '*Aaaaarrrrh!. . .*' and he threw himself at the barrels. They crashed like ninepins, and Kitty snarled and leaped. She jumped over Big Charlie and bounded down the rock embankment, ears back and tail streaming. She dashed for the bushes, and she was gone.

Charlie heaved himself up amid the scattered barrels, his face screwed up in agony; he gave another roar to terrify them all, Frank jerked backward, and Charlie threw himself at the cage. He wrenched open the door of Tommy's compartment and bellowed, 'Out, Tommy.' And Worthy's rifle cracked into the air above his head, and again. But Charlie was going to die anyway, and he shook the cage furiously and bellowed. Tommy bounded through the door and fled down the embankment; then Frank Hunt slugged Charlie.

Frank recovered his wits and remembered the cameras. Charlie's back was turned as he shook the cage furiously to chase out Princess, and Frank pulled out his .45 like a club and hit Charlie on the back of the head. Charlie lurched and clung to the bars, and Frank slammed the door in Princess's face.

Big Charlie sort of shook himself, and he turned murderously on

Frank. His fist pulled back slowly, the blood flooding out of his stomach and from his head; Frank staggered back, aghast, and swiped him with the pistol across his temple.

# seventy-eight

Something even more spectacular was happening in Hawkstown, though no television men were there to cover it. That afternoon Sheriff Lonnogan brought in David Jordan and the elephant which had killed his son.

He had radioed for an ambulance and had Davey Jordan sent straight to Knoxville hospital, lest he be accused of not doing his duty. He brought in the rest in Jeb Wiggins's *You-Wreck-'em-We-Fetch-'em* tow truck, with the dead Sam tied across the bonnet, and the wildcat doctor handcuffed at the back, gagged to stop her hollering. And, best of all, the killer elephant was in tow behind the truck, dragged by the stout break-down chain around his neck.

Fred Wiggins and Freddie Bushel sat on the back of the truck, keeping the elephant covered with their rifles, in case he gave trouble. Rajah stumbled along behind, half-running, half-dragged by the tight chain, the noose digging into his hide, squeezing his windpipe so he had to keep up to be able to breathe. Sheriff Lonnogan watched him in the rearview mirror and made sure he kept the chain good and tight, accelerating when it went slack, to wrench the elephant on his way. When he fell, the sheriff slammed into low gear and kept going, dragging him along by his neck for a while, to teach him a lesson. If he charged at the truck in his desperation, as he had done in the first few miles, or tried to charge off the road into the forest, Lonnogan accelerated hard and jerked him off balance, which was not only very funny to watch, but it taught the bastard not to mess with Sheriff Boots Lonnogan.

It was very spectacular, the sight of the sheriff driving into town. Rajah had fallen so often that his knees were raw from being dragged along the road, and his neck was swollen by the big chain biting his hide; his eyes were bulging bloodshot, and he was making sucking noises, rasping for air as he staggered along, trying to keep up with the truck.

Lonnogan had radioed ahead to his wife and told her to spread the word, so the whole town was standing down Main Street to applaud their sheriff—who had done what the hired-gun from South Africa had failed to do. Dr. Elizabeth Johnson was handed over to Prissie Lonnogan on a holding charge of obstructing a law officer, and lodged in the cells.

Then the trial of Rajah began.

The trial was held in the *You-Bust-'em-We-Buy-'em Scrapyard*. A jury of twelve honest men was empanelled, and Turkey-George Sparks, the auctioneer, was sworn in as judge. The elephant was towed before the court and kept chained by the neck to the truck in case he gave trouble, although his feet were chained too.

The prosecutor and principal witness was Sheriff Lonnogan. He took the oath to tell the truth, whole truth, and nothing but the truth, and he loudly, and with real tears in his eyes, told the court exactly what had happened; how this here elephant had charged and killed his son in the course of his son's duty. Thereafter Judge Turkey-George Sparks asked the elephant if it had any cross-examination of the witness, and Rajah just blinked, bleeding and rasping. As there was no cross-examination, Sheriff Lonnogan rested his case, and Judge Sparks called upon Rajah to present his defense, to call witnesses and give evidence himself. The elephant just stood there, groaning. So that closed the case for the defense, and Judge Sparks put the case to the jury. The jury did not have to retire to consider the case, and loudly returned a verdict of guilty, to roars of applause. Judge Turkey-George Sparks then sentenced the elephant to death.

Rajah was dragged off by Jeb Wiggins's tow truck down Main Street, with the judge and jury and the crowd all following, to the timber and papermill company. The timber yard had a very big crane for lifting logs off railway flatcars.

Jeb Wiggins's tow truck dragged Rajah over to the crane, and townsfolk clambered up onto the stacks of logs to watch. Sheriff

Lonnogan tied Rajah's feet together again. Logger-Bert Waller, the owner of the mill, swung the crane over the rasping elephant and lowered the chain. Sheriff Lonnogan and two men, standing on crates, hefted it over the elephant's neck and hooked it. Rajah did not understand what was happening and he just stood there. The execution began.

Logger-Bert Waller revved the crane's engine, and the big winch rattled up the slack in the heavy-duty chain; the noose began to tighten around Rajah's neck. Rajah stood there, wheezing, his trunk hanging down. Logger-Bert changed to low gear, and for a moment there was complete, expectant silence. Then he opened the throttle again, and the chain began to tighten.

First it just gouged, so Rajah lurched in panic, and almost fell over because of his bound feet; then it ground his head upward, strangling him so that he gave a terrified squeal and tried to wrench backward. But the chain held him, biting deep into his gullet. He scrambled his bound feet desperately to get up and fight, but the chain dragged his head higher. Trunk upflung, he screamed in the panic of strangulation, and now his back was stretched. His bound forefeet were pawing the air, his hind feet were scrambling, and his eyes were bulging wide; he screamed again. Then the chain was so tight that his hind feet were just scrabbling the earth, his body almost vertical, his forefeet thrashing, and he flung his trunk up around the chain.

Squealing, his eyes bulging, his trunk wrapped around the chain, he heaved with all his might, trying to lift his great body upward to take the weight off his neck; then his hind feet were winched off the ground, his whole body twisted, and he was hanging.

Logger-Bert Waller winched him twenty feet up into the air, above the walls of the yard, for all the world to see, and there he hung.

But the noose was made of chain, and it took Rajah a long time to die, almost an hour of twisting and kicking, his rasping trunk trying to heave himself up. Then he was exhausted; his trunk slowly, jerkily, unwound from the chain, and he just hung there, his giant body slowly turning, his trunk and ears hanging down.

# seventy-nine

Only one cub reporter from Knoxville covered that hanging, and he arrived late. But his story went worldwide on radio and television, and the next morning the photograph of Rajah's hanging was on the front page of almost every newspaper in the world.

Before dawn it was on the desk of the president of the United States. Dr. Elizabeth Johnson had released a statement to the press and television men through a famous Houston lawyer, who flew up in a chartered airplane to Hawkstown and got her out on bail. Elizabeth Johnson had a hell of a lot to say. The whole world was up in arms.

That morning the president called off Operation Noah, and appointed a commission of inquiry to investigate the viability of the Great Smoky Mountains as a 'suitable habitat for certain exotic species of animals,' and to inquire into the conditions in zoos and circuses throughout the United States of America.

But it took longer than that day for the presidential order to become effective in the vast valleys, and for local huntsmen to be flushed out and forced to quit.

That day the three men from Sylva crossed Jamba's spoor. It was fresh, and heading up the Tennessee side of the mountains toward the crest. They started tracking her. And five young men were tracking them.

They had been doing so for several days, ever since the three hunters had been reported setting out from the house in Sylva with the dogs. Now they were only a mile behind. It was midafternoon when they sighted them, fifty yards ahead, sitting, eating, their rifles propped against a tree. The young men pulled handkerchiefs over their faces as masks.

The first man from Sylva was smashed across the head, then the others. They sprawled, stunned; then the young men set upon them, kicking with all their might, in the ribs and in their crotches, and the air was full of the thudding and grunting, the gasping and the smashing in the undergrowth. The young men kicked them senseless, bloody, and broken; then they tied their hands behind their backs. They pulled a boot and a sock off each one; then they dashed water over their faces to bring them around. The three men lay gasping, faces contorted.

'What the hell? . . .'

One masked man slowly held up his hand. It was bandaged, and one finger was missing.

The man stared, aghast.

'Now wait a minute . . .'

The young man swung his leg and kicked him in the ribs again. He kicked him over onto his stomach. Then sat astride his back. He pulled out a big hunting knife. He held it up to the other two men from Sylva.

'Now watch . . . because the same's gonna happen to you two. It's gonna take you a long time to get out of these woods. And a doctor's gonna be too late to fix you . . .'

The young man slowly brought the big sharp knife down onto the man's hamstring, above his heel.

He paused a dramatic moment: then he slowly began to saw the knife through the tendon.

The man from Sylva bucked and writhed, and his screams rose up out of the wilderness.


It was sunset when Jamba came toiling up the steep sides of Thunderhead Mountain.

She stood on a rocky bald of Thunderhead, the sunset glinting on the two silver darts that hung from her hide, getting her breath back. She lifted her trunk, searching for a familiar smell; she slowly turned her head, getting her bearings. Directly below lay the steep wooded slopes leading down to the Garden of Eden. But she did not want to go down there while there was still light, for fear of hunters. She wanted to wait until it was dark.

Thus she stood on top of the Great Smoky Mountains, a giant silhouette against the sunset, waiting for the safety of darkness. On all sides stretched the vast misty mauve of America, with the faraway clusters of town lights coming on, then more mauveness all the way to the horizon.

She waited. Way up there, high overhead, another leviathan

screamed silently, slowly overhead in the sunset, trailing its long white tail of pollution. Down in the valleys the mauve had turned to darkness.

She started cautiously down the steep mountain, to look for Davey Jordan and Rajah.

# eighty

It took both Professor Ford and Stephen Leigh-Forsythe three days to make it out of the Great Smoky Mountains, and they were exhausted. Then they heard that the president had suspended Operation Noah, pending the determinations of the Commission of Inquiry.

Jonas Ford was dismayed, though secretly, grimly pleased that he had not been the only one to fail—and he was very relieved to have the respite. Forsythe was furious, and he stormed to his tents and started packing. He refused to speak to reporters. He left that night by taxi for Nashville, flew to New York, and got on the first connection to South Africa.

Jonas Ford left immediately to go to Elizabeth. Charles Worthy was angry that the show had been cut short, but he was consoled by his spectacular film footage from the capture of Princess. Frank Hunt was delighted that Operation Noah was suspended and promptly disappeared on a well-deserved bar crawl of Knoxville.

The charges against Elizabeth were dropped by the district attorney, and she was advised by very competent counsel to sue Sheriff Lonnogan for a great deal of money. She spurned that advice, but personally laid criminal charges against the sheriff and every member of his posse. That trial is still pending. But, as folk around Tennessee see it, even pundits in legal circles, there 'ain't no jury round here that going to hang a man for hangin' the elephant that killed his son, nor for shootin' the sumbitch's keeper who started the whole danged thing.'

The Commission of Inquiry set to work, sitting first in New York and then in Gatlinburg. The commissioners were a senior supreme court judge, a veterinary surgeon, and a prominent conservationist from the Audubon Society. Twelve lawyers, representing various interest groups, led testimony from one hundred eighty-one witnesses. Dr. Elizabeth Johnson was the most important witness; She was asked a general question.

'What is my opinion of David Jordan?'

She paused, then slowly shook her head.

'What can one say about a man who had such love for his fellow creatures that he was compelled by both compassion and . . . human *honor* to act, when all the rest of us looked on and did nothing to alleviate such misery? Even *me* . . . What do you say about a man who had such understanding of God's creations, who gave such love and understanding, and natural leadership, that they would follow him through the wilderness, through thick and thin; across rivers and through gunfire and a host of other civilized savageries; who would cluster about him by night and day, who would follow him to the ends of the earth? What do you say about a man who refused to abandon those animals even though he knew a crazed sheriff . . .' (Here there was a loud objection from counsel holding a watching brief for Sheriff Lonnogan, and the commissioner warned her not to usurp their function, nor to prejudice Mr. Lonnogan's position.) 'What do you say about a wonderful young man like that, who was mercilessly gunned down?' (Again there was objection, which was also sustained.) She looked at the commissioners fiercely. 'Listen to me! In another age I think he would have been called a saint.'

'I think you were asked for a scientific opinion rather than an emotional one, Doctor,' the commissioner stated.

'What does science know about a man who had such compelling sweetness that he could call wild birds out of the trees? Can science explain that? No. A man who could almost talk to animals. Who could project his thoughts into an animal's head, and they obeyed him because they loved him? Can science explain that? No. What can science say about a man who had the vision of putting God's creatures back where they are meant to be under the sky and sun, *free* . . . as God made them. Who looked at the misery man has made of life and who had the courage .. to do what had to be done. What

376

does science know about a man like that? Science lets animals suffer for its own ends. Science makes factories belch fumes to pollute the sky and kill the streams and oceans, and does not lift a finger. Science lets man rape his own earth and gives him the wherewithal to do it—more, better, cheaper, faster! And you ask me for a *scientific* opinion, sir? About a man who knew it was possible and necessary to re-create a Garden of Eden?' She had tears in her eyes. 'I tell you, sir—as scientifically as I can—that science is a bumbling, dangerous, self-destructive infant, and it does not understand the likes of David Jordan!'

Later, she was questioned by counsel for Sheriff Ernest Lonnogan: 'Do you know where David Jordan is?'

'No.'

'Would you tell us if you did?'

'Do I have to answer a hypothetical question?'

'No,' said the commissioner, and counsel interrupted, 'It is relevant to her general credibility, sir,'

'Then I will answer, sir! And the answer is a resounding no!'


For, while Rajah was being hanged, surgeons had struggled to save David Jordan's life.

Six weeks later he was transferred in custody to a mental hospital for psychiatric observation pending his trial. Big Charlie Buffalo-horn was also there, recovering from intensive surgery.

The psychiatrists could find nothing mentally unsound with either of them, and they were finally declared fit to stand trial. But first they had the right, if they so wished, to give evidence before the Commission of Inquiry.

The lawyers assigned to them, pro Deo, advised them not to do so, but both Davey and Big Charlie insisted on behing heard, and the commission was certainly anxious to hear them. There were large crowds of people gathered in Gatlinburg on the day Davey Jordan and Charlie Buffalohorn were brought to start their evidence, including hundreds of Cherokees, many in full war paint.

Two heavily armed police cars escorted the prison truck holding Davey and Big Charlie, honking and crawling through the crowds in Gatlinburg. But they never made it to the civic center where the Commission of Inquiry was sitting. The two police vehicles were surrounded by whooping Cherokees; when the officers rolled down their windows to shout them out of the way, a tear gas cannister was thrown into each vehicle.

Thereafter it was almost child's play. By the time the police stopped coughing and clearing their eyes, their car tires were flat, their distributor arms missing, and the prison truck was gone, hijacked, roaring through the street of Gatlinburg, heading up into the Great Smoky Mountains.

All the Cherokees had disappeared. It was impossible for the officers later to identify any of them, behind all that warpaint.

The prison truck was found abandoned up on the Newfound Gap road. Hundreds of men were pulled in to search the vast mountains for Davey Jordan and Big Charlie Buffalohorn. But all the lawmen found were hundreds and hundreds of Cherokees popping up out of the undergrowth and appearing from nowhere, with big smiles and lots of unhelpful suggestions.

Davey Jordan and Big Charlie Buffalohorn were never seen again. Some folks say they never went back into the Great Smoky Mountains, that a car was waiting for them at Newfound Gap, that they're in Mexico now, or South America, or up there in Canada.

Dr. Elizabeth Johnson was telling the truth when she said she did not know where Davey Jordan was. She returned to her job at the Bronx Zoo, but she was very unhappy. Then, one day, she walked out of her Animal Hospital, got into her car, and she was never seen again.

Nobody knows what happened to her. It is only known, through the zoo's switchboard operator, that she had received a long-distance call that day from a public telephone box, and that she appeared to be very excited and happy when she left. Eventually, when her apartment was searched, it appeared that she had taken only her medical bag, her knapsack and bedroll.

# eighty-one

After nearly four months the Commission of Inquiry delivered its findings. These are lengthy and include the excerpt that follows.

We are greatly assisted by a number of expert witnesses, particularly by the Senior Wildlife Officer who has been conscientiously, and with great difficulty, keeping track of these animals during the time this Commission has been sitting. He has testified that, without exception, the animals have reverted successfully to nature, that they are healthy and that they pose no threat to people. While it would prove necessary to provide some shelter for the gorillas in winter, the Great Smoky Mountains, with its wide range of climates at different altitudes, provides a satisfactory environment.

On the question of human safety, we heard a great deal of evidence from people on both sides of that fence, as it were. We will give detailed reasons for all our findings presently, but wish to say now that we find the bulk of the evidence is alarmist, and based on ignorance. In short, the *expert* evidence, confirmed by the very thorough observations of the Senior Wildlife Officer, are that these animals are *harmless* if not molested. This applied equally to the grizzly bears, and to the two lions. We have heard very convincing evidence that lions and elephants in the numerous game reserves in Africa do not pose any threat to tourists, even to hikers, provided they are not molested. Nor do they come out of their reservations, which are unfenced. Lions, we are satisfied, are not natural man-eaters, and we have heard from several expert witnesses that they only hunt when hungry and, when not, walk through herds of game without causing alarm. As for the grizzly, we were impressed that hundreds of grizzlies live in the Rocky Mountain National Park without hurting anyone. Further, as the Senior Wildlife Officer pointed out, there are over six hundred black bears in the Smokies already; there appears, therefore, to be little difference in having one or two bears more.

Of course, these findings do not purport to decide the legal rights of the owners of these animals to get them back, nor the rights and wrongs of what David Jordan and Charles Buffalohorn did, nor of what Sheriff Lonnogan did: those questions are outside our terms of reference and are for other courts, and perhaps for God, to decide . . .'

The gorillas and chimpanzees were not allowed to remain. This is because the experts deemed it would be too cold for them in winter, and the government refused to build them a shelter, despite funds offered by the public. They were eventually recaptured. King Kong and Auntie can be seen to this day, sitting on their concrete floor under their concrete tree in the artificial light, staring with dull eyes at the people who come to look at them. Auntie gave birth to a healthy male.

The bears were allowed to remain. Of course, Smoky was no problem. There was considerable indecision about the grizzly bears; much correspondence between the Smokies and Washington. What tipped the scales in the grizzlies' favor is that only Pooh could be traced. It was concluded that hunters had claimed Winnie, in the confused days after Operation Noah ended. This is correct. Her fur is now a much prized and admired rug in a man's den in Tennessee, and her head is mounted on a wall. The taxidermist did an excellent job in rebuilding her eyes and snout which a shotgun blasted off.

So Pooh was allowed to stay, because he could not breed. There was considerable public pressure to release a female grizzly, but the Government ruled against that. Pooh was no problem, but why *attract* a problem?, the findings of the Commission and the experience of the Rockies notwithstanding. The same argument prevailed against suggestions that another female elephant be released so that breeding strains would improve: government ruled that although these animals were no problem *now*, a significant increase in their numbers might disturb hikers and motorists.

For quite a long time Pooh and Smoky stayed together, grubbing for food and sleeping together. Then came the mating season for black bears, and Smoky heard the call. Pooh followed, but he was not wanted. Now they never see each other. Pooh doesn't really want the other animals any more. Now he browses alone through the wilderness. He is perfectly happy. He never goes near the hikers' shelters along the Appalachian Trail, nor near picnic sites. Sometimes he is seen, alone on a rocky outcrop, the breeze ruffling his shaggy fur, his big nose sniffing the wind.

The elephants were allowed to remain, too. Almost two years after Operation Noah, Jamba gave birth to Rajah's calf. It was a beautiful little female, and she weighed four hundred pounds at birth. Dumbo is now a fully grown bull, with big tusks. They are often seen in the lush areas of Cades Cove, where they are a great attraction to motorists, and in the winter they sleep in a barn there. Sometimes they cross the Newfound Gap road.

But mostly they stay along the shores of Fontana Lake, in and around the Garden of Eden. In the middle of the day they roll and send up clouds of dust, blowing soil over themselves to keep their skin healthy. And in the late afternoons, when bellies are full and elephants feel frolicsome, they wade into the lake and bathe, squirting the water in rainbows over their backs, splashing and wallowing.

But Kitty and Tommy were not allowed to remain, despite the Commission of Inquiry's finding and despite loud public outcry. This was partly because Washington disagreed with the Commission that lions are no hazard to human life, and partly because Charles Worthy insisted on recovering that much of his property. Those lions were the most spectacular aspect of The World's Greatest Show because of the story behind them and because all normal folk are just naturally scared of lions. So the department sent in a team to capture them. It took a long time.

But when they were back in the circus, Kitty was impossible. She had tasted freedom. Frank Hunt flatly refused to work with her, and finally Charles Worthy had to donate her, with considerable publicity, to a zoo, where she can be seen to this day, pacing up and down; four paces up, blink, turn, four paces down, blink, turn; on and on. Every day for the rest of her life. She is very popular, and a great many people come to see her because of the story about her, especially on Sundays when parents take their children to the zoo to entertain them.

## David Graham
### Sidewall £1.75

In tomorrow's world the problems are so dangerous that the solutions are targets for anyone with the necessary quantities of high explosive. In Hamburg, the new Baader Meinhof operation explodes a government nuclear waste processing plant. In America, the war of black secession is in its second year. In tomorrow's world, Don Savage is a security man. It's a job no sane man would want.

## Wilbur Smith
### A Falcon Flies £1.95

Set against the ocean swell of the South Atlantic, the fever-ridden shores of the Indian Ocean and the vanished Eden of the African continent, this is a master storyteller's sweeping narrative, bursting with passion, quest and conflict.

'Stirring adventure . . . a genuine sense of excitement and wonder SUNDAY.TELEGRAPH

'I read on to the last page, hooked by its frenzied inventiveness . . . piling up incident on incident . . . mighty entertainment' YORKSHIRE POST

## Jack Higgins
### The Last Place God Made £1.50

World War I ace Sam Hannah was down to pushing ancient planes across the worst jungles in the world. Mallory was one of the new generation who would rather fly anything than not fly at all. Mallory needed a job and Hannah needed a partner. Two men in patched-up planes . . . against the savage Huna Indians of Brazil's Rio das Mortes – The River of Death.

'High octane adventure' NEW YORK TIMES

## Fiction

| | | | |
|---|---|---|---|
| ☐ | **Options** | Freda Bright | £1.50p |
| ☐ | **The Thirty-nine Steps** | John Buchan | £1.50p |
| ☐ | **Secret of Blackoaks** | Ashley Carter | £1.50p |
| ☐ | **Hercule Poirot's Christmas** | Agatha Christie | £1.25p |
| ☐ | **Dupe** | Liza Cody | £1.25p |
| ☐ | **Lovers and Gamblers** | Jackie Collins | £2.50p |
| ☐ | **Sphinx** | Robin Cook | £1.25p |
| ☐ | **Ragtime** | E. L. Doctorow | £1.50p |
| ☐ | **My Cousin Rachel** | Daphne du Maurier | £1.95p |
| ☐ | **Mr American** | George Macdonald Fraser | £2.25p |
| ☐ | **The Moneychangers** | Arthur Hailey | £2.25p |
| ☐ | **Secrets** | Unity Hall | £1.50p |
| ☐ | **Simon the Coldheart** | Georgette Heyer | 95p |
| ☐ | **The Eagle Has Landed** | Jack Higgins | £1.95p |
| ☐ | **Sins of the Fathers** | Susan Howatch | £2.95p |
| ☐ | **The Master Sniper** | Stephen Hunter | £1.50p |
| ☐ | **Smiley's People** | John le Carre | £1.95p |
| ☐ | **To Kill a Mockingbird** | Harper Lee | £1.75p |
| ☐ | **Ghosts** | Ed McBain | £1.75p |
| ☐ | **Gone with the Wind** | Margaret Mitchell | £3.50p |
| ☐ | **The Totem** | David Morrell | £1.25p |
| ☐ | **Platinum Logic** | Tony Parsons | £1.75p |
| ☐ | **Wilt** | Tom Sharpe | £1.50p |
| ☐ | **Rage of Angels** | Sidney Sheldon | £1.75p |
| ☐ | **The Unborn** | David Shobin | £1.50p |
| ☐ | **A Town Like Alice** | Nevile Shute | £1.75p |
| ☐ | **A Falcon Flies** | Wilbur Smith | £1.95p |
| ☐ | **The Deep Well at Noon** | Jessica Stirling | £1.95p |
| ☐ | **The Ironmaster** | Jean Stubbs | £1.75p |
| ☐ | **The Music Makers** | E. V. Thompson | £1.95p |

## Non-fiction

| | | | |
|---|---|---|---|
| ☐ | **Extraterrestrial Civilizations** | Isaac Asimov | £1.50p |
| ☐ | **Pregnancy** | Gordon Bourne | £2.95p |
| ☐ | **Jogging From Memory** | Rob Buckman | £1.25p |
| ☐ | **The 35mm Photographer's Handbook** | Julian Calder and John Garrett | £5.95p |
| ☐ | **Travellers' Britain** | Arthur Eperon | £2.95p |
| ☐ | **Travellers' Italy** | Arthur Eperon | £2.50p |
| ☐ | **The Complete Calorie Counter** | Eileen Fowler | 75p |

| | | | |
|---|---|---|---|
| ☐ | The Diary of Anne Frank | Anne Frank | £1.50p |
| ☐ | And the Walls Came Tumbling Down | Jack Fishman | £1.95p |
| ☐ | Linda Goodman's Sun Signs | Linda Goodman | £2.50p |
| ☐ | On the House | Simon Hoggart | £1.50p |
| ☐ | How to be a Gifted Parent | David Lewis | £1.95p |
| ☐ | Victoria RI | Elizabeth Longford | £4.95p |
| ☐ | Symptoms | Sigmund Stephen Miller | £2.50p |
| ☐ | Book of Worries | Robert Morley | £1.50p |
| ☐ | Airport International | Brian Moynahan | £1.75p |
| ☐ | The Alternative Holiday Catalogue | edited by Harriet Peacock | £1.95p |
| ☐ | The Pan Book of Card Games | Hubert Phillips | £1.75p |
| ☐ | Food for All the Family | Magnus Pyke | £1.50p |
| ☐ | Just Off for the Weekend | John Slater | £2.50p |
| ☐ | An Unfinished History of the World | Hugh Thomas | £3.95p |
| ☐ | The Baby and Child Book | Penny and Andrew Stanway | £4.95p |
| ☐ | The Third Wave | Alvin Toffler | £1.95p |
| ☐ | Pauper's Paris | Miles Turner | £2.50p |
| ☐ | The Flier's Handbook | | £5.95p |

All these books are available at your local bookshop or newsagent, or can be ordered direct from the publisher. Indicate the number of copies required and fill in the form below                                                                8

.............................................................................................................

Name_____
(Block letters please)

Address_____

_____

Send to Pan Books (CS Department), Cavaye Place, London SW10 9PG
Please enclose remittance to the value of the cover price plus:
35p for the first book plus 15p per copy for each additional book ordered
to a maximum charge of £1.25 to cover postage and packing
Applicable only in the UK

While every effort is made to keep prices low, it is sometimes
necessary to increase prices at short notice. Pan Books reserve
the right to show on covers and charge new retail prices which
may differ from those advertised in the text or elsewhere